"Absorbing, salted-peanuts reading filled with detailed and fascinating descriptions of weapons, tactics, Green Beret training, Army life, and battle."

—*The New York Times Book Review*

"A major work . . . Magnificent . . . Powerful . . . If books about warriors and the women who love them were given medals for authenticity, insight, and honesty, Brotherhood of War would be covered with them."

—William Bradford Huie, author of
The Klansmen and *The Execution of Private Slovik*

THE CORPS
The bestselling saga of the heroes we call Marines . . .

"Great reading. A superb job of mingling fact and fiction . . . [Griffin's] characters come to life."

—*The Sunday Oklahoman*

"This man has really done his homework . . . I confess to impatiently awaiting the appearance of succeeding books in the series."   —*The Washington Post*

"Action-packed . . . Difficult to put down."

—*Marine Corps Gazette*

MEN AT WAR
The legendary OSS—fighting a silent war of spies and assassins in the shadows of World War II . . .

"Written with a special flair for the military heart and mind."   —*The Winfield Daily Courier* (KS)

"Shrewd, sharp, rousing entertainment."

—*Kirkus Reviews*

"Rich with witty banter and nail-biting undercover work."   —*Entertainment Weekly*

PRESIDENTIAL AGENT

The war for freedom is fought in the shadows . . .

"Cutting-edge military material." —*Publishers Weekly*

"Griffin once again mixes mystery, adventure, and the . . . internal workings (and politics) of the U.S. intelligence and diplomatic communities . . . Highly Recommended." —*Library Journal*

"Heavy on action and tough-guy dialogue . . . Griffin is a solid, dependable writer." —*Booklist*

"Mega-selling Griffin is well on his way to a credible American James Bond Franchise. It's slick as hell." —*Monsters and Critics*

CLANDESTINE OPERATIONS

A new kind of war demands a new kind of warrior . . .

"A thrilling new series has begun, opening doors to special ops and investigating the path to the Cold War. An incredible mix of intrigue and diplomacy from a literary team that ignites suspense lovers everywhere. Readers will be panting for the next novel." —*Suspense Magazine*

"A Griffin adventure to bring out the Walter Mitty in every red-white-and-blue-blooded American male." —*Kirkus Reviews*

"It's a testament to the authors' skill and wide experience that the pages seem to turn themselves." —*Publishers Weekly*

"The period between WWII and the Cold War offers raw material for several books, and as fans of Griffin's body of work are well aware, he really sinks his teeth into politics and history. An excellent series." —*Booklist*

BOOKS BY W.E.B. GRIFFIN

HONOR BOUND

BOOK I: HONOR BOUND

BOOK II: BLOOD AND HONOR

BOOK III: SECRET HONOR

BOOK IV: DEATH AND HONOR
(and William E. Butterworth IV)

BOOK V: THE HONOR OF SPIES
(and William E. Butterworth IV)

BOOK VI: VICTORY AND HONOR
(and William E. Butterworth IV)

BOOK VII: EMPIRE AND HONOR
(and William E. Butterworth IV)

BROTHERHOOD OF WAR

BOOK I: THE LIEUTENANTS

BOOK II: THE CAPTAINS

BOOK III: THE MAJORS

BOOK IV: THE COLONELS

BOOK V: THE BERETS

BOOK VI: THE GENERALS

BOOK VII: THE NEW BREED

BOOK VIII: THE AVIATORS

BOOK IX: SPECIAL OPS

THE CORPS

BOOK I: SEMPER FI

BOOK II: CALL TO ARMS

BOOK III: COUNTERATTACK

BOOK IV: BATTLEGROUND

BOOK V: LINE OF FIRE

BOOK VI: CLOSE COMBAT

BOOK VII: BEHIND THE LINES

BOOK VIII: IN DANGER'S PATH

BOOK IX: UNDER FIRE

BOOK X: RETREAT, HELL!

BADGE OF HONOR

BOOK I: MEN IN BLUE

BOOK II: SPECIAL OPERATIONS

BOOK III: THE VICTIM

BOOK IV: THE WITNESS

BOOK V: THE ASSASSIN

BOOK VI: THE MURDERERS

BOOK VII: THE INVESTIGATORS

BOOK VIII: FINAL JUSTICE

BOOK IX: THE TRAFFICKERS
(and William E. Butterworth IV)

BOOK X: THE VIGILANTES
(and William E. Butterworth IV)

BOOK XI: THE LAST WITNESS
(and William E. Butterworth IV)

BOOK XII: DEADLY ASSETS
(and William E. Butterworth IV)

BOOK XIII: BROKEN TRUST
(and William E. Butterworth IV)

MEN AT WAR

BOOK I: THE LAST HEROES

BOOK II: THE SECRET WARRIORS

BOOK III: THE SOLDIER SPIES

BOOK IV: THE FIGHTING AGENTS

BOOK V: THE SABOTEURS
(and William E. Butterworth IV)

BOOK VI: THE DOUBLE AGENTS
(and William E. Butterworth IV)

BOOK VII: THE SPYMASTERS
(and William E. Butterworth IV)

PRESIDENTIAL AGENT

BOOK I: BY ORDER OF THE PRESIDENT

BOOK II: THE HOSTAGE

BOOK III: THE HUNTERS

BOOK IV: THE SHOOTERS

BOOK V: BLACK OPS

BOOK VI: THE OUTLAWS
(and William E. Butterworth IV)

BOOK VII: COVERT WARRIORS
(and William E. Butterworth IV)

BOOK VIII: HAZARDOUS DUTY
(and William E. Butterworth IV)

CLANDESTINE OPERATIONS

BOOK I: TOP SECRET
(and William E. Butterworth IV)

BOOK II: THE ASSASSINATION OPTION
(and William E. Butterworth IV)

BOOK III: CURTAIN OF DEATH
(and William E. Butterworth IV)

AS WILLIAM E. BUTTERWORTH III

THE HUNTING TRIP

BROKEN TRUST

A BADGE OF HONOR NOVEL

W.E.B. GRIFFIN

AND WILLIAM E. BUTTERWORTH IV

G. P. PUTNAM'S SONS

NEW YORK

G. P. PUTNAM'S SONS
Publishers Since 1838
An imprint of Penguin Random House LLC
375 Hudson Street
New York, New York 10014

Copyright © 2016 by William E. Butterworth IV

The Library of Congress has catalogued the G. P. Putnam's Sons hardcover
edition as follows:

Names: Griffin, W. E. B., author. | Butterworth, William E.
(William Edmund), author.
Title: Broken trust : a badge of honor novel / W. E. B. Griffin and
William E. Butterworth IV.
Description: New York : G.P. Putnam's Sons, [2016] | Series: Badge of
honor ; 13
Identifiers: LCCN 2016036565 | ISBN 9780399171208 (hardback)
Subjects: LCSH: Payne, Matt (Fictitious character)—Fiction. |
Murder—Investigation—Fiction. | Murder—Investigation—Fiction. | BISAC:
FICTION / Action & Adventure. | FICTION / Mystery & Detective /
Police Procedural. | FICTION / Suspense. | GSAFD: Mystery fiction.
Classification: LCC PS3557.R489137 B67 2016b | DDC 813/.54—dc23
LC record available at https://lccn.loc.gov/2016036565

First G. P. Putnam's Sons hardcover edition / October 2016
First G. P. Putnam's Sons premium edition / June 2017
G. P. Putnam's Sons premium edition ISBN: 9780515155679

Printed in the United States of America
1   3   5   7   9   10   8   6   4   2

BROKEN TRUST

I

"Target is moving," the man behind the wheel of a white Chevrolet panel van called back through the partition after reading the burner phone's text message. "Get ready."

The driver—a short, small-framed, skinny male in his mid-thirties who wore faded blue overalls and a black woolen knit cap—had parked almost an hour earlier at the curb in front of the iconic Smith & Wollensky steak house. After walking around the van and placing two reflective orange safety cones at the front and rear bumpers, he had returned to the driver's seat and waited for the signal on the throwaway mobile telephone.

The position gave him an unobstructed view twenty yards up the red-bricked drive to the valet kiosk and the entrance of The Rittenhouse, a high-rise that housed a five-star hotel and ultra-luxury condominiums.

If Center City was considered the wealthiest section

of America's fifth-largest city—and it unequivocally was—then The Rittenhouse, overlooking the heavily treed and expensively landscaped Rittenhouse Square Park, which William Penn first designed in the seventeenth century, was without question one of the city's classiest addresses.

The white panel van had magnetic three-foot-square signage on its front doors that read KEYCOM CABLE TV INSTALL CONTRACTOR, PENNA. LICENSE 3-246. Just to the left of the passenger door signage, midway up the body of the van, was a chromed, twelve-inch-square door, above which was a sticker with red lettering: A/C POWER 110 VOLTS ONLY!

Inside the back of the van, behind the chromed door, sat an obese, olive-skinned forty-year-old with a puffy, pockmarked face and thinning, greased-back hair. He wore a gray hooded sweatshirt and heavy denim workman's overalls and was slumped in a heavy chair that had been salvaged from an Italian restaurant's dumpster. The wooden chair was bolted to the metal floor of the van directly behind the passenger seat, the chair's back to the partition.

Across his lap he held a black Remington twelve-gauge pump shotgun that had a short polymer pistol grip mounted in place of the longer standard shoulder stock.

"What's he doing?" the obese man said.

"It's *they*," the driver said. "Target's got some jagoff with him."

Approaching the kiosk were two well-built, clean-cut men in their early thirties, one blond and the other dark-haired, both over six feet tall and dressed some-what identically in sweaters, blue jeans, and pointed-toe Western boots.

The man in the back chuckled.

"Sucks to be that guy," he said.

He fought the urge to crack open the chromed door, from which they had removed the original plug recepta-cle, and have a quick look.

"They're getting their car at the valet stand," the driver said.

"About damn time," the obese man replied, then in-haled deeply. "This smell of grilled steak is making me starved."

"Tell me about it," the driver said, nervously drum-ming his gloved fingers on the steering wheel. "We're gonna eat like kings after this job."

The driver watched as one of the three valets—*That really is one fine-looking bitch to be parking cars,* he thought—trotted to the far leg of the A-shaped drive, where more than a dozen vehicles were neatly backed into a row of parking slots along the drive's exit.

She passed a silver Bentley Mulsanne sedan, which was at the far end, and a red Aston Martin Vanquish coupe before getting into a glistening black Cadillac SUV.

"It's an Escalade," the driver said. "And that Caddy's brand-fucking-new. Still got the window sticker on it."

She quickly maneuvered the enormous SUV around the fountain in the center of the drive and brought it to a stop in front of the two tall men at the kiosk.

The valet hopped down from the driver's seat and

stood erect, putting her right hand, palm out, against her lower back as she held open the door with her left. One of the male valets went to the front passenger door, opened it, and assumed the same erect stance.

The dark-haired male came around the SUV, handed the valet what looked like a tip, then got in behind the wheel.

"Target is getting in the passenger seat," the van's driver said, starting the engine and pulling the gearshift down into low.

"Got it," the obese male replied, then, after a moment, grunted and added, "Not that it's gonna matter much where the bastard sits."

The man in back then began shuffling his feet in order to sit up in the chair.

He racked the action of the shotgun, loading a round of double-aught buckshot into the breech with a solid, metallic *Ka-Chunk-Chunk!* He then rotated the weapon onto its side, dug his gloved hand into a pocket, came out with another round of double-aught, and shoved it through the slot in the bottom, topping off the magazine tube.

The van driver saw the brake lights of the Escalade illuminate, then the backup lights briefly flash once, indicating the vehicle was being shifted into drive. The SUV started rolling—then, twenty feet later, its brake lights lit up again and it came to a stop.

"What the hell?" the driver said.

"What?" the man in back said.

"Hang on."

Beyond the kiosk, a tall blonde in a long dress emerged from the building. She looked to be in her thirties, and moved quickly toward the SUV. When the passenger reached his arm out the window, she handed him a thick envelope. Then the blonde blew a kiss, smiled and waved, and turned back toward the building.

"Okay, finally we're going!" the driver said.

As he began taking his foot off the brake, he quickly checked the mirror on his door for traffic—and saw a black Porsche 911 fast approaching with its right-turn signal blinking.

"Shit!" he said, pressing hard on the brake pedal.

The Porsche's horn briefly sounded twice, then the car cut across his front bumper and went up the drive, pulling in behind the Escalade.

The SUV began to circle the fountain at the top of the drive.

The van driver checked his mirror again and saw a line of four cars.

"Aw, come on . . ."

"While that might be a valid point, Chad, right now I really don't give a damn what my doctor says," Matt Payne said, steering the 911 into the just vacated spot in front of the valet kiosk. He was talking on his smartphone via the Porsche's audio system, the device plugged into the car's USB port. "The incision where they worked fixing the bullet damage still oozes a little, mostly around the sutures, but I'm getting better."

Payne was a lithely muscled twenty-seven-year-old who stood six-foot and a solid one-seventy-five. He had deep, intelligent eyes and dark, thick hair that he kept clipped short. He wore a white, long-sleeved knit polo shirt and khakis, with brown suede chukka boots and a navy fleece jacket.

Under the jacket, a Colt .45 ACP Officers Model semiautomatic pistol hung beside his left bicep from a leather shoulder holster. A bifold wallet held his Philadelphia Police Department ID card and badge.

"I'm really on Amanda's shit list right now," Payne went on. "If I'm going to surprise her with this condo that just got put on the market, I've got to do this meeting now—before someone goes and leases the damn thing out from under me. Then I can just get the rest of my stuff that wouldn't fit in Amanda's out of my place around the corner."

To meet a City of Philadelphia requirement that members of the police department reside within the city limits, Payne had been paying his father a pittance to live in a tiny apartment in the garret of a brownstone overlooking Rittenhouse Square. The mansion, which had been in the Payne family since being built one hundred fifty years earlier, had had its three lower floors converted to modern office space and now housed the Delaware Valley Cancer Society.

Watching the valet trot over to his door, Payne put the Porsche's stick shift in neutral and reached between the seats and pulled up on the hand brake. He left he engine running.

"I've got to go. Call you later," he said.

He broke off the connection by tapping the icon on the in-dash multifunction screen, then unplugged the phone from its cradle in the console.

The valet pulled the door open and assumed the erect stance.

"Welcome back, Mr. Payne," she said.

He stepped out of the vehicle, wincing at the sharp pain from the wound.

The valet noticed.

"Are you all right, sir?" she said, her facial expression one of genuine concern.

"Yeah, fine. Melody, right? Thanks for asking. Indigestion, I think."

He smiled at her—then, hearing the squeal of tires spinning behind him, jerked his head toward the street.

Payne saw that the white panel van he had just passed was racing away from the curb, an orange traffic cone flying off its front bumper. And, a moment later, he watched it screech to a dead stop in front of the Cadillac Escalade, which was approaching the brick drive's exit, about to pull onto the street.

The Escalade, its path now blocked, also screeched to a stop.

Payne then saw a chromed door in the side of the van swinging open. A black tube poked out of the hole.

What the hell?

"Everyone get down!" Payne shouted, pulling the valet prone behind the nose of the Porsche and using his body to shield her.

He reached inside his jacket and tugged the .45 from the shoulder holster.

At that exact moment there came the *Boom!* of a shotgun blast. Payne heard the distinctive sounds of the piercing of metal and the shattering of glass.

There were screams as people ran for cover, many fleeing into the park.

Payne looked over the Porsche's hood when he heard the Escalade's engine roar. He saw the SUV surging toward the van.

There then came another shotgun blast right before the SUV rammed the van.

The Escalade bounced off it, careened to the right, and accelerated down the street.

The van, tires squealing, raced after the Escalade.

Payne scanned the area as he got to his feet. With his free left hand, he helped Melody stand up.

He walked her quickly over to the kiosk, behind which the others were crouching.

"You okay?" he said, releasing her arm.

"Yeah. Think so," she said, her voice shaking. "Thanks."

Payne, running back around the Porsche, scanned the area. He did not see anyone injured. But he clearly saw that the passenger door windows of the Bentley were shattered and there was a defined bullet hole in its crazed windshield.

That's not from birdshot, Payne thought. *That's buckshot.*

He then heard behind him a woman yelling: "What's happening? Was that Johnny?"

Payne turned and looked.

Jesus. Is she fucking nuts?

It was the tall blonde he more or less recalled walking away from the Escalade when he had pulled up. He had not paid her any particular attention; Center City crawled with really good-looking women and he had been distracted by his phone conversation. But now he saw that she was extremely attractive and elegantly dressed. Her sweeping dress and long hair flowed behind her as she rushed out from the high-rise and past the kiosk.

"Police!" Payne shouted at her from beside the door of the Porsche, which was still open. He held the .45 in his right hand, muzzle up and trigger finger along its slide, and pointed with his left toward the building entrance. "Stay back!"

As the woman passed Melody, the valet intercepted her and tried persuading her to return to the building.

Payne squeezed in behind the wheel, wincing again at the sharp pain. After putting his phone and pistol on the passenger seat, he threw the stick shift into first gear, hitting the gas pedal while dumping the clutch.

The 911 leapt into motion and went screaming around the top of the drive. He caught a glimpse of the attractive blonde forcing her way past the valet and heading toward the street.

Payne shook his head.

She must be crazy . . . or have a death wish.

He laid steadily on the horn as he approached the brick drive's exit and then turned onto the street.

Ahead, the battered van now was racing almost side by side with the SUV. The two vehicles were quickly nearing the T intersection that was at the southwest corner of Rittenhouse Square. A line of nineteenth-century buildings loomed directly ahead. Around the corner was the brownstone with bronzed signage reading DELAWARE VALLEY CANCER SOCIETY.

There's no room for both to make that turn, Payne thought.

Damn—they could hit my place.

Payne then saw the black tube again slide out of the chromed door on the right side of the van. He waited for another shotgun blast—but then the Escalade swerved hard into the van.

The impact caused the van to go up on the sidewalk and almost into the park. The Escalade then sharply veered right. The driver overcorrected—and the SUV slid sideways, its right tires clipping the opposite curb, causing the SUV to tip and then roll onto its roof.

Sonofabitch! Payne thought.

Sparks sprayed out from the Escalade as it slid down the street and then onto the sidewalk. It struck a tree and a lamppost, causing it to spin. Its rear end then slammed into the heavy stone wall of one of the two-hundred-year-old buildings. The impact compressed and then ripped open the fuel cell. Gasoline flowed out, then erupted in flames.

The white van braked and skidded sideways as it returned to the street. It then managed to make the left turn, passing within feet of the upside-down SUV. Billows of dense black smoke now rose above the thick orange-and-red flames coming from the rear of the vehicle.

Payne had just decided on the closest spot ahead that he could park in order to extricate whoever was in the SUV. But then he saw two blue shirts—Philadelphia police officer, detective, and corporal ranks wore uniforms with blue shirts; higher ranks, including the commissioner, wore ones of white—run out of the park and approach the scene. They passed more people who were fleeing into the park. One of the officers was yelling into the Police Radio microphone clipped to the epaulet of his shirt.

Nearing the intersection, Payne waited until the last second before braking hard and downshifting, then shot through the turn, the all-wheel-drive sports car hugging the street as if it was riding on rails.

He accelerated quickly after the van.

Ahead, more people bolted from the crosswalks and sidewalks as the van approached Eighteenth Street. The van then made a right onto Eighteenth, tires squealing again as its rear end fishtailed.

Oh shit.

Wrong way—that's a one-way.

Payne scanned the intersection, looking for cross traffic. He could see across the southeast corner of the park clearly. But the building across the street on the right created a blind corner. It was impossible to see what was happening on the far side of it.

A second later, it did not matter—the shrieking roar of tortured metal reverberated off the tall buildings as a

Quaker Valley Foods six-wheeled box truck, apparently having dodged a head-on collision with the white van, came sliding up the two-lane street on its side. It then struck a pair of cars that had stopped at the light and wedged between them, completely blocking off Eighteenth to the right.

Payne carefully approached the intersection, looking beyond the truck and two cars, but could see only a half dozen other wrecked cars and boxes of frozen meat scattered along the street.

He smacked the top of the steering wheel with his open palm.

"Damn it!"

He quickly reached for his phone, connected it to the port, and thumbed the EMERGENCY prompt on the keypad.

"Philadelphia nine-one-one," a woman's deep, calm voice came over the car's audio system. "What is your emergency?"

An image of the police 911 dispatch center flashed in his mind.

The grimy room, in the bowels of the Police Administration Building at Eighth and Race streets, was cramped with rows of workstations holding antiquated computers, and stood in sharp contrast to the department's high-tech Executive Command Center.

That the dispatchers toiled in such conditions, each working an average of three hundred 911 calls over the course of an eight-hour shift, amazed him as much as he was disgusted by the petty interagency infighting at City

Hall over the modernizing of the separate police, fire, and non-emergency 311 facilities.

He knew that dispatchers had to very quickly discern which calls were genuine emergencies, and then how to properly respond to them, and which ones were, for example, pranks and worse. While bored middle school–aged kids still called in hoaxes to liven up a slow day in the neighborhood with sirens, dispatchers now also dealt with older, tech-savvy "swatters" calling in bogus hostage or active-shooter threats and giving a rival's address so that responding police SWAT (special weapons and tactical) teams would kick down the rival's doors, scaring the living shit out of him—or worse.

And now Payne had no doubt the dispatch center was already lit up with a flood of legitimate calls for help from Rittenhouse Square.

"This is Sergeant Payne," he said, and gave the unique identifier code that would confirm him as Badge No. 471. He turned left on Eighteenth, and announced, "I'm in a black Porsche in pursuit of the vehicle involved in a shooting at Rittenhouse Square that caused two major wrecks there. Shooter's vehicle is a white Chevy van with white magnetic signs on its doors that say KEY-COM INSTALLER . . ."

After taking the immediate first right off Eighteenth, which was Locust, he then took the next right and headed down South Seventeenth.

Payne kept the Porsche in second gear, repeatedly pushing the tachometer needle near redline. Its engine roared.

". . . Did you copy that?" Payne said.

"Sergeant, I can barely hear you."

Payne raised his voice as he spoke slowly: "I repeat, Rittenhouse Square shooter is in a white Chevy van headed south—the wrong way—on South Eighteenth. I am driving a black Porsche in pursuit—"

"Okay. Got it. Description of the doers? White? Black? Skinny? Medium build? Anything?"

"Negative. Only the vehicle, a white Chevy with significant damage on right side and door signs reading KEYCOM INSTALLER. Also, need Fire Rescue for vehicle fire and multiple collisions at South Rittenhouse Square—"

"Priority 1 call for service already made on the fire and collisions. Stand by."

Payne flew down Seventeenth, hoping he could maybe get ahead of the van and cut it off. The Porsche shot, block by block, from ten m.p.h. to nearly sixty, then back to ten as Payne slowed and looked down every cross street toward Eighteenth.

Finally, at Spruce Street, he again stepped heavily on the brakes, looked toward Eighteenth—and saw the white van. There was no missing it, especially because it now was dragging its rear bumper. A shower of sparks flew as the bumper bounced wildly off the street.

The van quickly turned onto Spruce, fishtailing as its rear tires lost traction. More sparks sprayed.

Payne raised his voice: "Shooter's vehicle now on Spruce headed toward South Nineteenth."

Payne turned and sped after the white van, relieved

that at least it now was going with traffic on the one-way street.

"Westbound Spruce at Nineteenth," the dispatcher confirmed.

He heard her relay that over Police Radio, then she said, "Multiple units on their way, Sergeant."

At Nineteenth, the traffic signal cycled red, and Payne had to cut between three cars blocking the intersection. Then, at Twentieth, he blew through the light that had just turned red, narrowly avoiding a SEPTA bus.

He shot through the next two intersections, barely slowing to clear them, each time the car becoming light on its suspension as it crested the crown of the cross streets.

The traffic signal at Twenty-second was about to cycle to green—he saw the DON'T WALK on the far corner, its flashing, upraised hand having turned solid red—but not in time. He had to brake hard to miss ramming a taxicab that was last through the intersection.

Still, he saw that he was closing the distance with the van.

As he raced even faster over Twenty-third, the street crown caused the Porsche to leave the ground. He pulled his foot completely out of the accelerator and, as a precaution, hovered it over the brake pedal as the vehicle tires returned to the street.

He watched the van make a sliding left onto Twenty-fourth, its rear end clipping the front fender of a rusty school bus that had CHRISTIAN STREET YMCA painted on its side. The impact caused the van's bouncing bumper to break loose. It sent out a spray of sparks as it spun beneath the engine compartment of the bus.

"Shooter's van now heading down Twenty-fourth just south of Spruce," Payne announced loudly as the car decelerated from fifty.

"Southbound Twenty-fourth between Spruce and Pine," the dispatcher said, then repeated the information over Police Radio to the responding units.

"Move!" Payne then muttered to himself. "Move! Move! Move!"

As the Porsche flew up on the bus, a series of enormous clouds of black smoke belched out from under it. It then started to slide sideways, coming to a stop when the front tires struck the curb.

"Damn it!" he said, smacking the steering wheel again.

Payne saw a shiny black slick spreading on the asphalt.

Bumper must have speared the oil pan, he thought. *Not good . . .*

He shoved the brake pedal toward the floor and instantly felt heavy vibration kicking back through the pedal, indicating that the antilock braking system was functioning.

The car stopped just short of the bus and the edge of the oil slick.

Payne looked up at the bus. Above its windshield a sign read OUT OF SERVICE. The emergency flashers came on and the STOP sign swung out from its side. The tall twin glass main doors opened outward and a big man wearing what looked like mechanic's clothing stepped out. He went to the front, where he began surveying the damage.

"Say again, Sergeant Payne?" the dispatcher's even voice came from the speakers.

In the distance, he heard the overlapping *Whoop-Whoop!* of multiple sirens.

"Sergeant? You okay?"

As the distinct heavy smell of hot tire rubber and brake pads started filling the car, Payne scanned the intersection. There was no way around the bus. And no time to turn back and take another route. He knew he could never catch up to the van now.

He shook his head in frustration.

"Pursuit ended," Payne announced. "Shooter's van still at large. Last seen southbound on Twenty-fourth. I'm headed back to scene of the shooting at Rittenhouse Square."

"Hold one," the dispatcher said.

He heard the dispatcher talking over Police Radio and then heard a reply, the labored voice of a male officer speaking rapidly.

After a moment, the dispatcher said to Payne: "Vehicle matching your description has been located on Twenty-fourth at Fitler Square. Abandoned. The units responding, ten of them, are conducting a search of the area."

"Thank you. Nothing further," Payne said, then reached over to the cellular phone and ended the call.

As he put the gearshift in reverse, the in-dash screen flashed with his phone's caller ID. It read RITTENHOUSE REALTY. He left it unanswered.

Damn it, he thought, looking back over his shoulder while shaking his head. *And so much for Amanda's surprise.*

[TWO]

Ten minutes later, Payne turned off Twentieth Street onto the narrow, tree-lined, one-lane Rittenhouse Street. He scanned the busy scene ahead.

Police, firefighters, and Emergency Medical Services technicians seemed to be everywhere.

Blue shirts strung yellow POLICE LINE DO NOT CROSS tape at the nearest corner, where the Cadillac Escalade was still on its roof. The fire was extinguished. Soot now darkened the front of the two-hundred-year-old building that the overturned SUV had struck. An acrid, burning smell hung heavy in the air.

Next to the police tape, firemen worked with practiced precision around Engine 43 and Ladder 9 from the Market Street firehouse.

Across the street, one fire department Emergency Medical Services Unit was departing the scene—the red-and-white ambulance's emergency lights flashing and siren sounding—while an EMT from a second unit was administering first aid to the two blue shirts who Payne had seen running to the burning SUV.

Another fire engine and ambulance were beyond that

scene, at the farthest corner of the park at South Eighteenth, where a Tow Squad wrecker was pulling one of
the cars away from the overturned wholesale-foods dis-
tributor's truck.

And a line of television news trucks was parked along
the southern end of the park. Reporters stood facing
tripod-mounted cameras, giving live reports on the
damage behind them.

Payne rolled halfway up the block, then eased the
Porsche over the low curb and onto the sidewalk. He
depressed the dash button that activated the flashing
hazard lights and got out.

Payne walked over to where the EMT stood with the
two officers at the open rear doors of the ambulance. He
saw that both officers had bloodstains all over their uniforms. The blue shirt whose black nameplate read FOS-
TER had his right hand neatly bandaged. The other, with
a nameplate reading HARKNESS, was getting his left
forearm wrapped in gauze.

The three glanced at him. Payne flashed his badge.
The EMT, a somewhat pudgy male in his twenties
whose uniform showed his name was SIMPSON, nodded,
then started to return his attention to wrapping the
forearm before quickly looking back at Payne.

"Is that your blood?" Simpson said.

Payne realized he was motioning toward his belly.

When Payne looked down, he saw that beneath his
unzipped navy fleece jacket there was a fresh stain about
four inches in diameter. Blood had seeped beyond the
bandage and onto his white polo shirt.

"Shit," Payne said.

He pulled back the jacket a little, and thought, *Must have got hurt pulling the valet to the ground and didn't notice it with everything else that's going on.*

"You going to be okay?" the EMT said.

"Yeah, I'm fine," Payne said, letting go of the jacket. He forced a smile. "Only hurts when I breathe."

"You better let me have a look at it," Simpson said as he began taping the wrapped gauze. "Soon as I'm done here."

"Really, it's fine. But thanks."

Payne looked between the blue shirts.

"What about you guys?" he said. "You okay?"

They nodded.

"Yessir," they said over one another.

Payne thought that the two looked like they could still be in high school. They had youthful faces, ones now caked in dried sweat and soot. Their eyes reflected the fatigue and shock that came after an enormous rush of adrenaline.

"That's a lot of blood," Payne said.

"Mostly the victim's," Officer Foster said, then shook his head. "Lots of it. That was my first time responding to a really bad scene. I only got out of the academy a few months ago."

Simpson said, "You oughta ride with us sometime. We average twenty runs a shift. Never a dull moment."

Harkness stared at Payne, then his eyes grew large.

He said, "I thought you looked familiar. You're Sergeant Payne, right? Homicide?"

Harkness glanced at the bloodstain.

He said, "And that's where you took the bullet from that fucking heroin dealer you chased down, right?"

Payne raised his eyebrows and nodded.

"Guilty," he said. "And a word to the wise: Try not to stand near me. I tend to attract bullets."

Simpson chuckled.

"Jesus, and you're already back on the job?" Harkness asked. "How you doing?"

"No need to worry about me," Payne said, and gestured toward Harkness's arm. "That going to be okay?"

He shrugged. "Yeah. Just scraped it up real good after cutting the driver's seat belt free. I mean, there really was blood all over. Had no idea that it could be so slippery."

"So, then," Officer Foster said, nodding toward the car, "that was you in that black Porsche, wasn't it? Chasing the van."

"Yeah, looked like you guys had this scene covered— and, clearly, you did. Decided that going after the shooter was the thing to do."

"You get the bastard?" Foster asked.

Payne raised his eyebrows again and shook his head.

"Unfortunately, no. But they just found the van, abandoned, and are searching the area for the doers."

Then he nodded toward the Escalade.

"Can you tell me about that scene?" Payne said. "Who was in the vehicle? Their condition?"

"Two white males, both from Florida, who are staying at The Rittenhouse," Foster said, and glanced at

Harkness. "Me and him hauled them out right before the fire spread to the inside. Didn't get much info before the EMTs went to work on them."

Harkness pulled a small spiral notepad from his shirt pocket. He flipped pages, read his notes, then looked at Payne.

"Driver's a guy from West Palm Beach named Kenneth Benson, thirty-two years old," he said. "He was unconscious. Shot up real good. That's where all the blood came from. The EMTs working on him said he took multiple hits to the upper body, with one to the neck. Said it looked like with buckshot."

Payne nodded.

"That's what it looked like back at the scene of the shooting—buckshot," he said. "How about the passenger?"

"The passenger," Harkness went on, "is a thirty-five-year-old named John Austin. He somehow missed getting hit. Suffered some cuts from glass, was pretty badly banged up, but that was it. Call it a miracle, or something. He got transported to Hahnemann first." The wail of the siren from the ambulance that just left the scene could be heard as it headed up Eighteenth Street, and he added, "The driver got put in that meat wagon. The paramedic said they'll probably pronounce him at Hahnemann's."

"That makes this job yours, right?" Foster said. "I mean, Homicide's."

"That's what's known in the unit as job security,"

Payne said, triggering another chuckle from the EMT. Then he added, "If it was single-aught buckshot, each round has nine pellets, and each of those lead balls is the size of a .32 caliber bullet. And I saw the shooter get off two rounds. How the hell did the passenger manage to not get shot?"

Foster shrugged. "Just damn lucky, all I can figure. Except for getting banged up. Didn't have his seat belt on and got thrown around the back of vehicle."

Payne just looked at him.

"No seat belt?" he then said. "Maybe that's it. He got lucky and saw the shotgun before the first round went off. Or got even luckier when it did, ducking down on the floorboard and using the engine block for cover."

Foster and Harkness exchanged glances.

"I just figured he'd left his seat belt off," Foster said, nodding thoughtfully. "Hiding behind the fire wall makes sense."

"Their friend . . ." Harkness said. "She showed up right after we dragged the two out of the vehicle. Said she'd run down from The Rittenhouse. That's how I found out they were all staying there."

"Good-looking blonde woman, mid-thirties, nicely dressed, right?" Payne said.

"Yeah," Harkness said. "A real beauty. The rich kind, you know? Wasn't happy she couldn't ride along in the ambulance. She calmed down real quick when I flagged a cab to take her to Hahnemann." He paused, then added, "So, then, you saw her?"

Payne nodded. "Near the shooting. Who is she?"

Harkness pulled from his notepad what looked like a business card and handed it to Payne.

"She gave me this."

Payne's eyes went to the card.

"I'll be damned," he said. "Camilla Rose Morgan. That was her. Didn't recognize her."

"She someone important?" Harkness said.

"That is what's known as a vast understatement, but you were right about the rich part," Payne said. He motioned with the card. "I can keep this? You have the info off it?"

"Sure thing, Sergeant Payne."

"By the way," Payne said, "nice work, you two. Pulling those guys out took real guts. Not everyone would've taken the risk."

"Thanks," they said over each other.

"You would have done it," Simpson, the EMT, said. He gestured toward Payne's bloodstained shirt. "You *have* done it. Just one example is ol' Ray-Ray damn near making you number 373."

The blue shirts nodded their agreement and obvious admiration.

The news media was still reporting, weeks later, on Homicide Sergeant M. M. Payne's foot chase of eighteen-year-old Rayvorris Oliver, a street-corner drug dealer, after Ray-Ray's partner had just shot up a North Philly coffee shop.

Payne, who had been in the coffee shop talking with a confidential informant who had been their target, took out the shooter when he attempted to aim the semiauto at Payne. Oliver fled the scene.

After running through multiple overgrown, weed-choked lots, Payne had been ambushed by Oliver—and took a bullet in the gut.

Payne returned fire, then collapsed from his wound.

Ray-Ray died at the scene, making him homicide number 372 for the year. His partner had become number 371 moments after his bullets killed an innocent bystander—number 370—who had been eating at the coffee shop's back counter.

The shootings had been, and remained, big news because the city was not only living up to its unwelcomed epithet of Killadelphia, it was doing so with record numbers of deaths. And there was no reason to expect a reprieve anytime soon.

"Thanks," Payne said to Simpson, then looked between Harkness and Foster. "But, fact is, I let you guys go into harm's way while I chased—and lost—the shooter. And you performed admirably." He paused, then added, "If you'll excuse me."

Payne took a couple steps away from them, then pulled out his cellular phone and thumbed a text message: *Can you meet me at Hahnemann ER in maybe 20?*

A minute later, his phone vibrated once with a reply message: *Once again, boss, you're a day late and a dollar short. I'm already at ER. And you've been requested by name.*

[THREE]
Hahnemann University Hospital
Broad and Vine Streets
Center City
Philadelphia
Thursday, January 5, 4:30 P.M.

Matt Payne took Sixteenth Street a dozen blocks up from Rittenhouse Square, then turned right onto Vine Street. He braked for the red signal light at Seventeenth Street. The emergency room entrance at Hahnemann's was a half block ahead on the right, and he could see a few marked police sedans and fire department ambulances parked along the curb out front.

He glanced left and then right, and his eye went to the enormous banner attached to the tall chain-link fence that had been erected around an old parking lot that was being turned into a construction zone.

The white vinyl banner read HAROLD MORGAN CANCER RESEARCH CENTER—COMING SOON!

In the middle of the banner was an architectural rendering of a new twenty-story tower that would have a skybridge over Seventeenth Street connecting it to the existing hospital complex.

The banner also had multiple listings of those involved in the project.

Under the largest heading, PLATINUM DONORS, he saw the names of at least forty companies and individuals, many prominent ones he immediately recognized. Payne was not surprised to see at the top was Morgan International, which Camilla Rose Morgan's father had built from a small pharmaceutical manufacturer in Philly. Directly beneath that was Richard Saunders Holdings, which he knew to be the parent company of Francis Franklin Fuller V's multibillion-dollar empire that included major media and real estate companies, among other ventures.

Along the bottom of the banner, in smaller lettering, under the heading FOR THE CITY OF PHILADELPHIA, was listed every politician from the mayor's office and the city council to the local state house representatives.

Camilla Rose spearheaded the fund-raising for that building to honor the old man and his losing battle with that aggressive cancer, Payne thought.

And I know this because Amanda had me write a nice check.

Damn sure not platinum level, but more than I wanted.

Payne heard honking behind him. He looked out the windshield; the traffic signal had cycled to green. He drove through the intersection, and after passing three of the red-and-white ambulances that were idling short of the ER drop-off, he turned in to the covered bay.

He parked the Porsche in a spot next to an unmarked Ford Crown Victoria. He could see the driver of the gray Police Interceptor, Detective Anthony Harris, standing inside the sliding glass doors of the emergency room entrance and talking on his cellular phone.

After entering the ER doors, Payne moved toward Tony Harris, who he now saw held a brown folder.

Harris, who was thirty-six and slight and wiry and beginning to bald, had fifteen years at the police department. Having worked cases with Payne—in Special Operations and now in Homicide—he counted himself among those who did not buy into what some had said, both behind Payne's back and to his face, after Payne had joined the department. To wit: that he was "just a rich kid with connections playing cop."

Tony not only liked and respected Matt, he enjoyed working with him. Harris had been around the block enough times to know that some cops would never be satisfied that Payne, who was both tough and smart as hell, genuinely had earned his stripes. Including his recent promotion to sergeant, after scoring number one on the examination.

Harris's eyebrows went up as he looked at Payne's midsection. He ended his call and slipped the phone in his pocket.

"Jesus, you here to be treated or what?" Harris said, motioning toward the dried bloodstain on Payne's shirt.

"Damn," he said, zipping up his fleece jacket enough to cover it. "I forgot."

"Is it okay?"

"Yeah. I apparently aggravated the wound ducking for cover when I saw the shotgun."

"What the hell happened?"

"Long or short story?"

"Make it a short one, or longish short."

"Okay," Payne began. "So, I ditched a doctor's appointment in order to meet with a realtor at The Rittenhouse—"

"Very nice," Harris interrupted.

"This will be the long, long version, if you intend to keep interrupting."

Harris gestured grandly with his hand for Payne to continue.

Payne said, "You were right about Amanda being really pissed about me getting shot. It's caused all kinds of serious problems. So, attempting to spread oil upon troubled waters, I went there . . ."

A few minutes later, he finished. "And they're trying to run to ground the shooter and driver and anyone else who may have been in the van. I went back to the scene. After hearing that it was Camilla Rose Morgan who was connected to the victims, and that she had followed them here, figured I'd see what I could find out."

"You mean what *we* could find out. You texted me, Sergeant . . . boss . . . sir."

Payne knew that Harris, who had a decade more time on the job than he did, took some pleasure in needling him about it. But Payne also knew that, though technically on paper he was Harris's superior, he had a helluva lot to learn from him.

When Payne transferred from Special Operations to

Homicide, Harris had been in Jason Washington's squad. Both were happy to have the newly promoted Sergeant Payne join it.

"Right, *we*," Payne said. "I checked in with the Black Buddha and he said I should find out all that I can—all that *we* can. He's sent McCrory with a bunch of other detectives to the scene."

Homicide Lieutenant Jason Washington, Payne's immediate supervisor, was enormous—six-foot-three, two hundred twenty-five pounds—and very black. Washington—who regarded himself, and was generally regarded by others, as not only the best homicide detective in Philadelphia but possibly the best on the entire eastern seaboard—took no offense to the nickname. He said a Buddha was wise and deeply thoughtful. And there was no denying his distinct complexion.

Payne added, "Jason also relayed the news that the van, which came up as having been stolen months ago, had in back at least two spent shells of double-aught buckshot."

"Jesus," Harris said after a moment. "You really do attract the bullets."

"How did you get here so quickly? And talk to the Morgan woman?"

"I was already here. Had to come get this file for the Polaneczky case. When I was headed out, they were wheeling in the Rittenhouse victims. One of the EMTs recognized me, and when I nodded toward the gurney, he said, 'ART.'"

"*Art?*" Payne parroted.

Harris chuckled. "Yeah, I wasn't familiar with it, either. He translated: *assuming room temperature*."

Payne grunted. "So that was Benson."

"Right," Harris said, and looked at his notes. "The deceased is Kenneth Benson, thirty-two. He's got a Texas ID—"

"Texas?" Payne interrupted. "Harkness and Foster, the guys who pulled him and Austin from the Escalade, said they were from Florida—specifically, West Palm."

Harris nodded. "Both victims have home addresses in Houston. Benson is—was—the CEO of a pharmaceutical company based in Boca Raton. It's called Next-GenRx. The ER doc, after pronouncing him, said he counted four hits of buckshot. Pellet that got him in the neck ripped open the carotid, and the severed artery clearly is what caused him to bleed out."

Payne nodded. "Harkness said there was an enormous amount of blood in the SUV. What about Austin?"

"John Tyler Austin, aka J.T. and Johnny, thirty-five, also of Houston, has a vacation home in Florida, in West Palm. He has his own investment firm that specializes in wealth management. Maybe more important: he's romantically involved with Camilla Rose Morgan. I got that from her. And that that new Escalade they were in was registered to her."

Payne nodded thoughtfully.

"McCrory should be grabbing copies of the surveillance videos," he said, "especially from the steak house and the hotel. Can you get someone to run deep background on Benson and Austin, including any social media? Hell, for that matter, Camilla Rose, too."

"That's one of the things I was arranging for on the phone just now."

"Great. I've already had the Black Buddha's mantra repeated to me." Payne then mimicked Washington's deep sonorous voice, "'Turn over every stone, Matthew, then turn over the stone beneath it.'"

Harris then said, "This Morgan woman said she knows you. Which is why I said you were requested by name."

"She did? Now, that's really interesting. I know some people who do know her personally. But I know her mostly by reputation."

"Which is?"

"Camilla Rose Morgan has been running charities since she was an undergrad at the Wharton School—"

"A *gala* is what she said she's here for," Harris interrupted. "Her Camilla's Kids fund-raiser is Saturday night. Something about special camps for children dealing with terminal diseases."

"Yeah, mostly cancer patients. They're probably holding it in the hotel ballroom at The Rittenhouse," Payne said. "She's one of those supersized personalities who is always happy and who everyone likes. The ultimate party girl."

"She sure as hell didn't look like that when I saw her just now."

Payne nodded, then went on. "And that partying has led to a long history of rehab visits. Not that that's been a big secret. She always called it 'going to the spa to get a cleanse.' And she readily pointed out all the Holly-wood celebrities and rock stars who did the same."

"She mentioned that more than a few celebrities—her 'special friends,' she said—are attending the event," Harris said, then chuckled. "You know, with any luck, you can get temporarily assigned again to Dignitary Protection."

"Not no—*hell* no. Been there, got the T-shirt. That did not work out well last time. I have no patience with the *special* types. Rather rip out my stitches with a dull knife first."

Harris snorted.

The protecting of VIPs visiting the City of Brotherly Love fell to the Dignitary Protection Unit. Sometimes there were a few VIPs in town requiring protection, sometimes dozens, and sometimes none at all—which caused staffing of the unit, dependent on demand, to fluctuate wildly.

The solution to supplying the surges was the tempo-rary reassignment of detectives from their divisions. Usually these detectives—who wore coats and ties, not uniforms—came from the Special Operations Division, as did the uniformed officers of Highway Patrol, which fell under Special Operations. Having citywide author-ity, members of Special Operations were more familiar with policing Philadelphia as a whole than, for example, an officer or detective assigned to patrol just a single dis-trict.

It didn't hurt that Highway Patrol officers were the

elite of the department. And that they put on quite a showing with their elaborate 1920s-style uniforms—gleaming black leather double-breasted jackets, Sam Browne belts, black knee-high cavalry boots with breeches tucked in and bloused—while riding massive Harley-Davidson motorcycles with lights flashing and sirens screaming.

Thus, a dignitary being escorted around town could have as many as a dozen of the city's best-equipped, best-trained street-savvy uniforms protecting him or her.

Payne went on. "But no surprise about the celebs. People flock to her like moths to a flame. Of course, doesn't hurt that the Morgan fortune is in the billions of . . ."

Payne didn't finish his sentence as he looked beyond Harris.

Down the hallway, a door had opened partially, and the tall blonde Camilla Rose Morgan was stepping through it. Payne saw that she had a weary face, one deep in thought, and she moved with slow, deliberate steps. There was dried blood on her clothing.

As Payne began walking toward her, she lifted her head and her eyes went to him.

"Matthew," Camilla Rose Morgan said, her voice strained. "How are you?" She made a faint smile. "You're not going to yell at me again, are you?"

"Ms. Morgan," he said, holding out his right hand. "I understand Mr. Benson was a friend. My condolences."

She stepped toward him and shook his hand.

"Thank you. And, please, it's Camilla Rose."

He nodded, then said, "Forgive me, but I don't recall our having met. And when I yelled at the valet stand, I did not know it was you. I'm afraid I didn't immediately recognize you. My focus was on the shooter."

"No apology necessary," she said. "And we haven't met formally, but I feel like we have. We have a number of mutual acquaintances. Daffy Nesbitt, for one. And your father's firm represents a number of my projects."

"I think I knew that Daphne was," Payne said, nodding. "Her husband, Chad, and I have been close since we were kids. I was not aware of the connection with my father's firm."

"Brewster always speaks so very highly of you," she added. "I suppose that getting shot did not change your mind about continuing with the police department. But, then, I do understand how it is sometimes not to see eye to eye with one's father."

"I don't think I follow you."

"You graduated top of your class at the University of Pennsylvania. Isn't it fair to say that everyone expected that you would be working at your father's firm by now? Or at least practicing law somewhere?" She paused, then added, "I'm sorry. I don't know why that came out. It's not my place to say."

"But you're right. It's what they expected," Payne said, and changed the subject. He gestured at Tony Harris. "I understand you have met Detective Harris?"

"I have had the pleasure," she said. "I asked him if he

could contact you for me. No offense to Detective Harris, but I thought I would feel more comfortable discussing this with you."

"Let me assure you that anything you want to tell me you can tell Detective Harris," Payne said. "When will we be able to speak with Mr. Austin?"

"The doctors said they're going to keep Johnny overnight for observation," Camilla Rose said. "In addition to some cuts and heavy bruising, he has a hairline fracture in his right forearm and a possible concussion. They've given him some mild medication for the pain. Before he drifted off to sleep, he asked that he not be bothered. With what Johnny's gone through, especially losing his friend, I'm sure you understand."

Payne nodded.

He said, "Did he say if he had any idea who would do this? Would you have any idea?"

Camilla Rose met and held Payne's eyes as she nodded thoughtfully.

"At first, I thought it might be a robbery. Johnny had an envelope containing fifty thousand dollars."

"Fifty grand in cash?" Harris said.

"Yes, cash. In hundred-dollar bills."

"Why?" Payne said.

"Certain vendors are due today an advance for the gala. They prefer cash, and offer a significant discount on their services for it."

Payne and Harris exchanged glances.

"Who, for example?" Payne said.

"It's not what I suspect you are thinking," Camilla

Rose said. "I run an aboveboard program. Besides, no one knew that he had the cash. I'd just given it to him. Johnny was in such a hurry, I had to stop them before they almost drove off without it."

"Where is the money now?" Payne said.

"The vendors still need their advances. I had my assistant come get the envelope. Johnny had stuck it in his sweater right before . . . before what happened . . . And when the EMTs came, Johnny told them to give it to me."

Payne thought, *In his sweater? Maybe that's why he was not wearing a seat belt.*

"So, aside from the cash," Payne said, "any other ideas? Because I really do not believe robbery was the motive. I saw the whole thing go down."

"I asked Johnny the same thing: if he had any ideas. Maybe someone had made any threats against him. Or against Ken?"

"And?" Payne said.

Camilla Rose hesitated, then said, "And all he said was, 'You know.' He repeated it."

"What did he mean by that?"

She glanced around the room.

"May I buy you a cup of coffee?" she said. "Or maybe something a bit stronger?" She absently wiped at a large patch of dried blood on her sleeve. "After I get changed?"

Harris held up the file folder.

"Matt, I need to drop this off in the case file," he said. "I'll get going on what we discussed, then head over to the scene and see how McCrory is doing."

"Thanks, Tony."

"Ms. Morgan," Harris said, "thank you for your help."

"You're welcome, Detective. A pleasure to meet you, despite the circumstances."

As Harris headed toward the glass doors of the ER entrance, Payne nodded in that direction.

"My car is right out there, too. Take you back to The Rittenhouse? How does going to the Library sound?"

She made a small smile. She knew the inside line about the small Library Bar. Simply saying one was "going to the Library" came across as completely innocuous.

"Excellent. The Library it is."

[FOUR]

As Payne drove down Broad Street, with City Hall, the world's tallest masonry building, looming in the distance, Camilla Rose said, "I don't know if you did this by design—I suspect that you did—but this is the perfect place for what I have to say. I won't repeat this in public."

As Payne glanced at her, he saw an open parking space at the curb ahead. He quickly pulled into it.

He turned to her, and said, "Okay."

"It's about what Johnny said when I asked."

"He said, 'You know.' So, do you?"

She met Payne's eyes and nodded.

On her lap, she held tight to a small clutch purse. She reached into it and produced a miniature bottle of vodka.

"My nerves are a mess," she said. "Do you mind?"

"By all means, help yourself."

"Would you like one?"

"I can wait."

"Then you're not going to judge me, are you? It's not like you haven't needed a nip or two at some point."

"With me, it's more like three or four. So, no judging."

She made a wistful smile.

"You're too kind, Matthew."

Payne watched as she twisted off the top and drained the bottle.

After a pause, Camilla Rose, carefully screwing the cap back on and putting the empty in her clutch, then said, "Johnny means that Mr. Morgan is behind the shooting."

Payne thought, *But Old Man Morgan is dead.*

She's not saying that he calls the shots from the grave?

"Mr. Morgan? Your father?"

"My father passed, Matthew," she said, her tone now cold. She looked out the passenger window and sighed. "Which is a great deal of why this situation is so grave."

"I'm sorry. I don't follow."

She looked ahead, out the windshield.

"My father and I were very close when I was young. I was a classic daddy's girl."

She pointed in the direction of the thirty-seven-foot-tall bronze statue of William Penn standing atop City Hall.

"He used to take me up to the observation deck there, then over to LOVE Park, before going shopping along Walnut Street. Lots and lots of time together. And despite the divorce and my mother moving the two of us out to L.A., my father and I stayed in close touch throughout the school years—he paid for my schooling in Beverly Hills, of course, and kept an active interest in how I was progressing—and I spent my summers here with him.

"As I grew older, he saw to it that I had jobs here that introduced me into the family businesses. After graduating prep school, I came back from California to go to Wharton, with plans to eventually get my master's at the business school. My father was a Wharton grad. I wanted to follow in his footsteps. And I did . . . until Mr. Morgan."

What the hell is she saying? Payne thought.

He said, "So . . . who is this Mr. Morgan?"

Camilla Rose sat silently, staring out the window. Then she inhaled deeply and let it slowly out.

"I really don't know how to say this," she finally said, still looking out the window. "No one will believe it, I know. And even if they did, Mr. Morgan has proven to be untouchable."

"I've heard pretty much everything."

She turned to look at him.

"I'm sure you have. That is fine for most folks, I

suppose. It's just that we do not air such dirty laundry. Heaven knows, the paparazzi makes up enough of it without our adding more."

Payne nodded. He had seen the wild headlines and photographs triggered by her family name.

"Mason Morgan," she began, practically spitting out his name, "has long despised my mother for what he considered her having broken up the marriage of his mother."

"Then Mason Morgan is your replace brother," Payne said, his tone making it a question. "I didn't know you had any siblings."

"*Half* brother, if you please. And after what he's done, after his brazen betrayal, I refuse to refer to him by his first name, especially to his face. Doing so would suggest we have at least, on some level, a cordial relationship. I can assure you that we do not. He was ten when my mother married our father, and I was born a year later. I can understand his displeasure with my mother—she is a five-star bitch, and she likely was a homewrecker—but I never did anything to harm him."

She looked back out her window and laughed.

"Five-star might be shortchanging her," she said. "I hated being a debutante. My mother made me. And she did so not for my sake—she really knew I hated it—but simply to spite my father, who tried to talk her out of it when I asked him. This was while he was fighting to cut off her alimony because everyone knew she was shacked up with that actor Tom Smyth—in essence, married to him. My mother knew that if she actually remarried—

Poof!—there went the two hundred grand a month that she had fought so hard for, as she said in the divorce proceedings, 'to maintain the lifestyle to which I have become accustomed.' My father had had to agree to pay it—he wanted out of the marriage because he would not tolerate her infidelity—and she knew it and she really stuck it to him."

"Two hundred thousand a month in alimony? Wow. That's—"

"A real five-star bitch," she said, looking at him and nodding. "And that's not all. That was on top of the lump sum she got, and certain assets, such as the houses in Coral Gables and Pacific Palisades."

Payne whistled.

"So, how is it that Mason is behind today's shooting?" he asked. "How would Johnny know?"

Payne had used their first names without thinking. He realized that using "Mr." struck him as awkward.

"Because he hates Johnny. Has since I met him. And it's all over pure greed. And power. Same as what happened right before my father became sick."

"Which was?"

"Father was grooming me to eventually take over the pharmaceutical business while Mason would continue running, also under father's direction, the commercial real estate companies. I was, as now, already running the Morgan philanthropic arm, which I had built at Father's request. He told me he was impressed with how I had started Camilla's Kids while I still was earning my master's." She paused, then briefly continued, "Unfortunately, I also was getting . . ."

Her voice trailed off as she looked back out her window.

After a moment, she cleared her throat and went on: "I felt absolutely invincible back then. And because of that, I made some mistakes."

"A lot of college kids do. Hell, most do. I did."

"Thanks, but not like I did. I had it all. And I could do it all. Juggling school and the fund-raisers and working with my father came to me fairly easily. I worked hard . . . and so I played hard. Really hard."

"And wound up in rehab," Payne said, softly.

Looking out the window, she shrugged.

"Everybody was doing it," she said. "I didn't see the problem, especially after I finished my MBA. I'd come out of rehab and picked up where I left off. Everything was wonderful. Except I didn't see how my father was really viewing my behavior."

"He didn't say anything?"

She turned and looked at him.

"Oh, sure he did. He made subtle suggestions. But we got along so well, and I told him I was fine, and my work did not suffer—I just thought all along that I still had earned his trust."

She inhaled deeply again, then let it out slowly as she looked back out her window.

"They first found the cancer while I was away for two months in West Palm," she said.

"In rehab?"

She nodded.

"Same place where I first met Johnny," she said. "Anyway, they decided—my father told me later—not to tell me because it would have interrupted my treatment."

"They?"

"My father and half brother, who really was the catalyst."

"Catalyst? For what?"

"For marginalizing me. He essentially convinced my father, as well as got some board members and other officers at the companies to agree, that I was too young and unstable to be in the positions I was. Especially without my father being there."

"Wow."

She looked at him.

"Yeah. 'Wow.' At first, my father was not convinced. But as that goddamn disease quickly progressed, as it ate away at him and his mental and physical capacities weakened, he began to agree to certain changes. Small ones at first, then the bigger ones. In the end, I was left overseeing only the philanthropy arm, with a set budget of five million a year. My father's estate, which held the vast majority of Morgan International shares, was redrawn to provide me personally with a million every quarter."

"I feel uncomfortable asking, but four million a year isn't exactly hardship, is it?"

"And that makes me sound like an ungrateful five-star bitch, too, right?" She did not allow him to respond, and went on: "I would agree. *Except* for the fact that he convinced my father that for the company's sake—specifically the preservation of the Morgan family fortune—that I would have no access to the principal, only the quarterly payments that would end when I died. Meaning, at that point my principal would be distributed to the surviving family."

"Which would be Mason."

"Precisely."

"But we're still talking about four million a year, no?"

"Matthew, the pharmaceutical company is valued alone at eleven billion. Everything else nearly doubles that. It is unjust and an outrage that Mr. Morgan manipulated my father in his weakened state so that he could take control while patting me on the head with quarterly payments. Greed, power, ego—that sums up the son of a bitch."

She paused, and when she looked him in the eyes, he saw tears welling.

"Do I need more money, Matthew? Or course not. Not personally. But, goddamn it, neither does he! So I'm pressuring for the release of my share of the principal—not just the payments, the whole principal—for two reasons. One, because I will see that the money goes to good causes now, as my father wished."

"And two?"

She smiled.

"Because it will drive Mr. Morgan absolutely crazy. He loves believing that no one can get to him."

Payne looked out the windshield in thought, then turned back to Camilla Rose.

"And you are saying that that is why Mason Morgan arranged for someone to shoot John Austin?"

"I told you, he hates Johnny. Especially after Johnny told him he was going to help me. For the record, I do not need Johnny's help. But I do like the fact that he thinks Johnny's interference could cause him problems, particularly if we married. There is a clause that says that should I marry and have issue, the quarterly payments on my death would continue."

"The payments would go to your spouse and child? Or just the child?"

"Just the child . . . or children. It was designed that way to cut off gold diggers looking to marry, then make out like bandits in a divorce. As my mother did."

"Interesting. And are you going to marry?"

She laughed.

"Certainly not Johnny. After all I've seen what marriage does? Would you? And I don't think I'm cut out to be an everyday mother. I have plenty of interaction with children at my ranches. Children I can really help. I've found that's my real calling. And I want the money to do more of it now."

"And to zing Mason."

She laughed again.

"There is that," she said, digging back in her purse and producing another miniature bottle of vodka. "Anyway, that's far too much about me. What about you? How long are you going to continue with this cop thing?"

She reached over and pulled back on his fleece jacket, revealing the bloodstain on his shirt.

"My God, Matthew, I saw the news reports, and then someone told me that you almost died. Is catching another miserable heroin pusher worth losing your life?"

She opened the bottle and drank half of it.

He said, "Another miserable killer, slash, heroin pusher, to be precise. But you're not the first person to make that point."

"Well then?"

"I don't have an answer right now. Except maybe to quote the great Marine Corps general Chesty Puller: 'If not me, who? If not now, when?' And I find it interesting you press the point while I'm trying to track down who killed your friend today."

"You've made a lot of headlines, Matthew. You don't need any more."

"I might say the same about you."

Once more Camilla Rose laughed, this time loudly. She smiled broadly.

"Touché," she said, holding up the miniature bottle of vodka in a mock toast. She swallowed the rest, then added, "Except my headlines have been fun ones. Mine never said I almost died in some godforsaken ghetto."

As Payne turned the Porsche up the brick-paved drive of The Rittenhouse, he felt his cell phone vibrate once in his pocket, indicating a new text message. He ignored it as he scanned the line of cars parked across the drive and saw that the shot-up Bentley was gone.

Before turning in to the drive, he had looked to the southern end of the park and noticed that those crime scenes were gone, too. Where the streets had been all blocked off, traffic now flowed freely. Only the soot on the stone façade of the building remained, and even it looked as if it had been mostly hosed off.

If this were anywhere but Center City, he thought, *the crime scene tape would be flapping in the wind for weeks, all faded and ragged.*

Here, thanks to those business-funded cleaning services, everything already is tidy. It's like nothing happened. Which is exactly the way they want it.

He stopped at the valet kiosk. There was a new crew of valets; two of whom trotted toward the car doors.

"Matthew," Camilla Rose said, "would you be offended if I asked for a rain check on the Library? I am suddenly exhausted and there is still work to do for the gala. I really don't think I have anything more to add to what I probably should not have shared already." She sighed. "But this is part of the fight I've chosen."

He waved off the valet approaching his door, then wrote on a business card and handed it to her.

"That's my personal cell phone number," he said. "The others are my work numbers. We'll talk more later. Please call at any time if you think or hear of anything else. And let me know the soonest I can question Johnny. The first forty-eight hours are the most critical in finding a murderer."

She nodded. "I will. Thank you."

"Oh, and would you happen to have your brother's number?"

"You bet your ass I do."

She tapped on the face of her phone, then looked at the card Payne gave her, then tapped again.

Payne's phone vibrated.

"There," she said. "I sent you all his numbers, addresses—everything. Good luck with getting to the bastard. Let me know how else I can help."

Payne, watching Camilla Rose walk away and noting that she again moved in her usual graceful fashion, wondered: *Does she really believe her brother put a hit out on Austin? Or is this just an opportunity to use me to stick it to him?*

He felt his telephone vibrate once more. He pulled it from his pocket and read the glass screen. Below a text message from Amanda, and another from Camilla Rose, he saw that the newest had been sent by Rittenhouse Realty.

He first read Amanda's text. *If you can get out of anything you might have planned tonight, I'd appreciate it. I'd like for us to have some quality time together.*

Then his eyes went to the other text. *Mr. Payne, an update, as you requested. We have an application for the unit. You're welcome to view the condo tomorrow and complete paperwork as the back-up applicant for it. I highly encourage you to do so, as it isn't unusual for there*

*to be a problem with the other's credit, references, et cetera.
Thank you.*

He went back and reread Amanda's message.

Quality time? he thought.

*She's been in such a funk, I cannot imagine she's think-
ing about getting naked.*

*I really want to surprise her with the damn condo. We
can't live in that one-bedroom of hers. Not if there's going
to be three of us. Or more.*

And how would she not love The Rittenhouse?

I'll do anything to get her past this, get her happier.

*Including not letting work interfere with tonight's
"quality time."*

Better give Tony a heads-up.

He thumbed a speed-dial number, and when Harris
answered, Payne said, "Two things. First, in case I get
hit by a bus or suffer some other calamity, let me share
with you what Camilla Rose just told me . . ."

II

Matt Payne, having showered at the garret apartment and changed his bloodstained bandage and clothes, walked across the brightly lit marble lobby of the luxury condominium high-rise. He wore woolen slacks—his Colt pistol tucked inside the waistband at the small of his back—with a camel hair blazer, crisp dress shirt, and striped necktie. Cradled in the crook of his left arm were two dozen long-stemmed red roses wrapped in a fine ribbon of white linen.

At the far end of the lobby, he approached a pair of sliding glass doors outside the bank of four elevators. He waved the electronic fob that hung from his key ring at a reader device. The enormous doors whooshed aside.

One elevator stood waiting with its doors open. He stepped on, swiped the fob at another reader device on the panel, and when the green light above it lit up, he pushed the 21 button.

As the elevator began its ascent to the penthouse floor, he could smell the delicate fragrance of the flowers. And that caused his mind to drift back to two weeks earlier.

Matt had been released from Temple University Hospital on the previous day. Amanda had brought home with them a few of the enormous floral arrangements that well-wishers had sent. In total, there had been more than a dozen, and as the newer ones had arrived, and begun to pack the room, Matt had insisted that their cards be kept but the flowers be distributed anonymously around the hospital for others to enjoy.

Now floral fragrances filled the condominium.

In the dining room, there was also the smell of beef tenderloin. Matt and Amanda had just finished a fine Chateaubriand with béarnaise sauce that she had prepared, knowing it was one of his favorites.

Matt marveled at the woman who was carrying his child. Amanda Law, who had just turned twenty-nine, was the chief physician in the Burn Unit at Temple. She stood five-five and weighed one-ten, and had an athlete's toned body. Thick, wavy blonde hair hung to her shoulders, softly framing her beautiful face and intelligent eyes.

Early in the meal, Matt had recognized that the conversation had been somewhat stiff and had tried to lighten it by again discussing the various plans in preparation for when the baby would come.

Amanda's mood brightened a bit. Yet, as they finished their food, Matt felt that something still was not quite right. He mentally debated telling her about his grand idea of looking for a condominium more appropriate for a young growing family, at least a two-bedroom, maybe in Center City.

He studied her across the table as she very carefully finished her glass of water.

"Are you doing okay, babe?" he said, reaching over and touching her hand.

"I don't know. For the last few days, I've just felt strange."

He chuckled.

"Strange? You've never been pregnant. The whole thing has got to feel really strange. You have a seven-week-old alien creature growing in you."

She did not respond to that.

"Just feels odd," she went on. "That, and I've been experiencing some lower-back pain. I'm thinking I need to get back to my exercise routine."

"You said earlier that there's no longer any nausea or tender breasts. That's progress, right?" He chuckled again. "I mean, especially for me. It's not like I can get you any *more* pregnant. And it does qualify as intense cardiovascular exercise . . ."

She did not respond. She turned to look out the window for a long moment.

She then pushed her chair back and stood.

"Excuse me. I'll be right back."

She went down the hallway and disappeared into the

bedroom. Matt heard the bathroom door close with a click.

When Amanda had not returned to the table after ten minutes, he carefully pulled himself out of his chair to go check on her.

He was almost to the bedroom door when she came out.

Matt thought that she now looked very pale. All the color was gone from her face. Her shoulders were slumped.

"Amanda?"

He saw that she was starting to cry. She buried her face in her hands. Her body trembled.

He quickly went to her and wrapped his arms around her.

The elevator made a delicate *Ding!* stopping at the top floor, its doors opening. As Matt stepped into the hallway, his mind flooded with all he had learned over the previous two weeks about miscarriages. And how sadly common they could be—and, arguably worse, how emotionally devastating.

At Unit 2180, he fed the key to the dead bolt of the heavy, dark-oak door. He could hear Luna whining on the other side, the two-year-old water dog's long tail thumping the wall. He gently pushed open the door.

Wish some of that happiness would rub off on your master, he thought, patting Luna's curly black head. Then he heard in his head his sister Amy's voice snapping:

You're such an asshole, Matt! Have some empathy, for chrissakes!

Matt found Amanda in the kitchen. She was emptying a bottle of cabernet sauvignon into a large wine stem that was on the black marble island. Another stem next to it was three-quarters full.

And that's not her first glass. There's a trace of lipstick on the rim.

Maybe she's making up for lost time—now that she's not pregnant, she can drink again.

"Hey, babe," he said, moving around the island to reach her. "You look beautiful . . . I got you something."

She smiled as he put his arm around her. He kissed her on the lips.

"You didn't have to get me anything," she said, gently placing the roses next to the kitchen sink.

"I wanted to."

"That's very sweet. Thank you."

Amanda handed the just filled wine stem to Matt, then touched hers to it.

"Salute," she said.

Matt smiled, said, *"Salute,"* then took a sip.

He looked at the wine bottle—*Nice red,* he thought, glancing at the label—then noticed the folded sheets of paper beside it.

She saw where he was looking and reached over for the papers. She held them out to him.

"What's this?"

"I'm afraid something we need to discuss. Again . . ."

Matt put his glass down. He unfolded the pages.

Oh shit, he thought, immediately recognizing what they were.

[TWO]

It had taken Matt a great deal of effort to get Amanda's attention when he first tried courting her. She initially had refused his overtures. Amanda, even though she had known Matt's sister since college, told him that she could not become involved romantically with a cop.

It wasn't, she said, that she did not admire cops— she, in fact, held them in high regard, even loved them. Especially because her father had been one. He had retired on a medical disability after taking a bullet to the knee while off duty and in the course of stopping a robber.

The reason, Amanda said, was that she did not want to again live with the daily fear. Her family always had wondered if when they watched him leave the house for work if that would be the last they saw him alive.

But Matt had been relentless in his pursuit. And eventually Amanda relented.

Her worrying about his safety, however, did not go away. It caused her to consider what-ifs. Her father had taught her how to approach a problem from both a best-case scenario and a worst-case—*Hope for the best but plan for the worst*—and to consider the latter, she had written an obituary as if it had been crafted by Matt's friend Mickey O'Hara.

Amanda had given it to Matt in hopes that it might cause him to see things differently.

Now Matt, his eyes skimming the obit, remembered it painfully well.

The Wyatt Earp of the Main Line:
KILLED IN THE LINE OF DUTY

Homicide Sergeant Matthew M. Payne, 31, Faithfully Served Family and Philly—and Paid the Ultimate Price.

By Michael J. O'Hara

Staff Writer, *Philly News Now*

Photographs courtesy of the Family and Michael J. O'Hara

PHILADELPHIA—The City of Brotherly Love grieves today at the loss of one of its finest citizens and public servants. Sergeant Matthew Mark Payne, a nine-year veteran of the Philadelphia Police Department, well known as the "Wyatt Earp of the Main Line," was gunned down last week in a Kensington alleyway as he dragged out a fellow officer who'd been wounded in an ambush.

Payne's heroic act amid a barrage of bullets sealed, right up until his last breath, his long-held reputation as a brave, loyal, and honorable officer and gentleman.

Friends and family say that part of what made Payne such an outstanding civil servant, one who personified the department's motto of *Honor, Integrity, Sacrifice*, was that he did not have to do the job.

He chose to do it.

A FAMILY THAT SERVED—
AND SACRIFICED

When, almost a decade ago, Payne graduated *summa cum laude* from the University of Pennsylvania, he could have followed practically any professional path other than law enforcement.

He'd enjoyed a privileged background, brought up in all the comfort that a Main Line lifestyle afforded. After attending prep school at Episcopal Academy, then completing his studies at U of P, he was expected to pursue a law degree and perhaps join his adoptive father's law practice, the prestigious firm of Mawson, Payne, Stockton, McAdoo & Lester.

Instead, Matt Payne chose something else: He decided that he should defend his country.

He signed recruitment papers with the United

States Marine Corps, only to have a minor condition with his vision bar him from joining the Corps.

Determined to serve in some capacity, Payne joined the Philadelphia Police Department.

Again, he didn't have to. If anything, Matt Payne had a pass. But, again, he chose to.

A pass because his biological father, Sergeant John F. X. Moffitt, known as "Jack," had been killed in the line of duty—shot dead while responding to a silent burglar alarm at a gasoline station. And Jack Moffitt's brother, Captain Richard C. "Dutch" Moffitt, who was commanding officer of the department's elite Highway Patrol, had been killed trying to stop a robbery of the Waikiki Diner on Roosevelt Avenue.

Payne's decision to join the police department came only months after his Uncle Dutch had been killed. Many believed he'd done so in order to avenge the deaths of his father and uncle and to prove that the eye condition that kept him out of the Corps would not keep him from being a good cop.

"Frankly, all that scared hell out of us," said Dennis V. "Denny" Coughlin, who recently retired as first deputy commissioner of police but at the time of Payne's joining the department was a chief inspector.

Coughlin long had been best friends with Jack Moffitt and took upon himself the sad duty of delivering the tragic news to Matt's mother—then pregnant with Matt—that she'd been widowed.

"I can confess now that when Matty came to the department," a visibly upset Coughlin said, "I tried to protect him. I sure as hell didn't want to have to knock on his mother's door with the news that now Jack's son—who was also my godson—had been killed on the job, too. Unfortunately, that duty fell last week to First Deputy Commissioner of Police Peter Wohl."

NEW COP, HERO COP

After graduating from the police academy, there was no question that Matt Payne was becoming both a good cop and a respected one.

"But no matter how hard we tried throughout his career," said Peter Wohl, to whom Payne was first assigned as an administrative assistant when Wohl ran Special Operations, "Matt wound up in the thick of things, bullets flying. That said, all his shootings were found to be righteous ones."

Before Payne had even put in six months on the job, he had already drawn his pistol. It had happened when he was off duty and had come across a van that fit the description of the one used by the criminal the newspaper headlines called the "Northwest Serial Rapist." When the van's driver tried to run him down, he shot him in the head. A young woman—trussed-up and naked in the back of the vehicle—was saved from becoming the rapist's next victim. And headlines hailed Matt Payne as a hero.

The next incident happened during an operation that was being covered by this writer.

Matt Payne had been assigned to provide protection for this writer in an alleyway that was supposed to be a safe distance from where tactical teams were staging to arrest gang members who had committed murder while robbing Goldbatt's Department Store.

"We thought that in having Matt sit on Mick," Wohl explained, "we could keep Mick out of our way and at the same time keep Matt far from any gunplay."

They were wrong.

As this writer reported then, one gang member who ran from the tactical teams came into the alleyway and began shooting. Payne, his forehead grazed by a bullet, returned fire and killed the felon.

The following day, a photograph taken by this writer of a bloodied Matt Payne holding his pistol while standing over the dead shooter appeared on the newspaper's front page with this writer's first-hand account of Payne's heroic actions.

The photograph's headline read "Officer M. M. Payne, 23, The Wyatt Earp of the Main Line."

A SHINING—BUT BRIEF—CAREER

Promotion followed. But so, too, did more gunfire.

Payne became romantically involved with a young woman named Susan Reynolds and discovered that a sorority sister of hers was caught up with a terrorist named Bryan Chenowith, the target of a nationwide manhunt by the Federal Bureau of Investigation.

In an attempt to trap Chenowith, Payne asked Reynolds to lure her friend to a diner in hopes that the fugitive would follow. The plan was for an FBI special agent to grab him, but the fugitive brought with him a .30 caliber carbine rifle—and shot up the diner parking lot.

Susan Reynolds took a bullet to the head and died in Payne's arms.

Later, Payne quietly admitted that the experience haunted him beyond anything he'd ever known.

Payne dealt with it as best he could, mostly by losing himself in his work. And that he did well.

When he was promoted to the rank of sergeant and transferred to the Homicide Unit, Matt Payne was given Badge No. 471, which previously had been worn by Sergeant Jack Moffitt, his father.

Other heroic incidents occurred—too many to be included here—but one of the most recent was among the most memorable, when the Wyatt Earp of the Main Line again found himself involved in a foot chase—and a shoot-out—with a murderer.

Payne happened to be at Temple University Hospital when Jesús Jiménez, a nineteen-year-old gang member, snuck into the third-floor Burn Unit and executed a patient. Payne pursued him out onto the streets, wounding him in the thigh, before Jiménez got away.

Jiménez, it turned out, belonged to a drug- and human-trafficking gang led by Juan Paulo Delgado, a Texican, age twenty-one. And the assassination in the hospital to settle a drug deal debt was only a part of Delgado's reign of terror—one that stretched from the streets of Philadelphia to the dirt trails of the Texas–Mexico border.

When Delgado abducted for ransom Dr. Amanda Law—whose patient Jiménez had murdered—Payne, Detective Anthony Harris, and Sergeant Jim Byrth of the legendary Texas Rangers law enforcement agency were already hunting him.

The men, acting on a tip from their informant, tracked Delgado's gang to a dilapidated row house on Hancock Street in Kensington. After a shoot-out, Delgado was dead. Payne and his associates then rescued Dr. Law, who they found bound and gagged in the kitchen, her head covered with a pillowcase.

And so now we come to today. One final time we declare Matt Payne a hero.

This courageous, dedicated son of Philadelphia gave the city his all. May he rest in peace.

"We know that Matt will always be a hero to the decent and law-abiding citizens of Philadelphia," his wife, Dr. Amanda Law Payne, said as she held their toddler daughter on her hip and as their twin sons clung to her legs following a memorial service that overflowed with attendees. "But first and foremost, he was our family's hero. While we must move forward, our children and I shall never ever forget that."

Matthew Mark Payne is survived by his loving wife of five years, Mrs. Amanda Law Payne; his sons, Brewster Cortland Payne III and John Francis Xavier Moffitt Payne, age four; his daughter, Mandy Law Payne, age two; his sister, Dr. Amelia Payne; his parents, Mr. and Mrs. B. C. Payne II; and numerous other relatives and friends.

The family requests that, in lieu of flowers, memorials be made for other officers in Matthew Mark Payne's name to the Widows & Orphans' Fund at the Fraternal Order of Police Lodge #5, 11630 Caroline Road, Philadelphia, PA 19154-2110.

Matt, feeling the deep frustration that hit the first time he had read the obit, slowly refolded the papers and gently put them on the marble countertop.

Amanda said, "And now to that can be added you being declared Public Enemy No. 1 and getting shot by that damn drug dealer."

"You know," he said, "all that Public Enemy nonsense basically evaporated when Skinny Lenny got crushed to death. He was the problem, and now it's over."

"I truly hope so, Matt. Just the thought of someone else taking a shot at you, well . . ."

Jesus! Does she know about today?

It was on the TV news when I got out of the shower.

But I only heard Camilla Rose being mentioned.
What do I say?

After a while, he said, "I don't know what to say."

Amanda nodded.

She took a sip of her wine, then said, "At the hospital, I deal with death on a daily basis. I'm not going to wear the loss of the baby on my sleeve. But it is causing me a great deal of reflection. I can't get past the emptiness."

"So, first we lose the baby. And now . . . what?"

"Damn it, Matt! I almost lost you. That obit almost came true."

She paused, bit her lower lip, then, clearly measuring her words, went on. "I am not in any way blaming the miscarriage on you. They happen in fifteen percent of pregnancies. That's an unfortunate fact. My mother said she had two before she had me. Intelligently, clinically, I can understand losing the baby. Emotionally, is something else. Something that I'm learning I'm coming to terms with."

She inhaled deeply, then slowly let it out.

"Matt, I let my mind get too far ahead, making plans for the baby, for us. And because of that, because now there won't be a baby, there's this . . . this horrible void deep inside me."

She turned and pulled a tissue from the box on the counter and blew her nose.

"I'm disappointed and angry with myself," she said. "I didn't recognize the signs and I should have."

"You were distracted. It's understandable. I take all the blame for that."

She remained silent, clearly in deep thought.

"But we can try again," Matt said. "Right?"

He met Amanda's eyes. They were puffy and red—and he saw that they did not appear to support what he just said.

"What I do know," Amanda then said, softly, "is that we now have more time."

"Time?"

She nodded. "Maybe . . . maybe we were rushing all this a bit because of the baby. And I think that maybe a little time apart can be helpful."

Matt felt a huge knot in his stomach.

He glanced at her left hand and was relieved to see she still wore her engagement ring.

"Amanda, what are you saying?"

"I've been approached to be a visiting professor in an emergency medicine residency program."

"What? Where?"

"It's a joint Army–Air Force facility, a military medical center in San Antonio."

"Texas?"

She nodded.

"When?"

"Initially," she said, "I turned them down—I've mentioned that I get requests regularly that I have to decline for many reasons, and this time I'd just found out about the pregnancy—and then I forgot about the offer. But then a follow-up e-mail came saying that the doctor who accepted it had had a family emergency and the position remained open. And the more I thought about it, the more it made sense to immerse myself in work in a fresh environment."

She paused, then added, "A family emergency. Some irony, huh?"

"When?" Matt repeated.

"Next week. For an initial thirty days."

Matt's eyes grew wide.

"You're leaving next week? For a month?"

Amanda bit her lower lip again. She nodded.

Matt could not believe what he was hearing. He absently reached up and loosened his necktie, then opened the collar button.

"Military medicine," she then said, "particularly burn and trauma as a result of the wars, and the IEDs—those evil, improvised explosive devices—has been making huge, innovative leaps. It's a chance for me to learn first-hand from their doctors' methods and teach their residents about what I know from all the work we get here."

Matt said nothing as he looked past Amanda, his mind racing.

After a long pause, Amanda said, "I think it'll be good for both of us, Matt."

He looked at her, then said, "I don't know what I was thinking. Sure. I should have no trouble taking the time off. And San Antone is beautiful."

She pursed her lips and shook her head.

"No," she said finally, "I need to go alone."

Matt tried to absorb that. The knot in his stomach grew even larger.

"I . . . I don't know what to say."

Amanda's stomach growled.

"Sorry," she said. "That's nerves, I guess."

She took a healthy swallow of wine.

He said, "Do you want to get something to eat?"

She shook her head slightly.

"I'm not really hungry," she said. "Haven't really had an appetite for some time."

"I understand."

"But you should eat. I'll go—"

"No," he interrupted, softly. "It's okay. I guess I'm really not hungry, either."

He drained his wine stem, then walked over to the bar. He took one of the squat heavy crystal glasses that Amanda had ordered for him—the monogram MPM was etched in an elegant, bold roman typeface—and reached past the bottle of black-label Irish whisky and grabbed the Macallan eighteen-year-old single malt. He filled the glass half full, then added water almost to its rim.

He took a big sip of the scotch whisky as he walked over to the wall of floor-to-ceiling windows. Wordlessly, he looked out at the view of the Delaware River, the massive Ben Franklin Bridge reflecting off it, and, far into the distance beyond, the twinkling lights of New Jersey.

He inhaled deeply, then let it out slowly. And then he swallowed the remainder of the single malt.

"Matt . . . ?" she said, almost in a whisper.

He turned and stared at her and frowned as he nodded slightly, then walked back to the kitchen island and put the empty glass in the sink.

He put his hands on her hips, then leaned in and softly kissed her on the cheek.

"I love you," he said, softly, before pulling his head back.

She looked in his eyes.

"I love you, too, Matt."

"I think—" he began, but his throat caught. He cleared it and went on. "I think it'd be best if I stayed at my place tonight."

Amanda did not respond.

Matt looked deeply into her glistening eyes.

She is not exactly rushing to stop me.

He nodded gently. His eyes drifted past her toward the wall of windows, then back to her. An enormous tear was slipping down her cheek. He cradled her head as he kissed the tear, savored its warm saltiness, then lowered his hands to her shoulders, squeezed her tight, and released her.

"We can talk tomorrow?" he said, it coming out as a question.

"Certainly."

He nodded again.

And then he turned and started down the hallway.

Luna got to her feet and padded over and intercepted him. He quickly knelt down and scratched her ears.

He stood and wanted to say "Good girl" but didn't trust his voice not to break.

Matt, stepping into the hall, pulled the heavy oak front door shut. After he locked the dead bolt and removed the key, he could hear Amanda starting to sob.

Numb, he stared at the key.

He thought, *It wasn't long ago that she said hearing the sound of my key in the door made her think,* Now the fun begins.

Now it's causing exactly the opposite . . .

[THREE]
West Rittenhouse Square
Center City
Philadelphia
Thursday, January 5, 9 P.M.

Matt Payne, making a left off Walnut Street, had every intention of driving directly to his apartment. His mind spun, trying to put all that had happened in perspective. He realized the wine and whisky on an empty stomach had not exactly helped his thought process.

As he went past, he glanced at the enormous, century-old Romanesque façade of Holy Trinity Episcopal Church on the corner. Then the entrance to The Rittenhouse came into view.

"Oh, fuck it," he said, and tugged the steering wheel. "That's as sure a sign from God, if ever there was one."

The Porsche made a fast right, its tires rumbling as it shot up the brick-paved drive.

"Welcome back, Mr. Payne," a teenage valet said, holding open the door.

Payne, with some difficulty, climbed out of the car.

"How you doing, Ryan? How's La Salle treating you?"

"School's okay, thanks," he said, then nodded toward the row of cars parked nearby. "You want me to leave it out, close, like usual?"

"Hell no! Don't you know what happens to cars that get parked there?"

The valet's eyebrows went up.

"Yeah," Ryan said, "we all heard about that. I just remembered they said you were here when it happened. I heard that Melody said you were amazing."

"Just lucky. Others were not so fortunate."

The valet nodded, then moved to get in the driver's seat.

"Ryan, are you familiar with Saint Timothy?"

"As in the Bible, sir?" he said, looking up.

"The good book indeed. Saint Timothy says, 'Drink no longer water, but use a little wine for thy stomach's sake and thine often infirmities.' You can confirm that next door, if you wish. Regardless, I'll be in the Library Bar, trying to drink away any memory of this day and my 'often infirmities.' Then, at some point, I plan to walk—quite possibly, stagger—to my place around the corner." He patted the roof of the 911. "Park this in a safe place. I'll get it tomorrow. Do not under any circumstances allow me to have its key until then."

The valet chuckled. "Yessir."

"And, Ryan, despite the fact that I may drive it like I stole it, you may not."

The valet, shaking his head, chuckled again as he closed the door.

A second later, the window came down.

"Can I ask a question?" Ryan said.

Payne saw that the teenager's expression had turned serious.

"Sure," he said, his tone no longer light. "What's on your mind?"

"If someone may have overheard something about what happened today, what's the procedure to—?"

"What did you hear?" Payne interrupted.

"Not me."

"Then who? The shooting is an active homicide case. We really need information and now."

"I only said *if* someone . . ."

Payne quickly pulled a business card from his pocket and handed it to him.

"My phone numbers are on there. And the tip line's. Give it to anyone."

"You can keep anonymous, right? And there's a cash reward?

"Yeah. Up to twenty grand. It's *that* important, Ryan."

"Right. Thanks."

As Payne watched the Porsche slowly rumble away, he thought, *That service industry is a huge network. Valets, bartenders, maids—they see and hear everything.*

He sure as hell knows something.

Just wonder if it's something useful?

*   *   *

The Library Bar was an open, airy venue that created the feel of being in a very expensive, very modern mansion. It featured crisp backlighting and highly polished dark wood trim. There were deep couches and leather-upholstered armchairs arranged facing one another over low tables. The white marble bar itself was an intimate affair, lined with only a half dozen tall chairs. The bookshelves on either side of the stone fireplace, containing rare volumes on Philadelphia history, projected the impression of an exclusive private library.

Payne could hear the elevated murmur from the bar well before he reached its ornate, double-door entrance. And he started having second thoughts about going inside at all.

"What the hell am I doing?" he muttered. "I'm not up for this."

When he glanced in, he saw that the room was nearly full, with a nicely dressed, animated crowd.

I'm not thinking clearly. I shouldn't be here now.

He turned on his heels and headed for the door, wondering if the bar at the Union League would be quiet at this hour and he could drown his misery in peace there.

"Matthew!" a woman's voice called behind him. "I thought that was you. Please wait."

As he turned, Camilla Rose Morgan, looking stunning in a black satin cocktail dress and extravagant high heels, came toward him. She was balancing a full martini glass in her right hand.

"What a wonderful surprise," she said, grasping his

arm and giving him an exaggerated head-to-toe glance. "And, my, how you *do* clean up quite nicely." She motioned with her glass. "Please come and join me . . . join *us*. I owe you that drink."

Payne looked closely at her. She had a flushed face and somewhat glassy, dilated eyes. He could tell that while she more or less was holding her own, she was far from sober.

Which is not surprising. She started drinking in the car—what?—some six hours ago.

Hail, hail, the return of the prodigal party girl!

But, what the hell? One friend is dead. And Johnny Austin almost dead.

Who can blame her? Certainly not me. I'm ready to crawl into a bottle just over a rocky relationship . . .

"I was looking for someone," Payne said, "and they're clearly not here. Thank you for the offer, Camilla Rose. But I should head home."

"Please stay. Just for one drink?" she said, stroking his arm. She then took one of the olives and slipped it slowly between her lips.

My God, he thought. *My brain really is not working.*

She made that look damn suggestive—borderline seductive.

But it couldn't have been.

She smiled and gave him a questioning look.

He glanced beyond her toward the crowd. He thought he recognized a couple of somewhat famous faces.

"I really can't. But, thank you."

She saw where his eyes went.

"You're right. That is a boring scene," she said, touching his arm again. "Listen, I've been thinking since we spoke and there's something else I really should tell you."

"Great."

"Not here. Not in public."

"Okay. Where?"

She glanced over her shoulder toward the bar, then turned the opposite way.

"Follow me," she said, and began walking quickly toward the lobby, sipping her martini.

As she went, Payne's eyes automatically dropped to her derriere. The black satin dress clung to her firm hourglass figure. She turned a corner.

She really is one stunning woman.

But where the hell is she going? Not to her room?

I would really be an unmitigated bastard if I wound up sleeping with her.

Especially since I am engaged. At least, I think I'm still engaged.

No, not a problem—jumping her is not even a remote possibility.

But given that I'm even considering the idea, however remote, with all that's happened today, proves that I am an unmitigated bastard.

He came around the corner in time to see her going into the entrance to the condominium lobby.

Oh boy.

Not only absolutely proves that I am the poster boy for unmitigated bastards but also that a stiff prick hath no conscience.

Keep repeating: Listen to what she has to say, then leave . . .

He went through the lobby and found her standing just inside an elevator. She held out her right foot, the high heel shoe keeping the doors from closing. She motioned for him to move faster. Standing behind her was an attractive, well-dressed couple, each holding what appeared to be a flute of champagne.

The elevator alarm buzzed.

"Matthew, hurry—please!" Camilla Rose said, and smiled.

Payne moved quickly to the elevator. As he stepped in, his phone began ringing. He looked at it.

She moved her foot from the door. The elevator doors started closing.

"I have to take this," he said, quickly turning sideways and stepping back off. "I'll catch up."

Out of the corner of his eye, he saw her watching with a perplexed expression just as the doors shut.

The elevator ascended.

Payne put the phone to his head.

"Nice timing, Tony. Think I just dodged another bullet. What's up?"

After listening to Harris, his phone vibrated and he quickly checked its glass screen. Camilla Rose had texted her unit number.

"Sure," Payne then said to Harris. "I'm free."

[FOUR]
The Union League
140 South Broad Street
Philadelphia
Thursday, January 5, 9:35 P.M.

Matt Payne was alone at the large, heavy wooden bar—
there were only two other men, both in business suits, at
the far end of the room—draining his third scotch
whisky with a splash of water. He saw Baxter step into
the doorway from the front desk stand, look toward
Payne, and then with his left arm make a sweeping gesture into the room. Tony Harris then appeared from the
corridor. He was carrying a large file folder.

Baxter, who had been at the Union League for as
long as Payne could remember, and had to be in his
eighties, scowled his disapproval as Payne raised his
scotch glass toward him and smiled and waved.

Baxter then bowed slightly and slipped away as Harris crossed the room.

"I never get tired of this place," Harris said as he took
the seat next to Payne. "It's like stepping back in time.
The ambience drips of Old World Philadelphia circa
1862."

Founded during the Civil War as a patriotic society,
the Union League of Philadelphia long boasted a

membership of great wealth and power. Its enormous historic brownstone—with its iconic pair of curved stone staircases dramatically leading up to the heavy wooden doors of the main entrance on the second level—occupied an entire Center City block in the shadow of high-rises housing the offices of Fortune 500 corporations and just steps south of City Hall.

Harris scanned the large, high-ceilinged room. The polished-marble floor highlighted the exotic rugs. There was rich wood paneling and leather-upholstered furniture. The corridors were lined with bronze and marble busts and sculptures, as well as presidential portraits and paintings of man-o'-wars sailing the high seas.

Harris then saw that Payne had his smartphone on the bar.

"Still having trouble not breaking rules, I see," he said.

A sign was prominently posted near the front desk—ostensibly for guests but certain members required constant reminding—that League policy prohibited cellular telephone conversations. The signs also stated that the devices should be turned off.

Payne, like many others, simply put his phone on SILENT and, except for now, out of sight.

"No one here for me to annoy, unfortunately," Payne said as the bartender approached. "What's your poison?"

"Club soda for now, please," Harris told the bartender, who nodded and turned away.

"You trying to make me feel bad? Or worse than I already do?"

"I might have something stiffer, in a bit," Harris said, pulling papers out of the folder. He slid the top sheet on the bar in front of Payne.

"Before we get into this," Payne said, "let me add to what I said Camilla Rose told me in the car. About an hour ago, I decided to grab a bite at the Library Bar after an interesting evening with Amanda—"

"You say that like it's not good," Harris interrupted.

Payne grimaced.

"And it really is *not* good," he said, "but I'll not burden you with my personal troubles."

"You know I'll be your sounding board anytime . . ."

"Yeah, I do. And I appreciate it, Tony. But not right now, thanks. I don't want to think about it, let alone talk about it. Label me as being in deep denial."

"Ours is a shitty business for relationships. If it's any consolation, we've all been through it."

The bartender placed a tall glass of club soda on a napkin in front of Harris and silently slipped away.

"Misery loves company—cheers to that!" Payne said, and touched his glass to Harris's. "So, anyway, I was walking up to the entrance of the bar full of beautiful people having a grand time when I decided I was really at the wrong place at the wrong time, that I should be having my pity party here, quietly drowning my sorrows . . ."

A couple minutes later, Payne finished, "And that's how you helped me dodge another bullet."

"Jesus, you really think she was going to jump your bones?"

"Sure seemed like it. Then, right after I sat down

here, she sent a text that said *Where are you? I'm out on my terrace.* And followed that with this picture of herself by a roaring fireplace."

Payne tapped the glass screen of his phone, then Harris looked at it.

"Holy shit!" Harris blurted. "You took a pass on hooking up with that? You, my friend, have the strength of legions."

"Trust me, I'm as weak as the next guy. The thought crossed my mind. But while I went through my first drink here, I knew it was the little head doing the thinking. By the second drink, the big head weighed in and reminded me that party girls are dangerous. So, I called her—wound up getting her voice mail, fortunately—and apologized that work called—which was, literally, true—but that I was waiting to hear what else she said she wanted to share—also true."

"Coming on to you while her boyfriend is in the hospital—*dangerous* is right."

"You know, despite what she told you, I don't think he's really her boyfriend. She may just be leading him on. I told you she said she wouldn't marry him."

Harris grunted, then said, "Women—who the hell knows?"

Payne nodded, and thought, *And maybe that's what Amanda's thinking now about marriage.*

Taking a sip of his scotch, Payne's eyes went to the sheet of paper on the bar. He picked it up.

"So, what am I looking at?" he said. "Would appear to be a company's performance chart."

"This is the tip of the iceberg of what we found on Benson," Harris said, pointing to the printout. "The Krow started digging for data points with his scan software and—bingo! He's still collecting more open-source intel, but this was what he found after only a few hours."

Detective Danny Krowczyk was a Signals Intelligence analyst assigned to the Digital Forensic Sciences Unit. The skinny, six-foot-four thirty-year-old's office attire never varied—jeans, white polo shirt, black sneakers— and his idea of a seven-course meal consisted of a six-pack of diet cola and a package of yellow Tastykake Dreamies.

Harris went on. "In addition to CEO of NextGenRx, turns out Benson was basically the hands-on head cheerleader of the small start-up. He was aggressive. Had a short temper and was prone to yelling, or firing off rants on social media, at anyone who questioned the company. Actually called them idiots and worse."

"Sounds like classic small-dick syndrome," Payne said, studying the chart. "Maybe too aggressive? That's what caused the share price to tank?"

"Good question. All I can tell you is, don't ever come to me for financial advice." He gestured toward the sheet. "While I have never heard of NextGenRx before today, it damn sure is well known among the penny stock traders on the over-the-counter exchange. And especially on the investor websites, on their discussion boards, where you cannot count the number of postings by people frustrated and angry with the company. Judging by the posts, more than a few people would not be unhappy to learn what happened to Benson."

"Losing money on lousy penny stocks? You think that's motive to whack the guy? In broad daylight in Center City?"

Harris tapped his index finger on the stack of sheets of paper by the brown folder.

"First, I would've made fun of penny stocks, too, before I saw the comments on these discussion boards that referenced a Silicon Valley tech giant quietly snapping up a penny stock company that manufactured smart-home technology. When word got out, the share price shot from two-tenths of a cent to four cents—to the tune of three billion bucks. Then went up from there."

Payne whistled softly. "I stand corrected."

"Second, as to motive, I suppose it depends on how much one loses relative to how much one can afford to lose. And the Mob used to whack people in broad daylight all the time."

"Damn it. You're right again, of course. Jason's voice just popped in my head. It is a stone to turn over. And likely a big one. What happened with the company?"

"According to the discussion boards, investors lost confidence." He pointed to the chart. "Here, some people bailed at or near the top at a dime a share. Others lost money as shares collapsed back to around a penny. Many wrote online that they had given up on a return on investment. At this point, they would have been satisfied with just a return *of* investment."

"So, what caused the stock to nose-dive?"

"Apparently the company could not provide proof

that they (a) actually had a physical product that did what they claimed and (b) one that would be approved by the FDA. Medical device approval by the feds, from what I've picked up, is tough as hell. And without that, they had no marketable product. Remember the phrase *patent pending*? Well, that's about what they have. Lots of paperwork filed with the U.S. Patent Office. And when certain shareholders asked for independent scientific proof the device worked, Benson said that the company would not show a product until their intellectual property was safely under their patent, then berated them as short sellers bad-mouthing the company in order to profit on the share price drop."

"Sounds like *The Wizard of Oz*: 'Pay no attention to that man behind the curtain.'"

"Exactly. And when you get an idea of what the device is supposed to do, you really wonder . . . It's futuristic . . ."

Payne gestured for him to go on.

"Remember those eyeglasses they came out with that let you surf the Internet? You essentially are wearing a computer and no one knows what you're viewing."

"Yeah. That was futuristic by itself."

"This goes another step further. Instead of glasses, they're like contact lenses. The surface of an eyeball is a sort of one-stop shop. It can give these special lenses your body's vital information—temperature, pulse, et cetera. They claim the lenses can also monitor a person's level of medication. It works with a mobile phone—specifically, a smartphone—"

"Which is actually just a small, powerful computer that happens to also work as a telephone," Payne put in, tapping his on the bar.

"Right. And because it's also a phone, it can send a report to your doctor. Let's say you're diabetic. The user puts an app on the smartphone that checks blood sugar levels and warns you before it's too low or high. Or if you're, say, schizophrenic, the app can tell if you're on your meds—and, if not, then send a report to your doctor. They claim—again, key word *claim*—eventually the next level will be maintaining medication, so the doctor can send a command that administers your meds through another device."

"Jesus. Amazing. No more crazies? Or, at least, fewer? That's huge. So is reducing diabetic comas."

Harris said, "And that, supposedly, is the tip of the iceberg."

"What powers the lenses, and how do they communicate to the phone? I mean, you can't really have wires hanging from your eyeballs."

"Exactly. Good questions. And that seems to be exactly what the investors also want to know."

"So it's futuristic. And it's incredible. But, then, so was the smartphone not too many years ago. Still, if there's no patent and no FDA-approved device, it's all speculation. Investors are gambling—arguably, more than usual." He looked back at the chart. "What am I missing? What caused this spike in price at a dime?"

"News that there's been some interest by much larger companies, which suddenly gave the device and company some credibility. The suggestion was made—Benson was accused of using a shill to feed it on the discussion boards—that NextGen was the target of a takeover, and, if that failed to go through, then that the bigger companies would license use of the technology. Sound like another penny stock tale, one that has a happy ending?"

"And it went down again today," Payne said, pointing at the sheet. And then his eyebrows rose. "Maybe we should look into getting some shares. Damn, sure looks cheap now."

"Might want to wait and see what happens when news of Benson's death goes public," Harris said, then grunted. "But, then, I've already warned you about taking investment advice from me."

He took a long drink of his club soda.

"Right now," Harris then said, "until we talk with Austin, it's the best we have to go on. I also left a message for McGuire asking for a list, if there is one, of anyone requesting protection for the Camilla's Kids event."

Lieutenant Gerry McGuire, a somewhat plump, pleasant-looking forty-five-year-old, was the commanding officer of Dignitary Protection.

Payne nodded, and he said, "Let's plan on being at Hahnemann when Austin wakes up tomorrow morning. See what we can get out of him. Then, if I don't hear back from Mason Morgan—I've left voice mail messages on three different numbers—we'll make a surprise courtesy call at his office . . . Anything new on the shooter's van?"

"Well, the doers are still in the wind. Not a trace of

the bastards. And not much in the van. There was a little blood in back—like, maybe, from a bloody nose. And the spent shotgun shells. And a burner phone, which Krow's techs are going through.

"The security video files that McCrory got from the steak house cameras show the van turning off Walnut and parking at the driveway entrance about an hour before the shooting. The driver—a short, skinny white male—got out to put the orange cones at the front and back bumpers but was very careful to keep his back to the curb and keep his head down to conceal his face. All that can be seen of him is his clothing, including a black cap and gloves."

"And the gloves suggest the crime scene guys will be shit outta luck on getting fingerprints off anything—the phone, the shells, the vehicle."

"The plates that were on the vehicle came off another white Chevy van, identical make and model."

"Of course they did. All of which suggests these particular bad guys aren't exactly newbies to the trade."

Payne's phone vibrated on the wooden bar, its glass screen illuminated. Both their heads turned toward it.

Payne saw there was a red box with a text message from *215-555-2398*, a local number. It read *A guy on staff heard that Morgan lady tell the blond guy, "That's the last $100K he gets. Not another payment till the bastard produces." Maybe that's connected to the shooting?*

Payne showed it to Harris.

"A hundred grand?" Payne said. "If it's the same envelope, she said it held only fifty-large."

"Who's that message from?" Harris said.

"Not sure. Maybe Ryan, the valet. When I dropped off my car to go to the bar, he asked about how someone would submit an anonymous tip on the shooting. I think he knows something. But he denied it. I said we need information now, gave him my number, and told him to share it."

"The number for your department-issued cell phone, right? You're not giving out your mobile number to anyone."

"My department phone keeps crapping out, so I leave it plugged in at my desk and forward its calls to one of the throwaway lines on my smartphone. I can add and delete the throwaways all day long with the app. That way, I've got everything in one device and my personal number stays private. Don't need anyone trying to track me down with it."

"How do you tell them apart? Who's calling which of the numbers?"

"Caller ID usually tells me the name. But if it's just a number or blocked, the background colors for the ID box are all different." He pointed. "This throwaway line is red. See? My personal line's blue."

Harris nodded, looked across the bar, then rubbed his chin.

"You know," he said, "when we asked her about the cash, she dodged the question. Wouldn't say which vendors. But we didn't push her on that, either."

"That can be one of the first things I ask her tomorrow," Payne said, then thumbed a text reply asking when and where the staffer had overheard the conversation about the money.

He hit SEND, and, a moment later, an error message box popped up: NUMBER NOT VALID.

He sent another text, and the same message appeared.

"Maybe a burner?" Harris said.

Payne drained his drink.

"That," Payne said, waving for the check, "or maybe sent through one of those anonymous messaging websites that mask the sender's Internet address."

"Like the one that Temple University party girl who got dumped used to taunt the guy's wife—'Hey, your loving hubby's having a wild affair.'"

"And attached a photo of her Sugar Daddy in an extremely compromising act," Payne said. "That's it, the one Kerry cracked. I'll get him to see if he can run down this one after he's gotten the cell tower dump. Right now, there's nothing we can do until our early-morning meeting with Austin and then Camilla Rose . . ."

"Yeah."

"So I'm going home and feel sorry for myself."

III

When the ringing of Matt Payne's cellular phone on the bedside table woke him from a deep sleep at four-thirty, he immediately worried it was something to do with Amanda.

The last words he expected to hear were *Camilla Rose Morgan is dead*.

It had taken him five minutes in his foggy state of mind for the news to really register. Most of that fog, he realized, was because of all the scotch whisky he had consumed, the reminders of which were a throbbing head and a dry mouth that felt as if it was stuffed with cotton balls.

Then, through all that, the reason why he had hit the sauce so hard came back into painfully sharp focus. The thought of that made him feel there was a very good chance that he would become sick to his stomach. And right there and then.

He inhaled deeply, and let it slowly out, and the moment passed.

"Camilla Rose Morgan is dead," Tony Harris had announced. "I'm at the scene at The Rittenhouse."

Payne, rubbing his eyes, had then made out the sound of sirens once again bouncing off the buildings surrounding the park.

"Gimme ten," Payne had muttered, and broke off the call as he shuffled the short distance to the bathroom, delicately checking beneath his bandage as he went.

Tony Harris was in the hotel lobby of The Rittenhouse, talking with Detective Richard J. McCrory, when Payne arrived exactly ten minutes later. Dick McCrory, a native of Boston, was thirty-nine, of medium build, with close-cropped dark hair graying at the temples. He had served on the department for eighteen years, six of those with Homicide.

Harris watched Payne passing through the bright glare of a television news camera while waving off a reporter's questions. Harris motioned to McCrory, who turned and saw Payne and then disappeared around the corner.

Harris noticed that Payne looked somewhat pale and wondered how much of that was from a hangover or because he had inspected the scene before coming inside. Or both.

When the Crime Scene Unit blue shirts had arrived, they immediately erected a ten-by-ten-foot aluminum-framed canopy tent—one looking, more or less, like the square ones used by tailgaters in stadium parking lots—over a sleek silver Jaguar XJR sedan parked by the fountain. The tent's opaque vinyl top and side panels shielded the scene—and the dignity of the victim—from the lenses of the news media, as well as from passersby and those looking down from the windows of nearby high-rises. Only the vehicle's front and rear bumpers were exposed, and yellow police tape was strung around the XJR to create a protective perimeter.

Harris also noted that Payne had pulled on the clothes he had worn the previous night. His camel hair jacket was unbuttoned, and Harris could just make out the butt of the Colt .45 in the shoulder holster beneath it. The black leather case holding his badge hung from a chromed bead chain at the middle of his necktie. He hadn't shaved.

"Jesus H. Christ, Tony," Payne said, shaking his head. "The day that something like that doesn't shake me to the core, just shoot me. Please."

"No shit. Likewise."

McCrory came back from around the corner bearing two large, waxed-paper cups of coffee.

He held out one each to Harris and Payne.

"Black and black, gentlemen," he said, a distinct trace of his Southie accent still evident.

"I owe you, Dick," Payne said, and, before taking a sip, asked, "So, what do we know?"

"Right now," Harris said, "only that at oh-four-hundred she landed on the roof of that Jag, which is one of the chauffeured house vehicles. Made one helluva sound, then set off the car's alarm. The guy on concierge duty ran out and found her."

"Fell? Jumped? Pushed? What?"

Harris shrugged, and looked at McCrory.

"Door was open to her condo when they went up," McCrory then said, "but no one was there. They found the place trashed. Looks like a party that got out of control. Booze bottles and narcotics—some coke, Ecstasy—everywhere."

"Oh-four-hundred?" Payne said, exchanging a knowing look with Harris. "Security get any complaints?"

"None," McCrory said. "Hank Nasuti has been upstairs making lots of new friends by knocking on her neighbors' doors. So far, everyone has told him they know nothing, that they slept through whatever went on." He paused and looked at Payne, and added, "How much of that you figure is the Center City version of the hood's no-snitching bullshit?"

Payne considered that briefly, then said, "Some people here, for a number of reasons, can be very tight-lipped. But, by and large, people who invest in a place like this don't tolerate wild parties and would say something. There are families living here, some with small children."

He thought, *Like I was hoping to be—and still am hoping to be.*

McCrory nodded.

Payne looked at Harris, and said, "Last we know for certain is that she was in her condo, clearly alone, at nine twenty-five last night."

"How do *we* know that?" McCrory said.

"She told me."

McCrory looked at him, then glanced at Harris.

"Take his word for it, Dick."

"Short story is," Payne offered, "I ran into her as she came out of the Library Bar just after nine. She was drinking with some group there and feeling her oats. Minutes later, I watched her go up an elevator to the condos. And then I was on my way to meet with Detective Harris. She sent me, at the aforementioned time of nine twenty-five, a picture of herself on her terrace."

"Mary, Joseph, and all the fookin' saints," McCrory said. "Maybe someone else was there with her? The party maybe just getting going?"

Payne shook his head.

"She was alone then," he said.

"Ohh-kay," McCrory said after a while, looking clearly impressed with Payne's story. "I'd heard a rumor that you were quite the swordsman back in the day. That's some catch."

"Absolutely nothing happened between us," Payne snapped, his tone matter-of-fact. "She had something to tell me, she said, and whatever the hell it was, now she's dead."

They locked eyes.

McCrory then shrugged.

"Yeah, Matt," he said, looking genuinely embarrassed.

"I let my mouth run. Sorry. Anyway, so we need to grab video from her floor—"

"That's going to be a challenge," Payne interrupted, "as there are no surveillance cameras up there. People who pay a million or more for a condominium guard their privacy rather fiercely, which is one of the reasons why they tend to be tight-lipped, too. Different story here in the hotel, with a far more transient crowd. Its floors are all covered, stairwells, everything."

When Payne saw the questioning look on McCrory's face, he added, "I've been doing some research on the building. Long story."

McCrory nodded, and said, "Then we'll get the footage of her path between the elevators and the bar and start by building a time line after, say, nine, nine-fifteen. Maybe she came back down to the bar or people from the bar went up." He paused, then added, "Bartender, waitresses—they should know who was there and when."

"And/or they'll know someone else on staff who does," Payne said. "The condo residents have access to the same amenities as the hotel, from room service at any hour to housekeeping, the gym, the spa. Lots of eyes and ears."

"Yeah, and the service industry is pretty tight."

"Matt," Harris said, "Camilla Rose said her assistant came to the hospital for that envelope of cash. She—or maybe it's a he or maybe there's more than one—should know who, at least, some of them are. But we didn't get her name or number."

"We can reach her through the foundation," Payne said, then glanced at his wristwatch. "In maybe three, four hours?"

Payne carefully sipped his coffee, then his expression changed. He scrolled through his list of recent calls on his cell phone, then dialed one of them.

"I got this when I called her last night," Payne said, holding out the phone for them to hear. "Wait for the end."

"Hi!" Camilla Rose Morgan's voice came over the speakerphone.

Payne felt the hairs on the back of his neck stand up. Hearing her voice brought back mental images of her—in his car, drinking from the miniature bottle of vodka; in the tight black satin dress; in the picture on the terrace; and finally on the collapsed roof of the Jaguar—and then made him wonder if she would still be alive had he not fled the elevator . . . and her advances.

"So sorry I missed you," she said, her voice with its usual chipper tone. *"Please leave a message. If it's foundation-related and urgent, my assistant, Joy, is happy to help you at 212-555-5643."*

"New York City number," McCrory said, taking his cell phone out and quickly punching in the number.

Payne broke off his call as a pleasant young woman's voice, also chipper in tone, came over McCrory's speakerphone. There had not been a single ring; the call had rolled right into the voice mail function.

"Hello! This is Joy Abrams with Camilla's Kids. Your call is extremely important to us, so please leave a message

and we will get back to you right away. Thank you for your support!"

McCrory left a message, identifying himself as a police detective and saying he was calling about an emergency concerning Ms. Morgan. Next, he sent a text message repeating the same message.

"Stating the obvious," Payne then said, "the instant voice mail suggests that either she turned off the phone or its battery crapped out. Like most decent people at this hour, she most likely is enjoying her sleep."

Payne then held up his right index finger.

"Eureka!" he said. "And very likely doing so in the hotel here. Be right back."

Harris and McCrory watched as he walked over to the front desk. A female desk clerk, her attractive face not masking her sadness, appeared from an office door behind the desk. She forced a smile. Payne said something as he held up his identification. She turned her head toward it, nodded, and then she looked down behind the desk and quickly typed on her computer terminal.

A moment later, she was saying something while reaching across the counter to hand Payne a telephone receiver.

Putting it to his ear, he silently waited almost a full thirty seconds before gesturing to the clerk to redial the number. After another fifteen seconds, he finally spoke into the receiver. He then handed it back to the desk clerk, and crossed the lobby to Harris and McCrory.

"Joy Abrams said she will be down shortly," he

announced. "She was out cold. She finally answered the second time I called. I couldn't tell by her voice if the deep sleep had been induced by alcohol or maybe some other substance. Just sounded sleepy."

"Then she doesn't have a clue about her boss," Mc-Crory said.

Payne shook his head.

"Not yet," he said. "But I told her she'd find you, Dick, at the front desk. The clerk said their security guy will give you access to the Library Bar. You can break the news to her in private. It's small and quiet—"

"Good idea—"

"And you then can ask her (a) if she happened to be in the bar or the condo at any time last night, with or without Camilla Rose, and (b) if she knows who was with her, and (c) tell her we need to get our hands on the complete list of attendees for the fund-raiser. Meantime, get the security guy—or, failing that, someone in management— to pull a copy of Camilla Rose's lease agreement and see who she noted as her emergency contact."

"You got it, boss," McCrory said.

Payne turned to Harris.

"Let's go wake up Austin and ruin his day."

[TWO]
Hahnemann University Hospital
Center City
Philadelphia
Friday, January 6, 5:15 A.M.

A beefy nurse in her forties, wearing faded blue scrubs and carrying a clipboard close to her ample bosom, slowly trundled down the corridor escorting Homicide Sergeant Matthew Payne and Detective Anthony Harris to the hospital room of John Tyler Austin.

As they neared it, they found the door cracked open and the overhead fluorescent lights flickering. The television was on, the volume loud, and a perky female voice could be heard announcing, "Stay tuned. Action News weather is next."

The nurse looked at Payne and made a face, exasperation bordering on anger.

"That don't surprise me one bit," she said. "He's been more than a little trouble. Demanding this. Demanding that. Wouldn't break my heart if we could just treat-and-street him. But as bad as we need open beds, he really don't need to be up and moving just yet."

Payne and Harris nodded. They knew that hospitals constantly struggled to deal with uninsured patients, many of them homeless, who regularly showed up at the emergency room feigning yet another life-threatening illness. What these so-called frequent fliers really were after was *three hots and a cot*—food and a place to sleep—but if beds were full, what they instead got was *treat-and-street*—given whatever meds necessary, even if only an aspirin, and then discharged.

As the nurse began to reach for the handle and shoulder the door open, Payne said, "That's all right. We can take it from here. Thank you."

The nurse looked at him, then Harris, and seemed about to say something, then shrugged.

"Okay, Officers. I'll be down at the end of the hall, if you need anything," she said, then trundled back toward the nurses' station.

Payne rapped his knuckle on the door, and when he heard "Yeah?" on the other side, he swung it open.

John Tyler Austin was standing beside the bed, adjusting his clothing. He had his back to the door.

He was imposing. Payne figured that he stood six-foot-three and had to be at least two-twenty. He was muscular, with broad shoulders, and a square jaw. He was wearing a faded sweater, blue jeans, and pointed-toe Western boots.

"Mr. Austin?" Payne said.

Austin turned, moving very carefully, clearly in pain. He had a deep purple-black bruise practically covering his left cheek and ear. He favored his right arm, holding it delicately across his torso.

And he looked grief-stricken.

Payne thought, *He knows. He saw it on the news.*

"Who the hell are you?" Austin demanded, his voice deep, his intense gray eyes looking as if they could bore holes through cold steel.

Payne produced his black leather wallet containing his badge and ID.

"Sergeant Payne, Mr. Austin. Philadelphia Police Department. And this is Detective Harris . . ."

They stepped inside the room and Harris gently closed the door.

"I am afraid we have bad news—"

"I saw the goddamn news," Austin snapped.

He gestured toward the television, hanging on a bracket high in the corner, then looked around, found the remote control, and pushed a button. The sound muted.

"So, you're Payne, huh? What the hell happened to Camilla Rose? The news report said some unnamed source claimed she jumped from her balcony. But that had not been officially confirmed."

"I'm afraid I can confirm it's her," Payne said. "We just came from the scene. I'm very sorry."

Austin expelled air as if he had been hit in the gut. With his left hand, he reached back to the bed, then eased himself onto its edge. His head dropped.

"You need some help?" Payne said.

Austin, still looking down, silently held up his left hand, palm out, and shook his head.

Payne exchanged glances with Harris.

After a pause, Austin looked up, and said, "My God, why the hell would she do that? Do you know anything?"

"Very little on Camilla Rose, including if she did or did not jump—"

"What the hell does that mean, Payne?" Austin interrupted. "You just said she . . . Oh, I see. Maybe she fell?"

"Or possibly was pushed," Payne said. "We just don't know. Nor do we have much more on Mr. Benson. It's all very early and still being investigated."

Austin stared at him, his gray eyes turning more intense as he considered that.

Harris said, "Do you know how to get in touch with Mr. Benson's immediate family? They need to be informed of what's happened. And we need to ask them some questions."

Austin shook his head.

"He has no kin. We grew up in Houston, in the same neighborhood—River Oaks. He was an only child like me. Never married."

"Parents?" Payne said.

"They died in a plane crash two years ago in the Rocky Mountains. The old man flew their King Air into a rock-filled cloud on their way back from Colorado."

He paused, then added, "I can't believe it. First Kenny and now Camilla Rose? Since I first saw the news, I've been calling Joy but getting no answer."

"She's meeting with one of my detectives," Payne said.

"And, Mr. Austin," Harris put in, "we need to hear about what happened with the shooting, from your perspective. As well as what you can tell us about who Ms. Morgan could have been with prior to her death."

"What do you mean by that?"

"Do you know if she was using?" Harris said. "Or if anyone she was around was using?"

"Using what, exactly?"

"Any illicit drugs."

Austin met Harris's eyes. He shook his head.

"Far as I know," Austin said, "she was only doing booze. No recreational stuff. I'm guessing you know something different?"

Austin watched as Harris glanced at Payne, who nodded once.

Permission was not required. Payne knew Harris knew he would go along with whatever Harris decided was prudent. But both also knew it established a hierarchy in the eyes of others.

Harris said, "Security went up to her condo after finding her body at approximately four this morning and found the door had been left wide open. Evidence of alcohol and drugs was everywhere. There had been a party and everyone was gone."

Austin looked back and forth between them. He then sighed heavily.

"I was afraid that something like this would happen."

"Like this?" Payne parroted.

"That she'd get around the wrong people and relapse."

"And why would she?"

"Pressure, Payne. She's been under a lot, even more than usual. And then this shooting . . . It had to push her over the edge. She left here yesterday a mess."

Matt Payne nodded, and said, "I drove her back to The Rittenhouse. She admitted to being, as you say, a mess. But she did not strike me as being in a bad way. And when I saw her last night coming out of the Library Bar, she seemed pretty upbeat. Certainly not suicidal."

"She was probably entertaining her friends," Austin said. "That always makes her happy."

Payne considered that, then said, "You have the names of those 'wrong' people? And of her friends?"

"Yeah, sure. I can get you names. I'll need my computer. My phone disappeared in the crash. I imagine it melted in that damn inferno."

"Speaking of the incident yesterday," Harris said, taking out his notepad and pen from his coat pocket, "how about we go over what happened?"

Austin looked at the side table. It held a box of tissues, a small, insulated chromed carafe, and a short stack of white foam cups. With some effort, he used his left hand to take a cup from the stack, place it upright, and then, still using his left hand, pour water in it from the carafe.

"You guys thirsty? I called down the hall and tried to get some coffee, but that fat-ass nurse said it'd be at least another hour. Told her I'd pay her to get me some—I'd kill for La Colombe—but she said there's no coffee shop open this early." He sighed. "I don't even want to be here. Not in a goddamn teaching hospital. I want to be where the doctors already know what the fuck they're doing. You know, they even named this place after that Kraut quack doctor who believed in homeopathy? It's true. And that's ridiculous pseudoscience. I mean, come on . . . The guy declared coffee caused diseases."

Austin raised his eyebrows in question.

"We're fine," Payne said.

Austin nodded, then drank maybe half the water, put the cup back on the table, then looked between Payne and Harris.

"All right. Before we get into yesterday"—he groaned as he pushed himself off the bed with his left hand—"I need to drain the ol' lizard."

He turned and, in obvious pain, began moving toward the restroom.

[THREE]

John Austin, cradling his right arm, dropped back on the edge of the bed nearly five minutes later, and said, "Okay, Payne, where you want me to start?"

"How about the beginning?" Payne said.

"Then that'd be right after we had lunch. Me and Kenny were going to run errands while Camilla Rose went to the spa for a facial. We had just got the truck from the valet when she came running out of the hotel. I'd forgotten the cash."

"What cash?" Payne said.

"For the vendors. They were due their advance payments and they like cash." He chuckled. "Don't we all?"

"How much?"

"Does it matter? Is it illegal to pay people with cash anymore?"

Payne didn't respond immediately.

He met his eyes, and he said, "Depends, of course, on what you're buying."

Austin held his stare a long time, then said, "I think it was in the neighborhood of fifteen, maybe twenty grand. We were only paying two vendors, I think. Camilla Rose decided how much they got. I didn't have a chance to count it or even look inside, thanks to some asshole with a shotgun."

"Who were the vendors?" Harris said, looking up from his notes. "What service do they provide?"

"Hell if I know. I was just supposed to deliver the money, get a receipt, then get on with the day."

"Deliver the money where?"

"She said the addresses were on the individual envelopes."

"All right," Payne said. "So you came out of the hotel, then what?"

"I gave the valet the ticket for the Escalade." He shook his head. "Damn thing was brand-new. Didn't have fifty miles on it yet."

"Shame. Nice vehicle," Payne said. He was quiet a moment, then added, "Will your insurance cover the damage?"

"Not mine. It's registered in Camilla Rose's name. She bought it to give me . . . for my birthday, next week."

"That's very generous."

"What can I say, Payne?"

"If the Escalade's, basically, yours," Harris put in, "any reason Mr. Benson was driving it?"

Austin exhaled.

"Easy. He didn't drink near as much the night before. My head was hurting, so I asked Kenny if he'd drive." Watching Harris note that, he went on. "Then, just as we were pulling away, Camilla Rose ran out with that envelope of cash. And then we took off. I was looking down, stuffing the envelope in my sweater, when Kenny said, 'What the fuck?'

"I looked up in time to see, just as we about got to the street, that damn van squealing to a stop in front of us. Kenny nailed the brakes and the horn at the same time."

"That was the first you'd seen it?"

"The van? Yeah. And then the first I'd seen that chrome door open and then the shotgun barrel poke out the side. I didn't realize that that was what it was until a split second before the damn thing went off."

Harris made a note, then asked, "What did you do?"

"What the hell would anybody do? I fucking ducked! Kenny did, too. But he couldn't get to the floorboard like me."

"Did he get hit?"

"Not then. The guy missed. It was un-fucking-believable. Someone—Joy, I think—when Camilla Rose had her come here, said most of that round hit a Bentley parked behind us. But that's where our luck ran out."

He paused, and looked distracted. Then he made a wry grin.

"Ol' Kenny, he never took anything off anyone, and he really started cussing a blue streak. Then he got really pissed and hauled ass at the van, intending on ramming the hell out of it. But then another blast, and I guess since we were closer, that one really found the mark. I heard all kinds of rounds hitting the truck. And then Kenny said, 'Shit!' right before we hit the van."

"And you were where?" Payne said.

"All balled up, fetal-like, on the floorboard, trying to make this enormous damn body as small a target as possible. I mean, I had just looked up and seen Kenny's neck basically explode. He was screaming and trying to control the truck. There's blood going everywhere. And then he groaned this god-awful sound, and I saw his head droop. And when he slumped over, his foot floored the gas pedal.

"And I'm wedged down, knowing there's no way to get up and maybe get control of the truck. So while the truck's swerving, I'm trying to reach up to the keys to kill the damn engine. But they're just out of reach, so I'm trying to pull myself off the floor. Then, next thing I know, the truck's sliding. We clip something, and the damn truck rolls over. That throws me off the floor. And then there's all these noises—oh, man, the noises—they were deafening. And now I'm flying across the ceiling—or whatever you call the top of the truck—and bouncing from window to window. I can see sparks flying outside. Then, all of a sudden—*Wham!*—we smack something hard. And I go flying one more time."

He reached again for the foam cup of water, his left hand shaking.

After he had sipped from it, he looked back and forth between Payne and Harris.

"Scariest damn thing that's ever happened to me in my entire life," Austin said.

"I'm sure," Payne said. "So after that, after you went flying one more time . . . ?"

"Nothing. I mean, I don't remember a damn thing until I'm on the sidewalk and looking up at a couple of cops and the truck is all in flames and there's sirens screaming up to us.

"Then the EMTs started going to work on me. And Camilla Rose ran up. She kinda lost it when she saw all the blood. Those two cops tried to keep her back. When the EMTs found the envelope under my sweater, I asked them to give it to her. They told her I seemed okay, I was going to make it, but they had to take me to the ER. She told me later—here—that she wanted to ride along, but they said she couldn't and the cops got her a cab."

Everyone was quiet as Harris took more notes.

Finally, Austin broke the silence. "You never said . . . Did the bastards who did it get caught?"

"No," Payne said, "there was a chase, but they got away. We did recover the van, and some evidence inside."

"Do you have any idea who did it?" Harris said.

Austin remained silent a long moment.

"Let me tell you, Detective, that damn question's been going through my mind. I'm in wealth management. Sometimes people don't get the return on investments they'd hoped for and then they make some noise."

He paused, then added, "But do this? I can't imagine. So then I was thinking maybe it's something simple— like the wrong Escalade? I mean, legally, it was Camilla Rose's. But they could've been after someone driving another one? Lots of them around . . . And driven by people with money." He paused, then added, "Popular with the drug dealers in Miami Beach, I can tell you. Escalades . . . And those Range Rovers."

"It's a possibility," Harris said, writing again. He then looked up, and said, "Can you tell us more about Mr. Benson?"

"What's to tell?"

"You said he never took anything off anyone," Payne put in. "Any reason someone would target him? Maybe retaliation?"

Austin, in thought for a long moment, shook his head.

"What about his company?" Payne said.

"NextGen? What about it? Great start-up. And Kenny's got an amazing product that's going to revolutionize the medical markets. He is—was—going to be amazingly wealthy."

Harris said, "Then you've actually seen this device that—?"

"Yes," Austin interrupted. "And it will be huge, once it gets past the damn FDA approval."

"Are you aware," Harris went on, "that some owners of company stock are angry that Mr. Benson has withheld—"

"Yes, yes," Austin interrupted again. "And they're

just being impatient and greedy. And stupid. The government's the holdup."

"Some have claimed to have lost a lot of money. Are you aware of any threats to Mr. Benson that—"

"You're thinking that that would've led to this shooting?" Austin said. "Look, every company has shareholders complaining about something they think the company should or shouldn't be doing. The fact is, NextGenRx is about to make incredible money."

Payne said, "And, presumably, you were going to manage that wealth for Mr. Benson?"

"Well, it's what I do."

"How is your relationship with Mason Morgan?" Payne said.

"He's a fucking prick," Austin snapped. "And what's he got to do with any of this, Payne?"

"Interesting you say that. Camilla Rose told me that you said Mason Morgan was behind the shooting."

"She said I said that?" He shook his head. "She told me that that was what *she* thought."

"Did she say why?"

Austin appeared to think about that, then frowned.

"It's no secret she didn't like Mason," he said. "Despised him, actually."

"Any particular reason?" Payne said.

"I told you—he's a fucking prick. Isn't that reason enough?"

Payne didn't respond.

He finally said, "I need to ask a personal question."

"What?"

"Were you and Camilla Rose romantically involved?"

"What the hell?" Austin said. "How is that relevant?"

"Could you just answer the question?" Payne said.

Austin looked angry at first, then his expression changed, and he appeared to be measuring how he would respond.

"We were very close," he finally said, the edge in his tone gone. "It was—she was—extremely complicated."

"Were you intimate physically?"

Austin just looked at him.

"You mean, like, sex? Yeah, sure."

Payne turned to Harris, and said, "Anything further for Mr. Austin, Detective Harris?"

"Not for now," Harris said, tucking away his notepad and pen as he turned toward Austin. "Thank you for your time. I am sure we will be in touch soon. You'll be at The Rittenhouse?"

"Yeah, soon as I can get the hell out of here," Austin said, then added, "So, that's it?"

"We're all ears if you have something you'd like to add," Payne said.

Austin looked up at the television. The newscast was showing a live shot of a female reporter standing outside the yellow police tape, the exposed front of the tent-covered Jaguar ten feet behind her.

"What's going to happen with Camilla Rose?" he said. "I mean, right now? Next?"

Harris said, "She will be, as Mr. Benson was, taken to the medical examiner's office. An autopsy is required to determine exact cause of death."

Austin, stone-faced, looked into the distance, then nodded slightly.

"What about her fund-raiser gala?" Payne said. "Will it go on?"

"I suppose. Maybe, out of respect, it shouldn't. But I don't see why not. Everything's in place. People are coming, if not already here. Joy can run it. She's been there every step. And I can help her in some capacity."

"You might want to be behind the scenes," Payne said, "as opposed to some high-profile role."

"Well, I think that's a given, considering how I now look like the walking dead."

"I wasn't referencing that," Payne said. "Have you considered getting protection? Maybe a private security service? At least until we get a better idea of what all's happened?"

"Private security—as in, a bodyguard? I really haven't thought about that. I can take care of myself. I don't need some rent-a-cop looking over my shoulder for me."

Payne nodded, then handed him his business card.

"Here're my numbers. Call if you think of anything," he said, and led Harris out the door.

Halfway down the corridor, Tony Harris said, "You believe him?"

Payne, who was scrolling through the messages on his cellular telephone, said, "About what?"

"Any of it . . . All of it . . ."

"Some of it, yes. Saying the SUV was hers, for example, when I gave him the opportunity to say otherwise, tells me—granted, in a very small way—that he's capable of telling the truth. But other parts of his story, like the vendor cash and their relationship, make me think, no, I don't buy it."

"What the hell was that about? Asking if they had sex?"

Payne looked up from the phone, and said, "When I went to the front desk at the hotel and asked if there was a guest by the name of Joy Abrams, I also asked if the register showed Austin and Benson were guests."

"And?"

"No rooms registered under Benson, but two under Austin."

Harris's eyes lit up.

"Could mean anything," he said.

"Including," Payne added, "that Austin shares neither Camilla Rose's condo nor her bed."

"'Extremely complicated,' he called their relationship."

"Yeah, no shit," Payne said, his tone more bitter than he expected. "Ain't they all?"

He looked back down at his phone, and added, "McCrory texted that the Abrams woman had a meltdown when he informed her of what happened."

"Jesus . . . But I'm not surprised."

"He also said—and said Abrams confirmed—that Camilla Rose's emergency contact is her lawyer in Florida."

"I would have bet money that it was her mother," Harris said. "Or maybe her brother."

"Mother, sure, but a lawyer makes sense. Especially if you believe what they say about, to use Austin's phrase, 'that fucking prick of a brother.'"

Payne tapped the screen, then groaned.

"I really hate these calls with blocked IDs," he said. "Especially multiple ones, in a row, to my personal number. Just say who you are if you really want me to answer your call."

As he began listening to the voice mail message, he said, "I'll be damned . . ."

He held out the device, put it on speakerphone, then replayed the message. A male voice with a slight lisp announced: "Mr. Payne, Mason Morgan calling. My executive assistant just phoned me with some disturbing news, if true . . ."

[FOUR]
One Freedom Place, Fifty-sixth Floor
Center City
Philadelphia
Friday, January 6, 7:21 A.M.

"I'm not surprised at all that I wouldn't be listed as her next of kin," Mason Morgan said, solemnly. "As a matter of fact, I would be surprised if I was listed at all. As far as she's been concerned, I've long been dead."

Matt Payne and Tony Harris were seated in a pair of

overstuffed, leather-upholstered armchairs in front of a gleaming desk made of highly polished granite. Morgan's residence took up the entire fifty-sixth floor, three floors shy of the top of the glass-sheathed skyscraper, which was midway between Rittenhouse Square and City Hall. Payne estimated that the high-ceilinged office alone was at least four times the size of his garret apartment. He smelled a light vanilla-like fragrance and decided it was from the blooms of the potted plants in the corner of the room.

Behind the desk, Morgan, wearing a baggy suit and tie, paced the enormous wall of windows that reached floor to ceiling. His hands were clasped behind his back as he focused on Rittenhouse Square. Bright rays from the sunrise cast a warm, reddish orange glow over the city. From unseen high-fidelity speakers, classical music was playing at a low volume. Payne picked up on the distinct strings and thundering percussion of Mozart's Requiem Mass in D Minor and wondered if Morgan had chosen that or it was simply coincidence—and thought it to be dark irony, in either instance.

The forty-four-year-old chairman of Morgan International was big-boned and carrying at least two hundred fifty pounds on a five-foot-seven frame. He was pyramid-shaped—thick, tree-trunk legs and wide, heavy hips and narrow, sloping shoulders. He had a pointed head, bald except for a band of thinning, close-cropped hair that wrapped from ear to ear. His cleanly shaven face was florid, with pronounced jowls that tended to bounce at the slightest movement.

Payne idly wondered how someone the size of Mason Morgan managed to navigate the lobby's revolving glass door without getting wedged in it. And how he could possibly share any of the family genetics that had created the incredibly beautiful Camilla Rose.

Mason's mother must have been a gnome.

No wonder the old man dumped her for a younger model.

Morgan had had an elaborate coffee service waiting on the desk when they arrived, and now Payne leaned forward and picked up the silver-plated carafe. After Harris waved him off, declining more, he refilled his cup.

He returned the carafe to the desk, then sat with his elbows resting on his spread knees and sipped from the cup.

"From Camilla Rose's viewpoint," Payne then said, "she felt fully justified. She believed you were behind her being cut out of the family business. And responsible for the changes in how her trust was structured."

Morgan turned and looked at him. Then he walked past a credenza, on top of which were at least a dozen framed family photographs, and over to the gray granite desk. He wedged himself in the high-backed black leather chair. He locked eyes with Payne.

"You're calling my reputation into question," Morgan said, coldly, "and I will not stand for it."

"I'm not calling you out at all," Payne said, uncowed. He casually took a sip of coffee, and added, "I'm simply repeating what Camilla Rose told me yesterday. Actually, one phrase she used was 'brazen betrayal.'"

Morgan blurted, "I will—" then caught himself.

He narrowed his eyes as he looked off in the distance. Then he looked back at Payne.

"Don't you even begin to suggest where I may have failed my sister," he said, his voice trembling. "Everyone knows Camilla Rose as gregarious, larger-than-life. While her kindness and selflessness were genuine—she got that from our father—almost no one saw the other side of her that we did. No one, including her own mother."

He paused to let that sink in, then went on. "It was my wife who took time away from our young children to help Camilla Rose when her mental demons became too much. We accompanied her to see the doctors, and when the diagnosis pinpointed that she suffered from bipolar affective disorder, we then escorted her through the hell of rehabilitation clinics. Not once, but *five* times—and once after she overdosed!"

Morgan spun in his chair and went over to the credenza. He opened a wide lower drawer and dug around and then produced a brown folder. He opened it as he returned to the desk and spun back around in the chair.

The folder held a photograph, which he put on the desktop and slid toward Payne.

"Look at her!" Morgan said.

Payne put down his coffee cup and took the photograph in hand.

Two women, smiling awkwardly, stood on a curved concrete path leading up to an elegant light blue, two-story Mediterranean-style building. Above the red-tiled roof, tall palm trees soared into a cloudless, bright blue sky. The female on the left looked to be in her mid-thirties—and, clearly, the same woman who appeared in the family photographs on the credenza—and the other was an overweight strawberry-blonde in her mid-twenties who held a bouquet of yellow flowers. Beside them was a small wooden sign on a four-foot-high post. Its carved lettering read SANCTUARY SEASIDE GUEST PICKUP.

Jesus! The fat one's Camilla Rose?

She looks terrible. At least fifty pounds overweight.

But now I can see a very slight family resemblance.

The older one has to be Mrs. Mason Morgan.

Payne handed the photograph to Harris as he said, "That's Camilla Rose?"

"And my saint of a wife, Claire," Mason said, his voice calmer. "That was the second time we picked up Camilla Rose when she got out of rehab. She had been in rather worse-looking condition when she went in. She always ate heavily in her periods of depression. And, of course, all the alcohol she consumed was high in calories."

Payne thought, *That's one photo that never made the papers.*

Harris used the camera on his cellular phone to snap a shot of it.

Morgan went on. "Father set up the trusts for us when we were children. Camilla Rose's was set up separately, a decade after mine. She was Daddy's girl, and he made sure that she wanted for nothing. However, her trust stipulated that upon her death, if she were to leave no issue, her trust shares would remain in the family trust, eventually transferring to any nieces and nephews."

Payne's eyes drifted to the credenza of framed photographs.

"Just your children, correct?"

"Correct. My wife and I are blessed with four, two boys and two girls."

"Camilla Rose said that if she had had access to her full trust, not just these quarterly dividends, then she could have built whatever new facility for the disadvantaged kids at once. She said she wanted to name it after your father. I would assume in the same manner as the new cancer research wing going up at Hahnemann."

"No," Mason Morgan said, bluntly. "If she had access to the principal, she would have pissed it away, if you will pardon the phrase, or had it stolen from her." He paused, then added, "No money for her charity work and, worse for me, no money for her."

Payne looked puzzled.

"Worse for you? How?"

"Who the hell do you think she would have come to for funds when hers were all gone? She would have looked at what I have, decided that it came from family wealth, and, ergo, it was hers, too. With a name like Morgan, there would have been a long line of lawyers anxious to sue me to get her—and them—that money. I would have been forced to settle, if only to make the obscene flood of lawyers' fees stop."

He paused, looked off in the distance, then went on.

"No, the old man had it figured out when he structured it that way. She got a quarterly check—a very nice quarterly check—guaranteed, but absolutely no access to the principal."

"Which was declared to be not hers?"

Morgan shook his head.

"And it's not hers. Father wanted it to remain in the family—for the family—as his legacy, forever. And, properly managed, it will."

Payne, deep in thought, sipped his coffee.

"She told me," he then said, "that when she was in high school, she wanted to join the family business."

"That's right. I saw to it that, every summer she came from California, she had a different job she could learn. She particularly wanted to run the hotel chain we had at the time because she said she believed she understood the hospitality industry. Mind you, this was at age fifteen." He snorted. "That's like every blonde coed with Daddy's credit card devoutly believing she is God's gift to the fashion design industry. But she eventually proved herself. There was absolutely no question of her high intelligence."

He paused, then said, "Perhaps you have heard the phrase 'no good deed goes unpunished'?"

"Once or twice," Payne said.

Morgan nodded. "I actually was the one who lobbied our father to give her more responsibility. But her personal habits, her poor decisions, overshadowed things. That, more than anything, upset him. He was a private person, as I said, a kind man, who wanted the family name to be synonymous with good things, such as medicines that saved lives, and with philanthropic endeavors."

"And there went Camilla Rose making those headlines."

"Embarrassing headlines."

"What will happen now with the philanthropies she was running?" Payne said.

"The ones funded by Morgan International have board members who will come up with an interim head, then I'm sure I'll help recruit a permanent replacement. I can only assume that the same will happen with the other ones, such as Camilla's Kids, that she has independent of Morgan International."

After a moment, Payne said, "You're familiar, I'm sure, with a fellow by the name of John Tyler Austin."

Mason Morgan's eyes narrowed.

"Unfortunately, yes."

"And you heard what happened to him?"

Morgan shook his head.

"Something recently, you mean?" he said.

Payne said, "He and an associate were leaving The Rittenhouse yesterday afternoon at two o'clock in Camilla Rose's new Cadillac Escalade when parties unknown blocked their path, then shot at them with at least two rounds of buckshot."

"That was Austin?" Morgan said, evenly. "I saw the TV news."

"You didn't see the smoke and fire from the burning SUV?" Harris said, gesturing toward the window.

"I wasn't in the city yesterday."

"Mr. Austin's associate was killed," Payne said.

"And Austin?"

"He suffered some minor injury. We left him at Hahnemann just before coming here."

"Interesting," Morgan said.

Payne studied him.

"You don't seem at all surprised or concerned," Payne said.

"Excuse me? I'm absolutely upset about Camilla Rose. I will do everything necessary to find out how and why she died." He paused, then added, "She was family, for God's sake!"

Payne nodded.

Morgan then said, "Is there a connection between her death and this associate of Austin?"

"We're looking into that," Payne said. "What are your thoughts on Austin?"

"Right now?" Morgan said. "I hold him responsible. I'm sure he somehow shoulders a great deal of the blame."

Payne and Harris exchanged glances.

"Do you have any information that points to why he's responsible?" Payne said. "He was at the hospital when she died."

"He's a danger. I knew it from the minute they met in Florida. And so I had my security people check him out."

"You vetted Austin?" Harris put in.

"You are goddamn right I had him vetted, Detective. I knew he was—is—a danger."

"Would you say you in any way consider him a personal threat to you?" Harris said.

Morgan was quiet for a while, then said, "Financially? Absolutely. As I said, lawsuits can get expensive and time-consuming. But a personal threat physically? No."

"Where did you meet him?" Payne said.

Morgan gestured at the photograph.

"In West Palm, at the rehabilitation facility," he said, "when we went to pick up Camilla Rose. He came on so strong and charming that I felt he was trolling. I'd seen that behavior in others and naturally suspected that Austin smelled the money, a lot of it, and was working on getting his claws in Camilla Rose."

"It wasn't possible there was a genuine attraction?"

"Did you get a good look at her in that photograph?" Morgan said. "Let's be candid, Matthew. *Please!*"

Payne considered that, then said, "And so you had him investigated."

"For her sake, first and foremost, as well as the family's."

"And you found what? Did he just happen to wind up in Florida, in this particular West Palm rehab, or did he go there, as you say, trolling?"

Morgan took a sip of coffee, then said, "Aren't I doing your job for you?"

"I'm just asking questions."

Morgan made a sour face.

"And so you are," he said. "My apology. I said I would help and I will. I learned that Austin's wild side went back to at least age sixteen, when he caused an automobile accident that killed a young man. He had been drinking."

"He was found guilty of vehicular homicide, felony DUI?" Harris said. "Do you have the name of who died?"

"The name's in the file; I'll get it for you. But, no, Detective, Austin's parents had the financial wherewithal to hire that hotshot, high-profile Houston criminal defense attorney. He pled to a lesser charge and got off with probation. It didn't hurt his case that the driver of the other car, the one who died, also had a blood alcohol level in the double digits. And then there were lesser wild episodes during his college years."

He took a sip of coffee and then continued. "When Austin wound up in West Palm, it was because he had gone back to self-medicating the chemical imbalance in the brain, which is a fancy way of saying he was drinking away the mood swings. He had just spent three months at the Henninger House on Galveston Bay—arguably among the top-five clinics, if not the best—but because those who are bipolar tend to believe they have all the answers to everything, he said his diagnosis was suspect and wanted a second opinion."

"Three months?" Payne said.

"Yes. And, understand, that is at seventeen hundred dollars a day. West Palm runs around twelve hundred. Another clue that he has some money. Insurance does not cover such facilities."

Payne quickly did the rough math.

Jesus. That's close to a hundred fifty grand for ninety days.

All wasted when he went back to the booze . . .

"After the last time we got her out of rehab, which had been Henninger House," Morgan said, "she announced that she needed time for herself. I suspected she took off with Austin, but don't really know."

"Where did she go?"

"I'm not exactly sure. At some point—toward the end, I believe—back to California, to the Napa Valley and Carmel. One of her kids' camps is out there, on Monterey Bay. But, I think, first Santiago, Chile, then Mendoza, in Argentina."

"And she was clean and sober?" Payne said. "In all those wine countries, of all places?"

Mason Morgan shrugged. "All I know is, I did not hear a word from her. She communicated only through her lawyer, who handled her affairs, including her quarterly payments."

"You weren't bothered by that?"

"Absolutely not. Why would I be? Have you any idea what it's like waiting for a surprise call in the middle of the night, knowing you have to drop everything and rescue someone? Only to know that once you get them clean and sober, they're just going to relapse? It sucks the life out of you." He paused in thought, then finished. "So, no, it was a welcome relief not to hear from her. No news is good news, they say. Besides, my conscience was clear. We had time and time again rushed to her rescue. No good deed . . . et cetera, et cetera."

Payne nodded.

"How long was she gone?"

Mason Morgan rubbed his chin, then said, "A little over two years, I believe. Then I received a letter from her lawyer—an e-mail—that she was ready to return. And within days she was back in full form, once again overseeing the day-to-day running of her charities and the company philanthropies."

"Mr. Morgan," Harris said, "when was the last time you saw Austin and your sister?"

"Austin was four, maybe five years ago?" Morgan said. "Then he was out of the picture—I just assumed whatever relationship he and Camilla Rose may have had had run its course—but then recently she dropped his name during our discussions. So, I assumed they were back together . . . unfortunately. And now this happened . . ."

He was quiet as he looked across the room, then said, "To answer your question, the last I saw Camilla Rose was a couple months ago. Our corporate counsel had some papers for her to sign concerning one of the philanthropies."

He paused, then added, "To be clear, I only saw her; I didn't speak with her in person. As I said, we communicated by e-mail only, which was her decision."

"And she brought up Austin's name?" Harris said. "What did you think about that?"

"Like Camilla Rose, Detective, Austin is intelligent. You are aware that he now is in wealth management . . ."

Payne and Harris nodded.

". . . But he's not the good kind. And that, of course, concerned me."

"I'm guessing the bad kind is one who loses your money," Payne said, his tone wry.

"Indeed, that is an absolute truth. But the difference between good and bad is also about how they are compensated." He paused, and added, "You must know this, yes?"

"Kindly educate me. As Detective Harris can attest, I'm not very bright and can always learn something new."

Mason Morgan looked back and forth between them, not sure if he was being mocked or not, then decided to go on. "The good kind of wealth managers charge a very small percentage of your portfolio as their management fee. Ergo, the more money your investments make, the more they earn, too."

"Got it," Payne said.

"The other kind, the bad kind, is essentially a stockbroker—which my grandfather told me was 'really little more than a used-car salesman with shiny, expensive shoes.' They make their money from commissions on the buying and selling of stocks and bonds and various other financial instruments. If a stock's price starts to slide, for example, the broker may suggest getting out and investing in another stock that he declares, with great conviction, is undervalued and destined to rise in price. Which may or may not be true, especially if the brokerage firm is pushing certain financial products it has an interest in . . . But that's a whole other subject."

Payne said, "And this used-car salesman with shiny, expensive shoes gets a commission, and maybe a company bonus, from both the dumped shares and the newly acquired ones."

Morgan nodded.

"I knew you knew, Matthew. Thus, it is in the broker's best interest, not the client's, to do so. And, let me tell you, Austin is one remarkable salesman. Big, bright smile, a backslapper, your instant new best friend. Always with the next con going on. I would suggest always having your hand on your wallet when in his presence."

The multiline telephone on the desk began making a trilling sound. Morgan's eyes darted to its caller ID display, then he glanced at his wristwatch. He made a face of annoyance as he grabbed the receiver.

"Let me call you right back," he snapped, then more or less slammed the receiver back in its cradle.

Mason Morgan quickly pushed himself out of his high-backed leather chair.

"Gentlemen, I do have a meeting I must make. We can continue this later. Meantime, I'll get the file my security people compiled on Austin to you."

IV

[ONE]
The Rittenhouse Condominiums
Residence 2150
Center City
Philadelphia
Friday, January 6, 11:01 A.M.

Homicide Sergeant Matt Payne, standing on the terrace of Camilla Rose Morgan's leased unit, peered over the glass-topped, slate-tiled wall and saw, twenty-one floors below, the roof of the Crime Scene Unit's canopy tent. A panel van with MEDICAL EXAMINER'S OFFICE markings honked twice as it backed up and then parked just outside the yellow tape.

When he turned back, he had a clear view of the gas-fueled fireplace. Laying on the slate—next to a large crystal snifter and, on its side, an empty bottle of Rémy Martin VSOP cognac—were the extravagant high heel shoes she had worn the previous night, one of which she used to hold open the elevator door for Matt.

Now he could see in his mind's eye Camilla Rose at the fireplace, taking photographs of herself, while she waited for him.

I wonder, beyond what I have real reason to believe is an itch she anxiously wanted scratched, if she also really had something to tell me.

That telling me she did wasn't just a way of luring me into her lair.

He glanced beyond the fireplace, through the large windows, and saw Tony Harris peeling off his blue latex gloves while talking with a crime scene investigator who was balancing a digital video camera on his shoulder. The interior was brightly lit, and it looked as if every bulb in the three-bedroom condominium had been switched on.

The lighting made for an impressive sight—it was a remarkably beautiful unit, despite the detritus—and he could hear the realtor's nasal voice droning in his head.

"Mr. Payne, these truly luxurious condominiums were built with the finest of materials and superb craftsmanship. Of the one hundred and fifty units in the building, typical is the two-bedroom, two-bath, with eighteen hundred square feet. Then, at the upper end, we have the penthouse—a forty-two-hundred-square-foot property, with fourteen-foot-high ceilings, and a six-hundred-square-foot tiled terrace, featuring a natural gas fireplace.

"And the hotel itself is of five-star quality—indeed, it's world-class. Should you have guests, we have an arrangement for quite nice discounts on rooms. And, of course, our residents enjoy significant discounts in its restaurants and with the all-hours room service, and also use of concierge and housekeeping services."

Matt turned and went out on the terrace. In addition

to overlooking Rittenhouse Square, the view he scanned took in both big rivers, as well as such instantly recognizable landmarks as, to the east, the Mall, with Independence Hall, and, next to it, the Liberty Bell, and, to the north, the massive Museum of Art, and, just past that, on the eastern bank of the Schuylkill, the docks and buildings of Boathouse Row.

Amanda would love this, he thought. *We sure wouldn't need a place quite so big, but it would be every bit as nice.*

Matt could also see, just beyond the Museum of Art, on the far side of Fairmont Park, the 2601 Parkway condominiums, where his sister, Amy, lived.

That reminds me . . . wonder if she's home? Or maybe nearby?

He checked the time, then sent her a text message and slipped the phone in his pocket.

Payne then surveyed the terrace and tried once again to visualize what could have been Camilla Rose Morgan's last moments.

He looked—for what he figured had to be the twentieth time—from the slate wall down to the tent and then back up. He thought it was possible that she could have positioned herself in such a way—*Stupidly standing on the ledge to take another photograph with the city lights in the background*—that she then could have lost her footing and balance.

And her life.

But in listing the order of probability, Payne's gut had put "fallen by accident" last, behind "jumped" and "pushed."

And then, considering her mind-set—*She said she found her calling with helping sick kids, which included hosting the fund-raiser, and going after her brother to get her money*—and considering how damn terrifying the ground looked from this perspective, he simply could not come up with a logical reason that justified her ending her life by jumping.

Which leaves "pushed."

But by who? And, for the love of God, why?

And then he mentally went over what he and Harris had heard from John Tyler Austin and Mason Morgan.

After some time, he heard behind him, "Matt?"

Payne turned and saw Harris approaching.

"Crime scene guys are packing up," Harris said. "What're you thinking? I could smell the gears smoking from all the way inside."

Payne started pulling off his blue latex gloves, and said, "I'm thinking that I don't have a damn clue. But at least one thing bothers me for certain."

"About?"

"Camilla Rose clearly had her issues," Payne began, and shared what he felt in his gut.

Harris then nodded, and said, "Well, that's about as good as we have to go on at this point. We sure as hell haven't found a smoking gun here."

"And the one thing that bothers me for certain is the fact that she was (a) striving to build a facility to provide a better life for kids who are dealing with some seriously tragic situations, and (b) naming it for their father, who wished to be remembered for being altruistic."

"Why does that bother you?"

"It flies in the face of Mason Morgan's already stinking-rich kids winding up with the money. It's not like she hadn't proven herself capable. From all those billions, her brother couldn't, short of giving her everything that she wanted, make more money available for the charities? Something he knew his father would have approved? No. Instead, the sonofabitch squeezed her out."

Harris grunted. "They say life ain't fair."

"Understatement of the day." He paused, then added, "When I was at UP, there was no end to the cutthroats who were going on to business school. To them, everything's blood sport. And it's not just about making money—it's about winning *and* not losing. Those bastards devoutly believe in the Golden Rule."

"What? 'Do unto others as you'd have them do unto you'? That doesn't make sense."

"That's because it's the other one: 'He who has the gold rules.' They see no top end to what they can amass."

Harris nodded a couple times, then said, "Some kids who have jerks for parents turn out okay in spite of them. Maybe the Morgan kids will see the light and use the money for what she intended."

Payne looked skeptical, and said, "Yeah, sure—when pigs fly out their overprivileged asses."

Looking past Harris, Payne saw McCrory stepping out onto the terrace.

"Here comes Dick," he said.

"Hey, Matt," McCrory said as he approached. "We got from hotel management the names and info on the bartenders and servers working last night. Nasuti is running them down. And I'm supposed to meet with Joy Abrams in an hour. Looks like she's finally calmed down."

Payne's brow went up.

"You said she had a real meltdown when you broke the news?" Payne said.

"Oh, yeah. What did sailors call those things? Banshee wails?" McCrory said, looking almost embarrassed. "I mean, she made the effing bottles behind the bar rattle. It was difficult trying to console her, she was shaking and crying so bad."

"Jesus," Harris said. "Drama queen."

"You get anything out of her?" Payne said.

McCrory shook his head.

"About all she could get out between wails was that she hadn't been in the bar the night before because she'd been feeling under the weather. Then she popped to her feet, said she had to go to her room for some privacy, and bolted from the bar, crying and covering her face with her hands. When she called a little while ago, she said she was trying to contact Ms. Morgan's mother and lawyer and could meet with me at noon."

"What about what Tony just said?" Payne said. "Do you think that was genuine grief? Or just a dramatic display?"

McCrory made a face. "Painfully real. It's obvious she was really fond of the Morgan woman. Said she wasn't just a boss but a good friend, too."

Payne nodded.

"Anyway," McCrory went on, "when she called, she said she's got the master list of attendees for the gala and that she'd called around and came up with a short list of who was in the bar. I'll get Kennedy to go through it with me."

Thirty-six-year-old Detective Harold W. Kennedy, Sr., was an enormous—at six-one, two-eighty—African-American who had grown up in West Philly.

Payne said, "Split up the names of those in the bar with him and interview them first. And see if they're any of the same names Hank gets from the bartenders, et cetera . . ."

"Right."

"I got a glance at a couple through the doorway last night. They looked vaguely familiar, but I couldn't tell you who the hell they were."

Harris looked at his watch, and said, "I figured that by now I would've heard back from Gerry McGuire about Dignitary Protection's list. I'll try him again in a minute."

"Hey, I heard some rumor that Sandy Colt is coming," McCrory said, sounding somewhat star-struck.

"Oh boy," Payne said, dripping with sarcasm. "Stanley Coleman. My favorite pedophile."

Then he thought, *I wonder if Terry will be in tow?*

Long-legged, blonde, and beautiful, Terry Davis was vice president of the West Coast division of Global Artists Management, which had Colt as a client. Matt had met her while working with Dignitary Protection. She also happened to be an old friend from school of Daphne Nesbitt, who, playing matchmaker, had invited Terry and Matt to the Nesbitts' house for dinner. Their relationship turned out to be very short-lived.

I doubt she shows up. Not after being with me when those robbers shot up my car.

She'll probably never grace this city—not to mention me—with her presence again.

Shit! Kind of like Amanda? She heard that whole story—and the others she stuck in that damn obit—from Amy.

Maybe Amanda's worried she'll one day wind up in the cross fire, too.

McCrory was looking at Payne with a questioning expression.

"Stanley Coleman went to West Catholic High," Payne said. "Afterward, as a struggling thespian, he had his name legally changed to Sandy Colt. Then, for reasons that baffle me, considering his so-called talent, he became famous."

Colt, unbelievably handsome and muscular, had started out as lead singer in a rock band, then leveraged that fame to get minor parts in a police series on television, then used that to get a small role as a detective in a dramatic motion picture. When that motion picture exploded at the box office—mostly, Payne thought, thanks to its computer-generated special effects—he starred in a half dozen sequels.

Payne had seen only the first picture and quickly had lost interest after too many scenes stretched credibility, even by Hollywood standards. Especially one in which Sandy Colt's character had a shoot-out and, holding a full-sized Model 1911 Colt .45 sideways, fired twenty-two shots without reloading, from a semiautomatic that could hold, at most, eight rounds, and that was with one chambered.

"Last time Colt was in town," Harris told McCrory, grinning widely, "it was for a fund-raiser for his alma mater, West Philly High . . ."

"Why's that funny?" McCrory said.

". . . And newly promoted Sergeant Payne here got sandbagged by Monsignor Schneider, who grandly suggested that Payne's 'real-life exploits could serve as the basis for one of Stanley's films.'"

"Say, that's really something," McCrory said.

"Not really," Payne said.

"Colt," Harris went on, "had heard all about the famed Wyatt Earp of the Main Line. And he was as thrilled about getting to do ride-alongs with Sergeant Payne as Sergeant Payne was pissed off about having to babysit a cartoon actor. Colt's enthusiasm pretty much dropped more than a bit when Matt threatened what would happen to him if he (a) did not take a vow of chastity for his entire visit to our City of Brotherly Love, and (b) violated said vow."

McCrory's eyes went to Payne.

"Is he pulling my leg?"

Payne shook his head.

"I'd been told by his Hollywood agent," he said, "that Colt liked young girls—"

"Damn perverts," McCrory blurted, his eyes narrowed. "Sorry, but I got daughters . . ."

Harris said, "Rest assured that no harm had to come to Stanley's crown jewels at the edge of a dull knife. The vow was kept. And he did raise more than a half mil for the West Catholic Building Fund."

"And if he, indeed, is here," Payne said, "the same deal's in force."

McCrory said, "I didn't know all that."

"I'll bet," Payne said, "that Camilla Rose placed many tithe envelopes in the church's collection plate. Which strongly suggests that Monsignor Schneider, and maybe even the Archbishop, are listed as going tomorrow night. Which means there will be other politicians, particularly ones of the elected variety, which means I really don't want to go, if I can avoid it."

He paused, looked at McCrory, and added, "Let me know, too, what the Abrams woman says about that envelope of cash. Invoking the famous Jason Washington's *never leave a stone unturned* philosophy . . ."

He stopped when he felt a familiar vibration in his pocket and pulled out his cellular telephone.

"Aha, finally," he said, looking at Harris. "It's the family shrink."

Harris nodded.

"Good call," he said. "She's always been helpful figuring out these head cases."

Dr. Amelia A. Payne was the Joseph L. Otterby Professor of Psychiatry at the University of Pennsylvania.

"Sigmund!" Matt began. "How's—"

"I got your message," she said, cutting him off. "I'm meeting Mom at noon for lunch at the house. Come join us. And if, for once, you are nice to me and behave, I'll tell you more than you want to know about the bipolar roller-coaster ride."

"Define *nice* and *behave*," Matt said, but then realized that he was talking to a broken connection.

[TWO]
Providence Road
Wallingford, Pennsylvania
Friday, January 6, 12:01 P.M.

After getting his car back from the valet—which had taken some time because a large section of the Rittenhouse circle drive remained blocked with police units—Payne took Broad Street down to Interstate 95, the Delaware Expressway, then drove south on it toward Chester. He would, in about ten miles, then make the turn onto I-476.

Matt enjoyed the drive out to the family home in Wallingford. In addition to getting him out of the city, it gave him time to think—although, in the event there was bad traffic, sometimes far more than he wanted.

When Payne had eased himself behind the wheel of the 911 and plugged his smartphone into the USB port, he had considered calling Amanda while en route. He had not heard anything from her since he left her condo the previous night and he wondered if that was because she had seen the news about his involvement in the shooting and was now even more upset. So much so that she had nothing else to say to him.

But, he'd decided, even if she was not aware of what had happened, he really had no idea of what he could say to her right now. She had stated her case beyond question. And he simply did not want to think about it, let alone attempt talking about it. The whole thing was still too fresh—and left a gnawing ache in his stomach at least as painful as the damn bullet wound.

The overhead signage for Exit 7 to I-476 North came into view as he was thinking about how Mason Morgan had called into question John Tyler Austin's character, particularly describing him as a con artist.

It'll be interesting what that background folder on Austin has in it. And if any of it matches what we come up with.

Payne signaled to change lanes, then glanced over his right shoulder and finally found an opening and merged and made the exit.

His phone rang and he saw his private-number caller ID pop up on the multifunction screen in the dash. It announced that it was the bursar's office at Temple University.

Wonder how they got my number?

But apparently someone at Temple has put two and two together.

He tapped the on-screen prompt, sending the caller into voice mail.

Within the last month, after learning that he was going to become a father, Payne had quietly established academic scholarships in the name of his biological father, Sergeant John F. X. Moffitt, and his uncle, Captain Richard C. "Dutch" Moffitt.

The scholarships were made available to members in the Philadelphia Police Explorer Cadets Program, a coed, career-oriented arm of the Boy Scouts of America, who were studying criminal justice at La Salle University and, a couple miles south, at Temple University and Community College of Philadelphia.

The scholarships were fairly modest—he planned to add to them over time—but, depending on the school, they covered the cost of one or more courses.

Matt wanted no recognition for their creation and funding. Having taken the surname of Payne certainly aided that. Matt, of course, had never known his father, and a selfless Brewster Payne had adopted him, then reared him as his own. Accordingly, when the topic came up, Matt invariably became somewhat emotional, and would say that he had the great honor of having two fathers.

Matt's motive for the scholarships had been to help those wanting to serve the public. But perhaps more important personally, it had been to please, in some small way, Mother Moffitt, his sharply opinionated Irish-Catholic grandmother.

Still, being realistic, he deeply doubted the latter

would ever happen. He knew that good ol' Gertrude had never gotten over her daughter-in-law's remarrying after her son Jack had been killed in the line of duty and then—what Mother Moffitt really considered a mortal sin and told anyone she could get to listen—changing her grandson Matty's surname and then bringing him up as an Episcopalian.

Once her mind's made up, Payne thought, *damn-near nothing can sway that tough old Irish broad.*

Maybe that's where I acquired such a fine quality . . .

After turning off Interstate 476 at Exit 3, he eased the stick shift of the Porsche into third gear and then, after the vehicle bled off sufficient speed, down into second.

Payne, long before getting his first 911 as a college graduation gift, and then cutting hot laps on a track with a professional race driver in the passenger seat coaching him, had heard the old-school argument about whether it was better to slow a vehicle equipped with a manual transmission by a smooth combination of down-shifting and braking or by utilizing the brakes alone.

Replacing worn-out brake pads certainly was cheaper than replacing clutches. But he didn't give a damn. He knew that the 911 really responded with the downshifts, especially in tight, fast turns, which was why professional drivers employed both braking and downshifting.

And he admitted that he also liked how it sounded.

The exhaust made as nice a deep powerful note during downshifts as when he ran up through the gears, pushing the tachometer toward redline, which he was doing now as he headed down U.S. 1, which forever had been called the Baltimore Pike, toward Media.

A mile later, he downshifted and braked again to make a left onto Pennsylvania Route 252. And, finally, after a couple miles on that narrow two-lane, also known as Providence Road, he entered the small Philadelphia suburb of Wallingford.

While somewhat close to the Main Line, Wallingford technically was not part of the well-known upper-crust area, which derived its name in the nineteenth century from the Pennsylvania Railroad Main Line. That rail line, now long gone, had connected the towns incorporating the sprawling country estates that belonged to Philly's wealthiest families.

The present-day median income of Main Line residents was the same as that of residents of Beverly Hills, California. Similarly, sociologists would categorize those who lived in Wallingford as upper middle income, upper income, and wealthy, living in separate dwellings, some of which were very old, with many of the newer ones designed to look that way. Wallingford also had its own post office and railroad station and Free Library.

The residences were set well back from Providence Road. The two-lane macadam was lined closely with tall, overgrown pine trees that, while beautiful, made for blind driveways. And with the entrance to the Payne property coming up on the right, Matt, out of long-established habit, first hit his turn signal and checked mirrors for traffic—he couldn't count the many times he almost had been rear-ended by someone flying up on his bumper—and only then downshifted and applied the brakes.

He made the turn without incident. And after following the winding, crushed-stone drive through the four-acre property, the house came into view.

The property had been in the Payne family for more than two centuries. Brewster Cortland Payne II, Esquire, had raised his family, now grown and gone, in the large, rambling structure. What had been the original house, built of fieldstone before the Revolution, was now the kitchen and the sewing room. Additions and modifications had been made over the many years. While the result could fit no specific architectural category, it was comfortable, even luxurious.

A real estate saleswoman had once remarked that "the Payne place just looked like old, old money."

Yet it was not ostentatious—there was no tennis court and no swimming pool, as the Payne family used those facilities at the Rose Tree Hunt Club, where they also rode.

They did have a tennis court at the Cape May summerhouse on the southern tip of the Jersey Shore, as well as a dock that eventually would hold Brewster Payne's *Final Tort VI*, a Viking sportfisherman yacht that Matt was planning on eventually ferrying up from the Florida Keys.

Approaching the house, Payne saw two late-model GMC Yukon XLs, parked short of what a century before had been a stable and now was a four-car garage.

Both enormous SUVs originally had been purchased new by their father. The newest one, looking as if it had just come off the showroom floor, was still his. The two-year-old model, which also had been in pristine condition when Brewster had given it to his daughter, now was somewhat battered. It had been parked at an odd angle, its right tires up on the grass alongside the cobblestoned parking area.

Dr. Amelia A. Payne's inability to conduct a motor vehicle over the roads of the Commonwealth of Pennsylvania without at least grazing, on average once a week, other motor vehicles, street signs, and, on one memorable occasion, a fire hydrant, was legendary. Brewster had hoped that the big truck would keep Amy alive.

Matt shook his head—and parked his Porsche at the farthest possible spot away from her vehicle.

[THREE]

After crossing the big patio of old red brick and entering the house through a back door, he could hear his sister and mother talking in the kitchen. He found them both holding large coffee mugs and standing at opposite ends of a four-foot-square butcher-block island loaded with the makings for hoagie sandwiches.

"Matt, honey! How nice," Mrs. Patricia Payne said, smiling.

She was trim and youthful, with the fair skin of the Irish, and looked to be in her early forties when, in fact, she was a decade older. In recent years, she had changed her luxuriant head of reddish brown hair to blonde.

Matt quickly walked to the island and, after she raised her cheek, gave her a kiss. At the same time, he reached down and took a slice of salami from the butcher block. He folded it, then stuffed it in his mouth, while waving in an exaggerated fashion at his sister.

"I wasn't sure you'd find time in your busy schedule for us," Amy said. "Clearly, you couldn't find the time to shave."

"Don't start, you two," Patricia Payne protested. "You're starting to sound like Mother Moffitt."

Amy Payne, petite and intense and approaching thirty, while not a pretty girl, was rather naturally attractive. She kept her brown hair snipped short, not for purposes of beauty but because it was easier to care for that way.

She was unusually intelligent, having shortly after turning age twenty-two had a psychiatric residency under the mentorship of Dr. Aaron Stein, head of the school of psychiatry at the University of Pennsylvania and former president of the American Psychiatric Association. Many strongly suspected that Dr. Stein, who was short and plump and in his fifties—Brewster Payne described him as looking like a beardless Santa Claus— was responsible for Dr. Payne's current professorship at UPenn.

"So, Sigmund," Matt replied, after swallowing the

cold cut, "did you actually park your truck out there or give up and desert it?"

Dr. Payne gave him the finger.

Their mother pretended not to notice that, instead asking, "How's your wound healing, honey? Does it still hurt?"

"Only when I breathe."

"That's not funny," Amy said. "You could be dead."

"I just learned," Matt said, "that having dodged the Grim Reaper, I pissed off more than a few guys waiting on the promotion list. They thought that with the demise of the Wyatt Earp of the Main Line, there suddenly was about to be a sergeant's slot opening."

"And that's really not funny, Matt," his mother snapped.

Matt avoided her eyes and reached in the refrigerator. He came out with a bottle of Newcastle Nut Brown Ale.

"It's a little early for that, isn't it?" Amy said.

He held the bottle so that the lip of the cap was on the edge of the stainless steel counter. He then bumped the cap with the heel of his hand, catching it as it flew up off the neck.

"For medicinal purposes, Doc," Matt said, smiled, then raised it toward her in a mock toast before taking a big swallow.

"Amy said she saw you on the early-morning news," Patricia Payne said. "What was that all about?"

"Nothing good. But it's why I needed to see Amy."

"So, let's hear it," Amy said.

"Okay. I'll try to keep this brief. Yesterday, as I was

pulling into The Rittenhouse to see about leasing a unit that just came on the market . . ."

When he had finished five minutes later, Patricia Payne said, softly, "How absolutely horrible! Such a beautiful woman. And, from what I've heard, I mean that inside and out."

"Well," Matt said, "I cannot disagree with that. Everyone seems to say she meant well. Even her brother concedes it. But, apparently, the inside of her head had some real problems. Her brother said she fought mental demons forever. All the trips to rehab turned out to be little more than Band-Aids."

He looked at Amy. She was refilling her coffee mug.

"So, Sigmund, what do you make of it?"

"Interesting that you bring up Freud," Amy then said. "Erik Erikson, a well-regarded psychoanalyst, credits Freud for having said that for a person to have a healthy mental being, to be happy, there must be *lieben und arbeiten*—to love and to work."

"I seem to recall he also said, 'Sometimes a cigar is just a cigar.'"

"Bipolar is very real," Amy, ignoring that crack, went on. "And, tragically, it is quite common. How much do you want to hear?"

"Whatever you got, Doc," he said, rolling his hand in a gesture for her to go on.

She sipped her coffee, clearly in thought, then nodded.

"What's known as mania," she began, "defines the

disorder, and the mildest level is hypomania. Those with it tend to have lots of energy. They excite easily. Yet it can also make them highly productive. As the level of mental illness gets worse, the behavior becomes impulsive. Bad decisions are made. They're erratic. They don't sleep. When it gets really bad, they can become psychotic—their world is distorted."

"Jesus," Matt said, then took a swig of his beer.

"It's not pretty," Amy said. "There is no consensus on how many types exist, but there are three main subtypes, and another one that is a catchall for everyone not fitting the first three. Then there are other mental components that can complicate a bipolar description, from schizophrenia to borderline personality disorder."

"I heard Morgan say that the lithium helped—when Camilla Rose actually took her meds."

"A mood stabilizer is needed, and lithium has been found to be most effective. Depending on the severity of the symptoms, an antipsychotic drug can be used—for example, to help severe behavior problems."

She paused to sip her coffee, then went on. "The real problem is that despite how effectively we can diagnose the condition and create a treatment using a combination of psychotherapy and medication, the patient often chooses not to follow through."

"Like Camilla Rose," Matt said. "They stop taking their meds and skip their support group meetings. And self-medicate?"

"Yeah," she said, nodding. "And what's referred to as the true mania, a step worse than hypomania, can run for about a week, or even months. It simply varies from person to person. It's a kind of euphoria, during which they're prone to substance abuse. They speak quickly, their thoughts race, they focus really heavily on goals, and they engage in hypersexuality and other types of high-risk behavior . . ."

Payne, sipping his beer, felt his throat close involuntarily. He coughed, and a small amount of beer sprayed from his lips.

I'll be damned! Is that why she was trying to seduce me?

Amy stopped and shook her head.

"And," she then went on, "sometimes they attempt suicide."

"Camilla Rose didn't seem depressed, Amy," he said, wiping his mouth with the back of his hand. "Now that you describe it, I saw the mania. But no sadness."

"Matt, people mask the disease. They spend their whole lives knowing they're different. They're self-conscious about it. So they are very practiced at masking it, hiding it, from others. They also tend to gravitate to one another; there's a real comfort being among their own kind."

Which, Matt thought, *if he's also got it, maybe would explain her having Austin around?*

"At higher levels," Amy said, "they become delusional."

"As in, they believe the green meemies are coming for them?"

"Yeah. And not only believe it but think they see it. They sometimes hallucinate. It's terrifying for them.

Then after the manic episode comes the depressive episode."

"The mood swing," Matt said, making it a question.

"Yeah. And that's pretty much the layman's version. It's a treatable disease, but one of the biggest challenges is that the meds reduce the highs and lows to a mild middle ground. I've had plenty of patients say they don't like the 'dull' feeling and would rather deal with the lows—meaning, self-medicate—but especially the highs."

Matt nodded.

"I can see that," he said, then took a swig of beer. "Cheers to self-medicating."

Amy made a sour face.

"There's a lot more," she said, "but I already see your eyes are starting to glaze over."

Amy then motioned toward him with her coffee mug.

"How about we talk about you now?" she said.

"Amy," Patricia Payne said, softly.

"And what about me?" Matt said, his tone defensive. "Do you ever take a break from constantly analyzing people?"

"If you have this burning desire to stay a cop," Amy said, "why don't you figure out a position where you are not getting shot at?"

"That's not the way it works, Siggie. And you should know that. You have to work your way up the line, spending time in grade and taking the exam for a higher slot that may—or may not—be open." He paused, glared at her for a moment, then added, "Take Jason Washington. After the results of the sergeants exam, the lieutenants and captains results were released. Jason was at the top—not just in the top five but number one for captain. But there are no openings. Zero. So he just waits until some captain retires or gets—"

"Don't say it, wiseass," Amy interrupted.

"Promoted was what I was going to say," Matt finished. "White shirts at that level generally don't take bullets unless it's from a jealous lover or the lover's angry husband. Anyway, if nothing opens in two years, the whole process starts anew, beginning with retaking the exam. Rinse and repeat. And wait."

"You would think they would create an opening for Jason," Patricia Payne said, thoughtfully. "Such a brilliant man. But—"

"But there's no money, Mom," Matt put in. "The city council keeps cutting the department's budget."

"But as I was going to say before being so very rudely interrupted by my son . . ."

"Sorry," Matt said, shrugging.

". . . I would suggest that it's also as much about politics as it is about money. At least, that's what Denny and Jack would always say."

Matt had a mental image of his godfather, now the heavyset, silver-haired first deputy police commissioner, and his father around the time they would've been about his age. He could see them sitting at the wooden table in the kitchen of the South Philly row house, a half-empty bottle of Bushmills Irish whiskey between them, drinking from glass jars whose *Amish Apple Butter* labels had been soaked off years earlier, talking shop.

"Why?" Matt said.

"Jason's too smart," Patricia Payne said. "And that scares some people who think he might be after their job."

"You should see that, Sherlock," Amy said. "You didn't earn your promotion to sergeant . . ."

"Bullshit," Matt blurted.

". . . And go into Homicide," she went on. "You instead got a meritorious bump because of your connections. And if you don't believe it, just ask any cop." She paused, stared at him, then added, "That's the perception, Matt, and perception more times than not is stronger than reality. It becomes reality. And, like Jason, you may soon hit your ceiling, too."

Payne thought about that as he drained his beer.

"Where did you get that?" he said. "Not from Peter?"

Peter Wohl, at thirty-seven, was the youngest inspector in the department. After chief inspector, which was the next-highest rank, came the one- to four-star commissioner ranks.

It was no secret in the department that Wohl had been Matt Payne's "rabbi," his mentor. The function of rabbis was to groom a young police officer for greater responsibility—and rank—down the line.

Wohl's rabbi had been Inspector, then Chief Inspector, then First Deputy Police Commissioner Dennis V. Coughlin. And Denny Coughlin's rabbi, as he rose in rank, had first been Captain, then the Honorable Jerome H. "Jerry" Carlucci, Mayor of the City of Philadelphia.

Carlucci liked to boast that before answering the

people's call to elective public office, he had held every rank in the department except that of policewoman.

And Hizzoner had had a rabbi—one Chief Inspector Augustus Wohl, whose only son, Peter, would later enter the police academy at age twenty, two weeks after graduating from Temple University.

Peter and Amy had an on-and-off relationship.

"Yes," Amy said, "from Peter. But he simply was repeating it. He does not subscribe to it."

"Probably because people said the same about him," Matt said. He paused, then added, "So, what's the professional shrink term for him confiding in you? Pillow talk?"

Amy shook her head, clearly restraining herself from rising to the bait.

"You know, Matt," she said, "Penn Law and the Wharton School now have an accelerated course that combines JD and MBA programs. You can get both degrees in half the time it would take if you earned each separately."

"Is that so?" Patricia Payne said. "Business and law together. Interesting."

Matt's eyes darted toward his mother, and he fought back the urge to say, *Jesus! Not you, too?*

"Thanks, Amy," Matt said, his voice dripping with sarcasm. "That's nice to know. Duly noted." He paused, then added, "Is there a reason you're butting into my business?"

"Would you believe—as much as I right now want to smack you on the back of the head with one of those damn cast-iron pans—that I care about you? That *we* care about you?"

Matt did not respond.

"I know what's going on with you," Amy said. "I know the reason you're on edge. And, trust me, getting that place in The Rittenhouse really ain't going to cut it."

"What do you mean?" Matt said, his tone sharp.

"Amanda called this morning. I had to pry it out of her."

Matt saw his mother quickly turn her head at that.

He thought, *Shit! And you would.*

"Pry what, exactly?" he said.

"She told me she was taking that monthlong visiting teaching position in San Antonio."

"She say anything else?"

"About you two? No. She's never been the type who would do that. But, then, she didn't have to."

Matt was not surprised. Amanda and Amy, suite-mates in college before going on to med school, had kept up with each other ever since. They both had an uncanny sixth sense.

"Listen, little brother," she said in a tone that Matt decided was the same one she used with her more stubborn patients. "It's not as if this topic has not been broached before. And you really better start thinking hard about what it is that you want. *Really* want. Remember *lieben und arbeiten*?"

Matt felt his temper about to flare. There was a long pause before he trusted himself to speak.

"And do you remember what Dr. Stein said?" he said, finally.

Amy, eyes narrowing, looked at her brother.

"Which particular time?" she said, sharply.

"When he came to see me," Matt said, "after I took out those two in the parking lot of La Famiglia."

He paused, and thought, *The night Terry was in my Porsche and it got shot up and I shot the robbers. And that killed that relationship.*

Then Amy told Amanda that story.

And now . . . Shit!

"Well?" Amy said.

Matt went on. "He said, and this is almost verbatim, 'Your sister is a fine psychiatrist and a fine teacher. Perhaps for that reason I was terribly disappointed with just about everything she had to say, and certainly with her theories. She should have known that, and known that you should not even think about treating someone you deeply care for. It clouds judgment. In this case, spectacularly.'"

Payne paused, then added, "I think perhaps his point was flawed on the deeply caring part, but I agree with the rest of the premise."

"Matt!" his mother said.

"Sorry, Mom."

Payne's phone vibrated, and when he yanked it out of his pocket, there came a sharp pain from his wound. He automatically put his hand over the bandage as he checked the phone's screen. He grimaced.

"Are you okay, honey?" Patricia Payne said.

He walked over to his mother.

"I'm afraid I need to get back," he said, kissing her cheek again. "I'll take a rain check on lunch."

He went to the door and through it.

No one said another word.

[FOUR]

On the drive back, it took Matt a great deal of effort to keep a heavy foot off the accelerator pedal. In short order, he had gone through a wide range of emotion—first bordering on rage, then anger, then frustration, then, finally, a fair dose of self-loathing. Taking it all out on the car—which, by design, performed extraordinarily well when pushed hard—was easy to do.

His mind racing, he entered the on-ramp for I-476 South. There was no traffic ahead. And, seven seconds later, above the growl of exhaust, the alarm went off loudly in the dashboard—*Bong! Bong!*—and the instrument display flashed 90 MPH LIMIT EXCEEDED!

He immediately laid on the brakes and set the cruise control at 65, grateful that he had taken the time a month earlier to set up the onboard computer to warn him of the speedometer needle approaching triple digits.

He sighed as he touched the icon labeled PHONE on the in-dash screen, triggering the artificial intelligence interface on his smartphone that Kerry Rapier had had hacked and upgraded for him.

"Who can I call for you, Marshal?" the sultry, computer-generated female voice filled the car, triggering in Payne the mental image of the actress Kathleen Turner. He once had made the mistake of telling Rapier how much he'd liked her in *Body Heat*.

"Call Tony Harris mobile," he announced.

"My pleasure."

On the screen in the dashboard, a text box appeared that confirmed the request. Next, he heard two rings, and then Harris's voice. "Hey, Matt."

"You got my attention. I'm headed back from my family's place, and—"

"Hold one," Tony interrupted. "I want to conference in Krowczyk."

A minute later, Harris said, "Hey, Krow."

"What's up, Tony?" Danny Krowczyk, the Signals Intelligence analyst, said. "You get ahold of ol' Wyatt Earp?"

Harris chuckled.

"Yeah, and he's actually coming back from fighting evil criminals on the Main Line as we speak," Harris said. "He's on this conference call."

There was silence.

Payne's next mental image was of the gentle giant of a geek in his usual stance: hunched over his IBM i2 analyst notebook computer, his face aglow in its light, his eyeglasses reflecting a screenful of intel.

And, he thought, *right now probably with a look of* Oops! *on his face.*

"You've got the Marshal's attention, Krow," Payne said. "This better be good."

"Oh, hey, Sarge. Yeah, I got something that I think is better than good. Then again, with all I've had to dig through, it could be nothing better than a WAG."

"WAG?" Payne said.

"Yeah, that's short for a highly technical HUMINT term."

Human Intelligence WAG? Payne thought.

"Which is?" he said.

"Wild-ass guess."

Payne snorted.

"So, you making progress or not?"

"Sarge," Krowczyk said, "we can collect a shitload of data points round the clock till the cows come home, but unless they're sorta close to what we're looking for, there's a real chance of instead getting what we refer to as *analysis paralysis.*" He paused, then added, "That said, I think this will help. There's interesting stuff here, including a suicide. You swinging by the ECC anytime soon?"

"I'm on my way."

Payne saw movement on the in-dash screen, the caller ID reading DAD'S OFFICE.

Oh, for chrissakes!

"I've got to take this incoming call, guys," Payne announced.

"See you shortly," Harris said, and the connection went dead.

Payne tapped the screen to accept the call, and said, his tone disgusted, "I really can't believe they called you already, Dad. What the hell?"

"Hello, Matt," Mrs. Irene Craig said, a certain tone

of loving exasperation in her voice. She had served some twenty years as executive secretary to Brewster Payne, founding partner of Mawson, Payne, Stockton, McAdoo & Lester, arguably Philadelphia's most prestigious law firm. "You don't sound as if you're having the best day. I'm sorry. Please hold for your father."

"Thanks, Mrs. Craig. Nice to hear your voice. And you really don't want to know."

After enough time for Mrs. Craig to share what had just transpired, his father's voice filled the car. "Who called, Matt? What's this about?"

"I'm guessing my pain-in-the-ass sister."

"I haven't heard from Amy. Is it anything serious?"

"And Mom didn't call?"

"About what, Matt?"

"No, nothing serious," Matt said. "I just assumed that since I was out at the house with them now, and . . ."

"Well, Matt," Brewster said, when he had finished, "the one thing I can say unequivocally is that they do both love and care about you"—he paused, then added—"as do I."

Matt felt his throat tighten.

"Look, Matt," his father went on, "I've said it before and I'll say it again: You're a grown man. Do what you believe you must. Do what makes you happy."

Matt was quiet. He thought about his father—a tall, angular, dignified man in his early fifties—and how wise and fair he could be, and how he wanted to emulate that for as long as he could remember.

"Matt?" his father said.

"Yeah, I'm still here . . . And thanks for that."

"What was it that you called about earlier?" Brewster Payne said, moving the conversation on.

Matt told him about what Camilla Rose Morgan had said.

"I cannot right now confirm this," Brewster said, "but I'm almost certain she is not a client."

What the hell? Matt thought. *She lied about that? Why?*

Makes me wonder how well she knew Daffy. If it was only in passing.

Not that that really matters, but it could establish a pattern.

"Do you remember speaking with her?" Matt said.

"Oh, sure. How could anyone not, with that enormous personality of hers? Not to mention her gift for getting one to contribute to her charities. She's very good, very convincing. But just not a client."

"How come?" Matt said.

"Any firm as conservative as ours simply would not annoy a billionaire, especially a local one. Not when it's his or her business that we want. The firms going after those smaller lawsuits usually are ones in places like Seattle, Chicago, Dallas—"

"She has a Florida lawyer. Maybe more than one."

"Okay, even Miami, looking to make a name for themselves. The way it works—if, in fact, she had approached the firm for representation—is we would have said, 'Unfortunately, we have to decline taking your case.'"

"Because of what? Conflict of interest?"

"That's exactly the reason. And I'm sure the reason she didn't approach us was that she knew—or was told—that for decades we had represented Old Man Morgan in various cases. And none of the reputable local firms would take her case against Mason Morgan because they would rather have a billionaire's business. Even just the crumbs, which are serious crumbs."

"And that she wouldn't win."

"Yes, very likely that, too. The lawyer—lawyers, plural—taking her case will get plenty of billable hours. But if they don't win, that's all they get—there won't be a big payday. And whatever they get would be nothing like what they could get from the old man's company year after year. It would not surprise me if the old man, and now Mason, has put every heavy-hitting firm in town on retainer."

"So," Matt said, "when someone tries to hire them to go after Mason and/or Morgan International, the firms can say, 'Sorry, but our conflict check has found that they are our client. Said conflict check ensures that our commitment is to the client's best interest.'"

"Precisely."

"She had listed as her next of kin her lawyer in Florida."

"And not Mason or her mother? Interesting. That could mean something. Do you know who it is?"

"I should shortly."

Brewster was quiet a for a minute, then said, "There is a small chance it could be a firm to which we've outsourced work and that could explain her thinking she's our client. We've been looking at expanding into Florida, because farming out case work opens up a lot of other problems, such as inefficient conflict checks and disclosure of confidential information. When you do get the name, let me know. If nothing else, I can get you a clearer picture on who it is."

"Will do. Thanks," Matt said. "But, going off on a tangent, out at the house just now Mom mentioned the office politics of freezing people out of promotions because someone above them considers them a threat. I don't doubt it happens; I'm just wondering how much, and what you think."

"But you just got promoted."

"Not about me," Matt said, and explained. "We were talking about Jason Washington coming in at number one on the captain's list, and . . ."

After he had finished, Brewster Payne said, "In my experience, there very well is a great deal of truth to that. Happens all the time. And the reverse is true: promotions get made based not on one's superior abilities but on some connection." He paused, then added, "Apropos of nothing whatsoever, that is why I like what I do. No one limits how hard I can work nor how high I can go."

Matt was quiet.

"Look, Matt, call if you need anything. I have to deal with this deposition that just came in."

"Thanks for everything. And I really mean it."

"Anytime. You know that. Good luck."

Matt heard the connection drop out.

*   *   *

Ten minutes later, after thinking about what his father had said, Payne tapped the MESSAGES icon on the dash screen.

The sultry Kathleen Turner voice filled the car: *"Yes, Marshal?"*

"Text Daffy."

After a short pause came: *"Your goddaughter's mother has Do Not Disturb enacted on her communication devices right now."*

"Of course Daffy does. She's probably bent into a pretzel in some snooty yoga class and trying in vain to rein in her flatulence."

"Shall I ask Mrs. Nesbitt that?"

Payne chuckled.

"And you would. No, text her, quote, Quick question: How well did you know Camilla Rose Morgan, question mark, unquote."

The sultry voice repeated the message as it simultaneously appeared in a text bubble on the screen in the dash.

"Okay. How's this, Marshal?"

"Perfect. Send it. That way, it'll be waiting for her when she gets thrown out of the class for stinking up the place."

"Sent. Anything else I can do?"

"Yeah. You seem to be pretty intuitive. Always quick with the answers, getting me what I need. Why can't all the women in my life be as cooperative and accommodating as you?"

"Try making me mad and see what happens."

Payne was quiet.

"*Marshal? Does this have anything to do with Amanda?*"

"Play a Bob French album," he said.

"*Excellent choice. And I will cue up some new Emily Asher you might like. I love traditional Dixieland Jazz. Okay, Marshal, there, it's done.*"

Payne sighed as he heard the Original Tuxedo Jazz Band's crisp but mournful brass horns begin filling the car with "Someday You'll Be Sorry."

He formed a ball with his right fist, leaving the middle finger extended and pointed at the multifunction screen.

"*Are you testing me, Marshal?*"

V

[ONE]
Police Administration Building
Eighth and Race Streets
Philadelphia
Friday, January 6, 1:21 P.M.

This place is looking worse every day, Payne thought, glancing upward as he approached the aged police headquarters, its coarse concrete exterior stained with dark streaks from a half century of pollution.

The complex had two circular buildings, each four stories high. They were sheathed in cast concrete and connected in such a manner that some said the complex resembled a giant pair of handcuffs. The interior walls of the buildings, mirroring the exterior, also were curved, thus causing police headquarters to be known colloquially as the *Roundhouse.*

There had been some talk for years of replacing the Roundhouse with a larger facility, and now that idea finally was getting traction. Plans were in place to renovate the eighty-seven-year-old Provident Mutual Life Insurance Company Building in West Philly, which had been vacant and shuttered for two decades. The enormous structure would become home to all Roundhouse occupants, as well as consolidate certain other offices that, for space reasons, either had been forced out of the Roundhouse or that there never had been room for in the first place.

Further talk, mostly from city council members jockeying to get their names and, they hoped, their faces on the nightly news, said that it was going to happen—and soon.

What the city council members conveniently failed to mention was that the only thing the slowly-skidding-toward-bankruptcy city needed was the money to do so. Among its many other financial failings, Philadelphia was short nearly six billion dollars for funding just its pension obligations.

Payne, after displaying his identification to the overweight blue shirt manning the secure door, waited to get buzzed through. The officer punched the button for the solenoid release. There was a long pause before Payne heard the buzzing. He tried the door, found it still locked, shook it. Still nothing.

The blue shirt let out an audible sigh, then made more noise as he squeezed out of the chair. He ambled over to the door and manually opened it.

Payne, after passing inside, debated taking the elevator up or the stairs. He finally decided his wound dictated his use of the former.

He got on the elevator and pushed the panel button for the third floor. When the doors chugged, struggling to close, he immediately regretted his decision. Next came strange grinding, metallic sounds as the elevator ascended in a manner that he thought could be described as anything but smooth.

He thought, *What a dump.*

Getting off at the third floor, Payne turned and followed the curved corridor. It had windows looking out over the front entrance of the building and, diagonally opposite across Race Street, Franklin Park. The curved interior wall of the corridor was lined with steel filing cabinets that no longer fit inside the offices.

Twenty feet or so later, Payne came to the Executive Command Center. Its door—and every state-of-the-art item behind it—stood in stark contrast to the aged building itself.

The ECC was the electronic nerve center of the

Philadelphia Police Department headquarters. It was situated between the offices of the police commissioner and the deputy police commissioner in an area that had once been another office and a large conference room, the wall between them removed to form a larger space.

It had come into being thanks not to foresight from the elected officials in City Hall but, rather, from federal dollars having flooded in after Philly had been picked to host the Democratic National Convention.

Fears of a possible terrorist attack had been very real, and with politicians coming from across the nation, those voting on Capitol Hill in Washington, D.C., had not hesitated sending taxpayer monies to purchase the best technology that Philadelphia could acquire.

The Executive Command Center—what law enforcement members commonly referred to as a Fusion Center—aided in the collection, assimilation, and analysis of information from multiple agencies. The center had two enormous T-shaped, gray formica–topped conference tables in the middle of the room's charcoal-colored industrial carpet, each of which could seat twenty-six officers and staff. On the tables, beside a small forest of black stalk microphones and multiline telephone consoles, were outlets and ports to accommodate at least that many notebook computers and other devices. Gray leather office chairs on casters ringed the table. Additional seating was provided by forty armless leather chairs along two walls that formed a sort of continuous bank.

Mounted on the ten-foot-tall walls opposite the conference tables were three banks of sixty-inch flat-screen, high-definition LCD monitors. Each bank had nine monitors, frameless and mounted edge to edge, which either could create a single enormous image or be divided to display up to eighteen different images. These images generally were live video feeds from a wide range of secure sources, such as cameras in the SEPTA mass-transit system, as well as the broadcasts of local and cable news shows. A half dozen of the monitors were dedicated to the cycling feeds from the cameras of the Pennsylvania Department of Transportation, somewhat grainy black-and-white shots of traffic on major arteries and bridges and on heavily traveled secondary streets. If any of the Aviation Unit's assets—older Bell 206 L-4s and a new pair of Airbus A-Star helicopters acquired in the last year with federal funds—were airborne, the DOT images would rotate with the thermal and standard color videos sent from the aircraft.

The flat-screens also served as enormous computer monitors, broadcasting on a large scale anything that appeared on the computers plugged into the network ports on the conference tables. Some of these included the constant monitoring of calls coming into the 911 center so that when a unit was dispatched, a tech could check camera feeds in the area—and, if available, a helicopter's eye in the sky—and relay critical real-time information on the scene to the responding officers.

That the ECC pulled together a wide array of disparate data on people, places, and events, then connected dots and disseminated the findings in a highly efficient manner, was without question an impressive achievement.

But the fact that the ECC also furthered a political component, interagency cooperation, was equally impressive. While turf battles between local and federal officials were nothing new—and had the tendency to render the term *interagency cooperation* an oxymoron—the ECC helped alleviate that by linking its secure communications networks with those of state and federal law enforcement agencies, including the Federal Bureau of Investigation, the United States Secret Service, and all the alphabet agencies under the U.S. Department of Homeland Security.

[TWO]

Payne entered the ECC and scanned the room. There were at least a couple dozen people around the tables, working in the glow of the bright banks of TV monitors.

He saw Tony Harris at the far table, standing beside a seated Danny Krowczyk. Harris waved him over.

Detective Krowczyk, in jeans, white polo shirt, and black sneakers, was hunched over his IBM i2 notebook computer. The Signals Intelligence analyst had an open package of Tastykake Dreamies beside his computer. He held one of the cream-filled sponge cakes, absently taking bites, while repeatedly tapping the RETURN key with his right index finger. Behind the computer screen, with

its pages refreshing with every tap of the keyboard, Krowczyk had built a short pyramid of three empty diet cola
cans.

As Payne approached, the skinny, six-foot-four thirty-
year-old belched, then pushed his new black horn-
rimmed eyeglasses higher up his nose and returned to
tapping the keyboard.

"Gentlemen," Payne greeted them.

"Hey, Matt," Harris said.

"Sergeant Payne," Krowczyk replied, looking up. He
motioned with the sponge cake. "Want one? You need
one. Probably two. Or more."

"Really? Why's that?"

"They have mystical power."

"Oh, bullshit."

"You ever eat one?"

"Not after I read the ingredients. Those things could
survive a nuclear meltdown."

"That's exactly right. And that explains their super-
natural power to repel lead."

"All right," Payne said, then gestured with his hand
for him to go on. "I'll bite—"

"All I'm saying, Sarge, is that I eat them and have not
suffered a single bullet wound. You, however . . ."

Harris chuckled.

"Screw you two," Payne said, glancing around the
room. "Where's Kerry? I thought you said he was working on getting the cell tower dump."

"Yeah, and he did that," Harris said. "He sent the
subpoenas to the seven service providers of the cell

towers overlapping the scene, then said he'd have to come back later to help. There's going to be a ton of call data to filter through from this morning. And that's on top of what's coming in from yesterday's shooting, which, if we're lucky, we should have by the time he's back."

Corporal Kerry Rapier, the department's wizard of all devices electronic, was the ECC's master technician and, at twenty-five, its youngest tech.

Krowczyk, his tone somewhat disgusted, added, "Wafflin' Walker sent word down that he wanted Rapier, in uniform, at a conference at Temple. Kerry told me that since he had been one of the main techs the Temple guys had talked to when they planned the thing on data mining software, there probably wasn't going to be much for him to learn there, so he was going, as ordered, and would sneak out the soonest he could."

"Wafflin' Walker"—Deputy Commissioner Howard Walker, the fifty-year-old two-star chief of Science & Technology—was very tall and slender, with a cleanly shaven head and long, thin nose. He wore tiny Ben Franklin glasses and effected a soft, intelligent voice, much like that of a cleric with a somewhat pious air. His domain of Science & Technology included the Digital Forensic Sciences, Communications, and Information Systems units—the latter two with oversight of the Executive Command Center.

Payne was privy to the fact that Walker would never have been Denny Coughlin's first choice to work directly under him. Police deputy commissioners and above—the one- through four-star ranks—were appointed by the city's managing director with the blessing of the mayor. Ralph Mariana, the police commissioner, had quietly told First Deputy Commissioner Coughlin that he'd had his reasons for getting Walker the job, though, interestingly, had never shared them.

Payne had yet to find anyone who didn't think Walker had a highly inflated opinion of himself. He had earned the name Wafflin' Walker because he rarely made a decision that he stuck with the moment it was questioned.

Now that I think of it, Payne thought, *like someone afraid of his own shadow—and afraid for his job.*

Someone who would freeze out a person worthy of promotion.

He didn't like it one bit when I let slip in front of the mayor that the backup in the forensic lab was holding up that serial murder investigation.

"One of my guys," Krowczyk said, "is working on that burner flip phone they recovered from the shooter's van. It shows it was used yesterday—and yesterday only—with a bunch of texts sent and received right before fourteen hundred hours. He's running down all those data points."

"Okay," Payne said. "What else?"

"McCrory's second meeting with the Morgan woman's assistant didn't go worth a damn," Harris said. "She told him that after their first meeting she had called the lawyer in Florida to notify him of Morgan's death. He specifically ordered her, as a company employee, not to answer any more questions without a lawyer from the company present."

"Damn it."

"She did, though, give McCrory the list of those registered to attend the gala. Just over three hundred names. Frankly, I don't see them as high-priority, and, short of just seeing who's who, vetting them at this point would be a poor use of resources."

"And risk the real possibility of analysis paralysis," Payne said, glancing at Krowczyk.

Harris nodded, and said, "At least until we've run down other leads."

"What about names from the bar and her condo?" Payne said.

Harris shook his head. "Lawyer told her no. But—"

"What's this lawyer's name?" Payne interrupted.

"Grosse. Michael Grosse. He's got offices in Miami and New Orleans and Houston. McCrory has more details."

Payne pulled out his smartphone, and, as he typed an e-mail, said, "The old man offered to see what he could find out about him."

"But, as I was saying," Harris went on when Payne had finished, "thanks to the advent of social media and our attention-starved society, we don't need no stinkin' lawyer to give us names. At least, ones from the bar."

"What'd you turn up?" Payne said.

"You got it handy, Krow?"

Krowczyk put down his cake and typed rapidly. Payne and Harris looked up at the left bank of nine monitors. The individual images of Philly streets and traffic were replaced with one big image that also appeared on Krowczyk's computer screen.

"I found this picture posted on four social media sites," Krowczyk said, "the first belonging to that PR chick's."

Three women and three men, all with broad smiles, were leaning together in front of the fireplace in the Library Bar.

"I'll be damned," Payne said. "Nice group shot. And they even tagged names to the faces. How accommodating. Not that we don't know who they are."

"Yeah," Krowczyk said, placing the cursor over the head of each person, triggering a text box containing their name to pop up, "so there's Camilla Rose Morgan in the middle beside Sue Thomas, of Sweet Sue's Homemade Pies—man, I love those pumpkin whoopies she sells. And John Broadhead, the architect. Aimee Wolter, the smoking-hot public relations chick, who's obviously queen of spreading her face on social media. And City Council President Willie Lane, mugging it up with Anthony Holmes, quarterback of our beloved but besieged NFL team."

Payne grunted. "I was wondering where you were about to go describing Wolter's spreading . . ."

Harris and Krowczyk chuckled.

Payne added, "Well, I wouldn't exactly rush to get the district attorney on the phone and announce that we have the short list of doers."

"True," Harris said, "but hope springs eternal that through them we'll unearth the proverbial stone under the stone. Kennedy is down at his desk working on getting in touch with them all."

"So, nothing on who in the bar crowd could have gone to her condo?" Payne said.

"Hank Nasuti managed to track down the head bartender," Harris said. "Woke him up."

"Here, I'll pull up the interview," Krowczyk said.

The group image on the monitors was replaced with a close-up of Detective Hank Nasuti, who was looking into the camera lens. The thirty-four-year-old was a second-generation Philadelphian, his grandparents having moved to Philly from Italy in the 1920s.

The camera panned and eventually fixed on a narrow-faced male with disheveled dark hair and tired gray eyes in his mid-twenties. He held a Wawa to-go coffee cup. Payne saw that the timer box at the bottom indicated the interview was just over twenty-one minutes long.

"Guy's name is Harvey Wolfe," Krowczyk said, and began dragging with the curser to advance the video, the male's head moving in fast motion for a few seconds. He stopped when the timer read 14:50. "Here's the meat of it."

The video then played at normal speed, and Nasuti's voice came from the IBM computer's speakers. "Okay, so you said Miss Morgan had been in the Library Bar since happy hour?"

Harvey Wolfe nodded. "After you called, I called in and had them check her ticket. The bar register shows the ticket was opened with her first martini at six fifty-one."

"And she was there with her party until just after nine?"

Sipping his coffee, Wolfe nodded again.

"About then," he said. "I don't remember exactly. She told me to leave open her tab, to give her table whatever they wanted to order."

"And who was at the table?"

"The only ones I knew for sure was the football player and the city councilman."

"Tony Holmes and William Lane."

"Yeah. But there were a bunch of others who came and went. Someone said some actress, but I don't watch TV so I couldn't tell you."

"How long was Miss Morgan gone?"

"I'm not sure. It was a busy, loud night," Harvey Wolfe said. "I do remember that when she came back, she had me make her another martini. And that she looked a little annoyed for some reason."

Payne felt Harris glance at him, saw his knowing look, and shrugged in reply.

"But once she got her drink she brightened," Wolfe went on. "If I had to guess, I'd say that had to be about ten, ten-thirty-ish."

Nasuti said, "And she stayed until . . . ?"

Wolfe laughed deeply.

"What?" Nasuti said.

"She wanted to keep drinking until the sun came up, if she could."

"Why's that?"

"At one-thirty, I put out the word to the servers to tell their customers that last call was at one forty-five. When Miss Morgan heard that, she tried to get me to keep the place open later. And when I said I was sorry, that was impossible—the hotel strictly follows the city's two A.M. bar-closing law—she said she'd happily rent out the place, make it a private party."

"Why didn't you?"

"Well, I really don't have the authority, not that kind of flexibility. But, believe me, it was tempting—it was Miss Morgan, who's always really nice and a big tipper, and the extra money for the staff would've been sweet. I mean, the bar tab already was over a thousand bucks. She asked me to ask and I said I would."

"And?"

"When I first asked the other servers, before trying my manager, only a couple got excited, and we couldn't do it with only a couple. Some of us have second jobs, you know? And school. And even when we close at two, it's maybe not till three, sometimes four, that we get the place cleaned up so we can go home."

"Got it. So, what happened then?"

"I told Miss Morgan and she said she was inviting anyone in the bar to come up to her condominium for an after-hours party. Including us servers, which shows you how generous she was."

"Did you go?"

Wolfe frowned, shook his head.

"Thought about it," he said, "but management doesn't allow us to hang with guests."

"Do you know who *did* go up?"

He shook his head again.

"I was busy closing up the bar—wiping down bottles, cycling glasses in and out of the dishwater, the usual. People closed out their tabs and went out the door, but I can't say who actually went with her. I heard that city councilman saying he was exhausted and had to go home."

"And this was all at two, you say?"

"Starting at two, when I turned up the houselights. The stragglers trickled out by two-fifteen or so. Miss Morgan was among the first ones to leave, before the lights went up."

The video stopped.

Krowczyk said, "He adds nothing past that point. McCrory should anytime now have all the surveillance video taken of the condo lobby, going back to twenty-one hundred hours, and from the hotel."

"Okay," Payne said. "You find anything on Austin or Benson?"

Krowczyk shook his head.

"Not really. Austin has only a website for his wealth management firm. And it shows only the most basic contact information with a line that says, if I recall exactly, 'We offer investment and philanthropic advisory and strategic planning services for foundations, endowments, and individuals.' That's it. Nothing in-depth. And he has zero personal social media stuff."

"What about Benson?"

"He has a personal page, which appears to have been more or less inactive for about the last year. And besides a basic website, NextGenRx.com, he has a business social media page that's essentially a promotional site for the medical device. It doesn't allow anyone to post anything on it. So there's no paths to follow there."

"What about Camilla Rose Morgan?"

"Ah, now, she's the total opposite. She has social media pages for herself personally and for her charities. And they are packed with activity. Her picture is everywhere. Here, I'll show you the Camilla's Kids Camp website as an example."

The video interview of Harvey Wolfe was replaced.

"Now, that's impressive," Payne said. "It shows that more than five hundred thousand people follow her camps on social media."

"There's a reason for that. Just look at all they do," Krowczyk said as he clicked on the link to the camp calendar and read the screen. "Week one is for kids with cancer. Week two is diabetes. Then heart problems. Sickle cell. Asthma/Airway. Arthritis/Hemophilia. Spina bifida. Immune deficiency/kidney. Epilepsy. That's a lot of sick kids."

"The half million are ones who have attended and/or want to attend," Harris said. "The kids who get picked pay nothing to go."

"What's this Founder's Message video link?" Payne said, pointing. "Can you play it?"

Krowczyk clicked on the box and the screen changed to show Camilla Rose, clad in crisp khaki shorts and a white T-shirt and ball cap logotyped CAMILLA'S KIDS CAMPS, smiling and waving with both hands at the camera. Behind her, on a wooden pier jutting out into a river lined with moss-draped trees, a half dozen children in wheelchairs held fishing poles. Her voice came from the computer speakers.

"*Hi, I'm Camilla Rose Morgan. Welcome to Crystal River, Florida, home to one of my four ACC-accredited camps for children with extreme medical challenges. Every week at these twenty-million-dollar wonderlands, kids come to experience the excitement of the expected—and the unexpected.*

"*Our state-of-the-art medical facility features a full-time physician and nurse, plus volunteer doctors and nurses who specialize in the disease of each week's group of campers. And our superb staff counselors, one staffer for every three campers, are true professionals who have passed a rigorous vetting process.*

"*While parents do not attend—that would distract from the experience—they do know that all campers' needs are constantly monitored. Campers are provided their daily medications and any procedures, from chemo to dialysis, then they head out for a full day of sun and fun.*

"*Here on the Gulf Coast, for example, there's fishing, boating, swimming in the Olympic-sized pool, horseback riding on the beach, craft workshops, and much more. After dinners, we gather round the campfire for singing and skits and laughs.*

"*Lots and lots of the latter, as laughter is the best medicine. Just ask the campers themselves.*"

"Reminds me a great deal of Boy Scout camp . . ." Payne said.

They watched the image of Camilla Rose being replaced by a shot of what looked to be a girl of maybe ten or twelve holding out her right arm as she made a video recording of herself. She had a sweet, engaging smile and bright eyes that gleamed like the tiny diamond studs in her earlobes. And she had a very bald, very shiny head.

Payne added, "Except without the terminally ill kids. Guess the chemo got her hair."

The little girl said, her voice squeaking with emotion, *"I just had to say thank you for the best time I have ever had in my whole life! I didn't know it was possible to do all the fun things you taught me. I learned so much about staying strong and getting better. Thanks to you, no matter what, I'll always be a Camilla's Can-Do Kid!"*

Payne felt his throat tighten, and he caught himself wiping his eye.

"Wow," he said, after he cleared his throat. "Powerful. And another example of why my gut says she didn't jump. She said those kids were her calling in life."

"I hear you," Harris said, clearing his throat, too.

Payne looked at him and noticed he showed signs of also having had moist eyes.

Harris picked up on that and shrugged. "I'm a sucker for sick kids—what can I say?"

"She's got more of these camps on the coasts of California and North Carolina," Krowczyk said, "and one up on the Delaware River outside New Hope. That's eighty mil total, if each one's worth the twenty she said. What's going to happen to them now?"

"I'm guessing that their board of directors would carry on the mission," Payne said as he felt his phone vibrate. "As long as there's the money, that is. Which likely makes tomorrow's fund-raiser all the more critical."

He checked the smartphone's screen and saw that Daffy Nesbitt had replied: "I heard the terrible news about Camilla Rose. And, yes, I knew her. Why do you ask? It was from the fund-raising last year for the hospital. Chad was involved through the company. I thought she was delightful. Such a big, kind heart. We had plans to attend her gala tomorrow. Oh, and did you know Terry is coming back in town for it? With that horrid actor from here."

And another positive note for Camilla Rose, Payne thought.

Daffy can be cutthroat. She would not praise her unless she really meant it.

Payne gestured with the phone.

"Well," he said, "a back channel pretty much just confirmed that Stan Colt will be in town for the Camilla's Kids fund-raiser. Oh joy."

"Yeah, he's on the dignitary list," Harris said, then tapped a couple keys on the notebook computer next to Krowczyk's. "Meant to tell you on the phone that it came in while you were gone. Got it here. It's short."

Payne leaned over to look at the list. It detailed each VIP's biography and contact information and itinerary.

"Not as many as I'd expected," Payne said, tapping the keyboard's down arrow while scanning the scrolling screen. "A few actors; three, no, four pro athletes; and a mix of politicians. All with egos off the charts. I want no part of holding their hands."

Payne stood straight and looked between Harris and Krowczyk.

"Okay," he said. "So, what else? What was that WAG?"

"Right," Harris said. "Krow here, digging through the data points, found one bit of data—"

"Datum," Krowczyk interrupted. *"Data* is the plural form."

"Datum that eventually led him to a really interesting article."

"And that datum led to other data," Krowczyk said, "all of it open-source info."

Payne looked at him.

"You said something about a suicide?"

"That's right, Sarge," Krowczyk said, pointing toward the screen with his half-eaten sponge cake, yellow crumbs scattered across the keyboard of the four-thousand-dollar computer. "But first you should see some of these from the chat room on one investor website. They'll give you an interesting perspective."

"Remember how this guy Benson was the head cheerleader for his start-up?" Harris said.

"Yeah," Payne said.

"Well," Krowczyk picked up, "he also berated his stockholders and anyone else who did not blindly worship the company. For the Benson case file, I put together a ton of those comments. These are just a few examples."

The Camilla's Kids website was replaced by one filled with multicolored lines of text, each date-stamped posting a different hue. At the top it read PLEASE LOG IN HERE TO COMMENT ON NEXTGENRX.

"Okay," Payne said, "so tell me exactly what this is we're looking at. Looks like some sort of Internet electronic bazaar."

"It's definitely got a carnival atmosphere," Krowczyk said. "This is one of the chat rooms on the Investors Insider website. It has chat rooms for practically every stock and investment topic, and they're mostly used by day traders, though, in reality, anyone can post."

"That one says it was posted by Bull$Ball$," Payne said. "How do you know who's who?"

"You really don't," Krowczyk said. "While some people actually use a name, most are obviously made up, and there's no way to really know if those using what look like real names are actually who they say they are. Some, in fact, can be trolls."

"And these particular trolls are doing what here?"

"Actively trying to talk up, or down, a stock for their own gain. It's a lot like the free-for-all posting in a reader comment section that follows online newspaper and magazine articles. Except here there is money involved."

Payne read a few, then said, "Well, it's not exactly the black art of the old Soviet disinformation. But it looks like it's in the same vein. Remarkable how many are clearly pushing an agenda. 'This stock is poised to shoot through the roof. I just bought more at this low price.'"

"Yeah," Harris said, "while other posters are simply looking for answers, like that one from Tulsa Annie asking if the approval of the company patents, quote, is within the reasonable time frame of similar other patents, unquote. Want to bet what a troll's answer to that was?"

"Classic Salesmanship 101," Payne said. "'Tell your customers what they want to hear.'"

Krowczyk watched, and waited, as they read the rest of the page, and then tapped the keyboard to produce a new page on-screen.

"Okay," he said, "so now get a load of this exchange."

```
Charley411

RE: MarketMaven post# 22110

Post # 22116 of 22809
"Hang on for the next big announcement,"
you say? Are you kidding me? That's what
NGRx's mouthpiece said last time and the
only thing that happened was a five-cent
run-up in share price, followed by a
bigger drop after the profit takers were
done.
Fool me once, shame on you. Fool me
twice . . . is not going to happen.

1) There is no proof of a marketable
   product. It's all smoke and mirrors.
2) There are inexplicable spikes in share
   price, suggesting market manipulation, and
3) Then there's the mysterious death of the
   chief scientist.

I've had enough of this horseshit con job.
```

```
NGRxSocialMediaGuru

RE: Charley411 post# 22116

Post # 22117 of 22810
There's damn sure no smoke and mirrors. You
and everyone else making these baseless
claims are absolute fucking morons if you
can't see the upside to this! And there is
no market manipulation — otherwise, you
imbecile, don't you think the shares would
be even higher?
The world-changing product is there! The
patents are filed! This is the BEST time to
be buying!
Shareholders who hold a long position will
be aptly rewarded. It will be HUGE! The
rest of you, go ahead and SELL. Then go to
hell. Because the smart investors will snap
up your shares!
```

"So we're assuming that that guru is someone connected with the company," Payne said, "as opposed to a troll using a bogus name."

"From all I've read—and I've read countless exchanges just like that," Krowczyk said, "I'm convinced it is Benson. That business social media page of his I mentioned that's essentially a promotional site for the medical device? A number of items that appear on there—and only he or someone who works for him can post on it—have also appeared here, word for word."

"Amazing," Payne said, shaking his head. "On a public forum, calling people who invest in your company morons—and worse—it's really a *bizarre* bazaar."

"There are plenty of other examples in the file that I compiled. And he was well known for losing his temper," Krowczyk said.

Payne exchanged glances with Harris.

"That's what John Austin said about him," Payne said.

"Benson never took anything off anyone," Harris said.

"What's with the mysterious death?" Payne said. "Is that the suicide?"

Krowczyk nodded.

"After I picked up on that datum, I made a WAG and dug further," he said, then tapped the keyboard to produce another new page on the monitor, "and got this."

Payne whistled softly as he scanned the news article:

Death of Pharma Scientist Ruled a Suicide

Police Investigation Determines Dr. Zhong Han, Found Dead in His Garage, Succumbed to Carbon Monoxide Poisoning

By Jessie Dalehite

Business Staff Writer, *Miami News Now*

WEST PALM BEACH, Jan. 2nd—Police homicide detectives today closed the case on the death of Zhong

"Charley" Han, Ph.D., forty-five, declaring his death three weeks ago in nearby Riviera Beach was in fact a suicide. The ruling had not been unexpected. From the beginning, Dr. Han, a biochemist engineer, was said to have left a detailed note.

"The evidence always pointed to this being a tragic case of one taking his own life," Jeffrey Murray, the lead homicide detective on the case, said. "The forensic evidence, including the authentication of the suicide note, finally bore it out. Our condolences and prayers go out to the deceased's family and friends."

A family spokesman, Samuel Nguyen, addressing reporters outside the Hans' waterfront residence in Riviera Beach, said that Dr. Han's widow, Mrs. Ann Han, age forty, would have no comment.

"Not now or later," Mr. Nguyen added.

Mrs. Han as recently as two weeks ago had been actively courting media attention concerning the circumstances leading up to her husband's death.

Mr. Nguyen, when asked, said that "no comment" would include not releasing what Dr. Han had written in the suicide note. He did confirm that the note, written on NextGenRx stationery, had been found under the windshield wiper blade of a Lexus SUV in the garage of the Han residence.

Dr. Han, having been awarded numerous patents in the pharmaceutical industry by the U.S. Patent and Trade Office (USPTO), was well regarded.

Before his separation from NextGenRx six weeks ago, Dr. Han had been the chief scientist at the small company.

NextGenRx is a two-year-old start-up focused on the manufacture of medical devices and their technology. While it began with a modest venture capital investment, NextGenRx now is publicly traded in the OTC Markets Group. Of its 2.5 billion common shares, 600 million currently are traded.

Chairman and Chief Executive Officer Kenneth R. Benson declined repeated requests for comment on the ruling of suicide of his company's former number three officer.

However, in postings on at least one Internet chat room website, InvestorsInsider.com, a post using the screen name NGRxSocialMediaGuru has consistently, and at times in a caustic manner, denounced all who have suggested that the results of Dr. Han's clinical trials could not be duplicated.

The company's stock, which rose from an initial low of a half cent, had been trading last month at an all-time high of ten cents per share.

The rise in price had followed the release of what turned out to be Dr. Han's final patent application, and, the next day, news that Luoma Biologika GmbH of Germany, which manufactures and sells ophthalmic devices, had entered into a co-licensing agreement with NextGenRx.

The stock price plummeted by half on the news of

Dr. Han's separation from the company. It then fell even further, to two cents, after his death, when Mrs. Han went public with the accusations that Dr. Han had been coerced into endorsing papers containing falsified data from the clinical trials.

When first contacted last month, CEO Benson stated, "I consider Charley a friend, in addition to being a coworker. The sad fact of the matter is, unfortunately, he has suffered from some long illness and has rarely been able to even come to the office. His work suffered tremendously, to the point where he was unable to complete tasks, even remotely from home. We deeply regret that he decided that separation from NextGenRx was the best thing for him. He has made a lasting impression on this company and its game-changing medical devices."

In an extensive interview in the days after his death, his widow acknowledged that Dr. Han had missed a great deal of work due to illness.

"But," Mrs. Han stated emphatically, "it was brought on by the stress of the position, by the demands of Kenny Benson. Zhong was being forced to sign off on papers that he knew were false. He greatly feared his professionalism and character would be called into question. He had very much to lose, both professionally and personally. He would be first to remind you that his very name, Zhong, means *one who is devoted, honest*. No amount of money would change him."

One of the company's most vocal critics has been Texas businessman and venture capitalist Tom Brahman.

"Look," Mr. Brahman said, "my v.c. investment company gets pitched some five thousand start-up ideas a year. We green-light maybe a dozen. Of them, we know odds are that almost all will fail miserably, while a few will do really good—but only one will turn out to be a superstar. From everything I've seen about NextGen, unless there's some hole card Kenny's holding close to the chest, the company is ripe for absolute spectacular failure. Mark my words, that dog ain't gonna hunt."

Mr. Benson, in reply to other criticism, specifically mentioned Mr. Brahman's accusations and stated in a Securities and Exchange Commission filing that Mr. Brahman was making intentionally misleading statements.

"It is the type of conduct that one would expect of a classic short-and-distort scheme," Mr. Benson said.

When Mr. Brahman was asked if he was shorting NextGenRx stock, he replied, "I don't discuss details of my investments. But I will say that I would never do that. My strategy is not making money on another's bad luck. That's for vultures. I invest."

Mr. Benson added, "The simple—and, in fact, truthful—answer to those who are making accusations is, NextGenRx is currently at the mercy of the United States government. First, the USPTO's approval of our patents, and then the FDA's 510(k) clearance."

Manufacturers intending to market a medical device must file the U.S. Food and Drug Administration's so-called Premarket Notification 510(k) to gain approval.

The Securities and Exchange Commission stated that it has found no irregularities with NextGenRx.

Payne looked at Harris.

"You notice that even in talking about Han's death Benson slipped in a promotion for the company's 'game-changing medical devices'?"

"Uh-huh. If nothing else, give the guy points for consistency," Harris said.

"Well, hell," Payne said, "if Benson's company is a scam, that certainly opens up a whole new can of worms. If I was an investor, I'd want to whack him, too, just out of principle. Wonder if we're about to see Brahman's predicting its 'absolute spectacular failure' coming true."

"But the SEC gives it, and him, what appears to be a clean pass," Harris said.

"Yeah. That, and John Austin this morning raved that it's the real deal, that it would make Benson wealthy. Interesting." Payne paused, then said, "Anything on the widow? The suicide note could be insightful."

"I've got calls in to her," Harris said, "and that Detective Murray. And Brahman."

"What was she telling the media before she clammed up?" Payne said.

"I've added those news articles to the file," Krowczyk said. "It was essentially what's mentioned in this piece. That this Dr. Han was sick to death—literally, now that I think of it—from having to falsify the findings. He took leave of the company, hoping he could go back to his job in academia—Benson had poached him from Stanford's bioengineering department with the promise of fame and fortune. When getting back to academia didn't pan out, he checked out."

Payne shook his head, and said, "Damn shame. Can't imagine what the pressure is like that makes someone feel their only option is to off themselves. I guess, at least, it wasn't a messy way out . . ."

"I also did some drilling down on Han. He got spanked at Stanford—more like a slap on the hand, actually, since we're talking academia—for questionable practices with other clinical trials. Essentially, got caught taking shortcuts that, while not exactly unethical, were frowned upon by the scientific community."

"So we have a pattern. Smoke and mirrors at school and at the start-up."

"Maybe," Krowczyk said, and shrugged. "Maybe not."

Payne felt his phone vibrate again. He glanced at the screen and saw that this time it was a text message from Peter Wohl: "Meeting an old colleague for a beer. Come join. You might learn something. McGillin's in an hour."

What the hell is that about? he thought. *Sounds like an order.*

I guess that once a rabbi—"Yessir, Inspector Wohl, sir. McGillin's. One hour"—always a rabbi.

Must be more of Amy's meddling.

"Think you can spare me for a bit?" Payne said. "His Highness, Inspector Peter Frederick Wohl, has summoned me to his presence."

Harris snorted. "What's up with that?"

"Hell if I know, but I have my suspicions. Would you check in with the M.E. and see when he's scheduling the autopsies? Maybe we'll draw straws to determine who gets the thrill of being there. And can you see about that suicide note again, if you can?"

Harris pulled out a chair and slipped into it.

"I'll let you know," he said, reaching for the receiver of the multiline phone beside the computer.

"If you need me, I'll be with Peter at McGillin's, then headed over to The Rittenhouse. See if I can get that Joy Abrams to talk to me, with or without a lawyer. Or Johnny Austin."

"Good luck with that," Harris said without looking up.

[THREE]
McGillin's Olde Ale House
Center City East
Philadelphia
Friday, January 6, 3:21 P.M.

"Turn here, and it's the next left," Matt Payne instructed the taxi driver, who drove down Juniper, and a half block later made a left onto Drury, a narrow street that looked more like an alleyway than an active thoroughfare.

Payne, knowing that street parking was nonexistent here and not wanting to leave the 911 to the mercy of the public garages nearby, had left the car with the Rittenhouse valet, deciding that he could either walk or cab back after seeing Peter Wohl and company.

McGillin's, a freestanding, two-story Colonial surrounded by tall modern buildings, was midway down the block. Hanging from its red-bricked façade, the city's oldest, continuously operating tavern had American flags and matching bunting and, in neon lights, signage stating its name and EST. 1860.

Payne handed the driver a ten, then stepped onto the sidewalk. Across the lane were a dozen foul dumpsters filled almost to the point of overflowing.

Nice. Bet the truck shows up just in time for happy hour.

All the flags and bunting in the world can't get you to overlook that stench.

He moved toward McGillin's at a quick pace and went through the doorway.

Payne stood next to the end of the wooden bar that ran the length of the right side of the establishment. It was half full. But no Wohl in sight.

He scanned the large main room. On his second pass, he caught a glimpse of Wohl at one of the wooden tables at the far side of the room. Blocking Payne's clear view of Wohl was a beefy older male with wide shoulders and a thick neck. Hanging on the wall behind them were signs from out-of-business Philly landmarks—John Wanamaker's, Gimbel Brothers, among many others—all of which McGillin's had long outlasted.

The brown-haired and pleasant-looking Wohl—who was lithe and muscular and stood just shy of six feet tall—had on his usual well-tailored suit. The male sitting opposite him had close-cropped white hair and wore a tartan-plaid woolen shirt and dark slacks and brown leather shoes. Payne guessed he was in his mid-sixties.

Payne noticed that they both were drinking martinis.

He caught Wohl's eye, waved once, then crossed the red tile floor toward them.

"Hey, Matt," Peter Wohl said, motioning for him to take the seat beside him. "This is Tank. Tank, Sergeant Matt Payne."

"Stan Tankersley," the big man said, offering his huge

hand across the table. "But call me Tank. Howya doin', Sergeant? You look like you've pulled an all-nighter."

"Almost. A late night, then up at oh-four-thirty for another job," Payne said, shaking Tankersley's hand. "Pleased to meet you. Why is your name familiar to me?"

"Back in the Dark Ages," Wohl said, "when I was a rookie detective, I worked for a short time—too short, because he retired on me—under Tank in Homicide. Actually, I was under Jason Washington, who Tank charged with bringing me up to speed in the ways of the unit."

"That's it," Payne said. "You left one helluva legacy."

"Don't try to bullshit an old bullshitter, Payne," Tankersley said, and grinned.

A waitress, a young, attractive brunette, approached, and Payne quietly ordered his drink by gesturing at the martinis. She nodded and turned before even reaching the table.

"Tank taught me a lot," Wohl went on, "and quickly, which, because I'm a slow learner, was an accomplishment in and of itself."

"What'd I just say about bullshitting, Peter?" Tank said, and turned to Payne. "He was one of the sharpest guys in the unit back then. Picked up on things quick . . . Like I hear you do, Sergeant."

"Don't feed his ego," Wohl said, patting Payne on the shoulder. "As Commissioner Coughlin says—and not as a compliment—Matt's not exactly burdened with any semblance of modesty."

When Wohl patted him, he noticed Payne involuntarily winced.

"And," Wohl added, "he's got a fresh bullet wound to prove it. Sorry about that, Matt. Didn't realize it was still that tender."

Payne motioned that it was okay.

Tankersley's expression changed.

"How are you doing with that, son?" he asked.

"Sometimes I leak like a cracked sieve—I aggravated it during the Rittenhouse shooting yesterday—but I'll be okay."

Tankersley nodded.

"Glad to hear it," he said, then after a sip of his drink, went on. "I was really sorry to hear that Peter left Homicide. Especially when I found out he'd gone to Internal Affairs. That's a thankless job. But he was the youngest to make staff inspector, you know. And then—now—the youngest inspector."

Payne grinned. "Yeah, and speaking of modesty, Peter's never quick to let that slip in conversation—that is, never more than a time or two every other week."

Wohl, somewhat discreetly, gave Payne the finger.

Tankersley saw it, chuckled, and said, "He did a helluva job putting dirty cops, some of them high-ranking, in the slam. I don't have to tell you that most cops, of all ranks, while they don't like to admit it, really have ambivalent feelings toward dirty cops. And, unfortunately, toward the cops who catch the dirty ones and send them to the slam. That thin blue line can be hard."

Payne nodded wordlessly.

"But dirty cops damn sure do deserve the slam," Tankersley went on. "And guys like Peter, who put them there, deserve the gratitude and admiration of every honest police officer."

The brunette waitress delivered Payne's martini. It, like the others, contained no olives or other garnish.

"One Russian Standard vodka martini," she said, touched Tankersley's shoulder, and added. "No fruit, per Tank's orders."

"Perfect," Payne said. "Thank you."

Matt held it up in a toast. They followed with their glasses.

Matt began: "Here's to cheatin', stealin', fightin', and drinkin' . . ."

Tank grinned, and picked it up: ". . . If you cheat, may it be death. If you steal, may it be a beautiful woman's heart. If you fight, may it be for a brother. And if you drink, may it be with me."

"Hear, hear," Wohl said as their glasses clinked.

After taking a sip, Wohl said, "I was telling Tank about Washington's situation after coming in at number one on the list for captain."

"And the whole thing stinks to high hell," Tankersley said. "The Black Buddha is one of the brightest cops I know, and, on top of that, he's a damn good egg. But it happens. You don't have to piss in someone's beer, like I did, to have your career cut short."

"When I got to Internal Affairs," Wohl said, looking from Tankersley to Payne, "I learned that, years earlier, Tank had quietly turned in a couple guys, one of whom happened to be related by marriage to a future one-star, who he discovered were skimming cash and narcotics seized from the homes of dealers who got themselves whacked."

"Thinking dead men don't talk," Payne said.

"And then he helped take them down," Wohl, nodding, went on. "After that, Tank got passed over three times. He finally had had enough of the politics and decided it was time to just retire. It was a big loss for the department."

"Not for me. While I miss working with some of the men—like Jason, who was just cutting his teeth—I don't miss the bullshit politics one bit."

"Do you really think what you said, that Jason's career is getting cut short?" Payne said.

"I didn't say that. I said it was *my* career." He paused, sipped his martini, then added, "But Jason's situation doesn't sound good."

After a pause, Payne said, "Do you regret your time in? Would you do it again?"

Tankersley turned his head in thought.

"That's a good question. But, then, times have changed. It's a tough environment out there. Probably? Maybe? But, I don't know. Moot point anyway."

Payne nodded, looking around the room.

"I'm curious," he said. "How'd you guys wind up here? I've always liked the place. They've got a lot of interesting history on display"—he motioned with his head across the room—"including over there, every liquor license they have had since 1871, framed on the wall."

Tankersley held up his martini glass in another toast.

"Because," he said, "this place appreciates what it is. Here's to the old Liberties. R.I.P."

He drained his glass, then looked around and found their waitress and made a circle motion aound the table for her to bring another round.

"Since the bastards bought Liberties Bar," Tankersley said, "which I'm sure you know was forever the watering hole for us old Homicide guys, there's been a great hunt for the next one."

"There's a nice space upstairs," Payne said. "Used to be home for the original proprietors, Catherine and William McGillin. If Ma and Pa reared a dozen or so kids up there, it might be able to handle some slugs from Homicide."

Tankersley smirked and nodded.

"Anything would beat what those hipsters did to Liberties," he said. "Turned the damn thing into a artsy-fartsy place with fruity drinks, gave the food fancy names, and jacked up the prices on everything. I don't know what the hell is going on with this city. Gentrification is turning that whole NoLibs-Fishtown area weird. Guys shaving their heads while growing dirty beards damn near down to their navels. And the girls not shaving their legs and armpits. With all that hair, squirrels could nest."

Payne chuckled.

"Thanks for that mental image," he said, "but you're right. It's become a mini Brooklyn wannabe."

"And what the hell is a *craft cocktail*, exactly?" Tankersley went on, holding his martini up. "Just pour me a simple drink, for chrissakes."

"I'm working on moving my fiancée out of that area," Payne said. "I probably missed out on one place today. Someone put in an application on the condominium I wanted ahead of me."

"Hell, Matt, there's others," Wohl said. "There's always others."

"We talking condos or women?" Tankersley said.

They all chuckled.

"You know," Tankersley said, his tone turning solemn, "I was just thinking about how I once lost a really good friend—lost a great drinking buddy—to a tragic accident."

"Jesus," Payne said. "Sorry to hear that."

Tankersley nodded as he looked, stone-faced, back and forth between Payne and Wohl.

"Crazy part," he said, "is it was entirely avoidable."

"What happened?" Payne said.

Tankersley took a sip of martini, then said, "Poor bastard got his finger caught in a wedding ring."

Wohl snorted.

"Sorry," Tankersley said, looking at Payne. "Peter mentioned you were having—how do they say it these days?—*issues* with your relationship."

Payne glanced at Wohl, and thought, *Amy did stick her nose in this.*

"Girl troubles," Wohl said.

"That's redundant," Tankersley said, his tone somewhat bitter. "And I say that whatever the hell's going on, Matt, she's probably doing you a huge favor."

"How so?" Payne said.

"I just had this conversation with my nephew, who's probably about your age. Told him that forgetting marriage might not be a bad option. I've been married twice."

Payne grinned, shook his head, then made a grand *Go ahead* gesture with his hand.

"Okay, let's hear it," he said.

Tankersley nodded, and said, "They gamed the system, women did. Damn thing's rigged in their favor."

"What system?"

"Marriage and divorce. The days of most folks having a traditional long-term nuclear family are over."

Payne looked at Wohl.

"Have you heard this?" he said. "More to the point, has my sister? Clearly, you two have been talking."

Wohl shook his head.

Payne took a sip of his martini and gestured with his free hand for Tankersley to continue.

"Pray tell," he said.

"Okay," Tankersley said. "So after your glorious honeymoon's over and everyone gets back to the nitty-gritty of everyday life, then what? Maybe you make it to when the seven-year itch kicks in. Or, before that, boredom sets in. Or job stress. Whatever . . ."

"It's no secret that about half of first marriages *do* end in divorce," Payne said, a bit sharply. "But, call me naïve, I intend to be among the *happily ever after* other half."

"Oh, now, don't we all, Mr. Naïve?" Tankersley said.

"No one goes in thinking short-term. And for those really brilliant ones who go and get remarried"—he raised his hand over his head and pointed at it—"that divorce rate is even higher. And cop marriages that go kaput? Through the roof. It takes a really special woman to put up with us. They exist, God bless 'em, but they're really rare."

The waitress delivered three more martinis. Payne glanced at his first glass. It was still half full.

"I don't mean to suggest this applies in either of your cases," Tankersley went on, looking at Payne, then Wohl, "but, hell, there's a lot of females who don't even bother with the charade of dragging you to the altar. All they want is the kid. And then you get the court order saying, 'Congratulations, Daddy, you'll be paying child support until that little tax deduction turns eighteen.' And there it is: Game over."

He took a sip of his martini, and added, "So, word to the wise: You'd better keep that rascal wrapped when playing hide the salami. Even better, get the Big V." He held up his hand and moved his index and middle fingers together, simulating scissor blades. *"Snip! Snip!"*

Payne shook his head.

Wohl said, grinning, "With all due respect, Tank, you really are one cynical bastard."

"Cynical? After two marriages? You bet. And let me tell you, it ain't limited to baby mamas, though they pop out more little bastards—ahem, *children out of wedlock*, if you prefer—than anyone. I'm not making this up. You can look it up. The numbers track with the level of education. They're highest for those without a high school diploma, then drop for those without a college degree, and drop again, though do not go away, for those with a college education. Hell, just check out on-line dating services. My nephew showed me. They are packed—and, I mean, packed full—with single mothers in their twenties to forties who say they're either divorced or never been married."

His eyes moved from Wohl to Payne as he took a sip of his martini.

"Ask any lawyer practicing family law," he went on, putting down his glass. "They'll tell you that the vast majority of divorces end up with the wife getting at least fifty—standard, really, is sixty—percent of the couple's assets, plus custody of the kids. Which means they usually get the house, plus alimony to keep the house the way they like it, and, of course, child support, which they invariably spend on themselves and maybe their new boy toy. And you? Yeah, lucky you gets to drag your indebted ass back to your cheap rental apartment and work on growing hairy knuckles."

Making another visual aid, he formed a fist and jerked it back and forth a few times.

Payne shook his head and grinned.

"You a religious man, Matt?" Tankersley said.

"Well, I don't wear it on my sleeve. But you're looking at one who served as an acolyte and then an altar boy in the Episcopal Church."

"Then along the way you might've picked up on the teachings of Jeremiah, who is said to have warned: 'The heart is deceitful above all things, and desperately wicked: who can know it?' "

"At the risk of repeating myself," Wohl said, with a chuckle, "you really are one cynical bastard."

Tankersley shrugged.

"When did you start having a hard time accepting uncomfortable facts, Wohl?" he said.

"This all reminds me of what some rock star once said," Wohl said. "To paraphrase: 'When I considered getting married a third time, I got smart, and instead of an expensive diamond ring, I just gave her a new house.' "

Tankersley laughed, and nodded.

"Now you're getting it," he said. "And I just heard Rear Admiral Fellerman's voice offering me his sage advice on this issue."

"Which was?"

"Which was advice that I clearly chose to ignore. Twice. 'Tank,' the good admiral said, 'I've sailed the world and can counsel you unequivocally that if it flies, floats, or fucks, *rent it.*' "

Payne and Wohl laughed.

Payne said, "If it's any consolation, Tank, I've been told that, too, and mostly from married guys who also own airplanes or big boats. Classic case of do as I say, not as I do."

Payne felt his smartphone vibrate.

Maybe Amanda? he thought. *Considering the topic of conversation, her timing's impeccable . . .*

"Excuse me," he said, pulling out the device and scrolling the messages on-screen. He saw that he'd somehow missed two from Tony Harris, time-stamped twenty minutes earlier.

He looked up, and said, "Looks like we've found the doers from the shooting yesterday at Rittenhouse Square."

He then, in a slow, deliberate motion to avoid causing pain to his wound, rose from his seat.

Wohl picked up on it.

"You sure you're okay?"

"Harris says he's picking me up. I'm afraid I've got to get back to it," Payne said, nodding at Wohl, then holding out his hand to Tankersley. "It's been a genuine pleasure meeting you."

"Work never stops—I get it," Tankersley said, nodding as he took Payne's hand. "Good to meet you, too. Sorry I rambled on."

Payne pulled his money clip from his pants pocket. Wohl, just perceptively, raised his right hand, palm out—*stop*.

"I've got this, Matt."

"Thanks. Next time's on me, gentlemen," Payne said, looking back and forth between them.

"You ever get in a bind on a job," Tankersley said, "feel free to bounce it off me. Like I said, I do miss talking shop. Be careful out there."

Payne nodded.

"Will do. I appreciate that," he said, then saw Harris coming through the front entrance. "And there's my ride."

Tankersley drained his glass and slid Payne's untouched martini toward him.

"Waste not, want not," Tankersley said, flashed an exaggerated smile, and looked at Wohl. "You promised you'd feed me, too."

VI

[ONE]
Office of the Mayor
City Hall
1 Penn Square
Room 215
Philadelphia
Friday, January 6, 4:01 P.M.

"Before we get into the meat of this goddamn meeting," the Honorable Jerome H. Carlucci said, glancing anxiously around his elegant but cluttered office, "what's the latest on the Rittenhouse outrage?"

The fifty-nine-year-old mayor, wearing a dark, two-piece suit, leaned back in his leather judge's chair with his polished black shoes on his massive wooden desk. He held his hands together as if praying, tapping his fingertips together, as he looked at fifty-one-year-old First Deputy Police Commissioner Dennis V. Coughlin, who sat in a gray-woolen-upholstered armchair on the other side of the desk.

Both ruddy-faced men were tall, heavyset, and large-boned. A casual observer might take them for cousins, or even brothers, and the latter could be considered true in the sense that their relationship was measured by their decades of service since graduating the police academy.

Carlucci was quick to say that though he had left the job of top cop for the office of mayor, he still remained responsible for every aspect of the police department—perhaps more so now than ever.

Coughlin saw that Carlucci had gestured toward the large flat-screen television that was mounted in a wooden frame on the wall. With rare exception, Carlucci kept it tuned to the KeyCom cable system's *Philly News Now* channel that had round-the-clock coverage. The muted TV now showed video footage—the image shook, suggesting it had been made using a cellular telephone's camera—taken the previous afternoon at Rittenhouse Square of the Cadillac SUV upside down and erupting in flame, then picked up the black Porsche speeding past.

"One of the anonymous tips we got turned out to be solid," Denny Coughlin said.

"How so?"

"I'm not privy to all the details—it's still a fluid situation as we speak—but around noon a caller told the nine-one-one dispatcher where we could find the two doers responsible for the shooting. When I checked with Homicide just before walking in here, I was told that there were two bodies where the caller said they would be."

"Where?"

"At the old power plant in Fishtown. Apparently it's a pretty gruesome scene."

"How do we know they actually are the shooters?"

"We don't. Yet. As I said, it's fluid. We don't know a helluva lot more than what we released to the media"— he gestured at the TV—"that the driver, Ken Benson, was killed, and John Austin, the passenger, survived."

"And they're somehow connected to Camilla Rose Morgan?"

"Yeah, she and Austin were certainly close, and possibly romantically involved. The two men grew up together in Houston."

"And Matt Payne is the lead on this Benson's case?" Carlucci said.

"Matty owns it and the Morgan woman's."

"Then we know she didn't jump? It wasn't suicide?"

Coughlin shrugged.

"Too early to tell. Still awaiting autopsy results. Toxicology, too."

"I don't mean to speak ill of the dead," Carlucci said, "but her brother said she was certifiable crazy."

Coughlin's bushy gray eyebrows rose.

"Mason Morgan also said she was smart as hell," Carlucci added.

"I'm guessing he called you, Jerry."

Carlucci nodded.

"Morgan said he simply wanted the courtesy of being

told if there were any surprises he should know about concerning her death. So that he could deal with them, as he'd done in years past. I believe he was alluding to her trips to rehab."

"You know that she ran the family philanthropic arm," Coughlin said, "and that it recently donated thirty new Harley-Davidsons to Highway Patrol to replace their aging bikes."

Carlucci nodded. "Electra Glides. At over twenty grand each, that saved the city more than a half million. Old Man Morgan was a big supporter."

Coughlin nodded. He knew it went unsaid that friends like that received preferential treatment.

"The only possible thing that comes to mind that might be a surprise," Coughlin said, "was evidence of cocaine and Ecstasy was found at her condo. As opposed to just the usual fair amount of alcohol such parties have."

"In other words, nothing," Carlucci said. "Personal consumption."

Coughlin nodded. "Unless we want to start locking up a large number of Center City denizens for the same offense. In her defense, we don't know that she used the narcotics. No telling what was in her system, if anything. The toxicology results could come back clean."

Carlucci, nodding, looked out a window. Coughlin thought he had a somewhat pained expression.

After a minute, Coughlin said, "So, what is the meat of this meeting?"

Carlucci glanced at the TV again, and said, "That

killing was the tenth so far this year and we're not even a full week into January. And thanks to Payne shooting that heroin-pushing punk, even though we already had surpassed the previous year's total of numbers killed, we just hit an all-time record."

"And now we appear on pace to beat it, Jerry. Is this where I invoke our critics' favored term *Killadelphia?* Year after year, it's become a classic SNAFU."

Carlucci, staring at the TV, now clearly had a pained expression. Coughlin could tell something weighed heavy on his mind—something beyond the usual Situation Normal: All Fucked Up.

"Denny," he said, meeting Coughlin's eyes, "we go way back. What I'm about to tell you goes no farther than these walls."

"Of course, Jerry. You know that."

"A couple months back," Carlucci began, "Five-F waltzed his arrogant ass in here, uninvited, and proceeded to tell me pretty much everything that I already knew about this city's challenges."

There was a somewhat small circle, which naturally included Coughlin, that was aware that 5-F was shorthand for the derisive nickname of a well-known forty-five-year-old Philly businessman. The circle also knew that Matt Payne had come up with it, and the mayor, having heard Payne blurt it in a moment of anger, had immediately embraced it, on occasion repeating the longer version: "Fucking Francis Franklin Fuller the Fifth."

Fuller, who traced his family lineage to Benjamin Franklin, had been born to wealth. He had built that into a much bigger personal fortune, one that was over two billion dollars. Short and stout of stature, Fuller had a bulging belly and a round face and male-pattern baldness similar to his ancestor's. He embraced with enthusiasm everything Franklinite, beginning with the pen name Richard Saunders that Franklin had used in writing *Poor Richard's Almanack*.

Under Richard Saunders Holdings—his main company that was headquartered at North Third and Arch streets in Old City—Fuller owned outright, or had majority interest in, KeyProperties (luxury high-rise office and residential buildings), KeyCargo Import-Exports (largest user of the Port of Philadelphia docks and warehousing facilities), and KeyCom (a Fortune 500, nationwide telecommunications corporation).

Carlucci, jabbing his finger in the direction of the empty armchair beside Coughlin, went on. "Five-F sat in that chair and told me this city, the third poorest in the nation, is headed to becoming the next Detroit. Bankrupt, unless drastic changes are made. And chief among those drastic changes: the violent crimes rate."

"Which would be the job of the city council members," Coughlin said, his tone defensive but even. "They can talk to their constituents and figure out a way to stop the robbing and raping and killing. Beginning with cooperating with the police and the district attorney's office."

Carlucci, nodding, said, "I agree. And about that point Five-F said—and the research tends to prove he's right—that unless all that changes, the next generation just graduating college is going to marry and raise families where they feel safer. When they go, their tax base goes, too. And companies follow. And we start circling the Detroit bankruptcy drain faster."

Coughlin shrugged. "So, then, what's the magic solution?"

"I have ideas, plans," Carlucci said. "But what I may not have is time for them."

"I don't think I understand."

"The primaries are a year away. I can't turn this sinking ship around in that short time."

"You need another term as mayor," Coughlin said after a pause. "And guaranteeing that takes a lot of . . . support . . . from high places."

"Right. And it's been made clear unless there are changes, that support won't be there." He paused to let that sink in, then added, "But with that support, another term would have you, already my right hand, at the helm of the department. Four stars?"

Coughlin had been appointed—as had all deputy commissioners to commissioners, the one- to four-stars—by the city's managing director. But that happened only with the blessing—read *order*—of the mayor.

"And after that," Carlucci said, "perhaps even higher office."

Coughlin looked at Carlucci, mentally going over what he had just heard, and felt his eyes widen involuntarily.

The pieces had fallen into place.

On a Saturday a month earlier, as holiday celebrations were peaking, Coughlin had been called to an emergency meeting in the mayor's office to address that morning's gruesome slayings of a young college coed, who had been stabbed in JFK Park, across from City Hall, and of a young teenage boy, whose throat had been slashed in Franklin Park, across from the Roundhouse.

In addition to Carlucci and Coughlin, the meeting included only two others, Edward Stein and James Finley, both of whom had joined the mayor's staff no more than thirty days earlier.

Stein, a lawyer, held the new title of chief executive advisor to the mayor. Finley was head of the Philadelphia Convention and Visitors Office. Each was being paid, due to budgetary considerations, $1 per annum by the city. But this was not a hardship for them. While it was not broadcast, it was not exactly a secret that Stein and Finley continued to be well compensated—some believed in the middle to high six figures, plus generous bonuses and stock options—as senior vice presidents at Richard Saunders Holdings.

In short, Francis Fuller was loaning two of his top corporate executives to the city. It certainly was not the first time—nor would it be the last—that corporate businessmen would cycle into the political realm, influence the workings, then cycle back out to the corporate world.

In the meeting, Finley left no question that he was out to get rid of what he saw as the city's chief public relations disaster concerning killings—the Wyatt Earp of the Main Line, Sergeant Matthew Payne.

Stein, Coughlin believed, tended to be the voice of reason between the two of them, going so far as telling

Finley that he believed Payne was doing a great job protecting society from the barbarians—and that he didn't think Payne went to work hoping to get into another shoot-out at the O.K. Corral.

Coughlin had witnessed Carlucci's unwavering defense of Payne that day. He declared that he would not allow the decorated police officer, who risked his life protecting the city, to be sacrificed for what a sanctimonious Finley had called "the greater good."

In all the time that Coughlin had known Carlucci he could count on one hand, and still have fingers left over, the occasions that Carlucci had backed down from a fight. Now, however, Coughlin realized Carlucci's tone seemed different, familiar, but in an odd, distant way. And he realized it had been a decade since he had heard that tone of voice—a combination of wariness and resignation.

"What," Coughlin said, measuring his words, "are you thinking?"

"The Wyatt Earp of the Main Line is headed for the exit. Payne has to go. I'm sorry."

Coughlin was silent, then blurted, "You cannot fire Matty. He's done nothing wrong, Jerry. You said it yourself. That will cost the city a fortune. The FOP—and rightfully so, because all Payne's shootings were found to be righteous—will be all over this."

The Fraternal Order of Police Lodge No. 5 was the labor union for some fourteen thousand active and retired Philadelphia police officers and sheriffs. It fought to protect and improve the multiyear contract—the collective bargaining agreement—with the city that covered everything from pensions and benefits to working conditions and legal rights.

When, for example, an officer was handed a summons to appear before the Internal Affairs Division, the FOP provided legal representation for the interview. The FOP was damn effective at defending its members—on occasion, too good, getting some cops who the top brass felt did not deserve to wear a badge and gun back on the job.

"In this particular case, all that doesn't matter," Carlucci said.

"What? Any of the FOP's counsel could win the case. But if Matty's father's law firm takes it on, that proverbial fecal matter is going to hit the fan in ways unimagined. It's going to be one helluva mess."

Carlucci, who was frowning, nodded.

"You're right, of course," he said. "But we don't have to fire him. We simply have to help him realize that he would be happier doing something else."

"You'd railroad him out?" Coughlin said, his tone incredulous.

"This is what's known as being politically expedient."

Coughlin stared at Carlucci. He now really saw the pieces snapping together.

"It's what's known as a crappy setup, Jerry," Coughlin snapped, his florid face turning bright red and his voice rising. "Matty's a damn good cop. From a family of damn good cops. It's in his DNA. And you, of all people, damn well know it."

"I do indeed know," Carlucci said, the exasperation clear in his tone.

Coughlin went on. "Matty wouldn't take time off to even let that bullet wound fully heal. Hell, he's probably bleeding blue right now."

"Denny, I tried. I defended him. I had his back when that miserable little shit Finley first tried last month. But . . ."

Coughlin stared out the window, then nodded to himself, then turned back to look at Carlucci.

"Jerry—" Coughlin began, but his throat caught. He paused, cleared it, and went on, his voice wavering. "You know I have always appreciated your support and trust. And I devoutly believe that I have faithfully earned my three stars—"

"Damn right, you have."

"But if there's a sacrificial head to roll, let it be mine. I have my years in. Great years. And I would not—I could not—accept four stars knowing how they came about. Matty stays. I'll have my written resignation for retirement on your desk within the hour."

"And I will refuse to accept it. Period." He paused, then added, "Listen, maybe any other time I could have succeeded keeping Payne on. But after that mail-order preacher called Payne Public Enemy No. 1 and Payne killed that punk who shot him, it put the pressure way over the top. And the record killings for the year did not help. We have to get back the citizens' trust in our police department, restore what's been broken."

They met eyes and were silent for a minute that felt like an eternity.

Coughlin broke the silence with a deep, audible sigh.

"It's already a done deal, then?" he asked, but the disgust evident in his voice made it a bitter statement.

Carlucci nodded.

"Fact is, Denny," he said, "even you were worried when Payne first came on. You tried to hide him as a paper pusher under Wohl's son in Special Operations, true?"

Coughlin, looking resigned, nodded.

"True. I became his godfather after Jack's death. I sure as hell didn't want to have to tell his widow that she'd lost another." He sighed, and added, "Or have to face Mother Moffitt, who hasn't gotten over Jack and Dutch."

They again locked eyes.

"Look, Denny, I don't like it one damn bit. But sometimes we all have to swallow things we don't like." He paused to let that sink in, then added, "I knew Jack and Dutch, and I would bet they are looking down through those pearly gates, nodding, saying, 'Yeah, we paid enough of a price. And Matty's come close to paying the ultimate price. Get our boy out of harm's way.'"

"Yeah, maybe . . ." Coughlin began, then sighed again. "Well, I know for certain that parts, if not all, of Matty's family won't be disappointed."

"See? And it could be worse. Payne does have options. A lot of cops who find themselves off the force are lost."

Coughlin looked off in thought.

"Maybe I'll get Peter Wohl involved," he said. "Payne respects him. As his rabbi. And more."

"I suggest the first thing to do is rein him in, make him unhappy, let him figure out what's going on. The sooner he does that, the sooner he can make the right decision. With or without Wohl's help."

"I'm going to have to think about all this, but I will be shooting straight with him—"

"Not sure that's the best," Carlucci interrupted.

Coughlin stared at him, and said, "Maybe in someone's view. But I want to be able to look myself in the mirror when this is all over."

Coughlin grasped his armchair and stood up suddenly.

"I've had enough here," he said.

"It's the right thing, Denny," Carlucci said, also getting to his feet. "Just make sure it's done."

Coughlin met his eyes, then turned and left without another word.

[TWO]
Palmer and Beach Streets
Fishtown
Philadelphia
Friday, January 6, 4:35 P.M.

Two district patrol officers in their early twenties stood beside a marked police Ford Explorer, its light bar flashing red and blue, at the parking lot entrance of the deserted PECO Richmond Power Station. The blue shirts, their breath visible in the cold air, stopped talking and studied the approaching Crown Victoria.

Tony Harris, at the wheel of the unmarked Police Interceptor, hit the switch to light up its wigwags. The officers, in a casual, almost bored manner, motioned for the vehicle to pass through the gate, then crossed their arms over their chest and returned to their conversation.

The old, coal-fired plant—built in 1925 and shut down six decades later—covered more than eight acres on the bank of the Delaware River, adjacent to Penn Treaty Park.

"Did Kennedy give you any background on the scene?" Matt Payne said, looking up at the main plant as they drove toward the river.

"Only that we needed to see it for ourselves," Harris said. "When I pressed, he said, 'Words fail me.'"

"And two victims?"

"Uh-huh. Said they found the two dead males where I told him the nine-one-one caller had said. Then they checked the main plant in case there were others. Victims had no ID on them. But one did have a burner phone. Hal checked with Krow and confirmed that one of the numbers on the recent-called list belonged to the phone recovered in the shooter's van."

"The cell tower dump can show if that phone was at The Rittenhouse at the time of the shooting," Payne said, adding idly, "I thought that someone had plans to make something out of this place. That Romanesque architecture, even in its run-down state, is still pretty impressive."

"And maybe a bit spooky."

"Yeah, but the photos of it back in the day show that the place was really something. You know the enormous area that held the four huge steam turbines? It was designed to resemble the ancient Roman baths."

"I did not know that, and, frankly, wonder why you do," Harris said, and pointed out the windshield. "Fresh-cut pipes there. Looks like the metal salvage thieves have been busy again. Steel and copper."

"Adds to the creepy factor, along with all the broken windows," Payne said. "Since they shut this place down thirty years ago, there's been three, maybe four science-fiction movies filmed here. And you know what's the irony of that?"

"What?"

"They had to bring their own generators for power."

Harris grunted.

After rolling across the rough surface of what had been a parking lot, and bumping over sunken steel rails, they approached the back side of the enormous facility. A fat, long-tailed rodent scampered from the shadows, headed toward the Delaware River twenty yards distant.

"I hate rats," Payne said.

"Lucky you. You're apparently about to encounter a couple two-legged ones, too."

They made the turn at the back of the building and saw a half dozen police vehicles, including a Crime Scene Unit van and another unmarked Crown Vic. They were parked near the foot of a wide concrete pier that jutted out some two hundred feet from the seawall into the river. Another district blue shirt stood at the yellow crime scene tape that roped off the foot of the pier.

Approximately midway on the pier was a fifteen-story-tall masonry tower—bold lettering chiseled in stone across its top read THE PHILADELPHIA ELECTRIC COMPANY—into which vessels had off-loaded the coal that powered the plant.

A weather-beaten conveyor belt, wide as a two-lane street, rose on rusted iron trestles at a steep angle from the foot of the coal tower to the top of the main building, where eight smokestacks stood, stout but long-abandoned.

Harris drove over and parked between the rough-looking Crown Vic and a year-old marked Chevy Impala.

Payne reached to the floorboard and pulled from a cardboard box under the seat two pairs of blue latex gloves. He held out a pair to Harris.

"Don't say I never give you anything, Detective."

A bitter cold wind blew down the wide river. Payne and Harris approached a gray, rusted steel door next to an industrial overhead roll-up door that was beneath where the massive conveyor belt exited the tower. Both doors were covered in faded graffiti. The overhead door was shut. The smaller gray door had been opened inward and, Payne noticed, had fresh boot prints where someone had kicked it. A battered electrical generator, its noisy gasoline engine running at high speed, had been positioned just to the side of the tower. From it, four yellow extension cords snaked through the doorway.

Inside was dark, damp, and cold, but Payne was grateful to be out of the wind. Twenty feet farther in was another rusted steel door, also open, through which the power cords led. Beyond the door, a brilliant white light filled a cavernous space.

As Payne and Harris walked up to the interior door, they had to take care to let their eyes adjust from the darkness. Payne could not help noticing, above the dank odor of the neglected ancient structure, the distinct smell of decaying flesh.

They went through the doorway.

Plugged into the power cords were ten halogen flood-lights that were mounted on top of collapsible tripods. Half were aimed up the soaring interior walls, which were stained by more than a half century's contact with coal. The other lights pointed toward the center of the tower, illuminating the series of heavy, truss-like iron beams that were spaced approximately every ten feet all the way up to the top.

"Jesus Christ," Payne said.

"Yeah, I would say that's an appropriate response," Harris said after a bit. "They damn sure look crucified. Among other things."

Payne slowly shook his head.

"The word *macabre* leaps to mind," he said. "Looks like a mad scene from some opera."

"Or one of those sci-fi movies you said was filmed here."

Two human figures, their arms extended and wrists tied with rope, hung from the lowest iron beam.

Beneath them, the concrete floor was awash in a reddish pink pool of fluid—a great deal of blood diluted with an even greater deal of water—and in the pool directly below each body was a pile of shredded, pulp-like flesh.

A couple yards behind the two piles was an aluminum-framed, single-axle utility trailer, sitting at a nose-down angle. It appeared to be brand-new. Two Crime Scene Unit blue shirts, a male and a female, were working at pulling fingerprints off it.

Strapped to the trailer, also looking new, were a commercial-grade pressure washer powered by a gasoline engine and, beside it, a hundred-gallon polyethylene water tank that appeared almost empty. A sticker affixed to the fuel tank of the washer read SUPER SHOT—4,000 PSI AT 4 GPM.

A familiar voice from behind Payne and Harris said, "Four gallons a minute, spraying at that high water pressure, could probably strip the chrome from a trailer hitch . . ."

They both turned and saw thirty-six-year-old Harold W. Kennedy, Sr., approaching.

"Human skin doesn't stand a chance," the enormous black detective finished.

"They look like giant, badly peeled grapes," Harris said.

Multiple flashes of white light began pulsing as two crime scene photographers, one crouched and moving around the pool, the other halfway up a twelve-foot-tall folding ladder, worked to capture the scene from every angle. The photographer on the ladder let his still camera hang from its strap and began shooting with a video camera.

"Grotesque grapes," Payne added, taking a quick photograph with his phone.

"Told you that you had to see it," Kennedy said.

The body on the left was that of a short, small-framed skinny male, maybe in his thirties. The other, looking a bit older and bordering on obese, was an olive-skinned male who had thin dark hair that now partially covered his pockmarked face.

"They could have whacked them anywhere," Payne said. "There's a reason someone went to a lot of trouble doing this here. Even hauling in the equipment."

"We ran the trailer," Kennedy said, "and it didn't come up—no registration, no nothing. But when I called the manufacturer with the VIN and the serial number of the pressure washer, they gave me the dealer in Doylestown they'd sold it to. And the dealer, Bucks County Home Improvement, said they reported that it'd been stolen sometime last November."

Payne looked at Harris.

"And what did you say that male caller told the nine-one-one dispatcher?"

"Almost word for word," Harris said, " 'You can find the jagoffs that shot up Rittenhouse Square in the tower behind the old Richmond Power Plant.' When the call came in, from a blocked number, we saw it come up in the ECC. I gave Hal the heads-up, he checked it out, then I put the arm out for you."

Payne, looking up again at the bodies, said, "My God, that had to hurt."

"No shit," Kennedy said.

"You ever use a pressure washer, Matt?" Harris said.

"Yeah, all the time when I was a kid. Cleaning the brick patio at home, the boat at the Shore. Once, I got careless with the wand. I'll tell you, you let that jet of water nick you even a little bit and, after you're finished swearing at the top of your lungs, you make sure you never let it happen again. Took a long time to heal, for the scar to fade."

"So, then, you'd think someone would've heard their screams," Kennedy said. "Especially since sound travels so well across water."

Payne glanced around the interior of the enormous space.

"I'd bet that between the noise from that washer's gas engine," he said, "and these thick walls muffling it all, the screams were probably hard to hear—or, at least, hard to distinguish as screams. Add to that being closer to the sounds of the city and the traffic noise from the expressway . . ."

"Or, maybe, they just were dead," Harris said.

"But why make it look like torture?" Kennedy said.

Payne's mouth went on automatic: " 'The heart is deceitful above all things, and desperately wicked: who can know it?' "

Harris and Kennedy looked askance at him. Payne looked back at them.

"Tankersley, the retired Homicide guy," he said, looking between them, "just an hour or so ago quoted that a bit of Jeremiah to me. Maybe the doers wanted to make some *desperately wicked* point."

"Or just are psychopaths," Harris said.

"I'm betting both," Kennedy said. "And speaking of psychopaths making a point, come take a look at this. Just found it."

Harris and Payne, being careful not to step in the various pools of fluid, followed Kennedy over to a nearby wall. Kennedy pulled a small, black tactical flashlight from his pocket. Its bright, narrow beam cut the dark. They saw that the power washer had been used on the wall, the high-pressure jet of water having cut through the layers of coal residue. The lettering was faint and not well formed but legible.

"Talk about reading the writing on the wall," Harris said, holding up his phone to photograph it.

Payne read it aloud. " 'Austin got lucky this time.' "

[THREE]

Harris and Payne walked toward the Crown Vic after leaving the coal tower.

Harris had just punched in a number on his cellular telephone and now said into it, "Please connect me with Mr. John Austin's room."

He looked at Payne, who said, "Better try both rooms he has in his name."

"There's only one now. After the crime scene guys packed up the room Benson had used, Austin gave it up." Harris paused, then said, "Damn it. Got voice mail."

He broke off the call.

"Hank should still be there doing interviews," Payne said. "Have him get security and go check the room."

"You're reading my mind," Harris said, nodding.

Payne's phone vibrated, and when he looked at it, he muttered, "What the hell?"

"What?" Harris said.

Payne's head jerked up. He began a quick scan of the immediate area, looking from Penn Treaty Park to the left, then up at the main power plant building, then along the riverbank to the right.

"Is it just coincidence with the timing or is someone watching?" he said, handing the phone to Harris for him to read. "All I can make out is that pair of joggers on the trail."

Harris looked, saw that the two were in the middle of doing stretching exercises at one of the park benches, then glanced at the phone.

He read the text message aloud: "'We gave those ja-goffs to you. The dumbasses went rogue. The trigger-man is the big bastard, if that makes any difference. There could be others, but we'll handle it.'"

He handed the phone back, and said, "They found blood in the back of their abandoned van. Maybe they can match it to this guy."

"If he's got any left," Payne said as he wrote a reply message: *Tell me more . . .*

Immediately after he sent it, another message box popped up: NOT A VALID NUMBER.

"Damn it," Payne said. "Invalid."

"They sent that text to the same number you gave out at The Rittenhouse, right?" Harris said, meeting Payne's eyes. "The caller ID box is red."

"Yeah. And I handed out a bunch of cards, said to share the numbers with anyone."

They approached the Crown Vic and got in.

"What the hell could be The Rittenhouse connection to the killers?" Harris said as he started the engine.

Payne looked out at the tower, then said, "And what I'm wondering is why, instead of calling nine-one-one, they didn't also text me that we could find these guys here?"

"Maybe two different people? Or, if the same person, they were just given your number?"

"Or maybe they didn't want to establish a pattern," Payne said. "Hell if I know. But we need to find Austin now or find someone who can get a message to him." He read the text again, and said, "It makes my blood boil. The bastards abuse two human beings, then string them up like trophies. It's barbaric. Who knows what else they are capable of?"

"Apparently," Harris said, with a nod toward Payne's phone, "at least more of the same."

Payne looked out the windshield, then turned to Harris.

"You have Camilla Rose's assistant's number?"

Harris shook his head. "We can get it from McCrory."

"Wait," Payne said, and dialed Camilla Rose Morgan's cellular phone number. "This might be quicker."

Payne expected that his call, as before, would automatically roll over to voice mail—the forensics lab now had possession of her cellular telephone, the pieces of which had been recovered beside the Jaguar—and he could again get Joy Abram's mobile number from the end of the recording.

But there was no recording. Instead, following what sounded like two clicks, a familiar woman's voice answered.

"Good afternoon, Matt. It's Aimee Wolter. What can I do for you?"

After the initial shock—first, that a live person had answered, and, second, that it was a woman—the explanation for that fell into place.

Payne, who was familiar with Wolter both from her business and from the social circuit, knew there was a reason she named her firm Dignatio Worldwide. She was well known for protecting the *dignatio*—Latin for *dignity, reputation, honor*—of an international clientele. Corporations to celebrities, she handled the heavy hitters.

He remembered that Aimee Wolter had managed the publicity for the Harold Morgan Cancer Research Center's fund-raising campaign, which, of course, Camilla Rose had run. It logically followed that her kids charity was a client, too.

Aimee Wolter picked up on Payne's hesitation.

"You're not the first to be caught off guard," she said. "With the event still scheduled for tomorrow night, and Joy handling everything as best she can, we decided that I should cover Camilla Rose's phone calls and had her number forwarded to mine. Some I don't answer until I know what they're calling about, but your name came up on the ID. Is this about my interview this morning with your detective? Have you learned—"

"We need to talk," Payne interrupted. "But, first, do you or Joy Abrams know where John Austin is?"

"Hold on," Wolter said. Payne heard her raise her voice. "Anybody hear from that asshole Austin yet?"

Payne's eyebrows rose.

A second later, Wolter was back on the phone. "No idea where he is, Matt. We went to the hospital this morning and he'd signed himself out. And there was no answer when one of my assistants knocked on his hotel room door."

"What time was that?"

Payne heard her raise her voice again. "When did Samantha knock on that bastard's door?"

Wolter came back on the phone. "At nine this morning, and again around one this afternoon."

"Why do I get the feeling you're not exactly a fan of Austin's?"

"Because I'm not. I'm absolutely crushed about what's happened to Camilla Rose. She wasn't just a client; she was a friend. And I'm furious. I can't help but think that what happened is because of something he's done."

"Do you know of something?"

"No, nothing specific. Which is what I told your detective. I don't know what else I can tell you."

Payne was quiet, then said, "Okay. It's critical I find

Austin as soon as possible. There's reason to believe he's in more danger."

"Because of yesterday," she said, her tone questioning.

"I cannot say but . . ." Payne began, felt his phone begin vibrating, and said, "Sorry. Hold a second."

When he pulled it from his ear to look at the screen, he saw the caller ID read DENNY COUGHLIN.

"All right," he said into the phone. "I've got to take this call. Please let me know if you hear from him. I'll be in touch shortly."

"Sure thing, Matt," she said, and hung up.

Payne tapped the screen and answered the call: "Yessir, Uncle Denny?"

Harris looked at him.

"Yessir," Payne, after a moment, said. "I do believe I've been there a time or two. See you tomorrow."

[FOUR]
Ninth and Vine Streets
Chinatown
Philadelphia
Friday, January 6, 5:02 P.M.

A little more than a mile south of the deserted power station—and a block away from the Roundhouse—Philadelphia City Council President William G. Lane, Jr., stood on the brakes of his silver Mercedes-Benz SUV as he approached the broken curb beside a building construction site. Beneath a tall tower crane, a massive skeleton of steelwork rose more than thirty stories.

Lane was in his early forties, with an average build and a very black complexion. He kept his dark hair short and had a three-day growth of beard that almost masked the heavy pitting of acne scars. He wore designer sunglasses, a black blazer over a gray merino wool sweater, and dark slacks with Italian loafers.

The luxury SUV's large tires eased over the crumble of concrete, crunching to a stop alongside the fifteen-foot-tall, fabric-covered chain-link fence that encircled what months earlier had been a parking lot of asphalt.

Lane took a final pull on his cigarette, opened the sunroof and exhaled through it as he tossed the smoldering butt.

I really don't have a good feeling about this, he thought, checking his cellular telephone, then sending a text message to John T. Austin that simply read *I'm here.*

As he began to light another cigarette, he smelled fried food. He glanced at the two-story building directly across Ninth Street and saw a restaurant. Its big window had WONTON KING in faded red lettering and, under that, what he assumed was Chinese. By its door, a teenage male was putting a large white bag into the cargo basket of a battered moped. On the basket was plastic signage displaying a phone number and WONTON KING—SPEEDY DELIVERY.

Lane turned and looked through the windshield. There was an enormous double gate ten feet ahead, the gates folded open against the interior of the fencing. A driveway of crushed stone, rutted from the steady traffic of heavy-duty trucks and industrial equipment, led inside.

On the far side of the open gates was a black Chevy Tahoe. Lane wondered if the SUV was Austin's. It was parked on the broken sidewalk in front of a ten-foot-square vinyl banner. The banner had an architectural rendering of the construction project: a thirty-three-story, glass-sheathed tower. Above the rendering was HOUSE OF MING—LUXURY CONDOMINIUM LIVING—PRE-CONSTRUCTION PRICING FROM $1 MILLION. Under the dollar figure was a box that read REMAINING UNITS AVAILABLE, and then, on a sticker that clearly had been affixed over a series of similar stickers, the number 12.

Amazing, Lane thought. *Out of more than probably two hundred condos, only a dozen are left to buy before the place is even finished. Just like Austin said.*

Wonder how long the dives like Wonton King will last with the property values going up?

But, then, I bet the developer's brother-in-law—or cousin, nephew, whatever—have already used a straw buyer to get that property for dirt before anybody had a clue this high-rise was going in.

I do give Austin credit. He said the one big benefit of Chinatown being "the ugly stepchild of Center City" is it's got the last cheap real estate that can be converted into prime properties.

Chinatown—which covered about forty blocks, from Arch Street north to Vine, and Broad Street east to Seventh—was in Lane's district. He knew only a few parcels there remained diamonds in the rough. And with *councilmanic prerogative*—Philadelphia's city charter dictated that council members, because they knew their district and constituents best, were granted final approval over land sales in their districts that got the green light from the Vacant Property Review Committee of the Philadelphia Redevelopment Authority—he effectively controlled them all.

Lane looked back at the Tahoe but could not see anyone in it. He glanced through the open gates and saw a line of construction workers, all in heavy work clothes, reflective orange safety vests, and white polymer hard hats. They were on the far side of a wooden shack—a sign in front read ALL VISITORS MUST CHECK IN HERE—and looking as if they were clocking out for the day.

From around the edge of the open left gate, a tall white male came walking out. He also wore an orange vest and white hard hat. But instead of construction worker's clothing, he had on a gray parka over a black cardigan sweater and blue jeans. He also wore shiny black Western boots with pointed toes.

Is that him? Jesus Almighty, it is . . .

Lane immediately noticed two things about Austin: first, the blue-black bruise that covered the right side of his face, and then that he looked deeply saddened.

He really got beat up bad in that wreck. On top of losing two people he was close to.

Austin slipped off the vest and, using his left hand, tossed it and the hard hat onto the hood of the Tahoe. He turned and looked toward Lane's SUV.

Lane waved, and Austin acknowledged him with a short nod, before walking toward the front passenger door of the Mercedes.

Behind Austin, an eighteen-wheeled tractor-trailer rig was pulling in through the open gates. An enormous blue, shrink-wrapped modular unit was strapped to the flatbed trailer, dwarfing it. Seeing that made Lane recall the first ones Austin had showed him in South Florida. It had been two years earlier, at a manufacturing plant west of Miami, after they had visited the construction site of a condominium high-rise overlooking Biscayne Bay.

Austin drove Lane, in a white Ford Expedition with a license plate that read NEXTGEN05, the dozen miles from downtown Miami out to an industrial complex on the edge of the Everglades, the vast wilderness known as the river of grass.

They followed the eight-lane Dolphin Expressway out, passing Miami International Airport along the way. Lane, after adjusting the dash vent so that the cold air blew directly on him, stared out the window, taking in the sights, as he listened to Austin. He drank from a can of Jai Alai India Pale Ale that Austin had given him when they first got in the SUV. Austin had pulled two of the craft beers from a small cooler he had on the floorboard behind the driver's seat.

Lane had already decided that drivers in Miami were bad enough, but Austin was even worse, speeding through heavy traffic while drinking and talking a hundred miles an hour, either to Lane or on his cellular phone.

"The developer of that condo project," Austin now explained to Lane, gesturing with his right hand between sips of beer, "is handling the sales himself, including making all the loans on the individual units. And because these are private mortgages—the money comes from an investors' fund I put together—they are not held to the same lending rules as banks."

"No lending rules?" Lane repeated, his gravel voice incredulous.

Austin nodded as he exited the expressway just west of the Florida Turnpike.

"Right," he said. "Banks that make mortgages are required by law to confirm that the buyers are legit, that they're not, for example, laundering drug money. They make buyers prove where their funds come from. But private mortgage is like me reaching in my pocket and lending you the money personally. I come up with the terms—it's up to me what the interest rate will be, how much of a down payment I want, and if I care where your money comes from."

Lane looked at him. "You're laundering money?"

Austin shook his head as he glanced at him.

"Hell no. I am making money by bringing investors together in a fund that delivers a high return on investment, and taking my percentage from that. Each fund— in this case, the Morgan Partners Florida Capital Fund III—provides the developer with the money to build and market his project. Which includes handling the private mortgages."

Lane nodded.

"Now," Austin went on, "the developer is going to do his due diligence. But a lot of the buyers, to keep their names out of public records, have set up a corporation to be the buyer of record. These corporations, the sole purpose of which is owning the property, often are owned by another corporation the buyer has set up under the buyer's control. But the thing is, you can follow that paper trail only so far, especially because it can lead to foreign countries, and that gets complicated and expensive. So, the developer, after vetting the paper trail to his satisfaction, simply decides the terms of sale, including if there's a premium involved."

"That's never a problem?"

"Occasionally," he said, draining his beer. "But buyers really want the property. And with demand exceeding supply, those who balk are replaced by others who pay up. More and more, there's not even a note—buyers are paying cash in full."

"This investors' fund of yours sounds solid."

"Rock solid," Austin said, glanced at Lane, and went on. "And with that demand high, there's no end in sight. Take the Chinese. They are awash in cash they want to invest. Some of it is state-sponsored, some of it quiet money. They love America—and they really must: we owe them one-point-three trillion, which is mind-boggling money—and they've been on a buying spree. They're snapping up our existing landmark hotels—from two billion to buy the Waldorf Astoria in New York City to almost that much for California's Hotel del Coronado—and they're building these other high-end properties. And then Chinese individuals, as well as buyers from other countries—from Central and South America to Europe—are buying into them. This Miami condo you just saw? There're foreigners who've bought three, four condos at once."

"And before it's finished?"

"Oh, yeah. There's a lot of hidden wealth. With the Chinese, you're talking about a country with a billion more people than America. They're already showing huge interest in the House of Ming Condos, and we haven't even broken ground. So far, according to the developer handling its private banking, about a third of the pre-sold units were bought by Chinese parents planning for their kids to use." He paused, looked at Lane, and added, "None of which would been happening if you hadn't used your veto that got us that parcel."

"Councilmanic prerogative," Lane said. "If it's good for Philly, and especially my district, I'm all for it."

"And it is great for Philly," Austin said, nodding. "Every year, the University of Pennsylvania alone enrolls thousands of foreign students. Medical students, engineers—you name it, they want it. There're three hundred thousand Chinese attending U.S. universities. That's twice the number of five years ago. And, after graduating, you can bet many want to stay, especially if they can snag a EB-5. More than three-quarters of last year's—almost ten thousand EB-5s—went to mainland Chinese."

Lane nodded. He knew about the reasonably new visa program that was a fast track to U.S. citizenship. All a foreign national had to do was invest at least a million dollars in a U.S. business that created and maintained at least ten jobs for current American citizens, plus jobs for himself and his family members. In exchange, the U.S. Citizenship and Immigration Service issued green cards to the foreign national, to the spouse, and to their children under the age of twenty-one, followed by full citizenship.

Austin went on. "This is the next generation that will be their permanent bridge between the U.S. and China. Which explains why they're buying, why they're investing in solid assets, here."

As the SUV rumbled over a railroad track crossing, Lane noticed that the streets and roadsides now were coated in a white dust. And, after a moment, he saw why: next to a concrete manufacturing plant was a limestone quarry that looked like an enormous—at least twenty acres—white-rimmed pond filled with sparkling greenish blue water. Beyond it, there looked to be nothing but a swamp-like wilderness.

We're out in the middle of nowhere, he thought. *Or at least on the edge of it.*

Just up the dusty road from the quarry Lane saw, far out in the middle of an open field, chain-link fence and concertina razor wire. It encircled what he thought, considering its institutional design of heavy cinder-block walls inset with very small windows, had to be a jail.

"That's the correctional facility," Austin said, having

noticed where Lane was looking. He chuckled, and added, "No one tries escaping from there."

"Because of the fences?"

"Because of the alligators, which the fences keep out."

Lane wondered how much of that was true, as Austin sped though two more turns, passing distribution warehouses for a grocery store chain and an auto parts chain.

Finally, the SUV pulled through a gate and stopped before a two-story building, its sunbaked, corrugated-steel skin a faded blue. The manufacturing plant looked as if it covered at least four acres. Bolted to its front was a sign with bright lettering: FUTURE MODULAR MANUFACTURING, LLC.

Austin turned in his seat, and said, "I'm really glad you took Camilla Rose's suggestion and made the trip to see this. You'll get a good idea of how it will work in Philly."

"The lady is quite convincing," Lane said, nodding. "I'm happy to have her support. And, no surprise, she's right again. So far, I've been impressed with what you've shown me here."

"You ain't seen nothing yet," Austin said as he reached behind the seat into the cooler. "Another beer? Gets pretty hot here, even in January."

"Yeah, sure."

Austin passed one can to Lane, opening his just as his phone rang.

He took a quick sip, then answered the call. "Hey, Kenny. I'm showing Willie Lane around the plant." He paused to listen, then said, "Yeah, he just said he was impressed. Look, I'll call you back in a bit."

He broke off the call, and said, "Benson said to give you his regards."

As they stepped from the vehicle and walked toward the main door, Lane saw at the far end of the building that there were rows containing dozens upon dozens of multicolored, forty-foot-long metal boxes stacked ten high. He recognized them as shipping containers; he had seen them lined up in similar fashion on the docks at the port in Philadelphia.

"As you saw this morning," Austin said, "the iron framework of the condo is only half finished. When it's finally complete, that's when all this comes into play."

Austin pointed toward the back of the building.

"At that end," he said, "the trucks deliver the intermodal containers that come off the freighters at the Port of Miami. The containers have all the building materials—metal framing, sinks, toilets, floor tiles, whatever—that we have fabricated in China. The pieces are fed to the assembly line down at that end of the building and come out this end of the building as complete units."

He started walking toward the far front of the building, gesturing for Lane to follow. After a bit, Lane had a better view of the adjacent property. It was maybe ten acres, surrounded by chain-link fence, that contained giant rectangular-shaped pods stacked four high. He guessed each was twenty feet long, fifteen feet wide, and twelve feet high. They were individually shrink-wrapped, one section of what had to be at least fifty pods in blue plastic sheeting, the other section in yellow. There were large, four-digit numbers stenciled in white on their sides. Against the nearest fence line were a half dozen flatbed trailers, each with one of the shrink-wrapped pods strapped to it.

"So," Lane said, "what exactly are all these mysterious plastic-covered things?"

"The blue ones are kitchens and the yellow ones bathrooms."

"You mean, like, portable kitchens and toilets?"

"They're modular units," Austin said, nodding. He pointed at the trailers. "We load them on the trailers and truck them to the construction site, where we cut that shrink-wrap off and hoist them into place on each floor with the crane. Those numbers on the plastic are the numbers of the condos they're going in."

"Portable kitchens," Lane said again, his tone making it clear he still did not quite comprehend it all.

"Portable for now," Austin said, turning to look at Lane, "but not after they're slid into place and installed. See, the kitchens and bathrooms are all built as modules." He gestured toward the manufacturing plant. "They're done on the assembly line here. It's a helluva lot easier, and more efficient, to have the materials in bulk here than to bring the pieces on-site and send them piece by piece up into the building, where workers have to put it all together in each separate unit. That old way is highly inefficient."

"So these finished modules go into the buildings sort

of like those plastic building blocks that kids snap together?"

"Yeah. You ever notice how high-rise condos and apartments and hotels and the like all have pretty much the same thing on every floor? The bathrooms and kitchens, for example, are all situated in the same place on a floor plan so that the water lines all run in the same area and the sewer lines drain straight down."

"How about that?" Lane said, glancing back at the stacked boxes. "I never really thought about it, but they really are in the same place on every floor."

"So after we put them in place, we hook up the plumbing and electrical to the buildings and we're done. Same goes for the exterior of a building. The panels are fabricated off-site, trucked in, hoisted into place. We use electric cranes so we don't violate the city's nighttime noise ordinances and can work past the typical eight P.M. cutoff. That gets the building finished in a fraction of the time—the modular units can be built even before the building's steel framework goes up. Even better is the labor: there's plenty of craftsmen here from Central America and Cuba looking for steady work, so there's no threat of walkouts. We can run three eight-hour shifts forever." He nodded toward the building. "C'mon, I'll show you the assembly line."

Willie Lane nodded thoughtfully as they began walking.

"This is really amazing stuff," he said, glancing back at the field of blue and yellow modules. "Tell me again what's the initial investment for getting in one of these funds?"

John T. Austin took a big swallow of his beer, then grinned.

"I think we can work out something for the next mayor of Philly."

[FIVE]

The tractor-trailer rig with the blue-shrink-wrapped modular unit disappeared inside the construction fencing as John Austin approached the front passenger door of Willie Lane's Mercedes SUV. Behind him, an unwrapped bathroom unit, hanging from the end of the crane's cable, ascended.

After Lane pushed the master switch that unlocked the car, he noticed that Austin used his left hand to open the door and then, once inside, to pull the door shut.

He must've really messed up his right arm, he thought.

"How's it going, Willie?" Austin said.

"Jesus, you look like you got the shit beat out of you, Johnny," Lane said, his gravel voice sounding rougher than usual. "You okay?"

"It feels like I did. Thanks for asking. And, yeah, except for this nasty bruise and a hairline fracture to my arm, I'll survive, I guess."

Austin reached inside his jacket and came out with an envelope. He tossed it in Lane's lap.

"Fifty grand," Austin said.

Lane, looking nervous, pulled up on the armrest between the seats and stuffed the envelope in the console.

"You shouldn't have brought that here," he said, his eyes scanning outside the vehicle.

"I thought it would be better if you gave it to your favorite uncle."

Lane raised his eyebrows but said nothing. He looked at him, then realized that Austin's massive bruising was making him uncomfortable.

"I'm trying to lay low," Austin added.

Lane turned and looked out the windshield, and said, "What the hell is going on? First you get shot at and Kenny gets killed and then Camilla Rose dies."

"I'm pretty damn aware of that," Austin said. "But thanks for your concern."

"You're not worried who did that? You could be dead, too."

"Yeah, I'm concerned," Austin said, and shrugged. "But what the hell can I do? Except try to find out answers."

Lane shook his head, and sighed. "Man, I really am very sorry about it all. Don't know what to say. And she looked like she was fine when I left the bar last night."

Austin cocked his head, and said, "So, tell me about that. Who were you with?"

"Just a small crowd that she'd invited," Lane said, glancing at him. "There was Sue Thomas. Know her? She has that cake company."

"Yeah, sure. She's a member of the board of directors for Camilla's Kids."

"I didn't know that. And that architect, John Broadhead, he was there."

Austin nodded.

"Broadhead, too. His firm designed the camps for Camilla Rose. And the hospital wing for the cancer center."

"You know," Lane said finally, "I remember Broadhead talking with Aimee Wolter about that last night."

"Her company's handling the PR for the cancer research center, which is also being built with the modular units." He paused, narrowed his eyes, then said, "So, it was you, Sue, John, and Aimee . . . Who else?"

"As far as I know, just Tony Holmes . . ."

"Camilla Rose must've been using Holmes there to draw donations from the football crowd."

Lane nodded, and went on. "But there could've been others. I got there some time after ten, and Camilla Rose wasn't there."

"She'd already left for the night?"

"Not for the night. Aimee said that maybe an hour earlier Camilla Rose had seen Matt Payne—"

"The cop? That Payne?"

"Yeah, you know him?"

"He came by the hospital with a detective this morning. They were asking all kinds of questions."

"Really? I got a message they want to interview me."

"They asked all about Kenny and Camilla Rose," Austin said, paused, and then added, "Payne did want to know who had been in the bar, which doesn't make sense now that you're saying he was there."

"As I understand it, Johnny, apparently Payne wasn't there. In the bar, I mean. He was in the hotel. Maybe finished dinner there, or just work, I don't know." He sighed, and went on. "But Aimee said Camilla Rose left the bar when she saw him and didn't return for maybe an hour."

"What the hell?" Austin said, then, with a look of anger, stared into the distance. "I'll have to talk with Aimee about that."

He turned back to Lane.

"Look, Willie. There's something bigger, something serious . . ."

Lane thought Austin sounded odd.

A bit crazy? Paranoid?

But he did get shot at. And Benson got killed.

"Yeah? What?"

"You almost didn't get that envelope. And with what's happened with Camilla Rose, that's probably the last one . . ."

Lane involuntarily jerked his head toward Austin.

"Unless you pull some strings. Fast."

Lane, anxious, shifted in his seat.

"Like what?"

VII

William G. Lane, Jr., squeezed past a small circle of extremely attractive women as he entered the restaurant's almost full lounge, glancing around the elegant room as he went. The well-dressed crowd of Center City business professionals was unwinding from their workweek, their animated conversations giving the place an upbeat energy.

There were more than a few familiar faces, which did not give Lane comfort. He was not there to work the crowd—as he otherwise would be doing, especially the extremely attractive women—and he really did not want to talk with anyone he didn't have to.

A minute later, he saw a large mitt of a hand rise and wave above a group of three husky men standing at the end of the long black-marble bar. Lane then saw, peering around the group, the familiar white-haired, bug-eyed man he was here to meet. The beefy fifty-year-old wore his trademark gray-pin-striped three-piece suit and a maroon dress shirt with a white-specked blue silk necktie and matching pocket square.

Among the many legally recognized associations that represented Philly workers—for example, just as the Fraternal Order of Police looked after the best interests of its members, there also was an organized union for the city's electricians, one for its plumbers, another for ironworkers, yet another for teachers, and so on—there was one union that was, more or less, "first among equals." This was due to the fact that the head of United Laborers Local 554, while he had never held an elected public office, was as savvy a politician as anyone serving in City Hall.

Joseph Fitzpatrick, business manager of Local 554, had been raised Irish Catholic in South Philly. The son of an electrician, he had followed his father and older brother into the business, but only after "Fearless Joey Fitz" had given up on his dream of being a heavyweight boxer.

Joey Fitz still had his scrappiness—and a crooked, fat nose from having it broken twice—as well as a rough-edged charm that he used to rise in the ranks of the union. He knew everyone, and brought in business like no one else, while making the best deals for his workers. To show their grateful appreciation, the Local 554 union members—who earned thirty bucks an hour, or about seventy grand a year—saw to it that Joey Fitz took home a paycheck in the neighborhood of a quarter-million dollars a year.

Joey Fitz had learned early on the importance of culti-
vating politicians—from neighborhood-level ward leaders
on up to state house and U.S. representatives—and
knowing that they would return his telephone calls. That
took investment on the part of the union, from endorsing
candidates to contributing cash to their campaigns.

It also meant keeping an eye out for prospective candidates who would have the union's special interests at
heart.

One in particular had been the son of a politician
whom the union had first supported for ward leader,
then for a city council seat, and finally for mayor. Joey
Fitz knew the name recognition among voters alone
gave the son a solid chance of getting elected, and being
an African-American democrat in a city with a population that was mostly black certainly didn't hurt.

That young man was, of course, Willie Lane, who before deciding to go to Temple University and pursue a
political science degree had been an electrician's appren-
tice. His boss, who had handed him his first union card,
was an engaging young man that Lane had come to call
Joey Fitz with great affection.

Within a year's time on the job, however, Lane had
decided he didn't really care for laying wires all day. And
when he witnessed a coworker cross the wrong wires—
one of which had been hot as hell, a deadly two hundred
milliamps—Lane, then and there, experienced a moment of remarkable clarity.

First, he became a faithful believer in the electrician's
often uttered warning *It's not the volts that kill you, it's*

the amps. And, second, he realized he knew of no politicians—his father was at that time a freshman city councilman with his eyes on the mayor's office—who were risking death by electrocution.

Soon thereafter, Willie Lane had enrolled in poli-sci classes at Temple.

Joey Fitz kept up with Willie Lane over the next ten years, often prodding him about when he was going to run for office. So when it came time for Lane's first run for a council seat, he went to see his old friend at United Labor.

Joey Fitz announced that he was not only happy to support the candidate, he said he could also overlook the fact that Lane's union card had been long expired and issue him a new one, and add him as head of Local 556's Office of Public Policy. It was a new position, he told Lane, one paying sixty thousand dollars per year, and it reported directly to the business manager of Local 556.

William G. Lane, with the hardy public endorsement of Joseph Fitzgerald and the United Workers membership, was elected ten months later.

Philadelphia city council members each were paid an annual salary just over one hundred and thirty thousand. While the wage was one of the highest of any city council in the U.S., it had been decided that Philly's members could not be expected to make ends meet on that amount in the country's fifth-largest metropolis. Thus, the city charter allowed elected officials to hold outside employment in addition to performing their elected duties.

Members held one or more positions, some at for-profit companies, others at nonprofits such as charities, as a hedge against, God forbid, having to apply, as half the city's impoverished population had, for food stamps and the like.

There *was* the risk of business coming before the council that was connected with the employer of one of its members, thus creating a possible conflict of interest. In such a case, the member would simply abstain, in effect saying that they would remain impartial, that their vote was not for sale.

In reality, what then happened was the council member met in private with certain of his or her peers and made it clear that when it came time to vote, if one's back were to be scratched, it would be reasonable to expect, when those peers excused themselves from voting on business before the city, that they would have their backs scratched, too.

Because the general public appeared to accept that the system kept the esteemed members of the city council pure as newborn babies, Lane had felt more than comfortable announcing at the celebration of his second reelection to office: "If it wasn't for my good friend Joey Fitz, I really wouldn't be where I'm at."

It was very likely the only truthful statement to slip from the lips of Councilman William G. Lane in quite some time.

As Lane approached the group of men, Joey Fitz nodded toward him, and the three men turned.

"What ya drinking there, Willie? How about a bit of whiskey?" Fitzgerald said, holding up balled fists to feign shadowboxing before offering his enormous right hand to shake Lane's.

Lane nodded at the men in Fitzgerald's group. Fitzgerald introduced them first by name and then as union members. Lane noticed that they all held squat glasses dark with whiskey—and they all looked as if they already had had more than a few. Joey Fitz's fat, crooked nose and pudgy cheeks glowed red.

"And youse guys were just getting ready to leave, right?" Joey Fitz said, waving the bartender over. "So, what's your poison, Willie?"

Lane looked at the bartender and said, "Let me have a Woodford Reserve, a double, on the rocks."

A minute later, as the bartender slid Lane's Kentucky bourbon whiskey across the polished black marble, Joey Fitz nodded once at the union men. They drained their drinks, told the president of the city council that it had been a pleasure meeting him, then left.

"I didn't interrupt anything, did I?" Lane said.

"We were done when you called," Joey Fitz said. "You don't look so good. It have to do with why you asked to meet me?"

Willie Lane considered how to answer, deciding to say nothing and simply nodding twice.

"You're gonna have to give me more than that. I ain't a mind reader, ya know."

"We've got to talk."

"So you said on the phone." He gestured with his

glass at Lane's. "Drink up first, will ya? They don't call this happy hour for nothing."

Lane swirled the amber drink, savored its heavy oak smell, then took a healthy sip.

"Can we go someplace quiet?" he said. "I've got something for you."

"Ah, hell," Joey Fitz said, "that can wait. Relax. You look like shit!"

Lane raised the glass to his mouth, then said, "Well, I feel like shit."

Joey Fitz narrowed his eyes as he studied Lane.

"Okay, okay," Fitzgerald finally said, and motioned with his head toward the entrance to an adjoining room. "C'mon and follow me."

Lining the wood-paneled walls were ten booths with black leather seats and charcoal gray linen privacy curtains. Two of the tables closest to the lounge were taken, and Fitzgerald crossed the room and went to the farthest booth. As he pulled back the curtain, he waved to a waiter and called out, "Bring us menus."

Fitzgerald motioned for Lane to take a seat, and, as he did, Fitzgerald slid into the seat across the table from him. The privacy curtain fell closed behind them.

Lane reached into his black blazer and produced the envelope containing fifty thousand dollars that John T. Austin had given him. He put it on the table in front of Fitzgerald, who picked it up and, without looking inside, slipped it in his suit pocket.

"The usual fifty," Lane said, keeping his gravel voice low.

"How's our friend doing after that accident?" Joey Fitz said, changing the subject.

"Accident?" Lane parroted, his voice rising. He brought it back down as he said, "That was a damn hit job. The driver got hit with buckshot."

Joey Fitz did not reply.

Lane said, "And Johnny got banged up pretty bad. Not bullet wounds. But his face is one big ugly bruise. And he cracked an arm."

Joey Fitz's eyebrows went up. He took a sip of his drink.

"Well," he said, "at least he's better off than the other guy."

Lane nodded.

"Yeah. He's pretty upset over that. And Camilla Rose Morgan's death."

"They figure out what that was all about?"

Lane shook his head.

"No telling. I saw her a couple hours before it happened. She seemed fine. Drinking a bit. But, then, we all were."

"She fell, ya think? Had to. Girl like that wouldn't've jumped, no? Not when she's got everything going for her."

"Yeah. You'd think." Lane paused, then nodded toward where Joey Fitz had stuffed the envelope. "Austin said that could be the last one of those."

Fitzgerald, who was about to take a sip of his drink, looked over the lip of the glass and met Lane's eyes.

"You tell him he'd better think that through?" Joey Fitz said.

"Yeah. He said he needed a little time to sort out what happens next. I mean, two people close to him are dead, and he almost died, too."

Fitzgerald took a long sip as he considered that. He made a face of annoyance.

"We have an agreement," he said.

"And it's been lived up to."

Joey Fitz reached in his pocket, pulled out the envelope, ran a finger through its contents, then, apparently satisfied, stuffed it back in his pocket.

"So far, it has," he said. "But what you're now telling me—"

"I'm just saying what he said."

Joey Fitz shook his head. He stared off in thought.

"These rats in all these countries," he said, "they've been stealing our jobs for years. I was able to go along with Austin on this condo project this one time because he promised the payments and that future projects would use our workers. And also because you vouched for him, Willie. I went way out on a limb for youse guys."

"I know," Lane said. "And I'm sure it's gonna be okay. I know it will. You know I've always gotten the council to approve your projects."

Fitzgerald looked at him, shook his head.

"Willie, we've gotta keep our boys in jobs so they can put food on the family table. You know that way back when my grandfather's ironworkers union was putting up the Empire State Building, tallest building in the world, they were bolting them beams together that had been trucked in straight from our steel mills. That steel was coming from the furnaces so fast that it still gave off heat—"

"I'd heard that," Lane said, nodding.

"And when we were building ships down here in our Navy Yard, same thing. It was all made here. That Defense Department said we couldn't use no materials from outside the U.S. So the suppliers had to do the same. It was all U.S. of A. And now what? You got these Chinese—they're making half the world's steel these days, you know—selling here at thirty to fifty percent less than our mills can make it, and they're putting our boys out of work." He paused, then met Lane's eyes. "So you just might tell Austin that he really doesn't want to happen what could happen if he doesn't live up to his end of our bargain. And I tell ya, Willie, it'll be out of my hands. Some people do things I can't control."

Lane's eyebrows went up.

Joey Fitz's eyes dropped to his cocktail glass, and he took a sip. He looked up, and finally said, "I heard from some of my people that there's some kind of event Austin's having this weekend."

Lane nodded.

"It's tomorrow night," he said, "and it's not his. It's a fund-raiser for the Morgan woman's charity."

"Camilla's Kids," Joey Fitz said, and produced a small smile. "At the Bellevue."

Lane was surprised that Fitzgerald knew the name,

and the location, then realized that the union boss had known all along. Lane was disappointed in himself for being surprised. He knew, as everyone did, that Joey Fitz had a firm finger on the pulse of Philly.

"Nice charity, that one," Joey Fitz went on. "Be a real damn shame if something happened there."

[TWO]
Police Administration Building
Eighth and Race Streets
Philadelphia
Friday, January 6, 7:01 P.M.

As Sergeant Matt Payne entered the Roundhouse—this time, the solenoid on the secure door had actually worked after he kneed the door following its second buzzing—he noted that, judging by the waves of people already crowding the building, it was going to be a busy Friday night.

He thought, *Wonder what the over-under is on shootings and killings tonight?*

Whatever it is—probably two dead, ten shot—the bets will be even higher next week. Especially if Friday the thirteenth's a full moon.

He took one look at the line waiting at the elevator bank and decided to risk taking the stairwell up to the Homicide Unit.

The first steps he made fine. But after reaching the top of that flight, a burning needle of pain flared from his wound.

Damn it!

He stopped and squeezed the handrail as he gently pressed on the bandage and took measured breaths. He didn't bother checking the bandage; he had just changed it at his apartment. After a while, the pain subsided somewhat, and he felt he could continue upward.

When he finally got to the unit, the door was propped open. He looked across the room. He saw Lieutenant Jason Washington was in his glass-walled office, the door to it closed. Payne considered checking in with him, then saw that Washington was talking to someone who was obscured by a poster that had been leaned in the corner.

Payne looked toward his own desk. Tony Harris was sitting behind it, talking on his cellular telephone, while Dick McCrory used the desk phone. They both had notebook computers open on the desktop.

Harris waved, and Payne waved back as he crossed the room.

Harris broke off the call as Payne approached. Mc-Crory, his hand over the mouthpiece of the receiver he held to his ear, glanced up. Seeing Payne, he hung up the phone.

"Didn't need to stop what you were doing on my account," Payne said.

"Not a problem, Matt," McCrory said. "I'd been on hold for at least ten minutes. I think the secretary just parked my call and left me to suffer that gawd-awful country music they listen to down there."

"You feeling okay?" Harris said. "You look pale."

"I'm fine, damn it," Payne snapped, heard what he had said, and added, "Sorry. I'm annoyed. Nothing personal. Just came up the damn steps."

Harris nodded in understanding.

Payne looked at McCrory, and said, "Who's ignoring you?"

"John Austin's people. That was the third time I've called his office in Houston and asked how to find him. Each time they said that because of the shooting, they had been directed not to give out any information—"

"Did you tell them that his life's still in danger?" Payne interrupted, his tone impatient.

"Yeah, of course I did, but they said they were just doing what they were told, and took my name and number and said they would pass it along. Except this last time, when they put me on hold hell."

Payne shook his head. "They'd 'pass it along'? Damn nice of them."

"Yeah. Mary, Joseph, and all the fookin' saints, huh?"

Payne looked at Harris.

"Hank still sitting on Austin's hotel room?"

"After he got hotel security to do a safety check of the room and they found Austin gone but his suitcase and stuff still there, Hank posted a blue shirt at the door. He went back to working on the follow-up interviews while waiting to hear if Austin showed."

"Good. You're right about people feeling more at

ease talking to a detective in a suit, not to a uniform. Tell me about who you said had gone up to Camilla Rose's condo.

"From interviews and reviewing security camera video," Harris said, gesturing toward his notebook computer, "we cobbled together a short list of people—some known, some unknown—who left the bar and shortly thereafter appeared at the condo's elevator bank. Most were residents—who security ID'd for us—and their guests, and they all stated that they went home to their condos, not to Camilla Rose's. That left three others, a male and two females, none of whom security recognized, who went up the elevator with Camilla Rose. We were able to track down the male from the credit card he used in the bar."

"Who is he?"

He tapped the computer keyboard, and read, "Arthur Marx, white male, thirty-three. A dentist from King of Prussia." He looked up at Payne, and said, "Marx claimed he had just met the women in the bar last night. He knew them only as Keri and Pamela. They told him they were celebrating Keri's birthday."

"You talk with the women?"

"No. If he has their full names and/or phone numbers, he's not admitting it. He ran up a big tab, but not half as big as Camilla Rose did, and the women didn't use a credit card for us to run down."

Payne sighed. "Why do I get the feeling we may have trouble finding a solid stone to look under, never mind a stone under the stone?"

"Because you're right," Harris said. "Camilla Rose went off her balcony at oh-four-thirty . . ."

"Yeah. And?"

"And the condo's lobby security cameras clearly show these three going up with her. Then, just before oh-four-hundred, the cameras show the three coming off the elevators."

"Staggering off," McCrory put in.

"Yeah," Harris said, "they damn sure were feeling no pain. Anyway, Marx said there had been no one else in her condo. And the lobby cameras showed no activity after they left until oh-four-twenty-five, when one of the bellhops pushed a baggage cart by stacked with newspapers to deliver floor to floor. Finally, there's a bunch of activity at oh-four-forty-two when the security guys ran through the lobby, headed up to Camilla Rose's condo."

"You're saying nobody got off the elevator after oh-four-thirty?"

"Only the security guys. After they found her condo open and no one in it."

McCrory, picking up the thought, said, "So, all we know from video is that the three went up with the Morgan woman after the bar closed, stayed two hours, then left. But we don't know if other parties unknown were already up there."

Payne considered that, and said, "If there had been someone, they could've left her place and taken a stairwell. And to any floor, including a ground-floor exit."

"Yeah," McCrory said, "but there's cameras outside that are fixed on the exit doors and they didn't show anyone leaving. But another floor is possible—and the reason, I'm thinking, that the security camera video can't be expected to show our doer."

Payne thought for a bit, finally saying, "Then there's also the service elevator to consider."

"Speaking of which," Harris said, "that brings us to our other witness: a guy from room service. Camilla Rose ordered from the hotel kitchen a slew of appetizers, which got delivered around oh-two-thirty."

"What did he see?"

"The guy confirmed seeing the two women drinking with Camilla Rose. He didn't think the place was trashed, and saw no evidence of the drugs. Marx denied that there was any drug use—"

"Go figure," Payne interrupted. "If he got caught—*Poof!*—there would go his license to fill cavities."

"And he said that when they left her, just before oh-four-hundred, Camilla Rose was alive and well and living her usual large. Everything was hunky-dory."

"Of course it was," Payne said. "Okay, so all these people went up and then came down. But it still doesn't rule out the possibility of there being someone else."

"Yeah," McCrory said, "and it doesn't mean she didn't just take the high-rise equivalent of a long walk on a short wharf. That MDMA is powerful stuff—maybe it made her think she could fly."

Payne grunted. MDMA, street-named Molly and Ecstasy, was a synthetic psychoactive, what he referred to as "methamphetamine with a hallucinogenic twist."

Harris said, "There is one thing—Marx said he's lawyering up."

"I don't think that means anything these days," Payne said. "Seems everyone's got counsel on retainer. Hell, I would be, too, if I'd been in her condo."

That triggered a mental image of the photograph of Camilla Rose she had sent to his cellular phone, which in turn caused Payne again to think that if he'd gone up, she might still be alive.

"Has the forensic lab cracked her phone?" Payne said. "Could be photos of their little party on it."

"Along with that one she sent you earlier," McCrory said, was sorry he did, and expected Payne to snap at him. When Payne didn't, he added, "But no news that they did anything on her phone yet."

Payne nodded in thought, and said, "Aimee Wolter said she didn't have any insight. What did the interviews with Willie Lane, John Broadhead, Sue Thomas, and Tony Holmes turn up?"

"They all, with the exception of Lane, pretty much matched with what we saw in Hank's interview of that bartender," Harris said. "Which is to say, not much. They drank, avoided the subject of Benson's death, then went home at closing time. They said they had no interaction with Marx and the two women, who mostly stayed at the bar. None were seen on the condo cameras coming or going."

"Except Lane, you said?"

"We've got calls in to him. He's not gotten back in

touch. But since he wasn't on the condo cameras either, odds are his will be more of the same." He paused, and added, "At the risk of repeating what you said, without a solid stone, there ain't no stones under the stone."

Payne nodded.

"Well, we may be looking for something that's just not there. Okay, shifting gears, did we get any more background on Benson? And who is running the company now? That article said that the scientist that committed suicide was the number three officer."

"Han was three out of three," McCrory said. "You have Benson and a chief financial officer by the name of Ronald Johnson at the top. And then Han. That was the extent of their executive office. I called the office in West Palm and got a message center. They don't even have a receptionist or secretary answering the phone."

"Jesus."

"I did get a response when I tried reaching the widow," Harris said. "Listen to this."

Harris held out his cellular phone and played a voice mail message over the speakerphone.

"Detective Harris," the soft voice of a male said, *"my name is Samuel Nguyen. I'm down here in Riviera Beach, Florida, and returning the call that you left for Mrs. Ann Han. Your message said that you had questions for her about her husband and his death. I'm afraid that Mrs. Han will not be available. I'm sure you'll understand that she has suffered enough with the loss of Dr. Han. She considers the case closed and has nothing further to say. We appreciate you respecting that and her need for privacy. Thank you."*

There was a clicking sound, and the line went dead.

"No stone again," Payne said.

"After that," Harris said, nodding, "I gave that homicide lieutenant, Jeff Murray, another try and finally got him."

"He say if there was anything in the suicide note?"

"Yeah. That Han claimed to have been under extreme stress after being pressured to falsify lab findings for NextGen. He listed a number of processes that had been corrupted to meet Benson's demands. Han said he knew that ultimately the product was not going to work as described, rendering the patent application worthless."

"And the stock, too . . ."

"Right. But Benson was pushing the narrative that the stock was about to soar any day—he kept banging that drum on the Internet, telling everyone all that was needed was for the patent to be approved. And calling people idiots—whatever—if they could not see these great things coming—"

"Which would increase speculation, trigging more shares to be bought, which would cause the stock to rise."

"Exactly. Han said he figured out quickly what Benson was up to and that he had been duped into joining the start-up to give it credibility. When he took the leave of absence—Benson suggested that Han's stress was, in fact, a deep depression—Mrs. Han went public with the charges of corrupting the research-and-development process in the media."

"Did anyone else corroborate what Dr. Han claimed?"

"That's a good question, and the answer is no.

Because they couldn't. No device was released for a third party to determine if it did or did not work."

"That's right. Benson said he was protecting the intellectual property until the patent was issued. So it's one's word against the other's."

"Benson argued that it was simply the normal growing pains of a start-up, basically saying research and development is messy because you're creating something that's never existed before and it's expected that there will be mistakes made. The company's legal beagles fired off a cease-and-desist letter. Han, like all the other employees, had signed an NDA—"

"Nondisclosure agreement."

"Right. His discussing their methods of research and development violated the agreement—"

"Even though they were bogus."

"Moot point. In his suicide letter, Dr. Han said he felt shame, and felt he would never regain his good reputation. So, after his wife left for her yoga class, he popped a sleeping pill—an Ambien—then got in his SUV in the garage, started it up, put the windows down, and drifted off."

"Loss of reputation and feeling ashamed sounds damn depressing to me," Payne said. "And depressed people kill themselves all the time. I need to bounce this off my sister."

Harris nodded. "This Detective Murray said the reason the Han woman clammed up was because Benson threatened to sue her for making false accusations. He made it clear that he would pay whatever it took so that the costs of defending those lawsuits would leave her bankrupt."

"What a miserable sonofabitch."

"It gets better. Benson spelled it out for her that because Dr. Han was sick and that their income—stock in NextGen awarded as bonuses—was tied to the company, if the company didn't succeed, she'd be broke. That's why this Nguyen announced in the media that she would have nothing more to say. She'd become, fearing that threat, complicit. And even with Benson's death, that didn't change."

"Causing her to lose her husband sounds like reasonable motive to me," Payne said.

"Yeah, and I asked Murray about it. He said he really doesn't believe she's capable of that. On a good day, she's meek. Now she's frail, and genuinely frightened by the whole ordeal."

"I wonder how much of this John Austin knows," Payne said, "and when he knew it."

Harris shrugged.

"Well, they were old friends since childhood," he said. "You'd think Benson told him. And you heard Austin. He believes in the company, in the product."

"Two things," Payne said. "One, if the company is a sham, and Austin has a significant piece, they could have been working a pump and dump."

"What's that?" McCrory said.

"Talk up the product, inflating the stock price, then sell out."

"That's fraud, right?" McCrory said.

"Yeah, but hard to prove. And for the investor, speculation isn't illegal. People lose money in the markets every day. *Caveat emptor.* Or, as the master con man Phineas T. Barnum put it, 'There's a sucker born every minute.'"

"What's two?" Harris said.

Payne nodded.

"Not to defend Austin in any way," he said, "but money changes things. Best friends, even family members, will lie to each other over it. Whatever trust they have, it's quickly broken." He paused, and added, "And the more money there is, the worse it can get. Camilla Rose accused Mason Morgan of manipulating the old man into rewriting his will, calling it a 'brazen betrayal,' and refused to speak to her brother."

"So," Harris went on, "Austin could be completely innocent. Or be complicit, especially if he had money invested and it was to his financial advantage to say he believed in the product."

Payne said, "I don't think the phrase *completely innocent* has ever been applicable in Austin's case."

"That message they power washed on the coal tower wall," Dick McCrory said. "You think it means Austin was the actual target? Or both were? Either way, maybe that's how Austin 'got lucky.'"

"All we know is, three people are dead," Payne said, "and now he's in someone's crosshairs. I really don't like the sonofabitch. But keeping him alive is the best way to find out what happened to either Benson or Camilla Rose."

"Or, if there's any connection, it may solve both."

Payne felt another burning needle in his wound and grimaced.

"You sure you're okay?" Harris said.

"Define *okay*," Payne said, turning to leave. "I need to hit the head."

Harris and McCrory popped to their feet.

"Sit, damn it," Payne said, motioning with his hand. "Make yourself useful and find that damn Austin." He paused, then added, "Oh, and find out who's got tonight's over-under. I need to place my bet."

"I already did," McCrory said. "It's eleven. One dead. Ten wounded."

Harris's cellular telephone began ringing. He glanced at its screen, then answered it.

"Yeah, Hank?"

Harris looked up at Payne a moment later as he said, "Fifteen minutes ago? And you got someone up there to watch the door?"

As Harris put down his phone, he said, "The security guys got a computer alert that a radio frequency identification keycard coded to the Morgan woman's condo was just used in the elevator. Lobby cameras show Austin getting on."

"I'll go."

He then reached into his pocket and pulled out a dollar bill. He took a pen and sticky notepad from the desk, wrote "Sgt Payne 16" on the paper, and stuck it on the dollar bill.

He handed it to Harris, who then read the over-under wager.

"Betting really high? Such the cynic."

Payne nodded. "Guilty. Something's in the air. I feel it. And I'll let you know what I get out of Austin."

[THREE]
The Rittenhouse Condominiums
Residence 2150
Center City
Philadelphia
Friday, January 6, 7:20 P.M.

John Austin waved the plastic keycard that Camilla Rose had left him in the hospital at the door handle. He heard the lock click open, as the light on the reader glowed green, and with his left hand turned the handle and pushed the door inward.

Jesus Christ, this place looks spotless, he thought, making a quick scan of the main living room and, beyond it, the open kitchen and dining area. *That detective with Payne said there'd been a party. Booze bottles everywhere. Joy must have sent a cleaning crew in.*

"Hello?" he called out. "Anyone here? Hello?"

No one. Good.

He let the door click shut behind him, then threw the dead bolt, before tossing the keycard onto the glass-

topped table beside the door. It landed next to a Rittenhouse receipt and a business card.

He glanced at the receipt—it read "Your account has
been billed. Thank you for letting us serve you. Alicia,
Housekeeping"—and picked up the business card.

It's that damn Payne's, he thought. *Same as the one he
gave me, except he wrote another number on it.*

So, the bastard was here.

Or did Camilla Rose leave it? Or one of the cops?

Damn! I don't know.

He put the card back on the table, took out his new
cellular telephone, and, reading the number off the
housekeeping receipt, called the hotel and asked to be
connected with the front desk. After announcing who
he was, he said that he wanted one of the bellmen sent
to pack up all his personal items in his hotel room and
deliver them to Residence 2150.

Austin walked through the living room, trying not to
look toward the balcony, out where Camilla Rose last
stood. As he made his way to the kitchen, he reached
into the inside pocket of his coat and pulled out a small
zippered plastic bag. It held about a half cup of a grayish
white powder.

The kitchen had a large island, and on its polished-
granite top, behind the deep sink's gooseneck faucet,
was a stainless steel block holding a set of high-end
chef's knives. Austin poured a small pile of the powder
onto the stone and from the block pulled the smallest
utensil, a paring knife with a razor-thin blade. With a
practiced hand, he chopped the powder to reduce its

lumps, then formed four narrow parallel lines the length of the three-inch blade.

He placed the knife on the counter, pulled open a drawer beneath it, and came out with a short cocktail straw. He inserted an end of the straw in his right nostril, pressed his left nostril to form a seal, and leaned over and inhaled a line of powder with a quick, steady, deep breath. He stood, snorting as he rubbed his nose, then placed the straw end in his other nostril and repeated the process.

As he stood leaning against the island, he closed his eyes and enjoyed the wave of warmth that began flowing through him. Numbness set in, and he felt at ease.

The interlude was interrupted by his telephone ringing.

"Damn it."

He pulled the phone from his pocket. The caller ID showed WILLIAM LANE. He started to answer it but had second thoughts. He shook his head as the call rolled into voice mail. After a couple seconds, the phone indicated a new message. He listened to the deep gravel voice: *"Johnny, it's me. You need to call soon as you get this. I saw my uncle and did as you asked. There could be some real trouble."*

"Real trouble?" Austin said aloud, looking at the phone. "Well, Willie, no shit."

He slid the phone across the counter, leaned over, and inhaled the last two lines. There was a bit of powder left on the counter. He licked his finger, then wiped up the residue and rubbed it on his upper gums.

John Austin, his nose beginning to run, snorted as he

looked out the floor-to-ceiling windows. He felt his heart race. He was not surprised to see Camilla Rose standing there, martini in hand, her head back and laughing. He knew it wasn't actually her, only his memory of the last time he had seen her on the slate-tiled balcony. Yet the vision felt powerful.

He walked across the room and out onto the balcony. There was an icy wind, and he crossed his arms over his chest against it, taking care not to aggravate his injured right arm.

As he passed the darkened fireplace, it lit up with a *Whoosh!* of flames.

"Shit!" he shouted, jumping away from it.

His heart felt as if it would pound through his chest at any moment. He stared at the flickering flames, their heat cutting the bitter cold air.

Did she have something to do with this?

He glanced around the balcony and back through the condo's windows. He saw no one in the well-lit rooms, and only then remembered that the natural gas–fueled fireplace had a timer. Camilla Rose had told him that she set it to light up nightly at seven-thirty.

Still, it had unnerved him. And he took a deep breath, let it out.

He turned and looked at the thirty-foot-long railing along the balcony's outer edge. Its slate footing held thick, four-foot-square upright glass panels. They reflected the fireplace's red-orange flames.

He had no idea at what point along the glass rail she had been standing before going over. But he now visualized her at its center, the cold breeze blowing back her long hair and dress. As he approached, he saw her looking over the side, back at him, then reaching out to him, the soft dress clinging to her body and flapping on her outstretched arm.

And he saw her leaning over the side—and slip away.

He gasped, felt his heartbeat racing again.

Jesus!

He reached the barrier of glass and looked over the side. He saw nothing but the brick-paved drive at the building's entrance.

And the tears came.

Why . . . why did this have to happen?

After a minute, he shook his head, then used his sleeve to wipe away the tears. He turned and went back into the condo and over to the marble-topped island in the kitchen. He poured another small pile of white powder and, after reaching for the small knife, repeated the ritual.

He was halfway through sniffing the second line when he heard a knock at the front door. He jerked his head and looked toward it.

Who the hell is that?

Maybe it's my stuff already?

As he approached the wooden door, there was more knocking, rapid, impatient. He put his right eye to the peephole, saw an annoyed male's face, sighed with relief, as he shook his head. He opened the door.

Michael Grosse, a muscular, athletic thirty-five-year-old who had earned his law degree at the University of

Miami, stood in the corridor, holding the extended handle of a black carry-on suitcase. On top of it was a well-worn brown saddleback briefcase. Grosse had intense blue eyes, blond hair that fell to his shoulders, and the deep-tanned leathery skin of someone who had spent a great deal of time in the sun.

Austin thought Grosse, who he knew regularly wore tropical shirts and shorts to his law office but now was in a dark pin-striped two-piece suit and a collarless blue shirt, looked like a fish out of water.

Austin made a sweeping gesture with his left arm, and Grosse entered.

"What the hell took you so long?" Austin said, locking the door, then following Grosse into the living room.

"Nice to see you, too, Johnny," Grosse said, the sarcasm thick. "But to answer your question, I had to borrow a plane at West Palm, and got here as soon as I could." Eyeing Austin from head to toe, he added, "Jesus Christ, you look like shit."

"So everyone keeps telling me. In those exact words."

"I need a drink," Grosse said, and pulled his bags toward the kitchen.

He placed his suitcase beside the island, again putting the briefcase on it. He saw the lines of powder on the countertop.

"That what I think it is?" Grosse said.

"Help yourself to all you want. There's plenty."

"Not just no but *hell* no. And I thought you quit using."

Austin frowned as he shrugged.

"Call it extenuating circumstances," he said, then looked past Grosse to the glass railing of the balcony.

Grosse looked out in that direction, realized what Austin meant, and closed his eyes as he dropped and shook his head. He exhaled audibly.

"This all just gets worse by the minute," he said. "Did you have her doing that shit, too? You went back to self-medicating? Is that what happened?"

"Fuck you. I did not. In fact, I never made her do anything she didn't want to do. No one did, as you should know."

Grosse stared at him with a look of disbelief, shook his head, turned, and went to the wet bar at the far end of the kitchen.

The mirrored bar held a wide variety of expensive liquors, more than a couple dozen bottles. Many were unopened, causing Grosse to wonder if it had been recently restocked. He scanned them before grabbing a full bottle of Johnnie Walker Blue Label.

He turned and gestured with it toward Austin, who said, "Sure."

"Suppose that makes me an enabler," Grosse said, turning back to the bar and pulling down two crystal glasses. "But booze, I guess, is better than that crap you're abusing."

"Go to hell."

Grosse half filled the glasses with the scotch whisky, added a splash of water and a single ice cube to each, handed one glass to Austin.

Grosse held up his glass, tipped it to Austin, and said, "To Camilla Rose."

Austin did the same, adding, "And Kenny."

Grosse took a heavy sip, looked out to the balcony. He shook his head again, then looked at Austin.

"Anything new about what happened to her?"

"I've heard nothing since I called you."

Grosse glanced around the condominium. "This place looks untouched since I was here last week."

"It was cleaned this afternoon. Apparently she had a party before . . . before what happened."

Grosse nodded as he scanned the room. "I keep expecting her to make her usual grand entrance, floating in here from her bedroom, dressed to the nines, filling the room with that incredible personality of hers. This place feels eerily empty without her."

"I know."

Grosse took another sip of his drink, and said, "Well, anyway, first of all, I finally got in contact with Camilla Rose's mother. She took the news—maybe because she sounded half in the bag—rather well."

"When is she coming?"

"No time soon—"

"Jesus, why am I not surprised? She really is one cold bitch."

"Because she's on a cruise ship off Patagonia."

"Oh, that's right. I'd forgotten she was going on that. For some reason, I thought it was next month."

"Yeah, well, even if she skips the ten days in Mendoza and Buenos Aires that's scheduled before she gets off the boat, earliest she can be back in the States is a week from now. The boat she's on isn't big enough to land a helicopter, if she was up to that."

"Can't say I'm disappointed. I don't want to deal with her."

Grosse walked over and opened the weathered-leather flap of his saddleback briefcase.

"There is something you *do* need to deal with."

"What?"

He pulled out a manila folder and from it removed a single sheet of paper. He put it on the countertop.

"That's a copy of the e-mail I got at noon from Morgan International. Your firm should be getting notice, if you haven't already."

"About what? I haven't looked at any business e-mails today."

"It's about Morgan International's philanthropy arm. They want their investments returned."

"What? Which investments?"

"All of them," Grosse said. "They want all the money that Camilla Rose invested in your funds returned."

"The philanthropy does? Or Mason?" Austin said as he snapped up the sheet and read it. Then he blurted, "That miserable son of a bitch!"

Austin tossed the paper back on the counter, and stared at it.

"All of it?" he repeated, his tone incredulous. He looked at Grosse, and added, "Maybe Camilla Rose was right. The prick tried to have me killed. And, when that failed, he's now going after the money."

"She said her brother was behind the shooting?" Grosse said. "I remember her telling me a long time ago that there was a lot of friction between you and Mason."

Austin nodded, adding, "You don't think he went after her . . . ?"

Grosse was silent.

"Frankly," he said finally, "Mason being who he is, none of that makes any sense. What, exactly, was her proof that he was after you?"

Austin shrugged, started pacing. His whole body shook. He gestured out at the balcony, and, his voice quivering, said, "He pulls this shit when her body isn't even cold."

Austin slammed his crystal glass on the counter and began moving toward the hallway half bath, walking fast.

"I can't say that I disagree," Grosse said, watching him with interest. "The timing is more than a little . . ."

Austin sprinted to the bathroom and disappeared. He kicked the door shut. A second later came violent retching sounds.

"Distasteful," Grosse finished.

Now, that's damn interesting, he thought.

Grosse went to the bar, refreshed his drink, and stood by the sliding glass doors to the balcony, sipping the scotch whisky as he looked out at the lights of the city. He was halfway through his drink when he heard the bathroom door click open and then the hum of the fan.

Grosse watched Austin in the reflection as he went to the kitchen and retrieved his drink, guzzled it.

"Must've been something I ate," Austin said without conviction, his voice uneven.

Grosse turned toward him.

"You can't get them their money, can you, Johnny?"

[FOUR]

Matt Payne, driving fast westward on Walnut Street, downshifted and braked as the traffic signal at South Broad cycled to yellow, then red.

"Damn it," he muttered, coming to a stop.

He looked across the street at the elegant Bellevue—what old-timers still referred to as the Bellevue-Stratford, the enormous landmark hotel's name for most of its hundred-plus years' catering to the city's wealthy and powerful.

He saw parked next to its grand entrance were a pair of Highway Patrol motorcycles. The spotless Harley-Davidson Electra Glides gleamed in the lights of the entrance. And, next to them, he saw that there was a hotel welcome sign bearing the logotype of Camilla's Kids Camps.

And so the show goes on, he thought.

Those must be the brand-new bikes that Camilla Rose had the Morgan trust pay for.

Payne saw the car's in-dash screen show that he had an incoming call from his father. He touched the icon to answer it.

"Yes, sir?"

"Hey, Matt. You doing okay?"

"Sure. I'm afraid to ask why you ask."

"No particular reason, I guess. Just always concerned."

"Probably doesn't help with Amy's meddling."

"Don't be angry with her. She wouldn't hesitate pointing out that you're the one with a healing bullet wound."

"Point taken."

"Look, I made a couple calls on that Miami lawyer."

"And you found out that he's up to his ears in Bolivian marching powder."

"Which is . . . ?"

"If you don't know, then I guess he's not. It's cocaine, Dad."

"That's right. I did know that. Lord knows, there's enough of that down there in South Florida."

"And in South Philly. And heroin. It's everywhere. And bad guys needing legal counsel because of it."

"True. But, at least from what I gather, this Grosse isn't one of them. He's an interesting fellow, with an extremely successful practice. His firm has a high-end clientele—"

"Explaining why Camilla Rose had him."

"Right. And he handles the very complex needs of the very wealthy very quietly. From what I'm told, it's all aboveboard."

Matt watched the traffic light cycle and visually cleared the intersection before accelerating through it.

He glanced a second time to the right. A block up was the Union League, and, another block just beyond it, City Hall loomed.

"What, for example?"

"A lot of his work is in creating corporations. And a lot of that offshore accounts, some established here in Delaware and Wyoming, others in the Caymans and British Virgin Islands."

"Shell companies? Sounds like a slippery legal slope," Matt said, downshifting to turn left in front of the Episcopal church.

"Perhaps what gets put in them, but his work establishing them, from what I understand, is entirely legal."

Matt tugged the steering wheel to the right, and, tires rumbling, the car shot up the bricked drive to The Rittenhouse.

"Well," Matt said, "it's good to hear she had good representation."

"Did you find out any more about what happened with her?"

"Not really."

"Such a tragedy. Well, if I hear more, I'll let you know. Be careful."

Matt saw a valet trotting toward his door.

"Thanks, Dad."

When Payne got off the elevator on the twenty-first floor of the Rittenhouse condominiums, he found there was a uniformed officer sitting in one of the two linen-upholstered armchairs across the corridor from the elevator bank.

The blue shirt, a wiry, dark-haired male who looked to Payne to be all of twenty, had taken the chair that afforded him a direct view of the door to Camilla Rose's condo at the end of the corridor.

He had been hunched over, elbows on knees, reading something on his smartphone. But when the young officer looked up to see who was getting off the elevator, he snapped to his feet.

"Sergeant," he announced, "no one's gone in or out of 2150 the whole time I've been here." He looked at his wristwatch, and added, "Which has been precisely nineteen minutes."

"See anything unusual on the floor?"

"Pretty quiet. I got some strange looks from a couple people who got on the elevator, but nothing I'd call unusual."

Payne nodded. "Okay. Make yourself comfortable. I might need you in a bit."

"Yessir."

Payne reached the door to 2150 and knocked.

After a while, he could hear heavy footsteps on the other side of the door. There was a long pause before the sound of the dead bolt being thrown open.

The door swung inward.

"You sorry son of a bitch!" John T. Austin said, his voice booming down the corridor.

Austin cocked his uninjured left arm back, his hand making a fist.

He really thinks he's going to throw a punch?

"What the hell is your problem?" Payne said, holding his hands up, palms out. "Take it easy."

"I heard you left the bar with Camilla Rose last night, Payne."

"Well, you heard wrong."

"Bullshit."

Payne looked at him, and thought, *I wonder how many other times he's gotten jealous like this?*

Payne saw Austin's eyes looking past behind him, from where he heard feet fast approaching.

"What's this? You bring the junior cavalry?" Austin said, putting down his arm.

Payne turned and saw the blue shirt come to a stop five feet from them. He stood erect, hands at his hips, the right hand brushing the black polymer grip of his city-issued 9mm Glock service weapon.

The blue shirt did not say anything. His narrowed eyes, looking past Payne at Austin, and his stance telegraphed his intent.

"As you were," Payne said in a casual tone. "Mr. Austin, here, was just about to invite me in."

Payne, surprising Austin, strode past him.

"Yes, I think I will come in," he said as he did. "Very kind of you to ask."

Payne heard the blue shirt chuckle.

As Payne entered the living room, he saw on the far couch a well-dressed tanned man with long hair getting to his feet. Payne walked over to him, hand extended, and said, "Matt Payne, Philadelphia Police Homicide."

"Michael Grosse," the man said, shaking Payne's hand.

Grosse motioned with the cocktail glass he held out, and said, "Would you like a drink, or something?"

"Thanks, but no. You're Camilla Rose's lawyer."

"That's right—"

Austin stormed up to them, putting his face close to Payne's.

"We weren't finished, Payne."

Payne now could smell the alcohol on Austin's breath.

So, he's drunk?

"Johnny?" Grosse said. "You want to ease up?"

"This son of a bitch was with Camilla Rose last night."

Payne studied Austin, and thought, *It's possible he's using the booze for against the pain. Or maybe booze and pain pills, making for a nice toxic mix.*

Maybe it's more likely, as Amy said, that he's self-medicating.

Is this one of those mania episodes she mentioned?

"Two things, Austin," Payne said, his tone even. "First off, as I'm sure counsel here can tell you, you hit a cop, you go directly to jail. Do not pass go. Got it?"

"Fuck you—"

"And, two, I never went inside that bar. Not that there's any reason I shouldn't have. But the fact is, I happened to run into Camilla Rose in the lobby outside it. And not ten minutes later, the last I saw her, she was on the elevator, heading up here to her condo."

"Why should I believe you? You left the hospital with her after she was there with me. And then you're seen together in the bar later that night."

"I just told you, unequivocally, that I never was in the bar."

"But you were with Camilla Rose."

"I'm beginning to think that crash affected your hearing," Payne said. "I was never in the bar. Listen, she told me she wanted to talk, said she had more information that I could possibly use. So, at her request, I went with her to talk—"

"To here, to her condo?" Austin said, stepping in closer.

Payne sighed audibly. He looked between Austin and Grosse, then said to Austin, "She went up here alone, is all I can tell you. I, instead, wound up meeting a few blocks away, with Detective Harris, who you met this morning."

Austin took a step back as he considered that.

"Why didn't you go up and talk with her?" he said.

Payne met Austin's eyes as he mentally debated telling him about Camilla Rose having made a pass at him. And he wondered if he should also use the picture of her by the fireplace she had sent him as evidence. He dismissed both thoughts as fast as they had occurred to him. Damaging the virtue of any woman, especially one deceased and unable to defend herself, struck him as reprehensible.

There also was the very real chance that Austin, hearing such news, would really come unglued. It would be easy on Austin's part to make the accusation that Payne, in taking advantage of Austin being sedated in the hospital, had rushed to be her shining knight on a white horse.

"Camilla Rose," Payne said, "drank two vodka miniatures in my car when we were maybe a block from the hospital. She was clearly upset—she said that her nerves were shot—and, as far as I know, continued drinking until I saw her outside the bar. It was then my observation that in her condition she would not have information I could use."

He paused, let that sink in, and went on. "And when Detective Harris called and said he did have information, that was where I went."

He paused again, thought, *What the hell, why not?* and added, "In retrospect, I really regret not having gone with her, as that very likely could have changed the course of the evening."

Austin jerked his head toward Payne at that.

And now I feel a little shitty saying that, Payne thought, *but he doesn't know the details.*

And the fact is, it is damn sure true that the evening would have had a different outcome—and she could very well be alive right now.

Austin made what looked like a face of disbelief as he shook his head. But he did not challenge Payne on what he had said.

"You can believe what you want," Payne said, "but you've got bigger problems. Which is why I'm here."

Payne looked at Grosse.

"You should see this, too. Especially if you are planning to be around him, Counselor."

"To reiterate, I am Camilla Rose's lawyer," Grosse said as he watched Payne pulling out his cellular telephone. "Mr. Austin has his own, other representation."

Payne nodded, then brought up the photograph he had taken of the message on the coal tower wall. He held the phone out toward them.

"Where the hell is that?" Austin said.

"We came across it at the crime scene with the two guys we were told were responsible for killing Kenny Benson."

Austin looked back at the phone.

"I got *lucky*? Damn near dying is *lucky*? Just look at me!"

"We also were told that there may be another hit."

"On me?"

"We don't know."

Austin looked at Grosse, then at Payne, and said, "Those two guys. You get them to confess? They say why they did it?"

Payne shook his head. "Dead guys don't talk."

Payne had an image that combined only their heads—the faces, side by side, were contorted but did not reveal the abuse—and showed it to Austin.

"Recognize either of them?" Payne said, studying him.

"No. Who are they?"

Payne saw that Austin stared at it stone-faced. He detected no reaction. Grosse, when Payne looked at him, shook his head.

"You're late, Matty."

"Unfortunately, unavoidable, Uncle Denny," Payne said. "Had to change my bandage."

Coughlin grunted.

"I suppose I can let it slide for that. But apparently you found the time to stop for coffee."

"Priorities, sir. You really don't want to be around me if I haven't had adequate jolts of caffeine." He smiled while pointing at the cup. "And, as the Black Buddha would concur, good karma always is an admirable thing to aspire to."

Coughlin's expression showed that he was not amused.

"Actually, sorry I'm late," Payne went on in a more serious tone. "Tony Harris brought in the coffees. We've been going back over everything we have on the Morgan case and running down everything we can on the two males who were strung up in the PECO tower."

Coughlin came out from behind his desk and went to where a low wooden table separated a black leather couch and a pair of heavy armchairs. Payne followed, easing himself carefully into one of the chairs, while Coughlin sat on the couch opposite him.

"Jerry's keeping a close eye on her case and the shooting," Coughlin said, and gestured toward the nearby wall-mounted flat-screen television. "High-profile means top of the news cycle. There seems to be a new story about her every hour."

The TV was, like the one in Mayor Carlucci's office, constantly tuned to KeyCom cable's *Philly News Now* channel, the volume muted. The reason for that, Payne

"We're working on that," Payne said, putting away the phone.

"How did you find them?" Austin said.

"It's what we do."

Austin looked at him. "Real smart-ass, aren't you? How do you know for sure they're the ones?"

Payne didn't answer.

"Okay, so what was used to write that message about me?" Austin said.

"A high-pressure industrial power washer. It was also used to shred the skin off the shooters."

"Jesus," Grosse said in a low voice.

Austin was quiet. He appeared to lose color in his face.

"The question now is," Payne said, "were you the target? Or both you and Kenny Benson?"

"How the hell would I know?" Austin said, looking him in the eye.

Payne did not flinch.

But you do know, you sonofabitch. You know something. Time to play a hunch . . .

"You know because that cash envelope that Camilla Rose gave you right before the shooting held a helluva lot more than the twenty thousand dollars you said."

"What're you saying?"

"I heard it was fifty grand, in hundreds—"

"Did she tell you that?"

Yes, but you can't ask her if she did, can you? So I'll let you wonder about the source.

And that text said she'd told you that that was the last hundred grand.

Payne's eyes went to Grosse, then back to Austin.

"Who are you paying off with the hundred grand?" Payne went on. "And why?"

Austin avoided eye contact, turning to look for his drink as he forced a laugh.

"That's ridiculous. You're way out of line, Payne."

"Look, I'm trying to find who's responsible for these deaths. I can't help you if you don't help me. I really don't care who you're giving money. I want the killer."

"And I've got nothing for you. I've told you all I know."

Payne met his eyes, and, after mulling it over, thought, *What the hell.*

He pulled up the photograph on his phone showing the shredded bodies hanging from the iron beam in the coal tower.

"Suit yourself," Payne said, holding out the phone. "But here's something to think about."

Austin looked, and let out what Payne thought sounded like a deep primal groan.

"Jesus," Grosse said, again in a low voice.

"Feeling lucky now?"

"Get out, Payne!" Austin barked, his left arm stiff as he pointed toward the front door. "Just get the hell out!"

Payne saw that Austin was visibly shaking, beads of sweat forming on his brow.

Is that more of the mania manifesting itself?

Payne slipped his phone in his pocket and came out with a business card. He handed it to Grosse.

"I'd appreciate it if you called me later," he said, then glanced at Austin. "I'll let myself out."

VIII

[ONE]
Office of the First Deputy Police Commissioner
The Roundhouse
Eighth and Race Streets
Philadelphia
Saturday, January 7, 9:05 A.M.

The inner door of Dennis V. Coughlin's office was half open when Matt Payne stuck his head through it. He saw that Coughlin was seated at his desk, holding the receiver of his desktop telephone and nodding. Matt thought it was interesting that he was not in his usual suit and tie but instead wore his class "A" uniform, three gold stars shining on each epaulet of the dark jacket and on both collar points of his stiff white shirt.

"Okay, Jerry," Coughlin said as he began waving for Payne to enter, "I'll look into that before the presser and get back to you."

Press conference? Payne thought. *So, that explains the uniform.*

Coughlin put the receiver in its base as he looked up at Payne, who was sipping from a to-go cup imprinted with the logotype of the local Good Karma Café.

remembered Coughlin telling him, was that the mayor, who held the news media in utter contempt, regularly fired up his phone line, demanding, "Denny, are you seeing what those bastards are now broadcasting about us on the news?"

Coughlin added, "Are you getting any good leads?"

Payne shook his head. "A lot of leads that have gone nowhere. We finally interviewed the two women who had been in the bar with the dentist and went up with Camilla Rose to her condo. They're commercial realtors. They called in after hearing the news, then came in."

"And?"

"No smoking gun. Basically, they all just drank—and drank a lot. Their stories match the dentist's, and everything else we've established, including the time-stamped video of them staggering out of the lobby shortly before she died. The women were clearly devastated. They had even been planning to attend her fund-raiser tonight."

Payne glanced at his watch, and added, "Willie Lane is the last one from that crowd, and he's due in at ten o'clock for Tony to interview. Everyone he was with has been interviewed, and what few leads they gave us went nowhere. Hard to expect his will be any different."

"You never know. Still early, I would suggest. So, how is the wound? Besides freshly bandaged. The way you slowly lowered yourself into that chair was not lost on me."

"Better every day."

Coughlin studied him, his expression dubious, then said, "I damn sure hope so. That wound was bad enough, and easily could have been a lot worse. And I would have been the one obliged to break the news to your mother."

Payne nodded, and said, "I saw her at lunch yesterday, and she said to give you her love."

His mother, of course, hadn't, but he felt no guilt saying it because he knew she would have said exactly that had she known he would be seeing her son's godfather.

"Your mother is a wonderful lady."

"I brought up the Black Buddha—"

"You really have to insist on calling Jason that, Matty?"

"I don't understand why you object, Uncle Denny. He doesn't mind. And it fits him."

Coughlin, gesturing impatiently with his hand for Matt to continue, said, "Okay, so what about him?"

"When I mentioned *Jason*, Mom said something interesting that I wanted to ask you about."

"What?"

"I told her about how he came in at the top of the captain's list but apparently doesn't have a snowball's chance in hell getting promoted. And she said she remembered you and my father talking about it when you were blue shirts. That is, people getting frozen out of promotions."

Coughlin chuckled.

"What? Why's that funny?"

"It's not, Matty. I just had a flashback of all the Bushmills your pop and I put away at that wooden table in the kitchen. By God, we thought we solved, if not all, then many of the world's problems at that table."

"So she said."

"Solved a few cases there at that table, too. Anyway, Jack, your pop, to his credit, understood that early on."

"About getting frozen out?"

He looked at Payne, and nodded.

"Yeah. I suspect he got it from Dutch, who, as I'm sure you remember, was damn sharp. That's one reason why your uncle made commander of the Highway Patrol. Who knows how far he'd have risen had he not gotten killed by that punk at the diner. Same goes for your pop. Who knows how far? He was smarter than I was, and he'd probably have my job now."

Payne didn't know what to say and decided silence was best. He sipped his coffee.

"Even though I knew Jack was smarter," Coughlin went on, "I still was skeptical about people actually getting ahead who didn't deserve it, and others who had earned a promotion, genuinely deserved it, getting held back. But, hell, we were in our early twenties. I found out soon enough that even I could learn something new. Even today."

"Do you remember Tank Tankersley, big guy, retired from Homicide? Apparently has a multitude of ex-wives."

Coughlin nodded. "Absolutely. Good man. Great detective. I don't know about the ex-wives. But I can tell you that he got one lousy, rotten deal as a cop."

"So I heard. Peter introduced me to him. And told

me how, when Peter got into Internal Affairs, there was the story of Tank turning in the blue shirts who skimmed money and drugs they had seized in dead dealers' homes. Tank got painted as a gink."

Coughlin nodded again.

"One of the blue shirts was Harold Walker's son-in-law," he said.

Payne, taking another sip of coffee, almost sprayed it.

Wafflin' Walker? That sonofabitch!

That has to be one reason why Uncle Denny was pissed that they twisted his arm so that Walker reported to him.

"Walker was the one star in that story?"

Coughlin nodded.

"I heard that after that," Payne said, "Tank got passed over three times for promotion before tiring of the politics. He gave up and retired."

"As I said, he got a lousy, rotten deal."

Payne felt his phone vibrate.

"Sorry," he said, pulling it out.

Coughlin gestured that he understood.

Payne glanced at its screen. He grunted.

"What?" Coughlin said.

"Guess I'll be buying lunch. Looks like I won the over-under for Last Out with sixteen."

"Jesus, Matty," Coughlin said, shaking his head. "You ever give it a break?"

Payne looked up from his phone.

"Why? Payout's usually between two, three hundred bucks, cash. I'll find some place appropriate to donate it to, probably the Camilla's Kids fund-raiser tonight."

"Or maybe to one of the new scholarships for Police Explorer Cadets?" Coughlin said.

Payne's look was questioning.

Coughlin went on. "Someone in the bursar's office at Temple left me a message yesterday saying they had a question about the, quote, Moffitt brothers police scholarships, unquote. Putting Jack and Dutch together with the fact you're an Eagle Scout, I said they probably should ask you."

Coughlin hadn't been surprised to hear about the scholarships. In the last month, it had come to his attention that Payne quietly had been the one behind a new mentoring program for youth in Kensington, a hellhole neighborhood infamous for its street-corner drug dealers and the junkies overdosing on heroin in Needle Park.

The program's volunteers, most of whom were off-duty cops, worked with kids who were the product of single-mother homes and were otherwise destined to be lost to the streets—what Lieutenant Jason Washington described as "community policing, winning hearts and minds one at a time."

"I wondered how Temple got my number," Payne said, neither confirming nor denying responsibility. He went on. "The sixteen breaks down as four expiring and a dozen wounded. One of the dead was stabbed. And there was a double and a triple shooting. Busy night."

Coughlin sighed, and said, "Well, there won't be any lunch. Those sixteen are the reason—make that the *latest* reason—that Jerry is holding the presser for the noon newscasts. Big announcement on changes in the department."

"I guess that explains your uniform."

Coughlin nodded. "Yeah, and I'm afraid I've got some news that you won't want to hear. I damn sure didn't."

Payne took a long sip of coffee as he looked at Coughlin.

"Does it have something to do with today's big announcement?" Payne said.

"Indirectly, yes."

He paused to collect his thoughts, then went on. "Matty, it's interesting that you brought up Tank and Jason. And even Walker, for that matter. In each of those cases, there is an example of one having to deal with something that one has no control over. Tank, for example, had to deal with getting passed over. And Jason is dealing with a little of it, but I think with time he will get those captain bars."

"If too much time passes, he first will have to retake the exam," Payne said, "which doesn't seem at all fair."

"Life is not fair. You may want to write that down."

"You mentioned Wafflin' Walker?"

"He's my cross to bear. As you know, I'm not particularly thrilled he's reporting to me. I don't disagree with your nickname for him. But he has an in with Commissioner Mariana, who told me to deal with him. And I have."

"I'm guessing I'm about to have to swallow something."

Coughlin nodded.

"And it's interesting youse phrased it that way," he

said. "It's what Jerry said to me: 'Sometimes we all have to swallow something we don't like.' And let me tell you, Matty, I don't like it one damn bit. I made that clear to Jerry. I also made clear that I was going to be straight with you. What I'm telling you is not what I would do personally. But it's what I think you should know you can expect to happen."

Payne's eyebrows raised.

"Okay," he said, "I'm a big boy. What is it?"

"After last year's record homicides, and now this new year tracking to do the same, there is enormous pressure on Jerry to do something to lower the rate of violent crime."

"Especially if he expects to be reelected . . ."

Coughlin, meeting Payne's eyes, had a look of resignation.

"I told Jerry I wasn't going to beat around the bush with you," he said, "and I won't. You hit the nail on the head."

"It's not surprising. Every politician's priority from their first day in office is to get reelected."

"And this press conference is part of that." Coughlin paused, cleared his throat, and added, "As is having the Wyatt Earp of the Main Line resign."

Payne's eyes grew wide.

"What?" he said.

"I told you that you wouldn't like it. It's a lousy, rotten deal, Matty. No question."

Coughlin studied him, expecting Matt to explode any minute.

But he didn't. He simply shook his head in disgust.

"So, is Hizzoner going to announce I'm quitting?"

"Not today."

"And . . . if I don't obediently pack my bags and go away, Uncle Denny," he said, his tone even, "what then?"

"Think that through. It can get ugly, Matty. For starters, the citizen complaints against you have been steadily accumulating. They will be used against you."

"Those are bogus complaints. Most were made by ghetto ninjas." He paused, then added, "No income, no jobs."

"Still, if you were not to resign and those complaints were used against you—especially in this current hostile climate—that's all that's needed for a case to be made for suspension without pay for thirty days with intent to dismiss."

"That's, essentially, a firing, and a shitty way of firing."

"It's part of the process—"

"Which the FOP will fight tooth and nail, first in arbitration."

Payne did not have to state the obvious, that no matter what the Fraternal Order of Police accomplished, there would follow a lawsuit. One the city would have to settle for a high price.

"Some of the ugliness I mentioned," Coughlin said, "comes when there's generally the accusation made that the bad behavior happened because of failure of proper supervision."

"Oversight by my superior."

"It's one reason I said to think this through," Cough-lin said, nodding. "You really don't want Jason dragged unjustly through the mud. Among other things, that would very likely see his captain's bars even further de-layed . . ."

"This is bullshit!"

". . . And even if you win arbitration—and, frankly, I think that you would, and, further, that you should win—then it would just be hell coming to work. Car-lucci is a master, and the commissioner his puppet, and they'd see that your assignments ensured that you would be miserable."

Payne thought, *Jesus Christ. Here I thought it would be some petty prick like Wafflin' Walker who would come after me with knives sharpened.*

But it went all the way to the top.

Good ol' Hizzoner himself!

"Uncle Denny, I always felt there was a trust here. That sounds damn naïve now . . ."

"No, Matty, it's not. There is a trust. But when poli-tics is involved, and especially money and power, all bets are off."

Payne grunted again, loud this time.

"What?" Coughlin said.

"I know a little something about that. I just had, as a matter of fact, a similar conversation about trust when we were discussing the Morgan and Benson cases. And then there's Jeremiah's warning: 'The heart is deceitful above all things, and desperately wicked: who can know it?' Tank reminded me of that biblical gem. Fitting, huh?"

Coughlin sighed audibly.

"Matty, I can honestly say that Jerry had your back for a long time. I witnessed it firsthand. But he said that with the record killings year after year, and the public's perception of your shootings, the dynamic has suddenly changed. You should not take it personally that he's doing this. It's not about you. It's about the political perspective."

Payne, clearly in thought, was quiet for some time.

"I appreciate how you've handled this with me, Uncle Denny."

Coughlin nodded solemnly.

"What kind of time line are we looking at?" Payne said. "I'd like to see through Camilla Rose Morgan's case. I feel I owe it to her."

Coughlin shrugged.

"It's going to happen—Jerry as much as said it's a done deal—but not today, or tomorrow. I think I can buy you a little time." He paused, then added, "But, for the love of God, in the meantime just try and keep your head down."

Payne shook his head in resignation.

"This is bullshit," he said again.

"I know it is. But it's not the end of the world, Matty. Not like if that damn bullet had hit you elsewhere."

Payne sighed. He stared at his feet. His mind spun trying to process all of what had just happened. His ears rang.

First I have problems with Amanda, he thought. *And now this?*

I just can't fucking win.

But . . . I should have seen it coming.

He looked up and met Coughlin's eyes.

"I guess you're right, Uncle Denny. On all points."

[TWO]
The Rittenhouse Condominiums
Residence 2150
Center City
Philadelphia
Saturday, January 7, 9:15 A.M.

When Michael Grosse woke up and peered at the clock, he felt angry again. He had tossed and turned most of the night, unable to sleep as the anger built.

And now I've overslept, he thought.

Damn you, Johnny.

Grosse came out of his bedroom and found that the small flat-screen television hanging under the kitchen cabinets was on, its volume low. Grosse also saw that, next to the TV, the single-serve coffeemaker was on and warm, and he picked through the assortment of coffee cartridges. As the machine filled a white china cup and he smelled the rich dark blend, he glanced around the condominium and out at the balcony.

John Austin was nowhere in sight. But the two bottles of whisky that he consumed almost by himself were.

He has to have one killer hangover, Grosse thought.

Grosse picked up the steaming coffee cup and walked toward the bedroom that Austin was using. Its door was wide open, the lights on.

"Hey, you up?" he said. "We need to talk."

There was no answer. He sipped his coffee as he looked inside.

The bed was empty, its blankets pushed into a pile to one side of the mattress. The lights blazed in the bathroom, and when he looked in, there was a toilet kit on the counter and a toothbrush left in the sink. It was otherwise untouched. Towels still hung in neat rows on the wall rack, with another folded over the glass door of the shower.

Grosse felt a knot form in his stomach. He walked out of the bedroom.

"Johnny?" he called out, then repeated it louder. *"Johnny?"*

He went back to the kitchen and looked out the wall of windows. The sky was overcast, an ugly gray morning that looked bitter cold—and, he thought, depressing.

He ran his fingers through his hair, pulled out his cellular telephone, and tried calling Austin. Voice mail picked up on the third ring.

Grosse, thinking about all that Austin had said and done the previous night, began wondering how desperate he had become.

What the hell could he have done?

He put the phone on the island as he took a deep breath.

He glanced back out at the balcony—and his heart

sank. Against the glass panel wall, a white china coffee cup lay upside down.

Immediately after Matt Payne had left, Michael Grosse watched John Austin almost run into the kitchen. There, Austin fumbled pulling something from his pocket and eventually came up with a clear plastic bag containing a white powder. He removed a small knife from the stainless steel rack by the sink.

"Hey," Grosse said. "No more of that."

Austin ignored him. He poured a small pile on the counter.

Grosse marched into the kitchen and with a smooth, fast motion brushed the pile into the sink with his hand. He turned on the water.

"You son of a bitch!" Austin said.

"That shit has caused enough trouble, Johnny. You need to lay off."

Austin picked up the knife and held it tight as he concentrated on pouring another pile.

Grosse did not think that Austin would try to attack him, but it was clear the threat was made.

"You snort that, I'm calling Payne. I'm sick of this. You can spend the night in jail, for all I care. Then you can go back to rehab, or whatever."

Austin stopped. He turned his head and glared at Grosse.

"You don't like it," Grosse added, "then too goddamn bad. Call it tough love, or whatever else they say in rehab."

Austin stared at the bag in his hand.

"Have a drink, if you really need to self-medicate, Johnny. But not that."

Austin finally tossed the bag on the counter and started for the bar.

Grosse considered pouring that down the drain, too, but decided that could really cause Austin to turn violent.

"I understand you being upset about those pictures Matt Payne showed us," Grosse said as they stood on either side of the kitchen island, an almost empty bottle of Johnnie Walker between them. "But you have got to get yourself together."

"Easy for you to say. You didn't get 'lucky.'"

Austin took a big swallow from the drink he had just refreshed. Grosse saw that Austin's hand shook, and that, in addition to the deep bruising, he saw there was real anguish in his face.

"Johnny, you want to tell me about the money?"

"What money?"

"C'mon, man. First, the Morgan investments. And then that hundred-grand payoff that Payne said."

"I don't know."

"Damn you! I have to know. It involves Camilla Rose, and I'm here to start settling her affairs. Tell me now or I'll find out later."

Austin took a deep breath, slowly exhaling. Grosse could tell that he was considering what all he should share.

"In my private equity company," Austin began, his voice strained and uneven, "I set up funds that were venture capital vehicles for investing in real estate development, mostly high-rise buildings, and in start-up companies. I get investors to buy in. Camilla Rose was one of many—"

"I knew that," Grosse said, impatient.

"Including other private equity firms eager to place money in solid performing funds. What you may not know is that, over the years, Camilla Rose would oversee the investment of the Morgan International money, from which she would make her charity contributions. Morgan International moved money—the majority of it coming in cash, the rest stock in the Morgan parent company—into the philanthropy's accounts. Those funds were invested, and the dividends, the interest, et cetera, earned from those investments was what got distributed to charities."

"Okay."

"For the last five years, she has put tens of millions of the Morgan International philanthropy's money into my funds—like the recent Morgan Partners Florida Capital Fund III that funded the high-rise condo project on Biscayne Bay that's already sold out—which have been paying returns of fifteen to twenty percent—"

"Twenty percent!"

"And also gave some of the philanthropy's money to her own pet projects, such as Camilla's Kids and the cancer hospital. And then those charities had to have somewhere to park that money from the Morgan philanthropy, as well as the other monies that they raised."

"And so she also invested that in your funds."

"Not all of it, but enough. Because they were paying fifteen to twenty percent returns."

"She did not share this with me," Grosse said, sounding surprised, if not annoyed.

Austin took another gulp of his drink, and shrugged. "She didn't share it with anyone. Why would she? It was all really performing."

"I wonder what Mason Morgan thought of that."

"As far as I know, he thought nothing. Like I said, the funds were flush. The company accountants auditing her books were happy. So, he never said a word. But Camilla Rose knew it would piss Mason off no end if he knew that I was handling the money."

"Could he have overridden that?"

"If he wanted to push it. But I think he decided that it was a battle he didn't want to fight. She had already raised all kinds of hell about his hand in Old Man Morgan redoing the will. He left Camilla Rose alone."

"Until now," Grosse said. "He must have gone right to the books after she died, saw that she'd invested in your funds, and told the accountants to demand it back."

"Yeah, looks that way."

Austin met his eyes, then tensed up his bruised face and shook his head.

"But it's impossible to just pull out the money he wants," Austin said. "It's tied up."

"There's probably a huge early-withdrawal penalty . . ."

"Yeah, there is."

"What about offering to waive the penalty if they let

you return only a fraction of the investments? Mason might decide to wait."

"Not really possible."

"Why? Is there a problem?" Grosse said.

"The funds are illiquid."

"Illiquid? Why?"

Austin didn't answer.

"What is Camilla Rose's exposure?" Grosse said. "Twenty million?"

"Just over fifty mil of Camilla Rose's charities in the Trust III fund."

"Jesus Christ!"

"And another seventy mil, give or take, of the Morgan International's charity, the philanthropy's, in the Trust II fund."

"A hundred and twenty million? 'Give or take'?"

"I used some of the money to pay off the early investors their premiums, then put other money into projects, such as the Miami high-rise and Ming House here." He paused, then added, "And bought options on the Standard and Poor's index."

"Index options?" he said, shaking his head. "Are you serious? Betting on the market swing? For how much?"

Austin, crossing his arms, visibly started to shake. His eyes glistened.

"Twenty mil," he said, his voice strained. "The first time."

"And you lost your ass . . ."

Austin stared at him.

"All but two mil," he said. "But I got it back."

"And you bet again? Bigger?"

He nodded.

"How much?"

"I was on a roll—"

"How much?"

Austin began to weep.

"A hundred," he said, almost in a whisper.

Grosse felt the hairs on his neck stand up.

"A hundred million? My God . . ."

Austin tried to sound upbeat. "But I'm going to get that money back and more. I will."

"How?"

"I was planning on using proceeds from the sale of the Future Modular Manufacturing company and the stock in NextGenRx to cover the loss. NextGen, by itself, would more than cover it when the patents are approved and the stock soars. But the goddamn government keeps delaying that. So last month I started setting up another fund."

"Hold on a moment. Let me see if I have this straight. Because of this bind you got in, you're creating another fund to use to bail out—*illegally* bail out—the ones you took money from to pay artificially inflated returns and to gamble on the market."

Austin put his hands on his head, closed his eyes, and nodded. He wiped at his tears.

He opened his eyes, and blurted, "I could've easily ridden it out if Kenny and Camilla Rose were still alive!"

And then hunched over his big frame, his head in his arms on the counter, and began bawling.

"All I need," he added after a minute, "all I need is time. I . . . I still can do it."

Pathetic, Grosse thought, shaking his head in disgust as he looked at him.

"Jesus Christ," he said. "Stop conning yourself, Johnny. You don't have time. With Mason wanting back the investments, it's over. And wait until the Security and Exchange Commission gets a whiff." He paused, then jerked his head to look at Austin. "Did Camilla Rose know all about this?"

Austin stood back up from the counter, wincing as he rubbed his right arm. With a shaking left hand, he drained his drink and poured a fresh one.

"Johnny, did she?"

"Not all. She knew I was shorting. But just not to what degree. She was helping me with getting the Future Modular business to where it could be sold. And helping with NextGen."

"If she had found out she had that much exposure, that much risk, including her kid camps going broke . . . my God. What the hell were you thinking, Johnny?"

Austin met his eyes.

"I thought—no, I *knew,* because I already had been on a roll—that I was going to recover, get a windfall to make up for what Mason cheated her out of. Leverage the Morgan philanthropy money into a big payout that she could use to build more camps in other countries, like she wanted." He sighed, adding, "We were so close to telling that Mason to go fuck himself!"

Grosse was stunned at the depth of damage Austin had caused.

Grosse sipped his drink, and said, "I'm afraid to ask, but what about that hundred grand in cash that Payne brought up?"

"That's just chump change," Austin said. "It's grease to keep the union guys from squeaking."

"You're paying off the unions?"

"Have to," Austin said.

"What unions?"

Austin gave a brief explanation of his relationship with Willie Lane and Lane's close involvement with Joseph Fitzpatrick.

"We don't have union workers at the Future Modular plant in Miami," he explained. "And when we built the new plant up in Bucks County that's assembling the units for the hospital and the Chinatown condos, we brought in our own skilled laborers."

"Who aren't union?"

Austin nodded. "The higher cost difference would've been huge. We were stuck—and took a huge hit—using union workers to build the hospital and condo. But for the modular plant, it was cheaper paying off Joey Fitz and promising more later. Otherwise, they might've done a work stoppage, or even sabotaged the building worksites. I mean, they're already pissed off that the buildings' steel is coming from Korea, and that China's supplying all the materials for the modular units."

Austin drained his drink, then stared out at the balcony.

"A couple hundred grand doesn't seem to really matter now, though," he said, reaching for the bottle and realizing that it was empty.

Grossed watched as Austin looked toward the bar.

"More booze is not going to help anything," Grosse said. "The problems will still be here tomorrow."

Austin glared at him.

"I need to think about all this," Grosse went on, "and plan on what, if anything, I can do. I'm going to bed, Johnny. I suggest you do the same. And now."

Looking at the upside-down coffee cup, Michael Grosse now wondered if he had been too hard on Austin—and feared that the despondent Austin had done something really desperate.

He put down his coffee cup and went to the sliding glass door and through it. He tried to ignore the bitter cold as he quickly crossed the balcony and finally reached the glass railing.

His heart pounded as he looked over and down.

And saw nothing.

He realized he was holding his breath, then exhaled audibly. He realized he was shivering.

Oh, for chrissakes!

Damn that Johnny. That craziness can really be contagious. You start thinking like them . . .

Had I been thinking clearly I would've realized that if he'd actually jumped, there would've been police, ambulances, whatever.

Grosse heard his cellular telephone ringing on the kitchen island in the condominium. He walked back to get it. Just as the screen dimmed, he saw it had been Austin.

Well, at least the bastard is alive.

Why I care, I don't know.

Am I going to have to help him get Camilla Rose's money back?

A second later, the phone chimed, the screen showing a new voice mail message.

He tapped the glass face, and Austin's voice, its tone upbeat, came across the speakerphone: "Hey, you called me? I've got to take care of some things. All good. I'll call later."

Grosse shook his head as he put the phone down.

"'All good'?" Grosse said aloud. "Now he's all happy, like last night never happened? That bastard really is crazy."

He turned to the coffee machine and fed it another cartridge of dark-roasted coffee. As it hissed and filled the cup, his eyes went to the small television hanging under the cabinets.

Tuned to a local newscast, it showed video of a half-dozen police officers working behind a yellow tape imprinted POLICE LINE DO NOT CROSS. Then the same photograph of the two faces Payne had shown them appeared. He heard the well-built blonde anchor saying police needed help identifying them, then said something about the mayor scheduling a press conference at noon to address the city's record crime rate.

At the bottom of the screen, it flashed BREAKING NEWS! three times. The news ticker began its crawl, announcing POLICE CONFIRM 4 KILLED AND 16 WOUNDED IN OVERNIGHT VIOLENCE . . . SOURCE SAYS 2 FOUND YESTERDAY HANGING DEAD NEAR DELAWARE RIVER IN FISHTOWN HAD THEIR SKIN SHREDDED AND PEELED . . .

That caused him to remember that Payne had given him a business card and asked that he call. Grosse had decided he would pay him the courtesy but never had had the opportunity because of dealing with Austin.

He reached in his pocket and felt the stiff card was still tucked in his money clip.

He pulled it out and looked at it a long time. He picked up his cellular phone, then put it back down with the card.

He reached over and opened the flap of his well-worn brown saddleback briefcase. He removed from it a heavy file folder that was more than two inches thick.

He opened the folder, ran his finger down the printed sheet that had been Scotch-taped to the inside flap, and stopped at the contact information for Mason Morgan. He went over to the couch, picked up the telephone on the coffee table, and punched in Morgan's number.

"Good morning, Mr. Morgan," he said after a pause. "This is Michael Grosse—"

He paused and listened.

"Yes, I am calling from her condominium. Please accept my deepest condolences—"

He paused again to listen.

"That's correct. Please forgive me, as I realize this is

very last-minute and it's been some time since we spoke. But . . . could I perhaps impose on your time at your soonest convenience for a short talk? An *informal* talk?"

He paused, then replied, "Of course. A cup of coffee sounds perfect."

[THREE]
The Roundhouse
Eighth and Race Streets
Philadelphia
Saturday, January 7, 10:02 A.M

After a numb Matt Payne had left Denny Coughlin's office and eased the door closed behind him—he had feared he might snap and slam the damn thing shut—he crossed the curved hallway and went to the bank of curved exterior windows. He looked down at Race Street, to where his car was parked at the curb, then glanced across the street, off to the right, over Franklin Park.

Jesus! he thought. *What just happened?*

His mind was still spinning, his ears still ringing. His head felt hot, his temples throbbing with his rapid heartbeat.

It feels like my head is about to explode any second.

I need to get some air.

He turned and quickly followed the corridor around

to the stairwell and went down it as fast as he could, with every few steps feeling a sharp pain from his wound.

A blast of cold hit him as he went out the door of the front entrance. The air stung but also seemed to clear his head a little. He inhaled, and stopped walking. He looked for a minute at *The Friend*—the bronze statue of a uniformed Philadelphia policeman holding a young girl on his hip—before continuing down the steps to the sidewalk.

He walked past his car, heading toward Eighth. At the corner, out of mindless habit, he hit the button for the crosswalk signal, then, impatient, smacked it twice more.

Everything's broken in this damn city, he thought.

Aw, why do I bother? Screw it . . .

He started to step off the curb and cross the street before the traffic signal cycled—but was startled by two long loud blasts of an air horn on an eighteen-wheeled tractor-trailer rig.

He turned and saw the big rig slowly pulling onto Eighth Street through the fabric-covered chain-link fence of the House of Ming Condominiums construction site. The truck had an enormous empty flatbed trailer, which was rolling very close to the gate and a couple of parked pickups, one topped with a metal rack loaded with long iron pipes and the other covered with the blue-flame logotype of the city-owned Philadelphia Gas Works.

As the trailer cleared the pickups, and the gate, there came more honking, this time from behind the tractor-trailer. It was a steady, long blare from a smaller horn.

Suddenly, a black Chevy Tahoe shot out of the fencing and came around the tractor-trailer, then cut in front of it. Two cars coming down Eighth had to make evasive maneuvers to avoid hitting the SUV.

Just another jerk driver, Payne thought. *Breaking a half-dozen laws right in front of the Roundhouse.*

Insane . . .

The Tahoe ran the red light, its tires squealing as it took a fast left turn onto Race Street, flying right past Payne.

Sonofabitch! he thought when he got a clear look at the SUV's driver talking on a cellular telephone. *Even without the bruise, I could've made out who that is.*

What's Austin doing?

Payne watched as the speeding Tahoe passed where his Porsche was parked.

One damn way to find out . . .

He headed for his car.

Matt Payne, driving hard, caught up to John Austin's Tahoe right as it turned onto North Broad Street.

Staying almost a block back, he trailed it all the way up Broad, then out of the city.

Where the hell is he going? Not to Easton?

Payne glanced at his fuel gauge. The needle indicated he had only a quarter tank remaining.

I'll be on fumes if he does.

He plugged his phone into the console USB outlet, tapped the icon on the dash screen.

The sultry voice that sounded like Kathleen Turner filled the car. *"Yes, Marshal?"*

"Call Tony Harris's mobile."

There were two rings, then Harris's voice: "What can I do for you, Sergeant . . . boss . . . sir? How did your meeting with Coughlin go?"

Payne thought, *Well, he essentially told me that you won't be calling me boss much longer.*

He said, "I'll fill you in later. Right now, I'm tailing John Austin."

"Interesting. What is he up to?"

"He's going hammers of hell in a late-model black Tahoe. Headed toward Doylestown, maybe Easton. No idea why. But he's in a hurry."

"Anything I can do?"

"No, just keeping you updated. I'll let you know what happens. I'm guessing you have nothing new—"

"And you'd be wrong."

"What do you have?"

"I'm pretty sure I have a new sore on my ass from sitting here so long."

Payne heard McCrory in the background, laughing.

"And congratulations to you on that impressive achievement, Detective Harris."

"Actually, Matt, we got the vetting papers on Austin that Mason Morgan had sent over. I just skimmed them and am about to go back through them again. Was going to call you about it when I was done. It's got lots of detail on years ago, not so much lately. For what he probably paid for it, you'd think there'd be more. A helluva lot more."

"Mason told us he has not seen Austin for maybe five years, when Camilla Rose took off, too."

"Yeah. And this vetting pretty much peters out about four years ago. Guess Mason gave up worrying about Austin around that time. I'll see what I can find."

"Call if you need me."

"Will do, Matt."

For the next half hour, as the surroundings became more and more suburban, Payne kept focused on the taillights of the Tahoe—and on the dropping needle of his fuel gauge.

His brain still spun, but nowhere near as overwhelmingly as earlier, and he attributed that to the vehicle: Taking drives in the 911 always helped clear his mind.

Just south of Doylestown, driving past clump after clump of the usual mix of roadside stores—mostly fast-food joints and convenience stores—he began wondering if Austin just might be headed to Easton. Or farther.

He glanced again at the fuel gauge. The needle now touched the red zone.

This is not looking good, he thought just as the warning ping sounded and the exclamation point illuminated on the instrumentation. *Damn. Can't risk it much longer . . . but can't quit. He's up to something.*

Five miles later, near the exit for U.S. 202, Payne saw the Tahoe braking at a sign on the right that read BUCKS COUNTY HOME IMPROVEMENT.

It took Payne a couple seconds for it to register why the name seemed familiar.

So that's where the pressure washer trailer was stolen.

There can't be a connection between it and Austin. Can there?

Has to be coincidence . . .

Austin continued past the home improvement store, pulling into the parking lot of a mini-mart next door.

Payne saw that just beyond the mart was a gas station. He glanced at the fuel gauge. The needle sat as far as possible in the red.

"Damn. Too close."

Payne passed Austin as he entered the mart. He pulled up to a fuel pump island where he and the car would be mostly hidden if Austin happened to look that way when he came out.

As Payne filled the tank, he kept an eye on the mini-mart and the home improvement store. He tried to think if there was any significance to the fact that the equipment had been stolen way out here, some twenty-five miles north of the city, and way back in November.

What was their time line? Had the doers all along planned on using the pressure washer on the shooters strung up in the coal tower?

For two months?

Or had it simply been available, after having been stolen for some other purpose?

That text that fingered the shooters said they had acted on their own—"went rogue"—which really suggests a spur-of-the-moment act, not one more than a month in the making.

Austin came out of the mini-mart holding a small brown paper bag. Payne rushed to return the nozzle to the pump as he watched Austin pull a quart bottle of what looked like orange juice from the bag. Austin emptied about half of the bottle into a potted plant, got back in the SUV, and looked to be pouring two little bottles into the orange juice.

Making himself a screwdriver breakfast, Payne thought.

More miniatures for the self-medicating. Probably got them from Camilla Rose. Or she got hers from him.

Payne, watching as Austin's Tahoe blew past, put the car in gear and started rolling. He looked in the mirror for traffic, saw it was clear, then glanced back at the home improvement store. He decided if it worked out, he would stop there on the way back.

Spend ten minutes or so, ask a few questions, see if there are any stones under the stone that could be turned over.

Austin took the exit for U.S. 202, heading east toward New Hope.

So he's not going to Easton, Payne thought, hitting his turn signal to follow him.

After a mile or so, Payne saw the Tahoe's brake lights come on, and then, ahead of it, saw a line of slowing traffic. He could see up ahead, at the top of the rise, the emergency-flashing light bar on a police cruiser that had stopped on the roadway.

As the stop-and-go traffic crept closer, Payne saw an officer standing beside the cruiser, a silver Dodge sedan with DOYLESTOWN TOWNSHIP POLICE covering its side in bold, reflective lettering. He was directing a line of eighteen-wheeled tractor-trailer rigs that was exiting a manufacturing facility about thirty yards off the highway on the right.

On the browned-grass shoulder of the highway on the far side of the big rigs, he caught a glimpse of a folded-over, half-inflated cartoon animal that looked to be about the size of a school bus. Around it were a dozen beefy men—all wearing bulky winter coats and distinctive red hats—a few of whom were busy getting the animal fully inflated while the others set up folding chairs and coolers nearby.

What the hell is that inflatable thing doing out here?

Looks like one of those jump houses for a kid's birthday party.

The big-rig trucks rolled out and turned onto U.S. 202, headed in Payne's direction. He saw that they carried identical cargoes—enormous pods, shrink-wrapped in plastic, that hung over the sides of the trailers.

And he realized that the trucks were more or less identical to the one that had driven out of the construction site right before Austin raced out of it. Including signage on the driver's door reading FMM, LLC, DOYLESTOWN, PENNA.

After the last of ten trucks passed and the cop directed traffic to begin moving, Payne saw Austin turn the Tahoe in the plant's entrance.

Payne slowed and looked as he approached the entrance. There were steel gates on either side of a guard shack, one an entrance, one an exit, both now closed. On the shack was signage that read FUTURE MODULAR MANUFACTURING, LLC. / NO VISITORS / NO TRESPASSING.

A gate opened, and the guard waved with his clip-board for the Tahoe to enter.

Payne tried to get a better look at what was inside, but the solid fencing blocked his view. Then he heard the angry screech of a whistle being blown, and, when he looked, he saw the traffic cop by his bumper, motion-ing for him to move along.

Payne looked at the men setting up along the road-side. Two were pulling red signs from the metal rack of a pickup truck. Their red hats had bold white lettering that read PLUMBERS UNION LOCAL 324.

Payne drove up to the next large intersection and turned around.

Approaching the entrance again, he pulled into a fast-food joint's parking lot across the street from the plant, stopping when he had a clear view of the guard shack and gates.

He also had a perfect view of the inflatable cartoon animal, now almost fully blown up and rocking in the cold wind. What he saw was the exact opposite of kid-friendly. It was a rabid, teeth-baring rodent. And it held a red sign identical to those the men held: DON'T BE A RAT! UNION JOBS FOR UNION WORKERS!

Payne shut off the engine and studied the protesters.

He picked up his phone—the dash had gone dark with the ignition key off—and texted Tony Harris. *Please ask McCrory to see what he can dig up on Future Modular Manufacturing in Doylestown. And what, if any, connection to John Austin he can find.*

Payne settled back in his seat to keep watch on the

plant's guard shack. His mind drifted back to his meeting with Denny Coughlin, and ten or so minutes after considering all that had happened, he wondered if he should share it with Amanda. He decided that that could wait, at least until after Carlucci's press conference.

With the backed-up traffic finally cleared, the cop got in his car and drove off. Shortly after that, the protesters started marching back and forth in front of the entrance to the plant.

Payne's phone rang and he picked it up.

"What did Dick find out, Tony?"

"He's still working on it. But I just got word we ID'd the fat guy in the coal tower by his fingerprints. And his blood matched what was found in the back of the stolen van, so that backs up that anonymous text saying he's the shooter. Also, Krowczyk said that when they first looked at the cell tower dump from Thursday—specifically, at the window between twelve hundred to fourteen hundred hours—the burner flip phone recovered in the van is definitely on it. No surprise there—"

"Yeah. And?"

"And when they cracked that phone, all that was on it was a series of texts from one specific number—another burner phone that also was listed on the tower dump—a half hour before the shooting, then another text every five minutes right up until the shooting."

"Someone at The Rittenhouse was a lookout."

"That's what it smells like to me, too, Matt. But good luck tracking them down."

"So, who was the shooter?"

"One Daniels, Scott J., white male, age forty-one, with an address in South Philly. He had a meaty rap sheet. Mostly minor offenses. But one was for assault. He beat the living hell out of a construction worker with an iron pipe. Served six months of an eighteen-month sentence, got released three months ago. Still working on getting an ID on the smaller guy."

"Ugly way to go," Payne said, watching the line of marching protesters. "But looks like the bastard got as good as he gave."

"Dumbasses went rogue," Payne thought again. *"There could be others, but we'll handle it."*

Harris said, "I'll let you know what Dick comes up with."

There was a long silence.

"You still there, Matt?"

"Yeah. That construction worker this Daniels thug beat up. Was he union?"

"You mean, like an electrical union guy?"

"Or plumbers, carpenters . . ."

"I don't know. Can check. Why would it matter?"

"Never know, right? Stone under the stone and all."

Harris grunted.

"Must be a real challenge being a wiseass all the time, Sergeant . . . boss . . . sir."

"Sorry. Having a bad day."

Payne saw the exit gate start opening and the nose of the Tahoe pulling up. The Tahoe pulled through it, followed by a Mercedes-Benz SUV.

As the vehicles approached U.S. 202, the protesters,

two of whom were using cellular phones to take videos, hurried over to block them, then jumped out of the way when the SUVs accelerated.

Payne saw Austin at the wheel of the Tahoe as it turned onto the highway, headed back toward Philly. Then he saw the other driver.

"I'll be damned," he said aloud.

"What?" Harris said.

"New development. Ask McCrory to expand on that last request to include one Willie Lane."

"I could have asked him in the interview, but he postponed it."

"That's because I just saw him here with Austin," Payne said, starting the car and pulling onto the highway.

[FOUR]
One Freedom Place
Fifty-sixth Floor
Center City
Philadelphia
Saturday, January 7, 10:35 A.M.

"I do very much appreciate you taking time out of what I'm sure is a busy weekend," Michael Grosse said.

He followed Mason Morgan across the high-ceilinged office while looking out the enormous wall of windows that reached floor to ceiling. Morgan waved him into

one of the two overstuffed leather-upholstered armchairs in front of the desk.

"Happy to oblige," Morgan said as he gestured
toward the silver coffee service that was on the polished-
granite desktop. "How do you take yours, Mr. Grosse?"

"Black, thank you. And, please, call me Michael."

Grosse—whose regular routine in Florida found him
running on the beach or surfing or working out in his
private gym when it stormed—could not help but be
baffled by Morgan's obvious disdain for exercise.

How could someone with so much be so obese? Grosse
thought.

*He's got to be pushing two-fifty. It just hangs in folds,
from his jowls to those huge hips. Makes him look a lot older
than forty-something.*

*Is chasing money at the expense of your health really
that important?*

Get off your arrogant fat ass . . .

Morgan picked up the insulated, silver-plated carafe,
filled two fine-china cups, and placed one at the edge of
the desk before Grosse.

Morgan went behind his desk, lowered himself into
the leather judge's chair, then sipped his cup while waiting for Grosse to speak.

"As I'm here to begin getting Camilla Rose's affairs
in order," Grosse began, leaving his coffee untouched,
"I thought that there were a number of items you should
be made aware of before they became publicly known to
all." He paused, then added, "To give you time to pre-
pare for them, as opposed to being blindsided."

Mason Morgan nodded.

"That is quite considerate, Michael. And, frankly, unusual. I am not accustomed to such." He paused again,
then said, "Forgive me for asking, but do you feel comfortable doing that? Is it . . . ethical?"

*You're questioning my ethics? Screw you, you pompous,
arrogant ass!*

"Of course," Grosse said. "Absolutely ethical. These
events have already happened. And I am not violating
any lawyer-client privilege."

"I'm afraid I don't follow you."

"My office received from Morgan International's
charity office a copy of the notice sent to John Austin
demanding the return of its investments."

"It was absolutely necessary," Mason Morgan said,
stone-faced, his tone equal parts officious and defensive.
"As was the timing. And, I'm sure you'll agree, there
never is a good time for that sort of large-scale financial
separation."

"I do understand. Minimizing the pain is akin to the
docking of a dog's tail. Far better to do it all at once
than a little at a time."

Morgan made a face that suggested he found the
analogy distasteful, which pleased Grosse.

"As it's often said," Mason went on, "and quite cor-
rectly, I might add—it's not personal, it's business."

Grosse pursed his lips and nodded.

And you said that with a straight face, he thought.

Johnny was right about at least one thing. You are *a
fucking prick.*

"I did mention the notice to Mr. Austin last night when I arrived," Grosse went on. "He was not yet aware of it. Understandable, I think you would agree, considering the recent circumstances."

"True. I heard he was badly injured in the attack. But . . . I am sure he has staff he can direct to execute the necessary papers."

"He does have the staff," Grosse said, pausing before adding, "What he doesn't have is the funds."

"I'm sorry? What?"

Michael Grosse explained.

As he spoke, he could see anger building in the red-faced Morgan. When Grosse had finished, Morgan's entire body appeared to quiver.

"Absolutely incredible!" Mason Morgan exploded, his jowls shaking. "I anticipated bad things coming because of him. But not *this* bad. Now Camilla Rose is dead. And more than a hundred million dollars squandered."

"Mr. Austin did say she was not aware of his actions," Grosse said. "And, for what it's worth, I believe him. I certainly was unaware. She told me nothing, even as I arranged for some of her own personal investments."

Morgan was silent as he stared across the room. His face grew deeper and deeper red.

"Well," he said, "perhaps the saddest part is that her legacy, her children's charities, will be lost along with the money. Such a shame."

Grosse, shocked, just stared at Morgan.

You won't make sure that the philanthropy continues to fund that?

You would punish not only her memory but also all the sick children her work helps?

You are worse than a miserable prick . . .

An indignant Mason went on. "I will see that that son of a bitch Austin goes to jail and that they throw away the key!"

"I'm pretty sure that between the charges that will be brought by the Manhattan U.S. attorney's office and the Securities and Exchange Commission, that that will happen with or without your, no doubt, wide influence."

Mason Morgan's cold eyes glared at Grosse.

He put down his coffee cup.

"If there is nothing else," Morgan said as he began to get to his feet.

"Just one more bit of business . . ." Grosse said.

Morgan dropped his enormous frame back down, causing the big chair to rock under the suddenly returning weight.

"Yes? What is it?"

Grosse reached into his briefcase and removed the thick folder from earlier.

Mason Morgan saw that it was legal-pad size, its edges worn. There was a faded yellow label on the upper left tab: MORGAN, CAMILLA ROSE.

Grosse took out a sheet, and said, "This is something, I suppose, that might be most surprising."

"More than the lost hundred million? How is that possible?"

Grosse leaned forward and slid the sheet across the

desktop. As he did so, Morgan took a look—and his eyes began darting over it.

Morgan saw that it appeared to be some sort of government document. He saw "City of Philadelphia Marriage License Bureau—City Hall, Room 415." He noted that it was an officially attested copy, with an original signature in ink and a seal, and dated five years earlier.

Grosse watched, impressed that Morgan's expression, except for the darting eyes, remained unchanged.

After Morgan appeared to be finished scanning it, he looked up at Grosse, who produced a second sheet from the folder. Grosse slid the marriage license back and pushed the second sheet in front of Morgan.

"If you wish to keep these," Grosse said in a reasonable tone, "I have additional exemplified copies in my office." When Mason did not respond, he added, "Either way, I will see that copies are delivered to your legal department."

Morgan picked up and studied the second sheet. It was a certificate of marriage dated a week after the marriage license and signed by a Philadelphia justice of the peace.

"Who is this fellow, this O'Keefe?" Morgan finally said, putting the sheet of paper back on the desk.

"A very fine gentleman from a well-known and respected family in Orange County."

"Pennsylvania? There isn't an Orange—"

"California," Grosse said. "Camilla Rose was married in a quiet ceremony to the young man, James O'Keefe, who she met out there. He founded a Silicon

Valley start-up that had bid on a project for her camp on Monterey Bay."

Grosse, producing a third sheet of paper, went on. "They traveled widely for a while. Camilla Rose wanted to expand her camps to other countries. That got postponed because"—he slid the paper toward Morgan and watched his eyes slowly open wide—"exactly ten months later, she gave birth to a son, Harold Thomas Morgan II."

He paused, letting the name sink in.

Morgan saw that there was bold lettering at its top reading STATE OF CALIFORNIA, and there was an embossed official seal at the bottom. Mason picked it up and studied it, his eyes focusing on CERTIFICATE OF LIVE BIRTH.

"This child is now age three," Morgan said.

Grosse pointed to the birth date on the document.

"Turns four next month," he said.

Morgan's eyes went from Grosse to the birth certificate, and he shook his head just perceptibly before he slid it back.

"Unfortunately," Grosse said, then slid a final sheet across the desk, "the union was not to last."

Morgan saw that it was a court document, a certified page titled FINAL DECREE OF DIVORCE.

"The separation was by mutual consent," Grosse said, "with Camilla Rose waiving custody and visitation rights, although she could have had either if she wanted."

"She did *not* have issue!" Morgan blurted. "This is a sham!"

Grosse nodded thoughtfully.

"Camilla Rose thought it highly possible you might react that way. Great care was taken in securing irrefutable proof, beginning with all the proper documentation and ending with DNA samples. She even made sure that the marriage and divorce both took place here in Philly to ensure no out-of-state legal issues."

Grosse put his hand on the folder, and said, "In here are all the agreements and trusts for Camilla Rose's son. In a nutshell, they provide the boy with reasonable expenses until age thirty-five and then he gets the entire five hundred million—"

"What?"

"Plus whatever has not been released from the interest over the years to support Camilla Rose's charities," Grosse finished.

"I will have to have my legal team review any such purported papers before—"

"What you will have," Grosse interrupted, "with all due respect, is what I give you, Mason. I will petition the court to admit the Last Will and Testament of Harold Thomas Morgan for probate."

Mason Morgan, red-faced and breaking out in a cold sweat, looked off in the distance. His body began quivering again. He half closed his eyes and rubbed his neck. He groaned—and fell forward, his face striking the coffee cup, spilling it across the desk.

Grosse jumped to his feet. He rushed around the desk.

"Mason?" he said, feeling for a pulse.

Grosse grabbed the receiver of the desktop telephone and dialed 911.

IX

"Newscast's about to come back from the commercial break," Matt Payne called from the doorway of Lieutenant Jason Washington's glass-walled office in the Homicide Unit. Harold Kennedy and Hank Nasuti stood behind him talking next to the flat-screen television in the corner.

Dick McCrory and Tony Harris, at a desk across the room, got to their feet, Harris hanging up the desk phone while McCrory folded closed his notebook computer and tucked it under his arm.

They made it to the crowded office just as an attractive brunette talking head on the TV announced, "We're about to go live to City Hall, where Mayor Jerome Carlucci is scheduled to address the continuing soaring rate of vicious crimes in the City of Brotherly Love."

"Hey, that reminds me, Sarge, congrats on winning the over-under," Harold Kennedy, glancing at Hank Nasuti, said. "Who would've thought sixteen?"

"I thought you got banned from the pool," Nasuti said. "You've won, what, twice?"

"Why would I be banned?" Payne said.

"I just heard someone saying, 'Stop taking that Wyatt Earp of the Main Line's money.'"

"Because?" Kennedy said.

"'The marshal always bets high,' the guy said."

"How is that bad? Anyone can bet high."

"But with his reputation as a quick draw," Nasuti said, "he can influence the over-under by shooting someone."

Kennedy chuckled. "You're not saying he'd kill to win the bet?"

"Doesn't have to. Over-under is the number of homicides and shootings combined. Just has to wing one. Or two. Or if he really wants a sure win, trigger an O.K. Corral shoot-out in the 'hood."

Payne chuckled, then make a fist with the middle finger extended toward him.

"Matt," Harris said, "that was The Krow on the phone just now. They couldn't get anything off Camilla Rose Morgan's phone. Just too badly damaged from the impact."

"Great," Payne said, shaking his head.

"I've got good news," McCrory said, gesturing with the computer. "Found that Future Modular Manufacturing is owned by Austin Capital Ventures, which, of course, has John T. Austin shown as its president, slash, chief executive officer. One of the stories said the plant was built there in Doylestown to supply materials for a

Camilla's Kids camp near the Delaware north of New Hope. Now it's supplying the high-rise condo project across the street from here and the cancer research addition at Hahnemann's."

"Well, that begins to explain the connection," Payne said.

"I didn't find a connection with Willie Lane. But did you know he's got a gig with United Workers paying sixty-large?"

"Yep. And you can blame that on our fine city council members for making it legal to have jobs outside City Hall. Unions, especially Joey Fitz's, love Lane. And people wonder why this city is a disaster."

"You said you lost Lane in traffic?" Harris said.

"Yeah, he and Austin were going hammers of hell to get away from the protesters—almost clipped a couple of them who were taking pictures—and then, right as we got back in Philly, I got stuck behind two of the eighteen-wheelers that wound up crossways in an intersection. That was the last I saw of them."

McCrory said, "And, Matt, that guy you asked about who got bludgeoned by that thug Daniels? He was a non-union carpenter going to work when Daniels, a union plumber, took a pipe to him."

Payne, rubbing his face, nodded thoughtfully.

Heads turned to the TV as the image on it switched to what they recognized as the Mayor's Reception Room.

"Here we go," Kennedy said.

The ornate second-floor room appeared to have changed little since it was completed in 1890. It had rich

Honduran mahogany wainscoting. A grand chandelier hung from its two-story-high ceiling. And its walls held gold-leaf-framed oil paintings of former mayors of Philadelphia, who seemed to be looking down upon the proceedings.

Mayor Carlucci stood behind the wide mahogany lectern, on the front of which was a heavy bronze replica of the seal of the City of Philadelphia. Behind him, standing in front of a United States flag, were Police Commissioner Ralph Mariani and First Deputy Police Commissioner Denny Coughlin. On the other side, in front of the blue-and-gold-striped flag bearing the crest of the City of Philadelphia, stood three members of the city council who comprised the Public Safety Committee.

"There's the Black Budda talking with Coughlin," Payne said.

Jason Washington had leaned in close to Coughlin and was quietly speaking into ear. He then stepped out of frame.

"And look who just showed up," Payne said.

Willie Lane could be seen crossing the thick black-and-gold-patterned carpet. Lane joined the council members by the flag, positioning himself as the one closest to the mayor.

"Now you know why he was driving so fast," Harris said. "He's never been one to miss a photo op."

"You know, that's really one fancy room," Kennedy announced. "I heard that Carlucci spends the thousand bucks a day they get for renting it out on those slick suits and haircuts of his."

"Funny, I heard it was on hookers," McCrory said, snorting at his own joke.

"Well, it ain't finding its way into my paycheck," Nasuti chimed in. "I can tell you that for a fact."

They all chuckled.

"Hey, clam up," McCrory said as Carlucci reached up and tapped the microphones. "Time for the big address."

"Whoopee!" Payne said. "More hot air from Hizzoner."

Harris looked at him askance.

"Not a fan of his lately, eh?"

"Certainly not today. Probably not tomorrow, either. But let's see what he says."

Carlucci leaned into the microphones and in a deep, dramatic voice said, "Operation Thunder Road begins today."

"Anybody know about this?" Kennedy said.

"Nothing," McCrory said. "Seems we're always last to be told anything."

Payne and Harris shook their heads.

"Some months ago," Carlucci went on, "I quietly asked the Honorable Randle Bailey, Esquire, to spearhead an exploratory team."

A heavyset male stepped into frame, stopping almost directly behind Carlucci. He was in his mid-sixties. He wore a baggy two-piece suit, the jacket of which was pulled taut over his ample belly, looking ready to pop its two buttons. He had wisps of silver hair that tended to flop from one side of his scalp to the other. His beady dark eyes were set deep in a liver-spotted face.

Carlucci turned and took a long time shaking Randle's hand while they both mugged for the media.

"That Bailey," Harris said. "Yet another who just loves to be in front of the cameras."

"That is when Randy Randle's not groping the almost attractive women behind the cameras," Payne said.

"*Almost attractive?*" Harris parroted.

Payne grinned. "They apparently like the attention, and don't complain. It's when Randy Randle plays grab ass with the pretty ones—literally, gets touchy-feely—that the complaints start. He really has a thing for TV reporters, preferably the hot blonde ones, something that goes beyond his usual perversion."

"This *usual perversion* being . . . ?"

"What you said, his insatiable hunger for seeing himself on TV."

McCrory said, "I thought he lost his gig with the D.C. national political committee for doing exactly that, groping the local affiliate's ace reporter?"

"Dick, in Washington circles you get brownie points for that sort of behavior. The trick is, you have to do it *after* you're elected. Not like, say, that slick lawyer who, while running for president, knocked up his aide—which we later learned about shortly before his wife was diagnosed with terminal cancer."

Harris said, "Yeah. A real class act. No end of those types."

"And each party has its share," Payne said. "We just seem to have more than most in Philly."

Carlucci turned back to the microphones.

"As you know," he said, "Randle Bailey has long been a friend of our great city, first serving as the Philadelphia district attorney before becoming mayor. He then went on to be governor of the Commonwealth of Pennsylvania. I think that it goes without saying that Randle has unique insight into what works here in our historic home."

McCrory said, "That baggy suit of Bailey's looks like it was cut from a circus tent."

"Ha!" Kennedy said. "He could be a carny. Anyone want to start a betting pool for when he drops the first word that gets bleeped? First minute, second, third? Then how often each minute? He really lets them fly."

"I'm in," Nasuti said, pulling a dollar bill from his pocket, holding it out to Kennedy.

Kennedy, grinning, waved it away.

"In addition to the serious high crime rate we struggle with," Carlucci went on, "there is a confidence issue concerning our police department. Some people have gone so far as to describe it as a trust that's broken. We intend, beginning right now, to fix that, to regain the public's full faith. I assure you that we will get to the root of these problems."

"That's easy," McCrory said, "The problem is dietary. It's always something from the three major food groups—drugs, money, weapons."

Carlucci said, "These challenges are not unique to our city, of course. Others wrestle with it, too. But I was elected to lead. And that is why I recruited Randle Bailey. The result of his task force's work is Operation Thunder

Road, which will define law and order. We are assigning more veteran officers on Last Out, the midnight-to-eight shift when most violent crime occurs. Additionally, we are going to put two hundred academy grads on foot beats in crime hot spots. They will be supported by forty patrol cars rolling through known problem areas. Highway Patrol's elite officers will be a constant sight."

"Well, that's a good start, Jerry," Payne said. "But I bet it will result in more shootings—"

"You should know, Marshal," Nasuti said, grinning.

"And how can you field academy grads when no one is getting recruited?"

"To support this," Carlucci said, "as of today, those applying for consideration to join the department will no longer need college credits. A high school diploma or equivalent will suffice. There will also be a minimum age of twenty-two. And a new starting salary of fifty thousand dollars. Also, we are suspending the requirement that officers must live within the Philadelphia city limits."

"Jesus H. Christ!" Harris said. "Now, that's a huge one-eighty he's taking. Carlucci was the one who championed the higher standards."

"I've been told, in no uncertain terms," Payne said, "that he's under tremendous pressure to do something if he expects to get reelected. He's apparently taking a number of actions he otherwise wouldn't."

When a couple heads turned to look at him, Payne added, "You didn't hear that from me. And I damn sure never said it."

Carlucci said, "Many other changes are being weighed and will be announced at a later date . . ."

All heads were now turned to look back at Payne.

". . . We are confident that with these new changes we will fill the next class at the police academy with exceptional recruits who, after rigorous training, will complement all members of our exceptional police department."

"Does he really believe what he's saying?" McCrory said.

Carlucci looked around, then said, "Finally, I'm confident everyone will recognize, and welcome, the well-regarded Margaret Hart, who for twenty years was one of our city's distinguished news anchors, before transitioning to talk radio . . ."

"Carlucci hates that woman," Harris blurted. "When he was the commish, Maggie Hart called him out on everything. What else is he going to roll over for?"

Payne raised a brow but said nothing.

"Ms. Hart," the mayor said, "is joining the department as chief of the Communications Unit, which oversees Public Affairs. I believe we all can agree that Ms. Hart enjoys a genuine connection with our fellow citizens, who now will find her the confident, trusted face of the Philadelphia Police Department."

"My God," McCrory added, "she's the best face he could find? Her looks started going south in her thirties. By the time Baggy-eyed Maggie hit forty, you cursed the day they invented these high-definition televisions. When she finally got booted from TV—all the peroxide in the world couldn't save her—radio was her only real option."

"Wasn't there a rumor that she and Randle had a fling years ago?" Harris said.

"I think you're right," Payne said. "And that sure would go a long way in explaining why she just got a nice two-hundred-grand do-nothing job from a city so deep in the red that it owes the pension fund six billion."

"Okay," Mayor Carlucci said, "I am told that we have time for a few questions."

"Mr. Mayor," a female voice said, "what is your response to the charge from the Concerned Citizens for Philadelphia that your announcement today of this new operation is a false flag to take the focus off the recent pay-for-play accusations made against you."

Carlucci flashed a big smile.

"I'm afraid I don't understand the question. What does this have to do with Operation Thunder Road?"

"My point precisely!" the female reporter said. "And there is the fact that you recently added to your staff two of Francis Fuller's high-ranking executives who continue being paid by his corporate office. You just mentioned the public's lack of faith. Shouldn't these staffers have taken a leave of their company, at the very least, to avoid the appearance of undue influence on city business by Fuller—"

Carlucci's face flushed. "That is preposterous!"

"And gone so far as to put their holdings in a blind trust so as to avoid any suggestion of personally enriching themselves while in office?" she finished.

"And that's absolutely disingenuous," Carlucci said. "Putting one's investments in a blind trust does not stop one from being corrupt—"

"Mr. Mayor," a male reporter interrupted, "then you *are* admitting that there's corruption in your office?"

"That's an outrageous suggestion!" Carlucci said as a slender, dark-haired thirty-year-old executive in a well-cut conservative suit stepped up. "You're leaping to conclusions!"

"Ah, here's Mr. Stein now," the reporter said.

Chief Executive Advisor Edward Stein, Esquire, tugged at Carlucci's jacket sleeve, and Carlucci stepped back from the microphones.

There arose a chorus of reporter voices: "Mr. Stein, Mr. Stein—"

Margaret Hart worked her way up to the microphones.

"I'll be happy to take questions about today's announcement of Operation Thunder Road," she said. "Anyone?"

The look on Carlucci's face was a mix of shock and anger. Stein grabbed him by the shoulder and ushered him toward the exit.

When the camera cut to the city council members, Willie Lane appeared to be holding back a thin smile.

So, Payne thought, *a heavy dose of karma for Hizzoner.*

How's that working out for you, Jerry?

Maybe it is a good thing I'm getting forced out of here . . .

Payne's phone vibrated, and he glanced at it.

"Matt Payne," he said.

"Matt, Mason Morgan just had a heart attack," Aimee Wolter said, her usual upbeat voice now a monotone.

"That's impossible," Payne heard himself reply with the first thing that popped to mind. "You have to have a heart for that to happen."

He saw that that crack had gotten the attention of the others in the office.

"Wiseass," Wolter said. "But I take your point . . ."

"Was it adequate?" he went on.

"What do you mean, *adequate*?"

"Everyone's always saying, 'So-and-so died today of a *massive* heart attack,' when it really just takes an *adequate* one . . ."

There were chuckles around the room.

"Dead is dead," Payne finished. "But, then again, Mason is himself rather massive."

Payne noticed that Harris had turned his head at hearing Mason Morgan had had a massive heart attack.

"Jesus, Matt, who pissed in your coffee?" Aimee snapped. "He's not dead. He's having emergency surgery at Hahnemann. I think stents, to open some blockage." She sighed. "Look, I need you to come to my office. Michael Grosse is here. He said you wanted to talk. And you damn sure need to hear what he has to say."

"Sure. Be right there."

[TWO]
House of Ming Condominiums
Ninth and Vine Streets
Chinatown
Philadelphia
Saturday, January 7, 12:55 P.M.

"Call me when you get this damn message, Willie," John Austin barked into his cellular telephone as he raced up Ninth in the Tahoe. "I don't care about your public appearances. Something's going down. I got a text message that there's been an emergency at the Ming Condo site. Call me."

Austin broke off that call, then sneezed twice as he tried the project manager's number again.

"Damn it! No answer!" he said, sniffling and rubbing his nose.

He turned off Ninth onto the crushed-stone-drive entrance, tires crunching as he pulled through the open double-door gates.

"What the hell?" he said aloud as he scanned the construction site. "Emergency? Nothing's happening. Looks like there's no one here."

He braked hard, the SUV sliding to a stop behind one of the eighteen-wheeled tractor-trailers. It had a plastic-shrink-wrapped pod still strapped to its trailer. He grabbed the gearshift with his right hand and slammed it up into park.

A burning pain shot through his injured right arm.

"Damn it!" he said, cradling it with his left arm.

He used his left hand to open the driver's door, then stepped out.

Scanning the area, he could not believe his eyes.

"It's a goddamn ghost town," he muttered.

He looked ahead of the big tractor-trailer rig and counted the nine others that had left Doylestown that morning. The very first one in line was parked beside the condominium's main tower, where the bare iron-beamed skeleton of the building rose above the bottom three floors, which were mostly finished. The modular unit on the trailer had had its shrink-wrapping removed and had the lifting apparatus at the end of the tower crane's cable attached to it.

Yet, the crane was silent. And when Austin looked up, he couldn't see anyone in the operator's cabin.

He sneezed three times, then, squeezing each nostril in turn, exhaled and shot mucus onto the bare-dirt ground.

Damn, I'm getting a cold, too? he thought.

He walked around the site for five or so minutes, becoming more and more furious, then headed for the main construction office, which had been housed inside a section of the ground floor that had been completed.

His telephone rang as he entered an exterior door.

"Jesus Christ, Willie," he said, answering the call as

he walked inside and proceeded to cross a large open area. "What does that son of a bitch want from me?"

"Johnny, he said he didn't do it."

"Oh, c'mon, I'm not stupid. Someone had to send those union bastards out there to protest—"

"He agreed, and said he would find out and get back to me."

"And now there's a work stoppage!" Austin went on. "I don't believe him!"

Willie Lane sighed.

"Johnny, I guarantee you that Joey Fitz would tell me, and he said that he had nothing to do with it."

"And I'm saying that's bullshit! I'm at the construction site, and there is no one on the job."

"No shit?"

"Yeah, no shit."

"No one?"

"It's a ghost town."

"It's Saturday afternoon. Maybe they knocked off at noon? They are union, you know."

"Yeah, I fuckin' know!"

Austin reached the project manager's office. Above the window in the door the sign read CONSTRUCTION OFFICE / RESTRICTED AREA.

As Austin reached for the doorknob and found it unlocked, he thought he detected an odd smell. He looked through the window. It was dark inside.

"Look," Lane said, "I don't know what else to tell you. And I—"

"Hang on a second," Austin said.

He slipped the telephone into his shirt pocket and reached inside the door with his left arm, swiping at the wall for the light switch.

His fingers found it.

The office's overhead fluorescent blubs flickered on—and, a split second after that, from deep within the office came a deafening explosion. It blasted through the walls and blew out windows, its white-hot fiery plume incinerating everything in its path.

Eight blocks away at City Hall, Willie Lane jerked the phone from his head when he heard the loud boom. He stared at the phone as the windows nearby rattled.

When he put the phone back to his ear, there was only silence.

[THREE]
Dignatio Worldwide
Third and Arch Streets
Old City
Philadelphia
Saturday, January 7, 1:10 P.M.

"You know, Matt, that Aimee is the chair of the board of directors of Camilla's Kids," Michael Grosse said, sitting at the head of the conference table. "But Camilla Rose also made Aimee the alternate executor, after me, of her estate. Aimee, of course, has long been made privy to all legal and financial matters concerning the charity. And now, as the process of getting Camilla Rose's affairs in order begins, I'm sharing all I know with Aimee."

Aimee Wolter sat to Grosse's right, across from Matt Payne.

"Particularly, the financial irregularities," she said.

Payne's expression questioned this.

"It should go without saying that we've always had Camilla Rose's best interests in mind," Grosse said. "That cannot be said for others."

"It's not pretty, Matt," Aimee said. "In fact, it's criminal. And it's why I've asked Michael to share with you everything he's told me. I think it could help explain what happened with Camilla Rose."

"I hope so," Payne said, "because I have to tell you it's not looking good. There's that short gap in time that we simply can't find out what happened. One of our big hopes was what we'd find on her phone. But The Krow—he's one of my techs, supersharp—said that it was completely destroyed in the fall."

Wolter thought about that, then said, "How do I know that if you find a killer, it won't reflect badly on Camilla Rose?"

Payne locked eyes with her.

"I don't know if it will or it won't. That is out of my control. My job is to hunt down the miserable sonsofbitches who take others' lives. There's a Homicide saying that goes *I speak for the dead*. That may seem trite to some, but it's absolutely true. I give a voice to those who cannot defend themselves from the grave. Camilla Rose had her issues, but I don't think suicide was one of them, and I'm doing my best to find out what happened."

Wolter nodded.

"And I commend you," she said. "I do. But you said it's out of your control, if you find a killer, that it reflects badly on Camilla Rose . . ."

"Yes. Not that that's what I want. I count myself among her big fans."

"But, you see, it's not out of *my* control. I get paid a lot of money by important people to control the message. That's what I do, Matt, and I'm damn good at it. And right now it looks best for Camilla Rose, for her legacy, to have people believe the best. If there's a killer, I'll work around that, put her in the best light. But if you don't find one, then the narrative is that it was simply a tragic accident. She slipped. She's gone. And her kindness will continue to give to those in need. End of story."

Payne nodded.

Aimee went on. "If there is some miserable son of a bitch, to borrow your words, indeed responsible for doing that to Camilla Rose, I want him to pay, to suffer the consequences—and more. I just don't think, depending on what is learned, that there's any good reason to drag her through the mud."

"You say that like you know there's an ugly story." He paused, then added, "There was coke and Ecstasy— MDMA, the synthetic psychoactive—found in her place. The *MA*'s short for *methamphetamine*. So speed with a hallucinogenic twist. For all we know, she may have thought she could fly. Toxicology tests will detect what she took, if anything."

Michael Grosse said, "Johnny was snorting something last night. I assumed it was coke."

"Well, he's easily the source. But being in a hospital bed when she died clears him. At least of that."

"I don't know of an *ugly story*," Aimee said. "As far as I know—and I like to think that I know her very well—there's not one. And I personally have never seen her with drugs." She sighed. "Let's be realistic. I've done damage control for families who had loved ones murdered. You and I know that if someone did kill her, the odds against finding that person are high. What's that saying about the low clearance rate for homicides? *Three out of four murderers walk.*"

"Unfortunately, true. And it looks like Camilla Rose is likely going to become a cold case."

"As long as I can keep her name clear. I am not going to let anyone drag her name through the mud. She was an angel, a kind, caring, beautiful creature."

She turned to Grosse, and said, "Fill Matt in, please."

Fifteen minutes later, as Payne placed the birth certificate for Harold Thomas Morgan II on the conference table, he looked back and forth between Michael Grosse and Aimee Wolter.

"I don't know what to say. Camilla Rose certainly

was one of a kind. And that Austin . . . a hundred million bucks. Jesus."

"Johnny really went off the deep end when Camilla Rose got married," Aimee said. "Let's just say he was not sorry it ended in divorce. And when it did, he spent enormous energy trying to win her over."

"By exacting revenge on Mason Morgan," Payne said.

"Yes," Grosse said, "of which Camilla Rose was innocent. Her only, quote, crime, unquote, was caring too much about helping others. Unfortunately, including Johnny Austin."

"So," Payne said, tapping the birth certificate, "she had the child in wedlock, which means she met the provision of her father's reworked will."

"That's right."

"So the quarterly payments continue."

The lawyer shook his head.

"No?" Payne said. "Why not? She had issue."

"Yes. But it's not the payments the child gets. It's the entire principle that had created those million-dollar quarterly payments. They're shares in Morgan International, which are currently worth just over five hundred million dollars."

"A half-billion dollars," Payne said. "That's a fraction of what the company's worth."

"True," Aimee said. "But it's a lot of money, by anyone's count."

"Camilla Rose had trusts set up for her son. Some controlled the bulk of wealth, others her charities. They are structured to fund the camps entirely and to provide for the boy's reasonable needs, with him gaining access to all the principle at age thirty-five."

"The age she was when she died," Payne said. "And having the child . . . Do you think she did that just to spite Mason?"

Aimee said, "No, Matt . . . Well, yes, there was some of that . . . But she really wanted to have a child. She wanted to try to be a better mother than she had had."

"Tragic," Payne said, then heard Camilla Rose's voice in his head: *I don't think I'm cut out to be an everyday mother.*

Payne felt his phone vibrate.

"Sorry," he said, pulling it from his pocket. He glanced at the text message, boxed in red: *It's Ryan . . . FYI . . . Was gonna work valet at Bellevue tonight but heard rumor something bad might go down. Same guy who said he'd heard about that $100K from Morgan woman.*

"Well, this isn't good news," Payne said.

"What, Matt?" Aimee said.

"There's a kid I know casually who's putting himself through La Salle working part-time as a car valet. He says he was going to work tonight's event but got word something's going to happen."

"Could it be just someone talking?" Grosse said.

"Always could be that. And it could be a solid tip. His last one was. Service industry people are a tight community."

Payne began writing an e-mail.

"There will be a lot of cops there, escorting the VIPs," Aimee said.

"Guys working for Dignitary Protection," Payne said, nodding. "I'm sending a note now alerting the guy in charge of that."

"Earlier today," Grosse said when Payne put down his phone, "I put in a call to Tom Brahman."

"That Texan venture capitalist?" Payne said. "My guys never got their messages returned."

"No disrespect intended, but they're cops. And I'm a lawyer representing the heiress of a billionaire, among other wealthy clients. My calls tend to get returned promptly."

Payne made a face, and nodded. "Good point."

"I found it very interesting that Kenny Benson would accuse Tom of a short and distort in a filing with the Securities and Exchange Commission when it turns out that he apparently was doing exactly the opposite with NextGenRx."

"Why do you say that?" Payne said.

"Slideware," Grosse said.

"I haven't heard this," Aimee said.

"Brahman said he wanted to believe in Benson's technology, wanted to invest, and, of course, have it make a fortune. He's one of about seven hundred venture capital firms in the U.S. They invest some fifty billion bucks each year. Seeing, say, mere millions go up in smoke when a start-up dies, well, that's just the cost of doing business. Because the others are going to make money."

"But not NextGen," Aimee said.

Grosse shook his head.

"Brahman said his research people found that devices

measuring glucose through noninvasive methods simply don't work. That's a basic science that the fanciest computer coder cannot replicate. And that makes this Next-Gen contact lens just another so-called brilliant breakthrough known as slideware."

"*Slideware?*" Payne repeated.

"Yeah. That's what Silicon Valley calls things that work only in PowerPoint presentations. Nothing is going to replace the definitive testing of the glucose in blood because that's the most accurate reading of glucose levels. While, yes, there is glucose in tear fluid, its levels are easily altered by humidity and temperature and other factors. Not so with actual genuine blood."

"And that's what the scientist who committed suicide learned the hard way," Payne said. "So they were working a pump and dump."

"Brahman also told me John Austin is not a huge player. He cherry-picks the smaller venture capital types, as opposed to the enormous institutional investors, which have layers of oversight and don't invest off-the-cuff. But smaller shops can—and do. Especially when it's with a known name."

"Such as Morgan," Payne said, nodding.

"What Johnny does is solicit contributors to his funds with the Morgan name. They are legit funds—for example, Morgan Partners Florida Capital Fund III—but they're philanthropy funds that Camilla Rose controlled, not Morgan International's. He doesn't outright misrepresent the funds, as such, but he also doesn't go out of his way to disabuse investors, should they think that. He's promising people fifteen to twenty percent returns when the market is offering everyday investors three, four if they're lucky."

"It's a Ponzi scheme," Payne said.

"Pure and simple. Paying early investors high rates with the money from new investors who don't have a snowball's chance in hell of seeing even zero percent."

"How did that happen? You said even people who should know better got suckered by him."

"Camilla Rose had the latitude. Mason's hands were full, and, according to Austin, she raised enough hell about their father's will being changed that he decided it was a battle best not fought. So she gave the money to Austin, who used it to pay the high returns, which, in turn, brought in more investors."

He paused, then reached in his briefcase, pulling out what Payne recognized as a prospectus.

"You have heard, I trust, of the phrase *buyer beware*?" Grosse said.

Payne nodded.

"Austin's fancy version of that is: 'While we do our best to offer outstanding investment opportunities, we also make sure the buyer knows that nothing is guaranteed.'"

Grosse picked up the prospectus and began reading aloud. "'All potential investors in our offering (hereafter The Fund), before buying any security or investment instrument, must read and understand the entire prospectus and any memorandum. Be aware that these will contain what are known as forward-looking statements. And that these statements address the performance of investments into the future and are OPINIONS of the company. At the time of offering, these OPINIONS are considered factual BUT are subject to influences beyond The Fund's control, to include economic, business, and other unknowns that could effect the performance of The Fund.'"

He looked at Payne, and added, "Et cetera, et cetera."

Payne nodded. "So if the market tanks, or another bubble bursts, you've been warned."

"More or less. Certainly cautioned. What they like calling *an abundance of caution*. No one could sue for fraudulent enticement. But the investors, after hearing a twenty percent return, their eyes glaze over the fine print. Greed gets 'em every time. Even people who know better."

"Unbelievable," Payne said, shaking his head. "Austin raked in all that money, made a billion-dollar gamble, and blew it by going cheap—by not hiring union workers. It brought down his whole house of cards."

"And would have brought down Camilla Rose, had she not taken my advice and let me invest her personal funds."

Michael Grosse began returning the papers to his briefcase.

"Austin can't survive this," he said, "not when Morgan's lawyers get the feds involved. I wouldn't be surprised if he calls them from the hospital. Taking everything Johnny said at face value—which, I grant you, isn't exactly wise, but, in this case, it's adequate. Considering all he admitted to, he is looking at doing serious time."

"Yet he still thinks he can recover," Payne said, "pull a hundred-million-dollar rabbit out of his hat."

Grosse nodded, and began to say, "Well, he got away with it a long—"

Their heads all turned as they heard a thundering *Boom!* in the distance.

The lights dimmed. Windows rattled. Car horns up and down the street began honking.

Explosion, Payne thought. *Those are car alarms it triggered.*

"What the hell was that?" Michael Grosse blurted.

"Something big just blew up," Payne said, getting to his feet. "Could just be another of those PECO underground power transformers. Infrastructure in this city needs a lot of work. I'll be in touch."

[FOUR]
The Bellevue
200 South Broad Street
Center City
Philadelphia
Saturday, January 7, 8:55 P.M.

"It has not been a bad crowd, considering the circumstances," Aimee Wolter said, taking a sip from her martini. "A lot of cancellations—including Stan Colt, thank God, who *did* write a big check—but that's not surprising. Camilla Rose was the real draw."

She was standing with Sergeant Matt Payne and

Inspector Peter Wohl, both impeccably dressed in black tie and dinner jackets. They surrounded a high table covered with a white tablecloth near one of the eight well-stocked open bars. Between Payne and Wohl were drinks, two club sodas with lime in highball glasses, meant to suggest cocktails.

"I'd write that big check just to keep that pervert Colt away," Payne said, causing Aimee to laugh.

Matt Payne looked around the grand ballroom. In addition to blue shirts posted outside, including the immaculately dressed Highway Patrol, there were a dozen plainclothes detectives spread out among the two hundred attendees.

His eye stopped at Willie Lane, who was seated at his table, staring at a cocktail glass. Payne noted that he had been going to the bar often, and, judging by how long the bartender kept the bottles upended, ordering doubles or triples. A waiter, a teenage male with a short black ponytail and carrying a couple pitchers of water, was making another cycle around the table, topping off glasses.

Surprising to Payne, the dinner had been better than expected—he had devoured his filet mignon and grilled asparagus—and the comments from the four after-dinner speakers were mercifully short.

There had followed an onstage skit performed by a score of children who had attended Camilla's Kids Camps, and, after they had exited stage right—a few children in wheelchairs with IV drip lines hanging from bottles above their heads—the master of ceremony announcing over the applause that there would be a fifteen-minute break before the final presentation.

When the MC added that the open bars were awaiting, Payne had quietly said to Wohl, "Liquor becomes very cheap when it helps people write bigger checks than they would sober."

"It's been an impressive crowd," Wohl said. "All A-listers."

Payne grunted. "It's shocking—*shocking*, I say—who shows up when the party thrower is heiress to a fortune . . . and spends all her time deciding to whom she will donate."

Aimee chuckled.

"To include politicians," Wohl said.

"To *especially* include politicians," Aimee said.

"I heard that our distinguished former D.A., slash, mayor, slash, governor is in the house," Wohl said.

"He is," Payne said. "And you're right about *heard*. You're likely to hear Randle Bailey, Esquire, before you see him. Just listen for the growl of a guy letting loose with a string of profanities. If that doesn't narrow the crowd down enough, look for the dumpy, silver-haired guy whose baggy suit looks like, as McCrory said, it was *tailored from a circus tent*—"

Aimee Wolter leaned in close, and whispered, "He gives me the creeps . . . And I can handle anyone."

"A different-colored circus tent, from today's press conference."

"Speaking of circuses," Wohl said, "what about the elephant in the room?"

"What elephant?"

"Coughlin brought me up to speed on your meeting today."

"It's bullshit, Peter."

"Agreed."

Payne looked past him and saw Amy Payne coming toward them.

"Hold that thought," Payne said. "My sister's coming back from powdering her nose."

Aimee Wolter looked back and forth between them but decided not to ask.

Amy went up to Matt and put her hand on his sleeve and looked at Wolter and Wohl.

"I need a word with my brother. Would you please excuse us a second?" Amy said, pulling him aside.

"What'd I do now?" Matt said, when they stopped twenty feet away.

"I've been meaning to share something with you. And when I began missing Amanda here beside you . . . I suppose I'm not surprised Amanda did not come with you . . . I decided now was as good a time as any."

"Her plane landed in Texas this afternoon," Matt said.

"That was fast."

"Yeah," Matt said, the emotion evident in his voice.

"You shouldn't be upset, Matt. What's happening with her is to be expected."

"Mood swings?"

"Yes," Amy said. "You can expect hormonal levels to fluctuate wildly, affecting the level of neurotransmitters.

It can take weeks for the body to return to normal. The enormous surge of hormones in the first trimester is the worst. Remember how exhausted she'd been, and the nausea she went through. It was a roller coaster—excitement, then worry, then feelings of delight, followed by fear."

"And, boy, was it."

"And now it's panic attacks, depression, anxiety. Her taking this time alone I see as a selfless thing. She is sparing you."

Payne's eyes scanned the ballroom. "How?"

"By going through it alone. Not having you suffer, too."

"But I want to be there for her."

Amy nodded. "I know, Matt. And I wouldn't expect any less of you. But she's a tough one. Always has been. You can help her by being understanding. In a very real sense, those hormonal surges are no different than the chemical imbalances in the brain that cause mental illness."

"A *temporary insanity*?"

"I wouldn't term it that. Look, just know it's not her fault. The best you can do is be tender and patient until her body gets back to normal."

Payne was quiet.

"What are you thinking, Matt?"

"That I now appreciate why certain cultures segregated women from the general population and put them in menstrual huts on the far edge of their villages."

Amy shook her head.

"Those primitive practices are still in use. But don't be a caveman, Matt, if only for Amanda's sake."

As they rejoined the others, Aimee Wolters said, "Camilla Rose raised funds for everyone who opposed him in his mayoral and gubernatorial runs."

"Him *who*?" Payne said.

"Bailey," Aimee said. "It's hard, though."

"Raising money?" Wohl said.

She laughed.

"No, that's the easy part. What's hard is picking which of the pols is worthy of your support. Which ones can pass your smell test. Bailey didn't. But it didn't matter. Because he had Frank Fuller's machine."

"Five-F was the money behind him?" Payne said.

"Frank Fuller, and everyone who wanted to please Fuller. He starting raising money for Bailey behind the scenes after Fuller convinced him that he should run for Philly district attorney. Then he got Joey Fitz—Fuller owns all the unions, more or less, with the exception of the teachers, thanks to them working for his various companies, from the carpenters and electricians building his skyscrapers to the longshoremen—to rally behind him for mayor. Mayor Bailey, after eight years of spreading the city's wealth among his supporters—"

"Five-F and friends," Payne put in.

Wolter nodded. "And the unions, and passing out patronage no-show jobs to family and friends. You know, the usual. After eight years of that, with Fuller's machine laying the groundwork for a run on Harrisburg, Bailey announced his candidacy for governor. Meantime, anticipating that there would be a vacancy at the top in City Hall, Fuller went to work behind the scenes."

"He went to Carlucci?" Payne said.

"Not directly. He sent an intermediary," Wolter said. "Fuller and Carlucci are polar opposites. Plus, Carlucci, as police commissioner, had the reputation as a law-and-order hardass and couldn't be perceived as being bought."

"Perceived?" Payne parroted.

"Matt," Wohl said evenly, "every damn politician owes somebody something. You should write that down. It's simply a matter of how they pay that debt."

"Which is what got Bailey in trouble," Wolter said. "He put too many operatives in state jobs, and the kickbacks and bribes went off the charts. Bailey would have moved on to Washington, but there simply was too much stink sticking to him. He's lucky he didn't go to jail. So he crawled back to his law firm and now plays the wise elder statesman as he quietly works the machine, facilitating for Fuller and friends, doing their bidding."

Aimee nodded toward the corner of the room.

"And with the primaries coming," she said, "you can expect to see a lot more of that."

They all looked and saw Bailey having a quiet conversation with Carlucci.

Wolter added, "I give you the Commonwealth of Pennsylvania's former governor speaking with its presumed soon-to-be governor."

"My God," Payne said.

"Well, you can always come up with your own candidate," Wolter said, and brightened and smiled. "As a matter of fact, why don't you run, Matt? If you do, I'll be your campaign manager."

"Hey, now, that's not a bad idea," Wohl said. "You got my vote."

"Mine, too, baby brother," Amy Payne said a little too quickly.

"No way. Not no but *hell* no," Payne said. "The whole political mind-set is alien to me. I can't lie like they can, for starters. And what Peter said about being indebted to someone for his support, I refuse. I like having a clear conscience and being able to sleep at night."

"I expected you to say that," Wolter said. "But it's part of my job to test the waters. See who might be looking to do whatever."

"Really?" Payne said.

"Oh, not just for political office," she said. "I have powerful clients of all stripes who are always looking for select new people."

Payne nodded.

"But don't worry about not running for office," she went on. "There are plenty who are willing." She nodded across the room again. "There's Rapp Badde, for example. He is attending tonight not only because Camilla Rose supported his PEGI, which, in turn, introduced him to new investors for those urban-renewal projects, he's also here mostly because he had been pitching her to back his run for mayor after Carlucci has moved up the political food chain. He's been terrified she would back Willie Lane."

"Jesus," Payne said. "He's exactly what this city *doesn't* need. His father was a disaster as mayor. Almost as bad as Willie Lane's old man. Why in hell would she consider supporting either of them?"

"But those two disasters made it easy for Carlucci to get elected," Wohl said. "Were they bright enough, they might call it a case of unintended consequences."

"True," Wolter said. "And it will flip. After eight years of Jerry Carlucci, with the memory of the average Philly voter having a half-life of maybe six months, if not six minutes, another Badde or Lane will slide right in. So, they're both here because it just looks good for them to be part of this. It gives them a little cachet, and eventually, they hope, a lot of campaign cash, thanks to this chance to network—"

The lights flickered and dimmed.

"Damn," Payne said. "I was hoping for another explosion."

"That's bad, Matt," his sister said.

"Here comes the big sales pitch," Aimee Wolter said. "Cross your fingers."

On a half-dozen projection screens around the big room, Camilla Rose Morgan appeared. The murmuring crowd quieted.

"I've seen this video," Payne said, then added, "I think. Looks a little different. That looks like Pennsylvania."

"It's the New Hope camp," Aimee said. "We just opened it."

Camilla Rose was clad in the same crisp khaki shorts and white T-shirt, and ball cap with the logotype CA-MILLA'S KIDS CAMPS on it, and smiling at the camera. Behind her, a dozen helmet-wearing kids were riding horses along a wide river. Camilla Rose waved as her voice filled the ballroom:

"Hi, I'm Camilla Rose. Welcome to New Hope, the aptly named home to one of my four ACC-accredited camps for children with extreme medical challenges. At each of these twenty-million-dollar wonderlands, sixty kids come every week to experience the excitement of the unexpected.

"Our superb staff counselors, one staffer for every three campers, are rigorously vetted. Our state-of-the-art medical facility features a full-time physician and nurse, plus volunteer doctors and nurses, who specialize in the disease of each week's group of kids.

"Campers' needs are constantly monitored. They're provided their daily medications and procedures—from chemo to dialysis—then they head out for a full day of sun and fun. Here in Bucks County, Pennsylvania, for example, there's horseback riding, fishing in the Delaware River, crafts workshops, and much more. After dinners, we gather round the campfire for singing and skits and laughs. Lots and lots of the latter, as laughter is the best medicine. Just ask the campers themselves."

"Similar script to the one I saw on her Florida camp," Payne said to Wohl. "As I said last time, reminds me a great deal of Scout camp . . . with sick kids. Wait until you see what comes next."

The image of Camilla Rose was replaced with a young

girl with a sweet, engaging smile and very bright eyes and a very bald head.

The girl then said, her voice squeaking with emotion, *"I just had to say thank you for the best time I have ever had in my whole life! I didn't know it was possible to do all the fun things you taught me. I learned so much about staying strong and getting better. Thanks to you, no matter what, I'll always be a Camilla's Can-Do Kid forever!"*

Camilla Rose came back on-screen.

"Little Heather fought her cancer for four brave years. Then, a month after she became, as she said, a Camilla's Can-Do Kid forever, *she passed away."*

There were gasps as well as soft moans from the crowd. A man two tables over blew his nose.

"Jesus Christ!" Payne muttered. "That part was left out of the version I saw."

Camilla Rose came back on screen.

"And so you have some small idea of the impact that you can have on a child who may have lost all hope in life.

"Coming from a business background, I understand it is important for our corporation to be good neighbors, to give back to our community. Yet, while we are all very good at what we produce, we may have limited ability to vet the many charities that ask for support.

"In selecting a charity—which, essentially, will be viewed as an extension of your company—it is extremely important to align with one that will protect your company's image, its brand. You want something that will make your employees to say not only do they support something they're proud of but that they're excited to do it.

"*Here at Camilla's Kids Camps, our organization is completely open. We're ethical. Fiscally responsible. Transparent.*

"*And as to how we do, our campers say it all.*"

Camilla Rose held up a small note card, and, her voice on the verge of cracking, said it was one of many she received from parents. She read from it: "*Cassidy cried all the way home. She did not want to leave camp. She told us proudly that she wanted to always be a Camilla's Can-Do Kid. Thank you and your supporters who make the miracle camp possible.*"

Camilla Rose looked at the camera, and said, "*Yes, thank you, supporters, for your generosity tonight. We could not do it without you. Thank you for coming. Good night.*"

As the houselights in the ballroom came up, Payne heard Aimee Wolter and his sister sniffling.

"Rough, huh?" Payne said, pulling a white handkerchief from the inside of his coat pocket and offering it to Aimee. His sister already had a cocktail napkin to her nose.

She waved, declining the handkerchief.

"Thanks," she said. "I'll be okay. That just gets me every time. Camilla Rose was such a kindhearted person."

Payne scanned the room. People, pulling out checkbooks and credit cards, were beginning to crowd tables along the red carpet.

Payne quickly scanned the room again until he found Willie Lane. He saw him moving toward a back exit door. Payne's eyes went to the waiter, who he saw watching

Lane. The waiter then put down the tray of water glasses, pulled out the flip phone, and discreetly thumbed its keypad.

"I'll be right back," Payne said, and walked over to one of the undercover officers.

"Hey, Marshal, some video, huh? Got me choked up—"

"Yeah. See that kid over there, the waiter with the ponytail . . . ?"

"Sure."

"Take him aside and hold him till I get back. Don't let him touch his cell phone."

"Detain him? You got it."

Payne moved quickly to the exit.

Willie Lane was in the lobby, headed for the revolving front doors. Payne followed.

Outside, Payne stopped at the top of the stairs. He saw Lane down by the valet kiosk next to a heavy stone pillar. He was handing the valet a paper parking stub and pointing past the row of sparkling Highway Patrol Harley-Davidsons to his Mercedes-Benz parked nearby.

The valet grabbed the vehicle's keys from the kiosk's lockbox, then trotted to the SUV as Lane waited beside the pillar.

Payne scanned the immediate area, saw nothing unusual—then heard the racing of an engine coming south down Broad. He looked that direction and saw a dark blue Chrysler minivan flying up, the right-side door sliding wide open.

"Get down!" Payne shouted as he ran down the flight of ten steps.

Payne saw an arm extend from the open door of the van, a large black pistol in its hand.

Payne pushed Lane to the ground behind the heavy stone pillar, then pulled his Colt .45 from his shoulder holster.

As the gunman in the minivan began firing rapidly, Payne went down to one knee beside the pillar and took aim. He had a clear view of the driver and squeezed off two shots, then, as the van passed, finally had a full view of the shooter in the back—and emptied the magazine.

The horn of the minivan began blowing steadily, and the van swerved, striking a light pole. The impact crushed the front end, the sudden stop causing the sliding door to slam shut.

Payne, running at a crouch toward the van, kept focused on it while automatically ejecting and pocketing the magazine from the Colt, inserting a fresh one, then dropping the locked-open slide to chamber a round.

As he approached the minivan, he saw a pistol lying in the shadows at the curb—and, a few feet from it, a severed hand.

Payne went to the driver's side, scanning the interior of the vehicle as he went. There was no movement.

He threw open the driver's door—and found a middle-aged male slumped over the console, blood and gray matter from his head wound soaking the front seats.

Payne fought back his gag reflex and looked in the backseat. The shooter wasn't moving, either.

Payne heard the thunderous sound of multiple heavy footfalls. He looked and saw a small army of officers running toward him.

He thumbed the hammer lock upward on his Colt and slid the weapon back in his shoulder holster.

A young blue shirt came around the rear of the minivan.

"You gonna need a paramedic?" he said. When Payne looked at him, the officer added, "An ambulance?"

"Driver's dead. Check the shooter in back."

"No, I mean for you," he said, gesturing toward Payne's midsection.

Payne looked down and saw a circle of blood.

"Shit," he said, and as he pulled back his jacket he realized that his hands were shaking. He now felt an ache from under his bandage, but there were no new holes in his clothing. "I'm good."

"I'll say," the blue shirt said, opening the sliding door on the left side, then reaching in to feel for a pulse. "Man, you're really good. Two for two."

"Well, I think I just signed, sealed, and delivered my departure, Peter," Matt said as they stood watching yellow police tape being strung up. "It's not been twelve hours since Uncle Denny said to keep my nose clean. Carlucci is going to blow his cork."

"I wouldn't worry too much. Carlucci is busy putting out other fires."

"Yeah, and the clever sonofabitch will use this to deflect from the pay for play. 'Today, I fired Wyatt Earp.'"

The undercover officer came out with the teenage waiter in handcuffs.

"He had a flip phone," Payne said.

The undercover officer handed it to Payne, who scrolled to the most recent texts.

"I needed the money," the teenager said. "I didn't know this was going to happen."

"What did you think was going to happen?" Payne said.

The kid shrugged. "They said they were going to have a surprise for Councilman Lane."

Payne snorted. "And, boy, did they."

Payne hit the key that dialed the number. A telephone began ringing on the floorboard of the front seat.

The kid lost all color in his face.

ONE WEEK LATER

[ONE]
Police Administration Building
Eighth and Race Streets
Philadelphia
Monday, January 16, 1:21 P.M.

There was a double knock at the inner door of the office.

"What is it?" First Deputy Police Commissioner Dennis V. Coughlin said without looking up from the report he was reading at his desk.

"Inspector Wohl's here."

"Well, send him in."

The volume on the television across the room was low, and Coughlin heard the *Philly News Now* anchor announce: *"A visibly angry Mayor Carlucci today denied allegations of so-called influence peddling in his office. He has ordered an outside independent investigation into those allegations. And he dismissed as ridiculous the calls for his resignation."*

Coughlin heard Carlucci's voice and looked up at the TV.

The mayor, standing outside City Hall, was speaking into a half-dozen foam-ball-covered microphones that were held up to his face. *"And this is nothing but petty partisan politics. I brought to this office a long history of law and order and can assure you that all accusations will be found to be completely without merit. My good name and that of this office will be cleared of any wrongdoing."*

Edward Stein appeared in the shot as he put a hand on Carlucci's shoulder and began guiding him away.

"Thank you all very much," Stein said, leaning into the microphones. *"That's it for questions today. The mayor's office will release a press release shortly. Thank you."*

Coughlin thumbed the MUTE button on the remote control as the office door opened and Peter Wohl entered.

Wohl was wearing a well-tailored, two-piece dark gray woolen suit—and, Coughlin noted, an unusual expression. He carried a white No. 10 envelope in a somewhat delicate manner, as if he did not want any part of it.

Coughlin got to his feet and came out from behind his desk.

"Everything okay, Peter?" Coughlin said. "You look like somebody died."

"It's nothing quite that dire."

Coughlin tapped the report he had been reading. "If it hadn't been for Matty, Willie Lane would not be able to say the same."

Wohl gestured for him to continue.

"The two Matty shot who were trying to whack Willie Lane were union guys angry about their coworkers in the coal tower. When the photographs got circulated showing Lane almost running down the protesters in Doylestown, it got worse. Joey Fitz said the two in the minivan were out for revenge."

Wohl shook his head. "Makes you wonder about what happened with the explosion across the street. Gas Works said it was simply substandard iron gas pipe. Blamed it on China. Convenient . . ."

Coughlin looked at him with an eyebrow raised.

Wohl held out the envelope to Coughlin.

"I tried to dissuade him," Wohl said, "telling him to take time to think it over, maybe reconsider."

Coughlin saw that the envelope had been hand-addressed to him with his official title, FIRST DEPUTY POLICE COMMISSIONER COUGHLIN, not *Uncle Denny*, and that it was sealed.

He tore back an edge of the flap, poked his index finger in the hole, and ripped open the end. He extracted the single sheet of paper that was inside and unfolded it with a flick of his wrist.

"Jesus," Coughlin said after a time, then raised his eyes to Wohl as he refolded the sheet. "He finally did it."

Wohl nodded.

"Apparently so. He said he was adamant about his decision. Said he wasn't going to give in to Carlucci's henchmen. You know who he's referring to?"

Coughlin nodded. "And so do you, if you think about it. That's why I had him temporarily transferred to your unit before he could have been put . . . elsewhere."

Wohl nodded, then went on. "He didn't want to give

these henchmen the satisfaction of seeing him given thirty days with intent to dismiss. He gave me a similar letter"—Wohl reached into his pocket and produced the opened envelope—"said he had a plane to catch, and asked that I give you yours, with his apology for not doing it himself."

"Why don't you believe him?"

"I think he thinks he's failed the police department, in general, and you and me, in particular, and is willing to nobly fall on his sword."

Coughlin looked at the television. The footage was of ex-governor Bailey commenting on Mayor Carlucci.

Coughlin turned back to Wohl.

"Anyone else know about this?" Coughlin said, gesturing with the folded sheet.

When Wohl shook his head, Coughlin held out his hand.

"Let me see that one, too, Peter."

Wohl complied, and waited for him to read it.

Coughlin instead placed the two letters of resignation together in his big hands—and ripped them in half, then tore those halves in half again.

"He's my godson. You're his rabbi. Matty was born to be a cop. You know it. I know it. Most important, he knows it. This department, more so now than ever before, needs good cops. And minds like his—and yours, Peter—that think outside the box have to be the future of this department. Between us, we can find him a job that makes everyone happy." He pointed at the telephone on the desk. "Get him on the horn for me, please."

[TWO]
The Riverwalk
San Antonio, Texas
Monday, January 16, 12:22 P.M.
Texas Standard Time

At more or less the same moment that Inspector Peter
Wohl had entered First Deputy Police Commissioner
Coughlin's office, Matt Payne took a footbridge across
the scenic urban stream, which was maybe twenty feet
wide and hemmed with restaurants, hotels, and a variety
of retail shops. He crossed just in time to see Amanda
Law settling into a seat at a table of a small tree-shaded
cantina just downstream.

Next door to the cantina was the boutique hotel
where she had told him she was staying. And standing in
front of the hotel was a traditional Mexican mariachi
band—three Latin men wearing colorful outfits and
strumming acoustic guitars.

Payne carried fifty red roses that he had ordered by
phone from a florist a block off the Riverwalk. He went
up to the musicians and spoke in the ear of the lead gui-
tarist, and band leader, who nodded with enthusiasm.

Payne, balancing the enormous bouquet, dug his
money clip from his pocket and handed the man two
fifty-dollar bills. The man gave him a broad smile, re-

moved his Western-style straw hat, and put it on Payne's head.

With the band in tow, Payne approached Amanda's table. He tilted his head so that the long brim of the hat obscured his face, then pulled a single rose stem from the bouquet.

The three men began softly playing and singing: *"Besame, besame mucho / Que tengo miedo a perderte, perderte despues . . ."*

Amanda, absently surveying the menu, turned her head at the familiar music and lyrics.

"Señorita?" Payne said, holding the rose out to her.

She glanced at the flower, then slowly motioned with her left hand, palm out, toward it, and said in a soft monotone, "No, *gracias.*"

Matt smiled when he saw the diamonds of her engagement ring sparkling in the sunlight. But he thought that her face looked, as her voice had sounded, if not saddened, then simply devoid of any emotion.

Matt pushed the hat back on his head, motioned near the menu with the flower again.

"Señorita, por favor?"

Amanda looked up from her menu and in a polite tone had begun to repeat, "No . . ." when she gasped. "Matt?"

Payne, putting his open hand on his chest, joined in with the musicians, but in English, and completely off key: *"Kiss me, kiss me a lot / For I'm scared to lose you, to lose you afterward . . ."*

Amanda stood up, her face showing a mix of surprise and excitement.

"Oh my God," she said, "I've missed you so much . . ."

Matt Payne refilled their glasses with the last of the pitcher of frozen margaritas.

"So, they forced my hand," he said. "And, you know, I'm glad they did. It leaves me with no excuse not to broaden my horizons."

"What's your plan?"

"The initial plan, subject to modification, is that I'll be working in my father's Center City office while taking that new combined Law-MBA program at UP."

"What do you think you'd want to do with that?"

He shrugged. "Almost anything. Get this: Aimee Wolter says that I should consider running for district attorney, that she would run the campaign. But that's getting ahead of things. First things first . . ."

"Matt, listen. That all sounds great. But hold that thought. I have to tell you something . . ."

"Okay."

"I really went off prematurely. I like to think I'm pretty tough . . ."

"And you are. Incredibly tough."

"But losing the baby hit me hard. Really hard. You saw how I was, with my hormones raging off the chart. I'm grateful you tolerated me. That, and I've been talking with my father. Not about my hormones but about you. And me. *Us*. I won't repeat exactly what he said—he's not one to sugarcoat, as you know—but he helped convince me."

"About what?"

Amanda was silent. She met his eyes.

"Even though I get concerned and worried," she said, "I've always respected what you do, and what my dad did, as a cop. And now, tending to these warrior heroes here at the medical center . . . and seeing their amazingly strong families supporting them . . . has helped put it in another light."

She paused to sip her margarita, clearly collecting her thoughts.

"I came here to learn more about medicine," she went on. "And I have. The work that's done at Brooke is incredible, miraculous. But what I've also really learned about here is the inner strength, the extraordinary determination and perseverance, of the patients. They have been through hell, had their lives literally blown up, suffering horrific burns, losing arms and legs, and more. Yet they believe in who they are and what they do. The harder it gets, the tougher they get. And you know what? After all they've been through, and all they will go through, with multiple operations and then rehabilitation, they still would do anything to get back to serving with their brothers and sisters in uniform. It is awe-inspiring. And humbling."

She paused.

Matt felt his throat tighten.

"So I get it, Matt. And I don't want you to quit if you don't. I'll work this out. *We* can work this out."

"You're sure about this?" he said, his voice strained.

"Our world needs good men to overcome the evil. I know that to be an absolute."

Then Matt saw her eyes moisten, and a tear slip down her cheek. She leaned over and threw her arms around his neck. She buried her face in his neck and kissed it as he wrapped his arms around her waist and squeezed her close.

He ignored the vibrations coming from the phone in his pants pocket.